Ellie Da... romance novels and, after completing her English degree, decided to make a living from her love of books. As a writer and editor she finds her work now entails dreaming up romantic proposals, hot dates with alpha males and trips to the past with dashing heroes. When she's not ...rking she can usually be found running around after ...oddler, volunteering at her local library or escaping ... the above with a good book and a vanilla latte.

...spite a no-nonsense background as a West Point gradu-...e, army officer and Fortune 100 sales executive, **Caro ...arson** has always treasured the happily-ever-after of a ...ood romance novel. As a RITA® Award-winning Mills ... Boon author, Caro is delighted to be living her own ...appily-ever-after with her husband and two children in ...lorida, a location that has saved the coaster-loving ...eme-park fanatic a fortune on plane tickets.

Discover more at millsandboon.co.uk

SURPRISE BABY FOR THE HEIR

ELLIE DARKINS

THE COLONELS' TEXAS PROMISE

CARO CARSON

MILLS & BOON

First Published in Great Britain 2019
by Mills & Boon, an imprint of HarperCollinsPublishers,
1 London Bridge Street, London, SE1 9GF

Surprise Baby for the Heir © 2019 Ellie Darkins
The Colonels' Texas Promise © 2019 Caroline Phipps

ISBN: 978-0-263-27214-7

0219

MIX
Paper from
responsible sources
FSC™ C007454

Printed and bound in Spain
by CPI, Barcelona

SURPRISE BABY
FOR THE HEIR

ELLIE DARKINS

For Tess

CHAPTER ONE

'So, WHO DO YOU HATE? The bride or the groom?'

Elspeth frowned at the sound of the stranger's voice behind her. She turned to look and realised that she'd noticed this guy earlier. How could she not? Even among the sea of tartan and kilts he stood out. He was taller and broader than most of the other men filling the Royal Botanic Garden in Edinburgh, and his red hair had obviously been dragged into some sort of order at the start of the day but had been progressively rebelling ever since.

With her mouth open to tell him to leave, Elspeth realised that the man was already pulling up a chair to sit beside her, man-spreading with a confidence that showed just how comfortable he was in a skirt.

'Neither, of course,' she said, faking a smile, conscious that she was only at this wedding for appearances' sake, and clearly not doing a good enough job of keeping up the appearance of wedding joy.

'Then why do you look upset?' her new friend asked, looking at her astutely.

'Maybe I just have one of those sad faces.'

She wasn't sure why she'd answered him, given that it wasn't actually any of his business. She'd been wearing her best corporate fake smile for the best part of six hours, through the most ironically torturous day of her life. What was it to this guy if she'd let it slip for three minutes while everyone else had eyes on the bride and groom's first dance.

'Long story,' she added with a sigh.

She wondered briefly why she hadn't just shut the conversation down, as she'd originally intended. Perhaps something about the scene playing out in front of her was making her sappy. Or perhaps it was today's date—the one she'd inked into her diary with a simple 'my wedding'. Or the fact that this was the venue that she'd booked for her own nuptials. And the flowers were the ones that she'd chosen, and the food was the exact menu she'd tasted for the first time a little under a year ago.

In fact, the whole day had been the wedding that she'd spent a year planning and then had been faced with dismantling when she had split with her fiancé with just six months to go before their big day.

She remembered coming into the office the morning after they'd called it all off, eyes red and skin tight from lack of sleep, to find her boss, Janet, proudly showing off a diamond ring. And it had seemed that before she knew what was happening her boss was offering to take over all Elspeth's reservations, saving her from losing the deposits, so that she could have a whirlwind wedding.

She'd turned it into more of a circus than Elspeth had intended, of course, chucking in a hundred extra guests and adding a few zeroes to the budget. But her own wedding had been visible enough to sting throughout the day, like little brushes of nettles against her bare arms everywhere she turned.

She couldn't make herself regret it, though—the cancellation of her wedding or agreeing to the takeover. It made financial sense. Elspeth couldn't afford to lose the money, so she'd gone along with it, happily in denial about the whole thing until the invitation had arrived and she'd realised that she was expected to attend.

If she hadn't needed to impress everyone at the GP practice in order to be offered a permanent role when her training post ended she wouldn't be here. But she needed financial security, and that meant turning up, smiling, and making sure her boss never saw how much she was hating this.

Turned out she'd been doing such a shoddy job that a complete stranger had already rumbled her.

Elspeth took solace in the fact that on her wedding day Janet was hardly going to be paying her much attention. As long as Elspeth appeared in the photos and was mentioned in the inevitable office chat about the event on Monday morning it would hopefully be enough.

But for now she should really get rid of this man. The last thing her misery needed today was company. She just had to get through watching the first dance, and the cutting of *her* cake, and then she could go home.

A stiff drink was the answer.

She stood and headed to the bar, wondering whether he would follow her. The sensible part of her—the part of her she usually left in charge—hoped that he wouldn't. That she could just drown her sorrows in private. But there was something about the mischief in his eyes, something promising trouble, that had her intrigued. That made her want to ignore the part of her brain that had kept her together and her fear at bay for as long as she could remember.

'So, if you don't hate either of them, what's this long story about?'

Elspeth's stomach swooped at the soft sound of his voice behind her, his presence by her shoulder making her skin tingle in awareness. That answered her question, then. She'd been hoping for more of him.

'I'm not sure I want talk about it,' she said, lifting one of the flutes of champagne laid out on trays on the bar and taking a long sip as she turned to him.

He gave her an easy, relaxed smile, grabbing a glass for himself before leaning back against the bar. 'Well, will you at least let me try and distract you from it?'

Any way he wanted.

Wow, when her mind went there, it really went for it, she realised, as a host of ideas for how they could distract one another flooded her consciousness.

She studied him closely over the rim of her glass. 'Why would I do that?'

Just because her body was telling her in no uncertain terms what she wanted, that didn't mean she couldn't have a little fun with this.

He was still leaning against the bar, the picture of casual insouciance. 'How about because I'm also here under duress. I hate weddings—and I don't understand anyone who doesn't. I thought having an accomplice might be fun.'

Elspeth narrowed her eyes as she looked at him. Really, the only thing she wanted was to get out of here. But, as she couldn't do that until the formalities were out of the way, perhaps this would pass the time. And then there was the fact that her eyes kept being drawn to the calves exposed beneath his kilt, and to the way his hair was determinedly escaping whatever order it had been dragged into earlier. And the way those green eyes watched her, promising trouble if she wanted it.

'An accomplice? What exactly are you planning?' she asked. 'I could do without being arrested, so if we can keep it just this side of legal... But go for it. Do your worst.'

'In that case, would you like to dance?'

Elspeth glanced over her shoulder at the dance floor to see that it was filling with guests, joining the bride and groom, who were still wrapped around one another in the centre of the floor.

She laughed. 'That's it? That's your grand plan to distract me from my misery? Dancing in that syrupy mass?'

His eyes flicked to follow her gaze. 'Fair point. What about we cause a diversion, sneak something from the bar and go explore the gardens instead?'

Elspeth glanced around her and realised the bar was unattended and all eyes were still on the bride and groom on the dance floor. With a quick grin at her accomplice, she reached casually across the bar and snagged a bottle of champagne by the neck, then twisted her arm to hide it behind her back.

'Okay, so you really went for it. Good for you. I'm Fraser, by the way. I think we should probably be on first-name terms if we're embarking on a crime spree together.'

She widened her eyes at him in mock innocence. 'I'm sorry, I don't know what you're referring to. But I think I need some fresh air. Care to join me?'

Elspeth felt a shiver as Fraser draped an arm around her shoulder and tried not to think what anyone watching might be thinking. Maybe it was better that they thought they were sneaking out for a quickie or a snog, than realising that she was sneaking away with a very nice bottle of champagne.

He was using his body to shield the bottle from view, she reminded herself as her own body warmed beneath his touch. That was the only reason for him to be standing so close that it was making the hairs on her arms prickle.

Elspeth stepped out onto the decking and wrapped her arms around herself as the chill of the Scottish evening hit her.

Fraser grabbed a blanket from a pile that had been left in a basket by the door and draped it around her shoulders. She looked up and met his eyes, and only then realised how close they were. The sun was hitting the horizon behind him, making the light on the deck golden and glowing.

At her wedding they'd have been having photos taken now, she remembered. Her ex-fiancé, Alex, was a keen amateur photographer, and had scheduled a number of photography sessions into their day.

She shook off the memory of Alex, and the hurt on his face when she'd finally called time on their engagement. By then he'd known as well as she had that a marriage between them would never work. He'd wanted her to choose. To put him at the top of her priorities, even above her family.

But she was the one who'd actually ended it. Who had said that the compromises he wanted from her weren't going to happen. That she couldn't let anyone else take care of her family. That if he wanted to be with her he would have to accept that he would have to share her.

She took a step back from Fraser, breaking the connection between them and walking out across the deck.

'So, do you want to tell me this long story?' Fraser asked, following behind her.

'I thought you were meant to be cheering me up,' she replied, turning and looking over her shoulder as she reached the railing, leaning on it and looking out over the botanic gardens. 'Trust me, talking about things isn't going to be cheery for either of us.'

'Ah, but we have this to help us,' Fraser said, slipping an arm beneath the thick woollen blanket he'd wrapped around her and taking the bottle.

He ripped the foil from the neck of the bottle and started untwisting the wire cage around the cork.

Elspeth eyed the bottle. 'We'll need more than that.'

Fraser lifted an eyebrow as he twisted the cork, then pressed his thumbs beneath it. 'Sounds ominous.'

'Well, let's just say that today has come with a massive sense of *déjà vu*. Or future *vu*, or something weird like that.'

'You had a vision that you'd be stealing champagne from a free bar with a stranger in a kilt?'

She grinned involuntarily. 'Yes, this is what I planned for my Saturday night. Attending my own wedding as a guest and stealing the booze.'

'*Your* wedding?'

Elspeth let out an ironic laugh, wishing her tongue wasn't so easily loosened by alcohol. God, maybe she should just say it. Burying it and pretending these feelings didn't exist wasn't making the day bearable. Time to try something different.

'I was meant to be getting married today.'

She stated it baldly, with as little emotion as she could manage, but even she could hear the waver in her voice. Fortunately the cork popped out of the bottle with perfect comic timing, and Fraser directed the spilling white foam into her glass.

'Well, I wasn't expecting that,' he said, slightly flustered, in the classic manner of a man who has just been hit by an emotional confession he hadn't expected. 'Quick—drink,' he added, as the bubbles reached the top of the glass and threatened to spill over.

Elspeth drank, seeing no better course of action, and spluttered slightly at the tickle of the exploding bubbles in her nose. She laughed, fully out loud this time—the first genuine laugh she'd managed all day.

Correlation wasn't causation, and all that, but maybe Fraser was on to something, encouraging her to talk about what was going on. She did feel a little better. A willing ear from a stranger could be as good as therapy—and cheaper.

'I was meant to be getting married here, actually,' she went on. 'I called it off a few months ago and the day after my boss got engaged. She offered to take over my reservations…save me losing my deposits.'

'Wow,' Fraser said, holding the champagne bottle hovering just above his glass, frozen in the second of pouring.

'You said that already,' Elspeth remarked, raising her brows as she took another sip of wine, enjoying having him on the back foot.

He had been so cocksure, swaggering up to her, asking her to dance, suggesting they get into trouble together. It felt good to turn the tables: see him lost for words.

'And you decided you wanted to come because…what? You're a sadist?'

'I think that would make me a masochist, actually.' She dropped the word casually, as if her sudden thought of kinky sex with this gorgeous stranger had had absolutely zero effect on her heart rate. 'And, no, sorry to disappoint, if that's your thing, but I'm here because the bride is my boss and I was invited.'

He nodded sagely, thankfully not acknowledging her veiled question about his sexual kinks. She wasn't sure it would be good for her to hear exactly what he was into in the bedroom. Her mind was having plenty of fun making up the details by itself.

'Some big promotion in the offing?' Fraser asked, and it took Elspeth a moment to remember what he was talking about.

She took a sip of her drink and nodded. 'Something like that.'

'You're a doctor?' he said, after clearly searching through his memory banks for the bride's profession.

'A GP, yes. Well, a trainee, and hoping for a job when I finish.'

'Why did you want to be a doctor?'

Elspeth couldn't remember the last time someone had asked her that. And she didn't have a good answer. To her, it had never seemed like a choice. All she knew was that it had been a decision made long before she had chosen her exam subjects as a teenager. Probably around the time she had been sitting by her baby sister's bedside, incapable of doing anything that could help her other than sit there.

She'd trained as a doctor because she wanted to help people like Sarah. Be their advocate in the healthcare system and ensure that every single one of them got the best outcome that they could. Because she had seen the miracles the medical profession could perform. Keeping her sister alive, getting her home, giving her independence with an electric wheelchair and communication aids, among the million other ways it had helped her over the years.

And now Elspeth had the skills and the knowledge she hadn't had when Sarah was a baby, which meant she could be cared for by her family rather than by strangers. But her care responsibilities meant careful planning for the future, especially given that her mum had been in her forties when Sarah had been born, had arthritis herself, and wasn't going to be mobile, or even around, for ever.

But that was way more detail than anyone needed to know—especially dangerous-looking men in kilts brandishing bottles of champagne.

'I liked science and I wanted to help people,' Elspeth said, giving the standard medical school application answer.

It wasn't really much of an explanation, but it was all he would be getting. She had watched her relationship with Alex dissolve around her because he hadn't been able to reconcile family and romance, but she had no desire to go into the details. Perhaps talking about this wasn't the good idea she'd thought it might be.

'Anyway,' she said, keen to change the topic of conversation and shift the attention away from her sorry tale. 'That's my story. What's yours? Why are *you* here if it's so tortuous?'

Fraser shrugged as he leant his forearms against the railing, surveying the gardens in front of them. 'Nothing so exciting—just family duty. The groom is my mum's cousin. My mother insisted I be dragged into groomsman duty to make up the numbers even though I hardly know the guy.'

'Ah, a mummy's boy,' Elspeth said with a smile, echoing Fraser's knowing tone from earlier. 'Interesting…'

Fraser bumped her shoulder with his and Elspeth held her hands up.

'Hey, if it sounds like a duck, looks like a duck, and does what Mama Duck says…'

'Enough—drink your wine,' he said with a laugh, topping up her glass again. 'I did *not* lure you out here to talk about my mother.'

'Now, *that* sounds interesting.'

Elspeth looked up at him, pulling the blanket a little tighter around her shoulders, hyper-aware of the scratch of the fabric on her shoulders, the earthy smell of the wool, the barrier it put between her and Fraser.

'I'm not sure I remember being *lured*, as such. But what were your motivations if you weren't thinking about introducing me to your mother?'

Oh, she was sure that asking that question was going to get her into trouble. But that twinkle in his eye, the way he challenged her with his stare, egging her on, had tweaked at something inside her. She wanted to play.

He smiled back at that slight suggestion of innuendo, and she knew that she was right. She'd just got herself into trouble and she couldn't bring herself to be sorry about it.

'So you're saying you're not the kind of girl I want to take home to meet the parents, huh? Well, that's good to know. I thought we were going to explore out here. Wasn't that the plan?'

Elspeth drained her glass and gestured towards the steps down from the decking. 'Lead on. Where do you want to look first?'

They wandered through the gardens, their shadows long over the lawns, until they came across a gathering of redwood trees: Californian giants, hundreds of feet tall. Beneath their shade, the light was lost completely, and Elspeth realised what a secluded spot they had found.

She leant back against the trunk of one of the trees, feeling small, humbled by the scale of them. As Fraser approached, still swinging the bottle by his side, Elspeth held up her glass like a shield, suddenly aware of the intimacy of their surroundings, how her attraction to Fraser had been bubbling under the surface of their banter since he had first approached her, and how he was looking at her now, like the wolf in a fairy tale.

But she was no innocent Red Riding Hood, and she had no plans to run or hide.

'Do you think we've missed them cutting the cake?' Elspeth asked, breaking the tension, wondering whether they'd come too far to take their conversation back to something inane and safe.

'I'm not sure.' Fraser came closer, topping up her glass, then closer still, so she wouldn't have been able to lift it to her lips if she'd wanted to. The glass was trapped against her chest, along with her hands and her resolve. 'Do you care?'

'Not really.' The words escaped her before she could stop them, but she couldn't regret them. Not when they lit a spark in Fraser's eyes that made the night seem a little less dark.

'You don't want to go back?'

Oh, there was so much more to that question, and she could see from the look in his eyes, lit only by the moon, that he knew it.

Surely it was late enough by now that she wouldn't be missed at the reception? In her plan for the day, that was meant to be her cue to leave. To get home to her mum and her sister. Not to slope off somewhere with a stranger she would probably never see again.

Because if there was one thing she was sure about when it came to this connection she felt to Fraser, it was that it was never going to last more than a night. She had tried balancing a relationship, her work and family commitments before, and it hadn't been possible. She'd got hurt. Alex had got hurt. And she knew her family had been hurt too, as they'd seen all their hopes for her unpicked and falling away.

But one night with this man—well, that could be something interesting. More and more, it was feeling as if it could be something irresistible.

'I don't want to go back,' she said, looking up to meet his eyes, making sure that he couldn't mistake her meaning.

She let the tree take her weight, surrendering herself to her decision, to her desire. The champagne glass slipped from her hand and she heard it hit the ground with a soft rustle. With her hands free, she brushed the front of Fraser's jacket, taking a moment to really feel the fabric, the softness of well-worn wool on her fingertips. From his lapels she stroked upwards, inwards, and heavy fabric gave way to soft cotton.

His eyes never left hers as she reached the studs of his shirt and hooked her fingers into the fabric, pulling him down to her.

'What do you want?' Fraser asked, breaking their look at last and glancing down at her hands.

'I think you know.'

'Oh, I've got a pretty good idea. But I want to hear you say it.'

'It's going to be like that, is it?' Elspeth asked with a shiver, hoping very much that it would be.

He was still looking at her as if he wanted to consume her, and she was good with that. She had too much in her head. Too much in her life. She wanted to be devoured, to devour. To lose herself in her senses, in the present. To be so overwhelmed that she couldn't think about anything beyond the next second.

She slipped her foot out of her shoe and hooked it around Fraser's calf, noticing the feel of every hair that slipped beneath the arch of her foot, the line of his calf muscle, taut and defined and bared to the elements.

As she slipped her foot higher, feeling the slide of his skin beneath hers, she couldn't help imagining what she would find higher still. Wondering whether he was exposed to the elements, to her, beneath that kilt.

With the fingers of one hand still hooked in his shirt, keeping him close, she lifted the other to the back of his neck, feeling the softness of the hair curling at his collar. Meeting his eyes again, she smiled.

'Enjoying yourself?' Fraser asked, with a smile just the right side of smug.

'You know I am,' she murmured, dropping her eyes to his mouth and finding herself unable to look away from it.

She licked her lips, and watched as his mouth curved into a knowing, confident smile.

'Good. Don't stop.'

She had absolutely no intention of stopping. Gripping the front of his shirt tighter, she twisted the fabric between her fingers as she pulled him down to her. She held her breath as she closed her eyes, stretching up on tiptoes until at last her lips brushed against his. Sensation exploded at the touch of his warm mouth and she let out a quiet moan, revelling in every physical sensation assaulting her body.

In the press of hard wood and soft woollen blanket behind her, the creased cotton and tweed in front. The curling hair and soft skin beneath her hand. And the uninhibited mouth on hers. Tasting her, tempting her. Teasing her with its tongue and its lips.

Fraser's arms wrapped around her waist, pulling her away from the tree into his solid chest. Elspeth let her lips trace the line of his jaw until she was close enough to whisper in his ear.

'Let's go.'

Fraser woke to the sensation of silk sheets beneath his body and a warm summer breeze caressing his back. And soft, soft lips pressing against his.

Elspeth.

With his eyes still closed, he wound fingers into her hair, cupped his other hand around her cheek and kissed her lazily, slowly remembering the night before. He pulled her down on top of him, but she stiffened, drawing away until his body and his bed felt cold.

'Bye, Fraser.'

He lifted his head and blinked his eyes at the sound of high heels on deep carpet, heading towards the door, and it was only in the dawn light creeping round the edge of the curtains that he saw Elspeth's face.

'Bye.'

He croaked out the word and then fell back on the pillow as the door closed behind her.

He didn't have her number.

The thought occurred to him and then he was sitting

up without realising he'd decided to, and he had a foot out of the bed before he'd thought about what he was doing. Before he stopped himself, as he always had before.

No strings. They'd never actually said the words last night, but it had been clear enough in the way they had been with each other. Well, if he'd had any doubt she'd just proved it by walking out with barely a kiss goodbye.

For a fraction of a second he wondered if he could catch her before the lift reached their floor, but that summer breeze brushed him again, colder this time, and he realised what he was thinking.

He didn't do relationships. He'd seen when he had still been barely more than a child the harm they could do. What happened to people and their lives when they followed their desires rather than making sensible, objective decisions.

He'd sworn that he wouldn't make the same mistakes. Just the fact that he was even thinking of acting on a whim now was all the proof he needed that it would be a bad idea. Of all the women he might have a second date with, the one who was making him question all his carefully set ground rules was not the one to try it with.

He collapsed back, letting his arm fall over his eyes as he remembered falling into this same bed last night, with Elspeth pulling at his clothes and her body warm and supple beneath him.

Last night wasn't going to be easy to forget. *She* wasn't going to be easy to forget.

CHAPTER TWO

ELSPETH THREW DOWN her work bag by the door and shouted out as she walked through the hallway. 'Mum? Sarah?'

'In here,' her sister called back from the direction of the kitchen.

Elspeth crossed the hallway and smiled at the sight of the pair of them at the kitchen table, the huge pan of chicken and pasta she'd left in the fridge the day before sitting between them. Thank God. She was starving. All she wanted to do was carb-load and fall straight into bed. Again. She'd not made it past nine o'clock a single night this week, and she wasn't planning on breaking her streak tonight.

Her patients had been back to back from eight o'clock that morning, and the only food she'd had all day was a sandwich at her desk while she caught up on notes and phone calls. She was used to the workload, to the stress and the non-stop appointments, but for some reason this week it had caught up with her. Her body felt heavy, weary in a way she'd not felt since she'd been caught in an endless cycle of night shifts, studying and revision in her first years as a junior doctor.

She just had one last thing to do before she went to

help Sarah with her evening routine of medication, personal hygiene and changing for bed.

She had to pee on a stick.

It was just a formality, really. Just to rule out the flashing light that her inner doctor wouldn't allow her to ignore. She was a week or so late, but that wasn't unusual. She'd never had a cycle she could set the clock by. And she'd never taken risks—she always used a condom. But if she'd had a patient sitting in front of her, complaining of the sort of fatigue she had been feeling, she would have ordered a pregnancy test, so it only made sense to rule it out.

She smiled through dinner with her mother and Sarah, listening to stories of their day. Her mother's at work, her sister's at college. But in the back of her mind she couldn't shake off the thought of that little test sitting at the bottom of her bag.

As soon as her fork hit an empty plate she tidied the kitchen, thanked her mum for dinner, made her excuses and headed upstairs. Locking the bathroom door behind her, she thought for the thousandth time what a luxury it would be to be able to leave the door unlocked, free from the fear that her mum or Sarah could walk in on her.

Living at home in her thirties wasn't exactly ideal. But with her mum in her sixties, it wasn't fair to expect her to take on the full responsibility of caring for her sister. They all worked hard to ensure that Sarah was living as independently as possible, but she still required extra support and Elspeth was determined that her mother wouldn't have to take on all that herself. And she wanted to be able to buy a house. Somewhere for her and Sarah to live—a home that they could be certain would always be theirs—and that meant staying at home and saving for a deposit.

Elspeth peed on the test and set it on the side of the bath as she glanced at her watch. Three minutes and she'd be able to dispel this nagging doubt and get her head on the pillow. Which meant she had three minutes during which she could legitimately let herself think about Fraser.

Because for the past three weeks she'd not let herself do that. She'd pushed her memories of that incredible night out of her mind, knowing that with all the responsibilities in her life she couldn't afford the luxury of a relationship. No matter how good the sex had been. And, *oh*, it had been good. Better than good. Better than sex, actually. Because for those few hours there had been a connection between them. They had laughed, joked, challenged each other.

And when the sun had crept over the horizon in the morning she had crept out of his bed with a sigh of regret, wishing for a moment that her life could be different.

But here, in the cold, stark light of the bathroom, she knew that it couldn't be. She had responsibilities, and she and Alex had already done a fine job of proving that those responsibilities were not compatible with a romantic relationship.

It was a sobering thought, she realised as she kept her eyes averted from the pregnancy test. Looking ahead to a life without romance. Without marriage. Without a family of her own.

Elspeth loved her mum and her sister. She was devoted to them, and it was no sacrifice to set aside what she might want for herself for what was best for her family. But that didn't mean she wasn't curious. That she didn't wonder what sort of life she might have had if her decisions had been her own to make. Maybe she would have been peeing on one of these sticks hoping for it to show a smiley pregnant face rather than dreading the result.

She glanced at her watch. Three minutes. Well, there was no point putting it off any longer. All she had to do was check the test, put her daydreams and her sister to bed, and then climb in between the sheets herself.

She turned the test over.

Pregnant.

For a second she wished she'd bought one of those cheap, old-fashioned tests. Where you had to scrutinise the stick and the leaflet to work out if there was a line. What the line meant.

Seeing the truth just sitting there, so unvarnished, was a blow to her chest. She couldn't pull in air and sat heavily on the side of the bath, staring at it, unable to tear her eyes away.

She was pregnant. She did the maths in her head. Just a few weeks. Six weeks gestational age, at most. Barely a grouping of cells.

She had options. She ran through them as she would for any patient who wanted them, and in her head she was halfway through the referral process to end her pregnancy before she realised that the thought of doing so made her feel sick. Sick in her stomach, sick in her bones.

She realised that it wasn't the right choice for her.

And that was it, Elspeth thought, as she looked at herself in the mirror. Decision made. She was having a baby.

As she walked out of the bathroom Elspeth could hear her sister typing in her bedroom, and she knocked on the door before pushing it open.

'Hey, sis. Ready for bed?'

Sarah smiled and turned her head, gesturing for Elspeth to sit. 'What's up, Els?' she asked, frowning. 'You're completely white. You're not going to throw up, are you? If you are, you can get off my bed.'

Elspeth pulled a face, feigning ignorance. 'I'm fine. How was college today?'

Sarah gave her an insightful look. 'We already talked about that. Don't change the subject. You look terrible.'

'Gee, with a sister like you…'

'I know—who needs friends? But I'm not letting you off that easy. Come on. Tell me what's up.'

Elspeth considered her options. It wasn't as if she could keep it a secret for ever. And she could do with talking about what was on her mind. Maybe if she said the words out loud they would start to feel more real.

'I—' Her voice broke, stuck behind a lump in her throat. She coughed, took a deep breath and tried again. 'I'm pregnant.'

She heard the words for the first time, but it still didn't help. It felt as if she was talking about someone else. Except for the look on Sarah's face. That made it a little more real.

'Okay. Whose is it?' she asked after a long pause. 'Not Alex's?' she added, looking aghast.

'No,' Elspeth said, unable to help smiling at her sister's horror at the prospect that she was back with her ex. 'It's someone…new,' she said eventually, not sure she wanted her sister to know she'd been picking up strange men at weddings. 'We're not really in touch at the moment.'

They weren't meant to be in touch at all. Not if it meant trying to cram a relationship into a life that she'd already proved had no space for one.

'Guess that's going to have to change,' Sarah said.

Elspeth threw her a look only an older sister could give. 'You're very insightful tonight,' she said.

Sarah turned her chair so that she was looking directly at Elspeth. 'You're the one throwing bombshells. I'm just trying to keep up. How long have you known?'

'I've just found out,' Elspeth said. 'Don't tell Mum. Not till I've had a chance to speak to her first.'

'Of course,' Sarah said, watching her more closely than Elspeth was comfortable with.

Elspeth picked up a book from Sarah's bed, fiddling with it in her hands, running scenarios through her head, none of which were helping.

'Can you grab my pyjamas?' Sarah asked, with a glance at her restless fingers. 'I'm not getting anywhere with this essay. I think I need to sleep on it.'

'Of course,' Elspeth replied, pleased to have the distraction. As she went through the nightly routine—helping Sarah in the bathroom, dressing her, administering her meds and going through her physio regime—her thoughts kept drifting back to Fraser, as hard as she tried to keep them in the present moment.

'Are you going to tell me about him?' Sarah asked, and Elspeth realised she had been looking out of the window for the past few minutes, Sarah's toothbrush in her hand, completely forgotten about.

'I'm not sure there's much to tell. I haven't known him long. I don't even know if he's going to want to be involved. I mean, we've done okay, haven't we?'

Sarah gave her a look that wasn't at all difficult to interpret.

'I know, I know… I'll tell him. I know that I have to. It's just… Don't be surprised if he doesn't stick around, you know?'

Sarah rolled her eyes. 'Don't judge them all by Alex's standards.'

'He wasn't—' Elspeth started to defend her ex. It hadn't been his fault that she hadn't been able to commit to their relationship. She had been asking too much from him—way too much—and she hadn't been surprised when he had taken the escape route she had offered him.

But Sarah interrupted her before she could explain. 'Save it, Els. You know he wasn't the one for you. I've got higher hopes for this new one.'

'You don't know a thing about him.'

'Exactly. I don't know a thing about him other than the look he's put on your face and I already like him more than the last guy.'

CHAPTER THREE

FRASER STARED INTO his coffee and could tell without having to glance at the mirror opposite him that his eyebrows were pulling together in a way that was giving him a line between them.

He was pretty certain that this was a bad idea.

His usual practice when he had unexpected text messages from one-night stands he'd thought he'd never hear from again was to say a polite but firm no, and he should have stuck to that today.

It wasn't that he didn't like spending time with women— he liked to have fun. But he'd seen first-hand what happened when you let yourself be swept away by emotions. Lust and passion were all well and good for a night or two. But when you gave in to them for longer than that they clouded your judgement and led to the people around you getting hurt.

He got hurt.

That was what he had learned as a teenager, when he'd seen his father throw away twenty years of marriage and move in a woman who hadn't lasted more than a couple of years. But when Fraser had given him an ultimatum— '*Either she goes or I do!*'—in the early, heady days of that relationship, his father had chosen his new partner instead of his son.

So Fraser had packed up his things, helped his mother into the car—with her white face and her shocked silence—and left his home, the ancient seat of his ancestors and his title. The estate he had been preparing to inherit from the day he was born.

And he didn't know if he would ever get them back. All because his dad hadn't been able to say no to a pretty face and walk away. Seeing what that had done to his mother had made the decision for him. Nothing and no one, no relationship, could be worth the sort of pain that she had gone through.

Meeting with Elspeth now went against every rule he had made for himself and stuck to so rigidly for the past fifteen years. But she had found his phone number somehow and invited him for coffee.

She was clearly keen. Keener than most. And that meant he had to be even firmer than usual. He had to tell her, face to face and in no uncertain terms, that he wasn't interested. He didn't do relationships. He'd assumed that she'd known that when she'd taken him home halfway through a wedding and then barely woken him for a goodbye kiss the following morning. Had assumed that she wasn't after anything serious.

So why had she tracked him down? The time for swapping numbers had come and gone without either of them suggesting it, and he had assumed that meant that she felt the same way he did.

Whatever. The whys of the situation didn't matter. All that mattered was shutting this thing down. And it seemed more effective to do that in person than by text. He could show her that he really meant it.

And show himself.

Because he'd been thinking about Elspeth far more than was reasonable or desirable over the past few weeks. Perhaps it was the way that she had sneaked out in the half-light of dawn. The colours in the room faded in the early morning, the silhouette of her face the only clear thing.

But that was no excuse. He'd shared plenty of dawn kisses goodbye before and hadn't had any problems forgetting them.

The door of the hotel lounge where he'd suggested they meet opened and he glanced up. Even though he was expecting her, he still felt his stomach dip at the sight of her.

He'd forgotten how petite she was. Her shoulders were half the width of his, and her head barely reached his collarbone. Her ankles and wrists were so tiny he could wrap them with his thumb and little finger. And so sensitive that she'd moaned every time he'd done so. And those freckles over her nose and her cheekbones…like a constellation of stars. He'd stared at them so intensely that night he had been able to see them even when he'd closed his eyes—like the negative image left by a bright light.

And wrapped up in that delicate exterior was a desire and a strength and a passion that had given his six feet and two hundred pounds a run for their money for a whole, blissful night.

But he wasn't meant to be thinking about that, he reminded himself as he schooled his face back into something neutral. He had to remember that this meeting was about breaking things off, not about picking up where she'd left him, naked in bed, wanting more.

'Hi,' Elspeth said as she approached his table.

Her smile was wary and it made his forehead crease

again. She was the one who had asked to meet him, so why was she looking so guarded? So very much as if she didn't think being here was a good idea any more than he did?

He stood to kiss her on the cheek—a polite habit, he told himself, rather than anything meaningful. The hand that he dropped to her shoulder met firm, tense muscle, and he realised that she was really nervous.

'Have a seat,' he said. 'What do you want to drink?'

'I'll have tea. Thanks.'

He could see her looking around the richly decorated interior of the hotel lounge as he summoned the waiter with a glance and wondered whether he'd made a mistake, choosing somewhere so intimate. But he hadn't wanted to have this conversation in a crowded restaurant or bustling coffee bar. Though that would have had its advantages… He'd have loved a reason to step away from her right now and catch his breath.

The sight of her had brought memories flooding back, and he wanted some space to remind himself that it didn't matter that she was beautiful. It didn't matter that she was funny. It didn't even matter that they had killer chemistry together. What mattered was that he couldn't trust himself around her, and he had to make sure that she knew this wasn't going to go anywhere.

He ordered her tea, and a fresh drink for himself. Something to do with his hands. To keep them distracted. To try and forget the memory of the delicate bones of her wrists trapped between his fingers.

'Thanks for meeting me,' Elspeth said eventually, gazing at a point somewhere past his left shoulder.

Alarm bells started ringing. There was definitely more to this meeting than he understood, and he didn't like it.

'What's going on, Elspeth?' he asked, his voice brusquer than he had intended. But he couldn't regret it. He had to know what she wanted from him because his body was growing increasingly tense, and the suspicion that this conversation was going somewhere he wasn't going to like was becoming impossible to ignore.

Elspeth took a deep breath, and—finally—looked him straight in the eye. Her face was set defiantly, as if she were expecting a fight, and a shiver travelled the length of Fraser's spine. A flash-forward—a presentiment, perhaps. An acknowledgement that, whatever it was that had put that expression on her face, he wasn't going to like it.

'I'm pregnant.'

The words hit Fraser like a bus, rendering him mute and paralysed. He sat in silence for long, still moments, letting the words reverberate through his ears, his brain. The full meaning of them fell upon him slowly, gradually. Like being crushed to death under a pile of small rocks. Each one was so insignificant that you didn't feel the difference, but collectively they stole his breath and would break his body.

'Are you sure?' he asked.

He didn't know why. She wouldn't be here if she wasn't sure. The look on her face *told* him that she was sure. And he wasn't going to insult her by asking if he was the father—she wouldn't be here if he wasn't.

'I'm sorry. Of course you're sure.'

But this couldn't be happening. He didn't *want* this. He'd seen the danger of giving in to romantic feelings. His mother had married the man she loved and then found herself turfed out and having to start her life again more than a decade and a half later. His father had given in to those feelings a second time, destroyed his family in the process—and with what to show for it? Two ex-wives and a son who hated him.

Fraser had decided a long time ago that that sort of commitment—the family and marriage sort—wasn't something he was interested in. It couldn't possibly be worth the heartache for everyone involved. Okay, so when he looked ahead maybe he *did* see a couple of kids in his life, in between the dogs and the lambs and the horses. But that didn't mean they were a realistic part of the picture, because they didn't come on their own. The thought of committing to any woman was completely off the cards. And to *this* woman—someone who had already caused him too many sleepless nights—it was impossible.

The commitment of raising a child was an unimaginable complication—how could it not be? He was happy with his life the way it was. With a string of casual attachments and the distant thought that one day, when his father was dead, he would return to his family estate and finally do the job he had spent his whole life waiting and working for. Put into practice all the preparations he had been making in the meantime, developing property and managing estates all over Scotland and being responsible for the lives of the people who lived and worked on them.

His father had always impressed upon him as a child that his money and his title came with responsibilities, and he was determined to be worthy of that privilege. In the years since he had left Ballanross he had been training to take up that position. Learning how to make land profitable; investing the small trust he had inherited from his grandfather and turning it into a fortune. Watching this fall and rise of the property market and ensuring that he was on the right side of it, amassing the cash and the property that had gone some way to filling the hole in his life that the loss of the estate had left.

He'd not been able to return home for fifteen years. His father had made it clear that he wasn't welcome in his home or in his life. Even after his dad's second marriage had broken down, when it had turned out that leaving his wife and the mother of his child *wasn't* the cure for a midlife crisis that he had expected it to be, Fraser had not gone back. How could he when his father had made it perfectly clear that he didn't want him in his life?

So he had taken the heartbreaking decision to wait until the land was his before he returned.

But if he had a child… That would change everything. Because that child had every right to know its inheritance. Its place in the world. On their land. How could he deny him or her that?

'Are you going to say anything?' Elspeth asked, breaking into his thoughts at last.

He met her gaze and saw that it had hardened even further—he hadn't thought that was possible. But he could understand why. He'd barely said a word since she'd dropped her bombshell. He needed time to take this in. Surely she could understand that.

'I'm sorry. I'm in shock,' he said. Following that up with the first thing that had popped into his head. 'We were careful…'

'Not careful enough, it seems.'

Her voice was like ice, cutting into him, and he knew that it had been the wrong thing to say. He wasn't telling her anything she didn't know.

Fraser shook his head. He'd never expected to be so unlucky. Nor had Elspeth, from the look on her face.

'What do you want to do?' he asked, his voice tentative, aware that they had options. Equally aware that discussing them could be a minefield if they weren't on the same page.

'I want to have the baby,' Elspeth said, using the same firmness and lack of equivocation with which she had told him she was pregnant. How someone so slight could sound so immovably solid was beyond him—and it was a huge part of her appeal, he realised. Something he should be wary of, then.

He nodded, though, his chest a little lighter, and realised that he was relieved that was what she wanted. Selfishly glad that she had spared him having to come to a conclusion himself. That picture of his future with children—it was what he wanted, he realised. He couldn't imagine growing old on his land with no one to pass it on to. It wasn't the child that wasn't wanted—it was the relationship, and the woman, and the commitment, and everything that came with it that was completely terrifying him.

'How are you?' he asked.

Elspeth shrugged. 'Tired, hungry. Everything that you'd expect, really. I'm only about eight weeks along. It's still early days, but I called in a favour and got a scan. Everything looks good so far. We've no reason to think that anything will go wrong.'

'That's good,' Fraser said.

His lips involuntarily turned up into a smile. He wasn't even sure why. He couldn't even think about what he was meant to be feeling at this news.

'So, what do we do now?'

What did they do now?

How on earth was *she* meant to know? She'd only been able to see as far as this. As far as telling the father of her child that the child existed. From here on in it was up to both of them to figure it out.

It would help if she had a clue where to start.

She didn't even know the basics about Fraser. Where he lived. Where he was from. His surname…

They'd come back to this very hotel the night of the wedding, so she didn't have many clues there, apart from the fact that it was one of the most discreetly expensive hotels in the city. She'd gone along with it, surprised, when he'd suggested meeting here.

If she was honest with herself, she was more surprised that he'd agreed to meet her at all. He had money, she gathered, wondering what he would make of her usual coffee shop and feeling suddenly uncomfortable.

'I guess we try and figure out the practicalities,' she said. 'If you want to be involved.'

She'd decided that this was the best tactic. She didn't want to force him to be in their lives if he didn't want to be. This child had every right to know its father, but it also deserved a father who *wanted* to be there. Not someone who was only doing it because they thought that they should.

A harsh look crossed Fraser's face, and Elspeth realised that somehow she'd touched a nerve.

'Of *course* I want to be involved. What kind of person do you think I am?'

She raised her palms. 'I don't know what kind of person you are, Fraser. All I know so far is that you get bored at weddings and what you like to do in bed. How am I meant to know what you think about kids? So far, this conversation isn't filling me with confidence.'

'I'm sorry,' he said. 'It's a shock.'

'I know that.' She replaced her cup rather too emphatically on the table and reached for a napkin as the liquid sloshed over the side. 'It wasn't exactly easy for me to find this out either. I had plans, you know. I *have* plans. I have responsibilities that don't exactly fit well with an unplanned pregnancy.'

'Of course—your permanent role at work. Have you had any news? I guess a baby's going to throw all your plans out of whack.'

She wasn't sure whether to be impressed that he'd remembered or annoyed that he was making light of the massive upheaval her career was going to have to go through. She decided quickly on the latter. 'Don't you dare be flippant. I need this job, and my career plans are important. I have responsibilities. Responsibilities and a career that are going to be hard enough to make work without you cracking jokes about it.'

Saying the words out loud was making the reality sink in. How on earth was she going to cope? She'd spent the last God knew how many years asking herself that same question. How was she going to care for her sister when her mum was gone? Or when her mum was older and needed a lot of care too? And now a baby in the mix? It was just too much.

She took a long drink of her tea, letting it wash away the lump that was threatening to form in her throat.

'So—what? You want *me* to take the baby?' Fraser asked.

'What? *No.* Are you deliberately making this harder?'

How could he jump to that conclusion? It made her realise that he really didn't know the first thing about her. Any of her friends, her colleagues, anyone who had met her for more than a random night at a wedding would know that she would *never* let someone else raise her child. And here she was, planning on co-parenting with a man who didn't even understand the basics about her.

'What I want, Fraser,' she said, slowly and deliberately, knowing that her temper wasn't going to help this situation, 'is some sort of plan for co-parenting this child that doesn't completely derail everything I need to happen in my life.'

'Well, it might be a bit late for that. Babies have a habit of derailing things.'

It was Fraser's turn to shrug, and she narrowly avoided the temptation of throwing her tea at him. How could he be so damn casual about it? Simply brush away her concerns?

'Well, in this case it can't.' She ground out the monosyllables, her temper still on the up.

At some point she was going to have to tell him about her life. Her responsibilities. The reason she had called off her engagement. And what would she see in his eyes? Pity? Fear? Horror at what he had got himself involved in?

'Okay, are you going to tell me what this is about or do I have to read between the lines and guess? Are you going to throw me a clue?'

Well, it looked as if she was about to find out.

'It's not a secret,' she said. 'I already have caring responsibilities. I have a sister with a disability and a mother who's getting older, whose arthritis is getting worse by the day. I need to get ahead with my career now, because the time will come pretty soon when I'll need the money I've banked, and I'll need to have reached a point in my career when I can work flexibly.'

'You were engaged before?' Fraser said thoughtfully.

Elspeth bristled. 'I'm not sure what that has to do

with anything. I'm talking about the baby, here. I'm not proposing.'

'I'm just saying you must have thought at one time that you could have both. I don't want to marry you, Elspeth. I just want to understand you.'

She tried to throw off the feeling that he was criticising her and answered as calmly as she could. 'You're right. At one time I thought that things could be different, and then I proved myself wrong. When my family and my relationship were both suffering because I was being pulled in opposite directions I had to choose, and I chose my family.'

Fraser's face creased, and Elspeth had a moment to see pain in his eyes before he wiped his expression clear.

'What?' she asked, when Fraser's silence stretched.

'Nothing,' he replied.

But she could tell that something she'd said had touched him. Had resonated with him. She knew he was keeping things from her. But why shouldn't he? He barely knew her. Other than the cells dividing and multiplying inside her, they shared nothing in their lives. They might as well be strangers.

Not quite strangers.

Not when she knew the curve of his buttocks and the scratch of his stubble. The deep, bass notes of his groans and the gentle huff of his breath while he slept.

But not familiar either. Unfamiliar enough for her skin to tingle when it sensed him close. New enough for her heart to pick up its pace a little every time her eyes flickered to his face. Enough of an unknown that she had to resist the temptation to reach out and touch his mouth, just to remind herself of how it had felt pressed hard and hot against hers among the giant trees of the botanic gardens.

Elspeth finished her tea and replaced her cup and

saucer on the table, wondering where they were meant to take this next.

'So, what do we do now?' Fraser asked.

Elspeth wondered why she was meant to have all the answers. Just because she was the one doing the gestating? But the answer suddenly seemed straightforward enough—not that that made it easy.

'Well, if we both want to be involved in this baby's life, then I guess we ought to get to know one another,' she said.

Then Elspeth's phone buzzed; she glanced at it and gave a start.

'I'm sorry,' she said. 'I have to get back to the surgery. I'll call you soon and we can arrange something. We've got lots still to talk about.'

Fraser stood as Elspeth did, and for an awkward moment he didn't know whether to offer his hand or lean in to kiss her cheek. A look of alarm on Elspeth's face betrayed that she was as confused as he was and she took a step backwards, making either action impossible.

'We'll speak soon, then,' Fraser said. 'Look after yourself,' he added.

And look after our baby.

He didn't say it out loud, but she must have known that he was thinking it. He was still trying to get his head around the fact that he was going to be a father. What would his mother say? She'd be excited—he had no doubt about that. But he was pretty sure that this wasn't how she'd imagined it happening, with a woman he had only known for one night of passion, and with whom had he had no intention of settling down.

Not that Elspeth wanted to settle down either. He'd

breathed a sigh of relief over that—the fact that she didn't want a relationship any more than he did. But there was no question that it would make the whole 'practicalities of parenting' thing harder. He had no intention of being an absent father, but he didn't want to live in the city either. Which meant he'd better get used to being in his car, driving in and out of Edinburgh's busy roads on a—what? A weekly trip to see his child?

It wasn't going to be enough, he realised. He didn't want to miss a day of his child's life. He wanted to be there for all of it.

A shudder went through him as he thought about what his father had missed out on when he'd chosen his stepmother over him. All those years he had lost that couldn't be retrieved. Fraser was not going to let that happen to his baby. His child would always know, unquestioningly, that his father loved him. His child would always come first.

At least he and Elspeth saw eye to eye on that one. He thought back to what she had said about her family—her responsibilities. He had to respect the choices she had made. They were the choices he wished his father had made. Choosing family and responsibility over the passion and lust that everyone knew would fade a couple of years into a relationship.

Emotions like that could not and should not be trusted. They certainly shouldn't be the basis of important life decisions.

So why did his mind and his body have to torment him with reminders of just how much passion and lust he had felt for Elspeth? He was trying to make smart decisions. Trying to do the right thing, But all his brain cared to remind him of was how good it had felt to be with her. How satiated and content he had felt, exhausted and sweaty, with her lying in his arms. How still he had felt in that moment, just holding her close.

But it couldn't happen again. Because he'd seen how the lure of those feelings clouded judgement and screwed up priorities. His only priority now was his child. And that meant that any thoughts of a rematch of that wedding night had to be shelved. If there was one woman in the world that he couldn't have, it was Elspeth.

CHAPTER FOUR

ELSPETH LACED UP her trainers and wondered at what point she would stop being able to tie her own shoes. At just about twelve weeks pregnant her body barely felt any different from before. Her jeans were maybe a little tight, and her breasts a little sore. But the nausea that had coloured the last few weeks was starting to fade, and she could feel a surge of energy building to carry her through the next trimester.

There were no obvious outward signs of the life that was growing inside her, and even her mother hadn't guessed what was going on until she'd confessed all a week or two ago. But now Elspeth was booked in with a midwife and had a scan appointment in a few days. There was no escaping the fact that this baby was real.

She wondered whether Fraser would be able to see a difference in her and thought back to that night after the wedding, how he had touched her and held her and caressed her. Would he notice the very slight roundness of her belly? The subtle changes in her breasts?

Not that he was getting anywhere near her breasts, she reminded herself. The last thing this situation needed was the complication of a romantic relationship. They had enough to worry about without their feelings getting involved.

Since that morning in the lounge of the hotel they had exchanged a few brief texts, mainly about how the pregnancy was going, and relaying any news about the baby. Other than that there had been nothing said between them that would have given away how intimate they'd been just a few months ago. No hint of the chemistry that she couldn't deny had been seriously hot that night.

The sudden arrival of an enormous muddy black four-by-four beside her broke her train of thought, and she looked up to see Fraser behind the wheel, disconnecting a cable and tapping on his phone so she had a minute to watch him before he realised what she was doing.

The stubble on his jaw looked more than a day old, and his hair was wild and unkempt. He couldn't look more different than he had at the start of that wedding, with his hair dragged straight and under control and a smooth jawline. But she suspected that this was closer to the man he really was, with no regard for his hair and mud spattered up the sides of his car.

She smiled, pleased to have been gifted this unguarded moment, and then started as Fraser glanced out of the window and saw her watching. She refused to blush, breathing deep and evenly, forcing her body not to react. It was a trick she'd learnt young, not wanting her pale Celtic skin to give away her every emotion.

Fraser swung down from the car and, remembering their awkwardness the last few times they'd seen each other, Elspeth decided to take the lead and reached up to give him a peck on the cheek. A handshake would have been ridiculous, given everything that had happened between them, and she'd been thinking about how this was going to work.

They needed to be friends. It was important for their

baby that they got on with one another. That they worked together to give this child everything it needed. If they couldn't manage a kiss on the cheek, then they were in serious trouble.

'Hi,' she said, trying to make her smile seem natural as she lowered herself from her tiptoes. She'd forgotten how he towered over her. How much she'd loved the feeling of her body being literally overwhelmed by him.

'Hi,' Fraser replied, and for a few moments he didn't move away.

She didn't want to either. She stayed close to him, smiling up, caught in the memory of how good it had felt to have his body tight against hers. How naturally they had read one another, how in sync they had felt that night.

And then Elspeth's smile dropped as she remembered where it had led. The consequences of that intimacy.

Basking in the warm glow of a smile and a physical connection was all well and good if you had no responsibilities. But that wasn't her life—and she had to remember that. The days when she had been able to indulge herself with romantic fantasies were long gone—if they'd ever really existed at all.

She took a deliberate step back, and Fraser seemed to sense her change in mood, his face falling and darkening as she could only assume her own had.

'Are you sure you're up to a walk?' he asked. 'I don't know much about this pregnancy stuff, but I read a couple of books and I'm pretty sure you're meant to take things easy.'

Elspeth couldn't help her smile returning at the thought of him poring over mother and baby manuals.

'I'm fine, really. I'd tell you if it wasn't. We'll take a gentle route up.'

Fraser nodded and looked out over the park, up towards the climb to Arthur's Seat—a jagged rocky peak that towered over the city of Edinburgh, the remains of a long-extinct volcano. 'Do you come and walk up here often?' he asked.

'Not as often as I should,' Elspeth said, realising it was true. 'I suppose it's that thing of stuff being on your doorstep—you forget to do all the things that the guidebooks flog to the tourists.'

Fraser gave an offended snort, digging his hands in his pockets. 'It's not just the tourists, you know. I walk up here whenever I'm in the city.'

'I'm calling you out on not being a tourist,' Elspeth said, clicking the button to lock her car as they walked towards the path leading out of the car park. 'You might not be wearing tartan trousers and touring a distillery, but you're not part of the city—I can tell that much.'

She'd had to go on her instincts, fill in some blanks, she realised, because she knew so little about him. This man had donated fifty per cent of the genetic material she was growing inside her, and yet she didn't know even the most basic things about him.

Time for some digging, she realised. Time to work out who this man was and how she was going to fit him into her life.

'I lived here for a few years when I was a teenager,' Fraser said. 'Before I went back north.'

'That explains the accent, at least.' Elspeth smiled. 'The city's softened it.'

Fraser returned her smile, but it didn't quite reach his eyes. 'You'd make my mother weep.'

'I live to make mothers weep.'

'I like the sound of that.'

She caught his eye and enjoyed the heat in his expression as they stopped and took one another in. It was so easy. Like it had been that night at the wedding, talking with him was so natural. And afterwards, falling into bed with him had been effortless. He'd known everything that she'd wanted. She'd seen everything that he'd needed.

And then she jerked back to the present and self-consciousness set in as she remembered that she shouldn't be thinking of him like that—that the life growing inside her put anything else entirely out of reach.

'What about you?' Fraser asked. 'Edinburgh born and bred?'

'Yep, that's me,' she said, gratefully leaping on the change of subject. 'I've never left the city limits. God, I'm kidding,' she added, when she saw the look of horror on his face. So much for lightening the mood. 'You don't like the city?' she asked.

'Edinburgh's my favourite city. Does that count?'

She narrowed her eyes. 'Well, that kind of depends on what you think of all the others.'

'I don't feel natural in a city.' He shrugged. 'It feels… constraining. I need fresh air. Open spaces.'

Elspeth smiled. That much she'd started to work out for herself. 'So you left as soon as you could?' she guessed. 'College? University?'

He nodded and named a specialist agricultural college near Inverness.

'When you say you're a country boy…'

She found that she was somewhat impressed, though she couldn't put her finger on why. But his commitment to a way of life, to the countryside that he so obviously loved, was commendable. And there was something sexy and grounded about a man who was so connected to the earth.

'I mean there's mud in my veins, rather than blood.'

Elspeth realised that even with as long as they had been talking about what he loved she still had no actual idea what he did for a living.

'So you work in—what? Farming?' she asked, pitching a guess towards the only countryside occupation her city-bred mind could think of.

She knew that she sounded ignorant, but in all honesty she couldn't think of a time in her life when she had even thought about how the countryside worked. That someone had to be out there *making* it work.

'Not really. I had a little money from my grandparents' will when I turned twenty-one, and I invested it in some land I wanted to see developed in a sustainable way. The development made a profit, so I bought more land, built some more properties,' Fraser replied.

Elspeth raised her eyebrows, encouraging him to tell her more.

'Well-developed and well-managed country estates generate an income, which means I can buy more land, which I manage profitably… You can see how it goes.'

'Okay…'

With those titbits of information, and what she'd already seen of where he stayed when he was in Edinburgh, it was becoming increasingly clear how different their lives were. She hadn't given much thought to the luxurious hotel suite he'd taken her back to the night of the wedding. But when he'd suggested the same luxury hotel when she'd met him for a second time she'd guessed that he had money. Serious money.

Great. Money wasn't exactly known to *un*complicate

situations—and what was he going to make of her less than glamorous lifestyle? The nineteen-fifties bungalow that she shared with her mother and her sister? Was his money a part of him that she would ever understand, or would it always be a gulf between them? A part of one another that would always be alien.

It didn't matter, she reminded herself. She didn't want to date him. All she needed from him was to be a good father to their child.

'Are you okay?' Fraser asked, looking at her with concern.

Elspeth waved away his worries and looked out at the view. 'Fine,' she said. 'Just need a breather for a moment.'

She stood looking out over the city and realised how close Fraser was behind her. So close she could practically feel the heat radiating from his chest and his torso. Those tight abs that she'd explored, and then owned, the night of the wedding.

It would be too easy to lean back into him, to let the chemistry that had led them astray that night be back in charge. But it would only lead to trouble, she reminded herself. She was taking on enough with this baby, the baby that was making its presence known by literally stealing the oxygen from her lungs, without trying to make space in her life for a relationship as well.

No, it didn't matter how attracted she was to Fraser. Falling for him meant devoting less of herself to her mother and her sister, and that wasn't an option. Sarah needed her, and Elspeth's feelings came a distant second to that.

She let the breath go and started walking again, determined to reach the top of the hill before they had to turn around, looking for a change of subject. 'Have you told your family about me? About the baby?' she asked, not sure where she wanted this conversation to go, but aware that she needed a change of subject.

'I told my mum,' Fraser said, with a nod and a smile. 'She was pretty shocked, but she's excited about being a grandmother. And desperate to meet you.'

Elspeth grimaced nervously. 'Mine too. My mum, I mean. And my sister. Well, once the shock wore off and they regained the power of speech. What about your dad?' she asked as an afterthought, remembering, as she did sometimes, that most people had more than one parent to consider.

'I've not told my dad, actually,' Fraser said. 'We're not in touch.'

'I'm sorry,' Elspeth said, slipping without thinking about it into her sympathetic doctor's voice. 'Do you want to talk about it?'

'No.' Fraser's tone made it clear that the topic was not up for discussion, and he turned back to the path, picking up his pace. 'What about you?' he asked. 'You mentioned your mum and your sister. Is your dad around?'

She shook her head. 'He never has been.'

Fraser's expression told her exactly what he thought about a father who abandoned his children, and she wondered about his relationship with his dad. How long had it been since they had spoken? What had happened to drive them apart? Was he the reason Fraser bristled as much as she did every time that chemistry sparked between them?

'Probably better that way,' Fraser said.

Well, that was one way to look at it, she thought, surprised at his reaction. But was it really better to have been abandoned by one of her parents? And did she really want to raise a child with someone who thought that way? If she had the choice, two parents seemed like a pretty good deal.

'You know,' Fraser said, his tone still brusque, 'we haven't spoken at all about how this is going to work. I mean, where I'm working now—it's not quite the Highlands, but it's more than an hour from the city. I don't even know where you live. Do you live with your mother?'

Elspeth bristled, wondering whether that was a criticism. 'And my sister. It's not like we have a choice. We all rely on each other.'

'Right. So we're both stuck where we are, and somehow we have to come up with how we give this baby the family that it deserves. And we've got six months—more or less—to figure this out. Shouldn't we be concentrating on that?'

He said it as if it hadn't occupied just about every free moment that she'd had in the last three months. Her shoulders rose as she prepared to defend herself against his implied criticism.

'Brilliant. If you've got this sussed, then I'm all ears.'

'I didn't say that I had the answers,' Fraser snapped. 'Just that we need to start thinking about it.'

'*Start* thinking about it?' Well, if he wasn't going to hold his temper in check, she wasn't either. 'Fraser, I've thought about nothing else since I took that pregnancy test. The fact that I haven't come up with an answer doesn't reflect the amount of effort I've put in.'

'I'm sure you've been thinking about it.' Fraser said, stopping and grabbing her hand so she had no choice but to look him in the eye. 'I have too. But we've not been *talking* about it. Thinking about this separately isn't the same as thinking about this together.'

He squeezed the hand he was still holding and a jolt of electricity went up her arm—a warning of the danger that still existed just from being close to him. A reminder that if she wanted to keep her head she couldn't get too close.

The sun was behind her. She could feel it warm on the back of her head as the gentle breeze caught at her hair. The sun gleamed off Fraser's hair too, and fine lines appeared around his eyes as he squinted in the bright light. High above the city, in the quiet they had found up here, it was harder to ignore that insistent nagging feeling, the reminder of everything she had felt for him that night. Of how hot their chemistry had been. Of how easily the conversation and the laughs had come.

'I'm not going to be an absent dad,' Fraser said, and the *like my own* was so clear it didn't need to be said out loud.

Elspeth shook her head, glad that he had brought her thoughts back to the baby, where they should be. Not on that night.

'I'm not going to be some bit-part player in my child's life.'

'I don't want that either,' Elspeth admitted. It wasn't going to be easy, having him in her life. Not when her body had its own very firm ideas of what it wanted from him, which were strictly off-limits. But they both owed it to their baby to work out how to be around each other.

'I'll look at my property portfolio,' Fraser said at last. 'See if there's a place in the city that's suitable for us. For me and a room for the baby, I mean. If not, I'll see what's on the market.'

'What about your work?' Elspeth asked.

He shrugged. 'I don't have to be there twenty-four-seven. I can work from the city some of the time if I have to. I'll work it out. This is too important not to.'

Elspeth nodded, and they walked on.

'Are you going to carry on living with your mum?' Fraser asked.

'I don't have a choice,' Elspeth said. 'My mum and I take care of my sister. My sister and I help Mum out. They both help me put in the hours at work that I need to do so that we can pay the mortgage. If I leave, the whole ecosystem stops working.'

Her sister had mentioned once or twice that she would like to move out one day, but Elspeth had been trying to break it to her gently that there was no way it could happen. Elspeth needed to oversee all her care, and it just wouldn't be possible if they weren't under the same roof.

She glanced across and saw Fraser nodding. 'I understand that—sounds like a lot of pressure on you, though. And there's enough room for you all, when the baby gets here?'

'For now.' She nodded, with more confidence than she felt. 'The baby will sleep in my room. And when that's not possible any more...'

Well, I'll cross that bridge when we come to it, she thought.

By the time the baby was born her training post would have finished and she should have been offered a permanent job. Janet was happy enough with her, and the shortage of GPs across the country was in her favour. But... But what if she didn't get the job? What if she couldn't find anything else near her home, so that she would always be nearby if she was needed?

She felt a twinge of anxiety. This was when she was meant to be making big commitments in her career—while her mum was still mobile, before her responsibilities grew even more. She had intended to spend her thirties working every unsociable hour, taking every extra shift, every on-call, covering for colleagues, all to build up a pot of money and goodwill that would be sorely needed when they all needed more help.

She'd never made the conscious decision that she wouldn't have children—she just hadn't thought about where in her plan it might happen. But then Fraser had come along and all her carefully made plans had been worth less than nothing.

'What are you thinking about?' Fraser asked, and Elspeth realised they had been walking in silence for a good ten minutes.

'Work,' she replied, knowing that she was holding back.

'Anything I can help with?'

'Not really.' She shook her head. There was no point. Fraser couldn't fix this situation any more than she could. 'Just thinking about what I'm going to do when my training post comes to an end if I don't get this job.'

'You'll get it,' he said, with a confidence she had never felt. 'They must love you. You dragged yourself to that wedding…'

She smiled, knowing that he was thinking about the first time they'd met.

'I definitely earned some Brownie points with that.'

Janet had written a touching note in the thank-you card she'd sent after the event, saying how pleased she was that she had been able to come. And no one seemed to have noticed that she'd sneaked out early, so she was winning all round.

'I'll need you to send me your address,' Fraser said after they'd walked on a bit more. 'I'll start looking for somewhere nearby.'

'Nearby?'

So they might bump into each other in the supermarket, or out for a jog? She felt a shiver of apprehension at the realisation of how present Fraser was going to be in her life from here on in. How impossible it was going to be to ignore him. How much of a challenge it was going to be trying to ignore this chemistry between them. He never said his flat in the city would be *close*.

'Doesn't make sense for me to get a place if it takes me an hour to travel across from the other side of the city.'

'I know. I just hadn't thought…'

'What? That I'd be a part of your life?'

Ugh, she could do without him reading her mind right now.

'I think this is how it works from now on. We have to get used to that.'

Of course he was right. It was just that it had been easy to kid herself so far that nothing was going to change that much. Sure, she'd have a baby to care for, but her whole day was already spent caring for people.

There would be maternity leave, and then, if everything went as she hoped, she would be back at work, just with extra drop-offs and pick-ups to work into her day. Appointments with health visitors and childminders and looking for a nursery. A whole new column to add to her calendar and her diary and her to-do list.

That was the choice she had made. But at no point had she chosen Fraser. Well, she had, she supposed, in the half-light of the botanic gardens. But she'd chosen him for *right then*. For *pleasure*. For *that night*. Not for ever.

'I'm not going to disappear on you or the bairn, Elspeth. Like your dad or mine. I'm here. I'm always going to be here.'

Well, he didn't have to make it sound like a threat… But she felt his words in the pit of her stomach, the commitment that he had just made to her child, and a tiny part of her fear melted away with it.

And then another, larger part, doubled in size. She knew she was never going to be rid of him, and she was going to have to spend her whole lifetime resisting him. It was going to be exhausting, and she had no idea where she was going to find the energy to do it.

'Your dad…' Elspeth started, not really sure where she wanted the conversation to go, just knowing that she wanted it to move away from her, and the changes to her life. He could sit under the spotlight for a while. 'You said that he left. What happened?'

Fraser made a casual gesture, but she could see from the hard-set lines of his face that he felt anything but relaxed about the subject.

'He met someone else. I was fifteen. He and Mum broke up and I told him that if he married the new woman I wouldn't see him again. He chose her.'

Elspeth stopped in her tracks. 'You gave him an ultimatum?'

'And he chose her.'

She stood and looked at him for a moment, shocked by the strength of mind that he'd had at fifteen. The stubbornness that she knew he still had now. 'I'm sorry, Fraser, that must have been hard. And you've had no contact since?'

'He contacts my mum occasionally. But other than that… Nothing.'

She really didn't want to be on the wrong side of an argument with him. This was brutal, she thought, on both sides. Though she couldn't help but consider that his father had been put in an impossible position. There were rarely any winners when people started dishing out ultimatums. But Fraser had only been a kid himself at the time.

'How did your mum feel about this?' Elspeth asked, still trying to imagine the shockwaves that something like this would send through a family.

'She was devastated when he told her he wanted a divorce. It took her years to be happy again. I couldn't see him after watching her go through that. And I couldn't go back to… I couldn't go home. To see someone else in our home. He destroyed our family.'

'But surely…?'

Elspeth hesitated. She knew that she didn't have all the information, but to cut off any contact like that seemed so…*drastic*. It was heartbreaking when a family broke up, but plenty of people managed to keep relationships going in worse circumstances. People less stubborn than Fraser and his father, clearly.

'You don't think that was a little…?'

The look on Fraser's face told her that her opinion was not welcome on this subject. Well, fine. Not today. But she had a feeling that they would be revisiting this one.

'I suppose I'll have to see him now, though,' Fraser said eventually, and Elspeth whipped her head round to look at him.

'Why?' she asked. 'I mean, I'm all for it, if my opinion counts for anything,' she clarified.

The last thing she wanted was her baby to be born in the middle of a family feud, but this was such an about-turn. After what—fifteen years of silence?—he was suddenly going to change his mind?

'Because my father still lives in our family home. It's a part of me, and I want my child to know it. That's more important than how I feel about my father.'

She gave him a sidelong look, aware that there was something she wasn't understanding here, that Fraser was choosing to hold back.

She felt a shot of something cold. A protective instinct that she recognised as maternal. The first stirrings of her inner mama bear. 'The baby's home will be with us,' she said.

'Of course with us. But it's also...*there*. Where I grew up.'

Elspeth bit her tongue. It was as clear as anything that Fraser was still carrying a lot of emotional baggage about his father. But it wasn't her place to interfere. She wasn't his wife, or even his girlfriend. She was the mother of his child, and that was it. No opinions about his personal life were allowed. Or necessary, she remembered. This wasn't her fight, however sad she might be for that poor teenaged Fraser, feeling abandoned by his dad.

'Well, I can be there with you. If you want,' Elspeth said.

Fraser caught at her hand and gave it a squeeze. 'Thanks.'

She snatched her fingers back, surprised at the heat she had felt zipping from his hand to hers. The last thing she needed was to be reminded of that.

Fraser looked at her, his eyes narrowed as he took in her reaction. 'I was just saying thanks,' he said, raising his hands in a show of innocence. 'It didn't mean anything.'

'I know that. But it's just… I don't want things to get confusing.'

Fraser narrowed his eyes. 'Confusing how?'

She took a step back, needing to put some space between them. 'Confusing like thinking that it would be a good idea for something to happen between us.'

'All I did was hold your hand.' He shook his head.

'I know that. But it reminded me…'

It had reminded her of every skin-on-skin second they had shared before, and it had made her body crave more. And that couldn't happen. She couldn't allow herself to think like that. To want that. It was too dangerous. She fought to keep her body neutral. To quieten her pulse, to fight the rush of blood to her face. She was an adult, and she was in control of her body. Her decisions. Her desires.

'It doesn't matter what it reminded me of,' she told Fraser eventually, her voice admirably calm. 'I just want to be clear about what's on offer here and what's…*not*.'

'I think you're making that very clear,' Fraser said.

She searched his face and his voice for any hint of annoyance but couldn't find one. He seemed irritatingly nonchalant about the whole thing, if she was honest. Was she pleased about that? Was this easy for him? Did he not think about it at *all*?

She needed to make sure that he completely understood, though. Given how they had met, and all the changes in their lives since then, she had to make sure that they were on the same page when it came to their relationship. Had to make sure that he understood that they could only ever be friends. Anything else was too complicated.

'I think we need to acknowledge that there is chemistry between us. I mean, that's what got us here, isn't it? But we can't act on it any more. We can't be tempted. We need to be good parents to this baby. We need to be thinking straight. Making sensible decisions. We can't be getting distracted by whatever feelings we had for each other that night.'

He quirked the corner of his lip in an annoying hint of a smile, as if he was finding this whole conversation amusing rather than embarrassing. 'And what feelings *did* you have for me that night?'

Oh, she could have listed them: lust, desire, need, abandon, *want*. But someone had to be the responsible one here, so instead, she shook her head.

'We're not talking about that night. We're talking about now. And right now the only feelings I have for you are friendly. We are going to be friends. We are going to raise this child together. And we are never going to talk about that night again.'

'Never talk about it again? Might that not get awkward?'

He shrugged and she decided that, yes, his nonchalance was *definitely* annoying. 'Why would it be awkward?'

'People are going to have questions,' Fraser replied. 'Our friends. Our families. They're going to want to know what's happening with us.'

'Oh, and you usually spill all about your sex life to your friends and your family, do you?'

'No, but there's a baby on the way...'

She nodded emphatically and started walking again. 'Exactly. That tells them all they need to know about what has happened in the past. When they want to know what's happening with us now, we tell them the truth. That we're friends.'

Fraser fell silent, obviously thinking that through. 'You know, we never considered the alternative.'

For the first time she heard a shake in his voice, heard doubt in his tone.

'We've never talked about doing the right thing. Marrying. Making a proper family for this baby.'

Elspeth wasn't sure whether she was meant to laugh or not. That was the most unromantic proposal of marriage she had ever heard, and from the look on Fraser's face he'd dragged it out like needles through his skin. She was tempted to accept, just to see the look of horror on his face, but even she wasn't that cruel.

'Is that what you really want for our family, Fraser? The two of us pretending to be something we're not because we think it's the right thing for the baby?'

He looked relieved that she hadn't said yes, but aware that she hadn't said no either. She had no intention of doing so—she was more interested in exploring the reasons he'd asked in the first place.

'Aren't we meant to be putting the baby's needs first?' he asked, tiptoeing his way through the words.

'Why does that have to mean marriage? Your mum and mine have both done fine on their own.'

'But you're not on your own. You've got me; I'm not going anywhere.'

Elspeth crossed her arms. 'Exactly, so we don't need a marriage certificate to tell us that. Your name will be on the birth certificate, and that's enough for me.'

'You're not interested in the whole nuclear family thing?'

'I guess not.'

'What about when you meet someone else?'

The thought hadn't even occurred to her. It was hard enough accepting that she was going to have to make room in her life for Fraser and their child. The thought that she might meet someone else one day, make room for them too—it was laughable. She'd tried once before to make a relationship work with the other commitments in her life, and it had threatened to take her away from her sister. The person who needed her more than anyone. She wouldn't be making that decision again—not with him or with anyone else.

She thought back to the night she'd spent with Fraser, how they'd clicked from their first banter at the wedding to her first orgasm, to that first and last kiss of the morning when she'd sneaked out of his hotel room. If she couldn't find a way to make a relationship work with that kind of incentive, she didn't much fancy anyone else's chances.

'I don't want anybody else.'

It was easier to say that than to tell the truth. How would Fraser, with his money and his privilege, understand the compromises and the struggles that were an everyday part of her life? How was he going to react when she didn't finish work until long after she wanted to be in bed because the practice was overstretched and her patients needed her attention? When her mum had been in so much pain after work that she'd had to go straight to bed and so there were dishes and laundry to do? When her sister needed her? When her mother could no longer look after herself?

Alex had made it clear that it wasn't something you signed up for voluntarily.

There was no point pretending that she was looking forward to a life without romance, but some things took priority. If she had to choose—again—she'd make the same decision every time. Nothing would ever be more important to her than her family.

As they reached the top of Arthur's Seat she took a moment to look at the view, seeing the whole of the city spread out beneath them and realising how high they'd climbed. She was a little out of breath—no doubt courtesy of the baby now sharing her oxygen and blood supply.

But, having climbed up here with Fraser, she was sure of one thing. They were going to fight for this. Probably with each other at times, but hopefully on the same team too. They were going to be a family. They would make it work because they both loved this baby.

The fact that they didn't love each other wouldn't change that.

CHAPTER FIVE

WHEN FRASER HAD suggested grabbing something to eat after the twelve-week scan she hadn't realised that he'd meant *here*. She had shoes she'd be happy to wear to a Michelin-starred restaurant in one of the city's most exclusive hotels, but she didn't usually throw them on when she was expecting to go for a scan and then straight back home. And catching sight of her battered old trainers was making her mightily uncomfortable.

The interior of the restaurant was opulently decorated, and the pale September sun that braved it past the heavy velvet curtains and dark wooden panelling glinted on the crystal glasses and the chandeliers above them. She couldn't remember the last time she'd been in this part of the city, and she'd forgotten how packed the Royal Mile could be with visitors—even outside of the usual touristy times of year.

She would walk back through the closes and wynds, she promised herself, thinking of the quiet alleyways that snaked through the Old Town, down the steep hill towards the New Town and away from the main thoroughfare. No matter how familiar she was with the city she still found something new to see every time, looking up towards the sky at the teetering buildings, five or six storeys above the narrow cobbled passageways below.

The wait staff were hovering at the edges of the room, and she remembered that she was meant to be choosing something to order. The food looked incredible—all Aberdeen Angus steak and oozing egg yolks and local game—normally everything she could have wanted from a menu. But with pregnancy safety advice in the forefront of her mind after the scan she couldn't see a single thing that looked both safe to eat and appealing.

Fraser didn't seem to care that neither of them was dressed for a fancy lunch, and was still wearing the blissed-out expression that he had adopted when the sonographer had drizzled the cold gel on her belly, touched the probe to her skin and showed them their baby's flickering heartbeat just a second later.

Elspeth looked up from her menu and smiled across the table at Fraser. Seeing their baby on the screen had been a breathtaking moment, and she was so glad they had shared it together. At her first scan—when she'd gone alone, not sure whether this baby was going to have one parent or two, half convinced that she'd completely imagined seeing the word 'pregnant' on the test she'd taken a few weeks before—there had been nothing more than a tiny pulsing flicker.

But this time they had seen her baby—their baby—with its tiny arms and legs and fingers. Fraser had gripped her hand, and in that moment she'd known that it didn't matter how this baby had come about. They were both going to love it with an intensity that threatened to suffocate her.

But now they had left that little bubble, and the real world was creeping back in.

'I can't believe we saw our baby,' she said, for about the hundredth time since they'd left the hospital, trying to recapture their mood in the hospital.

'Pretty amazing,' Fraser said, nodding. 'When do we get to see him again?' he asked.

'Easy with the *him* stuff,' Elspeth reminded him. 'We don't know the sex yet. And the next scan is at twenty weeks. We can find out the sex then, if we want to.'

Fraser's eyebrows shot up. 'Not for another two months? What if something goes wrong before then?'

Elspeth bristled, sitting up a little straighter. 'Why would anything go wrong?'

'I'm not saying it will,' Fraser said. 'But it's a long time between scans. I want the baby to be checked more often.'

She shook her head. Here spoke a man with little experience of the NHS and none of pregnancy.

'Well, with most pregnancies there's no need to be seen more often,' she explained, as she would to any patient. 'Everything is fine.'

'But in some pregnancies there *are* problems, and I don't want us to be one of those pregnancies,' Fraser pressed on, seemingly unaware that her hackles were rapidly rising. 'As soon as we're done here I'm going to get us booked in to the private hospital. I want the best for you both, and waiting two months for another scan can't be the best.'

'And you're basing this on what?' Elspeth asked, her voice tart, annoyed at his high-handed tone. 'Your extensive obstetric knowledge?'

Was he really suggesting that she wouldn't do what was right for their baby? That she would cut corners to save money? *She* was the one who actually knew what she was talking about when it came to the medical side of things. She wasn't going to let him have his own way just because he wanted to throw his money and his privilege around.

'I just don't see why we wouldn't pay for extra care for our baby,' he said, laying down his menu and glaring at her.

Elspeth tried to tamp down her temper before she spoke, but she was finding it more and more difficult. 'This isn't a situation that you just throw money at, Fraser. You weigh up the costs and benefits of additional investigations. I don't see the need for more.'

Fraser took a sip of his drink and shrugged. 'I don't see the downside. I'm not going to change my mind.'

'Really? You surprise me.' Forget keeping her temper—it wasn't *her* fault he was being completely illogical. 'Well, with my five years of medical school, and seven more of training, I *might* have picked up something about weighing up the risks and benefits of additional testing in a medical setting. But if you think your gut feeling and your bank balance outweigh that experience—'

He held his hands up. 'Fine. If you feel so strongly, stay at your hospital—don't bother with the extra scans. But I'm not going to pretend that I understand. I think you're making a mistake.'

Too right he didn't understand. And if he wanted to go private now, when they'd had a textbook visit, with a ten-minute wait in a comfortable room and a friendly sonographer who had chatted as she'd talked them through the scan, what was he going to make of her family's regular middle-of-the-night trips to the emergency department? Of dealing with underfunded community services and appointments cancelled and moved at the last minute? The sort of things that made up most of the days of her life. And that was when she wasn't working extra shifts to cover their understaffed and underfunded GP practice…

'What?' he asked, and she guessed that some of what she was thinking must be showing on her face.

'Nothing…' she hedged. 'I was just thinking how different we are. How different our lives are. Wondering how this is going to work.'

'I don't think we're that different,' he countered, leaning forward on his elbows and fixing her with a look.

'You think this is the sort of place to come for a quick lunch,' she stated, glancing around her.

He drew his eyebrows together and frowned. 'I thought you'd like it. I mean, it's not where I usually come in my walking boots and my waterproof jacket.'

'Right—Fraser the country boy.'

He narrowed his eyes. 'I'll choose not to take that as an insult.'

'It wasn't.' She lifted her hands, not sure how to get across what she was thinking. 'But we're *different*. I love this city. You're clearly uncomfortable here. You'd rather be out at one of your estates—and when I say "estate" we both know I'm not talking about new-build semis,' she clarified. 'My life is spent in city hospitals like the one you thought wasn't good enough today, and you've spent the last week looking to acquire—what? A…a stately home?'

'A castle.'

'A castle? Right. And you're buying it from…?'

'A duke.'

Elspeth nodded—he had just proved her point. Even if her family didn't present its own challenges, they were too different. Their lives were too different for this ever to be anything other than impossible.

'A duke is just a person,' Fraser said, holding her gaze, not letting her look away. 'No different from anyone else.'

'Yeah, right. Castles notwithstanding.'

Elspeth watched Fraser as a cloud crossed his face.

'I'm serious. Titles don't mean anything,' he said.

Elspeth stopped and gave him a long look. 'You're taking this rather personally.'

He nodded. 'I have reason to.'

'You have a…a title?' Elspeth asked, noting the strain in her own voice.

'A courtesy title—at least while my father's still alive. When he dies I'll inherit the estate and the title that goes with it.'

She took in a deep breath, collecting herself, trying to keep a rein on her thoughts. 'Which means the baby…?'

'Will have a title too. One day.'

How could he have kept this from her? She didn't care about his title. About where he'd grown up and who his family were. But this was *her* baby he was talking about. She had seen him or her on the screen that afternoon, waving at them with its perfect, tiny little fingers. And now Fraser had dropped this bombshell, telling her that her baby was part of something that she could barely understand, never mind be a part of.

'And you're only thinking to mention this now?' she said, aware that her shock was making her words sharp. 'You didn't say a word about it when we talked about your dad.'

Fraser shrugged and held up his hands. 'It's not usually my opening gambit when I'm picking up women.'

'Wow—and doesn't *that* make me feel special?'

She glanced down at the menu again, using it as a handy way to hide her face. At least Fraser had made it very clear where she stood, she supposed. She was just some woman he had picked up—one of many, by the sounds of it. If there hadn't been a baby they never would have seen each other again.

'I imagine a castle and a title have a pretty high success rate,' she said, when she was sure she could speak calmly, determined to show him she didn't care that she had been nothing more than a one-night stand to him. That was all he had been to her as well, after all.

Fraser snorted, pouring them both a glass of water. 'Evidently not with you,' he said. 'You seem pretty annoyed about it, actually.'

Well, he was observant enough—she would give him that.

'I am *pretty annoyed* about the fact that you haven't mentioned it before. This is the sort of thing I think I should know about the father of my child. When were you planning on telling me?'

'I didn't really have a plan,' Fraser said.

He really wasn't helping himself here. Still, he was making it easier and easier for her to remember that under no circumstances should she be thinking about having a relationship with him.

'You were going to hide it from me?' she asked.

'That's not the same thing.'

'I don't even know what to call you,' she said at last, her frustration getting the better of her. 'Am I meant to curtsey?'

Fraser gave a frustrated bark of laughter. 'You call me Fraser, just like before. And don't be angry.' He reached across to brush the gentlest of touches against her fingertips, where she was clutching her water glass with a death grip. 'This isn't about you or the baby,' he continued. 'I don't like to talk about my family because it's complicated.'

'Well, I'm family now too. I think we should talk about this.'

He drew away, rested back in his chair and gave her a long look. 'I'm not sure what to tell you, apart from what you already know. I've not seen my father or been back to our estate since I was a teenager,' Fraser said after a few moments.

'So you're buying all this land, these other estates…?'

'Because I can't go back to my own.' Fraser nodded slowly, thoughtfully. 'I wish I could. I miss it like—'

Fraser cut himself off and took a long sip of his water. Elspeth kept her eyes on him, waiting until he was ready to speak again.

'Thank you,' she said. 'For sharing it with me now. I want us to be able to talk.'

He reached for her hand. 'I still can't believe we saw him,' he said, throwing a glance to a waiter, who had appeared beside them with a tray and two champagne flutes. 'It's non-alcoholic,' Fraser said, reading her mind. 'But I thought we should have a toast.'

She smiled. He was right. This wasn't about them. This was about doing what was right for their baby. Their feelings for one another didn't have to come into it at all.

'To the baby,' she said, clinking her glass against his and taking a sip.

But just because she had let this conversation rest for now, that didn't mean it was over. There was still so much that they didn't understand about one another's lives, and she wasn't sure how they were ever going to reconcile that. There was a part of him, and of her child now, that would always feel like a stranger to her.

CHAPTER SIX

'Is it going to be big enough?' Fraser asked a few weeks later, as they viewed an apartment in Edinburgh's exclusive West End.

Big enough? She looked around the room that she was standing in. The floor-to-ceiling windows flooded the old Regency room with light, which reflected back at her from the gilt work on the ceiling, the white marble of the enormous fireplace, the top of the grand piano and the polished floorboards beneath her feet.

You could have fitted her family's whole semi-detached bungalow into this one room. Okay, maybe she was exaggerating a little—but only a little. When Fraser had said that he was going to find an apartment in the city, she'd envisaged a two-bedroomed bachelor flat, just a room for him and a nursery for the baby. Not this luxury.

She was reminded once again of how different their lives were. How their homes would always look so different. His filled with designer furnishings and a grand piano, just 'because', and hers with medical equipment and stray stethoscopes.

'It's plenty big enough,' she said with a slightly brittle laugh. 'How big do you think this baby is going to be?'

'Ah, but I've done my research,' Fraser said, smiling and pointing a finger in the general direction of her newly apparent baby bump. 'A baby equals about seven or eight pounds and twenty inches long. The *stuff* that comes with one is approximately the size and mass of the Milky Way.'

Elspeth laughed again—properly this time. 'Well, I guess that depends on how much stuff you buy. Me and my mum and my sister manage in somewhere half the size of this, and we come with about thirty years' worth of accumulated junk and a shedload of medical equipment.'

Fraser's face fell, and she guessed he was only just starting to see how different the experiences they brought to this relationship were.

'But wouldn't you want more space if it were an option? Would you just "manage" if you didn't have to?'

'I'm not good with hypotheticals,' Elspeth said, any trace of laughter gone from her voice. Was he judging her? For having less money? A smaller house than he did?

'Okay,' he said. 'Let's make this less hypothetical.'

Fraser spoke quickly, and she wondered how much of her annoyance had shown on her face.

'This baby is going to have a lot of money at his or her disposal. I think we ought to talk about how we're going to approach that.'

Elspeth crossed her arms. Still wondering whether he was criticising. Judging. 'I don't want to raise a spoiled brat.'

Fraser raised an eyebrow. 'And do *I* fall into that category?'

Elspeth shrugged. 'I never said that.' *Out loud.*

'But you know that I was raised with money. Do you think it's made me a bad person? Am I a brat?'

Well, if he was going to ask a leading question…

'You know what you want,' she replied, not directly answering his question. 'You're good at getting it. You *expect* to get it.'

He oozed confidence and privilege with an ease that made it apparent he didn't realise he was doing it. It wasn't his fault. He couldn't help the position he'd been born into any more than anyone else could. But that didn't mean he should be ignorant of it.

'I'm not sure I should apologise for that,' he said.

She didn't point out that she'd never asked him to. They both knew her criticism had been implied.

'It's just not what I'm used to,' Elspeth said, trying to be conciliatory. 'I'm sure we'll find a middle ground.'

'I want to make sure that my child is provided for.'

'And I'm not capable of doing that?' Being conciliatory didn't extend to ignoring his criticism of how she took care of her family.

'I just don't see why you don't want me to spend the money I've worked hard to make on our bairn.'

She smiled, unable to help herself, at the words 'our bairn' from his lips. From the look on his face as he'd said it.

'Let me look after both of you,' he continued, sitting back on the arm of the nearest sofa, his body language relaxed and open. 'All three of us.'

Reluctantly, she smiled and nodded, intoxicated by the sight of Fraser in his new role as doting dad. She sat in the armchair beside him, tucking her feet underneath her.

'You know, we've never really talked much about your family,' Fraser went on. 'Tell me more about caring for your sister. How is it with the three of you living together?'

'It's the only arrangement that makes sense. I do as much of Sarah's care as I can myself. Sarah's mentioned getting her own place, but I don't think she really appreciates what that would mean. More care from strangers... less from me and Mum. I hate the thought of it.'

'And did your ex live with you too?' Fraser asked, throwing her a curveball by mentioning Alex.

She shook her head. 'No. In fact we called things off when it became clear that it wasn't going to work for him. And he was right. We never stood a chance—not with all the other responsibilities I have in my life. He would always have had to share me with my family. It wasn't fair on him.'

'I'm starting to think he didn't deserve you,' Fraser said. 'But tell me more about caring for your sister,' he added, looking genuinely interested. 'I want to understand what your life is like.'

She didn't bother correcting him about Alex. She had been right to call things off. But Fraser had asked about Sarah, and she smiled, much happier talking about her sister than her failed attempt at being a fiancée.

'My whole job is to make sure she can do whatever she needs to and to help her do as much for herself as she can manage. A lot of it is pretty basic: cutting up food, making drinks, driving her to medical appointments. Then there's the more specialised stuff, like physio, her medication—that sort of thing. She's stubborn and fierce and independent, so I'm just there to fill in the gaps when she can't do something she wants to. She was born when I was twelve; I've helped to care for her all my adult life, so I don't really know things any other way and nor does she.'

Fraser smiled. 'Sounds like you two are quite the team. Do you have outside help?'

Elspeth shrugged. 'Only in an emergency. Why would we have someone else in when we are such a good team?'

'It would give you more time,' Fraser suggested gently.

'I don't *want* time. Not if it means compromises for Sarah.'

'You love her very much,' he said plainly. 'I can't wait to see you love our baby like that.'

She met his eyes, and for a second they held each other's gaze, feeling all the potential of a future life, their future family, between them.

'I'll get in touch with my lawyer, then. Start sorting out some paperwork for our finances.'

Elspeth sat back, dropping her feet to the floor and straightening her spine, surprised by his change of direction. 'Lawyers? We're at *lawyers*? What happened to "We'll find a middle ground"? I thought we were working this out ourselves?'

'We will. We are—of course we are. But I want the baby to have security. For ever. I want you to know that whatever happens you'll be provided for.'

'Well, there's nothing melodramatic in *that* sentence to terrify me,' Elspeth replied, taking a step away from him.

What was he planning on happening? Was he creating an escape plan for himself?

'I'm not being melodramatic.' Fraser's voice was darker now. Serious. 'I'm being practical. Families break up. Parents make mistakes. I just want to know that our baby is always going to be taken care of.'

Her instinct was to bite back, to remind him that he was going absolutely nowhere and neither was she. They were going to raise this baby together, just as they had agreed. But then she remembered the look in his eyes when he had spoken about his father. That sad, confused teenager he had been was still just under the surface, still didn't understand why his relationship with his father had broken down, and she decided not to push it.

This conversation was just a symptom of a deeper problem. And the only way to deal with that was for Fraser to come to terms with what had happened between him and his dad.

She thought about the money too. Thought about the years of medical costs and on-call shifts and waiting for payday ahead of her. Knowing that at least her baby would be well provided for had relieved her of a pressure she hadn't even realised she was feeling.

'You're right. Have your lawyer do whatever you think is necessary.' She waited a beat and then asked, 'Have you thought any more about your dad?'

Fraser shot her a dark look, but she decided to press on. She and Fraser didn't know each other that well, but it was clear that his relationship with his father was going to affect his relationship with their child. She didn't want this baby born into conflict or uncertainty—if there was confrontation to be had, it would have to happen before the baby arrived.

'About going to see him?' she added, when Fraser stayed silent.

'It's complicated,' he replied, as if that was an end of the matter.

'Of course it is. That's why if it's going to happen I think it's best to do it well before the baby is here. The last thing we need is to be trekking up to the Highlands when I'm nine months gone.'

'We?'

Elspeth felt her cheeks colour. She'd assumed that she would be going with him. This was all about the baby, after all. And it wasn't as if the baby could go up there without her right now. But obviously Fraser hadn't been planning on introducing her to his family yet. Oh, well, she was too far into this thing to succumb to embarrassment now.

'Yes, *we*,' she said. 'I thought you wanted your dad to know about the baby?'

'I know I have to tell him about it. I thought I'd call him. He's not exactly going to demand to see the evidence. I'm not going up there and you don't have to either, Elspeth. It's going to be…awkward.'

'Of course it is. That's why I'm offering to be your wingman. Wing-woman. Whatever.'

She strengthened her resolve. He needed her there. This was going to be a hideously awkward family reunion, and a neutral observer would keep things on track.

'This is not the sort of conversation you have on the phone. I think you should just go up there and get it done. I'll come with you.'

'Really? You'd do that? Walk smack-bang into the middle of someone else's family drama?'

She shrugged. 'Well, I think *we're* family now. Your family drama is my family drama. And in my experience awkward family stuff usually goes better if you have a drinking partner.'

At last he cracked a smile. 'You're not going to be much use on *that* front.'

Elspeth threw up her hands and laughed softly, relieved that the tension in the room had broken. 'I will happily drink cups of tea while feeding you whisky and mopping up your tears.'

'Well, *that's* a definition of love if ever I heard one.'

Elspeth laughed again, but couldn't deny to herself

the warm glow of something that she felt in the pit of her stomach. Fraser was right. That was family. That was friendship. Wanting to sit with someone and share their pain. To offer support through something difficult even when you stood to gain nothing. That was what you did for someone that you loved. She'd do it unquestioningly for her mother and Sarah. For a handful of her friends. And now, it seemed, for Fraser.

Friendly love. Family love. That was what he had meant. Not *love* love. He didn't think she *loved* him. And she absolutely didn't—she was quite sure about that. But just the mention of the L word had done something to the atmosphere in the room.

The sun had set while they had been talking, and the lamps placed around the room now seemed more mood lighting than bright and welcoming. The soft throw rugs on the white sofa looked sensuous and inviting, and the candle burning on the mantel seemed romantic rather than staged to sell a house.

Suddenly she was standing too close to him, and yet not close enough. Before she realised what she was doing she had taken half a step forward, and he had done the same. Leaving only the space of a breath between her face and his chest.

Elspeth looked up, surprised all over again by how he towered above her, and she felt a shiver of desire as she remembered what it was to be dominated by him. How it had felt to be with him…how aware she had been of his height, his size…how powerful she had felt giving up control to him.

His hand landed on the small of her back at the same moment that her fingertips brushed against his chest, and she had a split second to decide whether she was pulling him closer or pushing him away. Her body swayed towards him, leaving her in no doubt about where her baser instincts wanted her to take this. But reason won out at the last moment and she held her breath, pressing gently against Fraser's chest as she retraced her steps, putting some much-needed space between them.

'I like the apartment,' she said, aware of how inane the words sounded given what had just almost happened between them.

She looked up, curious to see how Fraser would take the change of direction. He raised an eyebrow, and that tiny gesture showed her that he knew exactly what had just nearly happened between them, and that he had seen her swerve perfectly clearly. But he let it lie, and she figured he was as relieved as she was that they hadn't complicated things by giving in to a momentary spike of lust.

They had been perfectly clear with one another that nothing like that was on the cards between them. They just had to be sure to remember it when they were tempted.

'I'll take it, then,' Fraser said.

It took Elspeth a moment to remember that he was talking about the apartment. And then another to marvel at the fact that he could make the decision just like that on a property purchase that must run into seven figures. And then she took *another* moment to remember that this was the life her child was being born into. Would it feel normal for her child, one day, to drop upwards of a million pounds on a second home just because it was more convenient than the castle out in the country where it normally resided?

No, she reminded herself. Because regardless of where Fraser had been born, and regardless of whether he patched things up with his father, this baby would be living with *her*. Her and her mother and Sarah, in their comfortable bungalow with only a few decades of memories and zero coats of arms on the walls.

'We've not even seen all of it yet,' she reminded him.

Though, on reflection, reminding him that they hadn't seen the bedrooms maybe wasn't her most sensible move. He stood back, gesturing her towards the hallway from where several doorways led off. She tried not to feel self-conscious as she walked ahead of him. Tried not to wonder whether he was looking at her bottom in the close-fitting shift dress she had chosen to wear that morning.

It had seemed sensible and professional when she had chosen it. Now it seemed sensuous. She knew that it made the most of the few curves she had, and she couldn't help but wonder whether Fraser had noticed. Had that been what was really on her mind when she had taken it off the hanger a few hours before?

She opened the first door she came to and gave the opulent bathroom a nod. It was big, luxurious and marble. Exactly what she'd expect of a bathroom in an apartment in this part of town. The next door revealed a bedroom, its enormous bed piled high with more pillows, blankets, bedspreads and throws than a bachelor could ever need.

She had a brief thought, not quite fully formed, that this would be where Fraser would sleep—and that he wouldn't always do so alone—and shut the door. Both on the thought and on the bed.

She caught Fraser's eye, and knew that he had clocked something but decided not to say anything. Wise man.

She opened the next door, prepared just to glance inside and then close it as quickly, but the sight of an enormous white cot-bed made her pause with her hand still on the doorknob, temporarily winded.

'Wow…' The sound fell out of her mouth, barely a word, and she found she didn't have any more to follow it.

She couldn't look away from the cot. The changing table. The tiny wardrobe and the baskets stuffed with toys. This was where her baby would sleep. This was where they would change her or dress him. Rock her to sleep in the chair by the window. Would he learn to crawl on the plush rug in front of the fireplace?

It took her a few moments more to remember that she had the picture all wrong. Her baby might sleep here sometimes. Fraser might change him or her on that table. Might see first steps on that rug. But *she* wouldn't be here. This was where her baby would live when she didn't live with her.

A pain spiked at Elspeth as the knowledge that they were far from a perfectly nuclear family struck her afresh.

Her child would have two homes. It wasn't the worst thing that could happen to a child. Not least because it meant that it would have two parents who were completely devoted to it. But not to each other. There would always be hard choices. Awkward Christmases and long holidays without one parent or the other.

Elspeth reminded herself again of all the ways her baby was lucky. All the incredible advantages he or she would have in life. But she couldn't help feel a little sad that this unconventional but oh, so practical parenting arrangement meant that a lot of the time one parent or the other would be conspicuous by their absence.

'What are you thinking?' Fraser asked.

She didn't know how to put into words everything

that was racing through her mind. She realised that all her life she'd had an idea of how family life should be. Some dreamy half-formed image of breakfast in bed and acres of white bedding and a husband beside her. And now that she was expecting a baby, and part of that picture was coming true, the rest of it seemed further away than ever before.

'Just that our baby will sleep here,' she said eventually, filtering her thoughts down to their simplest component part. 'It feels weird,' she added, in case he hadn't picked up on the vibe in the room.

'Yeah,' Fraser added.

She could hear the wonder in his voice. Maybe he wasn't completely oblivious, after all.

'Do you like the room the way it is? I can ask them to leave everything?'

'I think it's gorgeous. Perfect.'

'You don't want to put your own stamp on it?'

'It's *your* home, Fraser…'

Perhaps he hadn't quite reached the same conclusions she had yet. Perhaps it hadn't occurred to him that their family was going to be stretched across at least two homes. That this little picture of familial bliss that the show home had created wasn't really going to apply for them.

'I know, but it's our baby. I want you to be happy with it too.'

'Honestly, it's lovely. Leave it just as it is.'

The atmosphere in the nursery was suddenly stifling, and Elspeth turned for the door. Fraser reached for her hand and she let him take hold of her fingers, but didn't let it stop her leaving. She needed to be out of that room.

As they reached the living room she glanced down at

their still clasped hands and Fraser followed her gaze, as if he hadn't realised what he had done. He pulled his hand away, a little more quickly than was comfortable for her ego.

'So, my dad…' Fraser said. 'You're right. We should go. And soon. I'll have to call him.'

Just like that? As if they hadn't been estranged for fifteen years?

'Well, just let me know when. Like I said, I'll be there if you want me.'

Fraser looked again at the number in his phone. Would it even still work? No one he knew answered their landline any more. But it was the only number he had for his dad. He didn't even know why he'd bothered to programme it into his phone. The number was ingrained in his memory, in his childhood—in that part of his life before he'd had a mobile phone, before his family had been torn apart.

He could ask his mum if she had a mobile number for him. He knew that they had been in touch over the years. He'd seen the evidence in his mum's red eyes whenever letters from the family solicitor had arrived on the mat at home. Worst of all had been the time they had found out that his father's second marriage had ended. Every time his father had made his mum cry, Fraser had sworn again that he wouldn't go back. He would never speak to him again.

What would his mum say if she knew that he was thinking of getting in touch with him?

The betrayal would undoubtedly hurt her. She'd been delighted when he'd told her about the baby, and had hardly batted an eyelid at the fact that he wasn't in a relationship with Elspeth. Had she guessed that he would want to go back to Ballanross? She hadn't said a word about it if she had. She'd never told him that she didn't want him to speak to his father. Hadn't had to when he had been able to see the pain that even the mention of his name caused her.

If ever he'd needed a reminder of what following lust and impulsive attraction did to a family it was now. *This* was why he wasn't going to give in to the feelings he had for Elspeth. *This* was why he was going to resist the fact that he wanted her with every bone in his body. Because he wouldn't subject his child to the pain that he and his mother had gone through.

But he couldn't deny his child Ballanross either. As formative as his parents' separation had been, Ballanross had been more so. That feeling of being connected to the land. Of belonging somewhere. Of standing on the ground where his grandfather, and his grandfather's father had stood. That was what had made him who he was today. He couldn't take that away from his child, however much pain it might cause in the short term.

What was he going to tell his dad about Elspeth? he wondered. His father wasn't entitled to know *anything* about his life. Maybe he wouldn't tell him anything. Just show up with a noticeably pregnant woman and let his dad work it out. It wasn't as if he owed him an explanation.

But that wouldn't be fair on Elspeth, he knew. It probably wasn't really fair to take her up there with him at all. If she hadn't suggested it—insisted on it—he wouldn't have thought about doing it. He shouldn't be letting anyone else see into the middle of the conflict between him and his dad. But he was going to—because she had offered and because, selfishly, he wanted her there.

He didn't know what was going on between himself and Elspeth. Other than that they were both keeping a sensible distance from the fireworks that had got them into this situation in the first place. When they had been looking at the apartment the chemistry between them had been so hot that he had been tempted—*so* tempted—to forget all the reasons why they both knew it was a bad idea to be anything other than friends.

And now he had to go and see his father—the perfect reminder of where things led when you made decisions based on what your body wanted, rather than making rational, sensible decisions that protected everybody.

Talking about his father had cured him of that temptation. Or had put it in its proper place at least. He wasn't sure he would ever be cured of wanting her, but the memory of what those sorts of emotions had done to his family was enough to keep his feelings in check. However much he might want Elspeth—and right now he wanted her in every possible way—the only way to keep his family safe and secure and together was to bury those feelings deep.

He dialled his father's number and felt a heavy roiling anxiety as he waited for him to answer.

CHAPTER SEVEN

ELSPETH WATCHED THE landscape change from the window of Fraser's muddy black four-by-four as they drove north. The busy city streets gave way to the suburbs north of Edinburgh, a view of the water as they crossed the new bridge over the Firth of Forth, and then miles of lowland motorway surrounded by fields.

As the motorway gave way to A roads, mountains appeared on the horizon, heavy with snow. The sunlight caught the jewel-bright greens of the grasses and the trees in the fields, popping against the layered taupes and greys of the hills and Munros. Clouds shrouded the higher peaks, and the tops of even the lower hills were covered with snow.

It would be bleak up here in a cold snap, she thought, noting the snow poles either side of the carriageway, just in case the snow hid the road completely.

Elspeth shivered and cranked up the heating, glad that they had taken Fraser's luxury car rather than her old wheelchair-friendly eco-wagon.

Elspeth was growing more and more edgy, she realised, as they racked up the miles between her and Sarah, but at least she knew her mum was there to keep an eye on things. After Elspeth, she knew Sarah's needs better than anyone. And, although they had arranged for some respite cover to help out with the stuff that arthritis made difficult—lifting and transferring Sarah, the physiotherapy that eased the tightness out of her muscles—her mum would be there to supervise.

'There are some blankets behind your seat if the heater's not enough,' Fraser said, spotting her fiddling with the controls and distracting her from her worry for a moment.

She reached behind her and tucked one of the blankets around herself, wondering what this journey would be like with a baby. They'd been on the road for a couple of hours now, and the landscape grew more beautiful, more dramatic, by the mile.

The lush greens of the lowlands had given way to the starker browns and greys of the Cairngorms, broken up by the rich greens of the pine forests. And as the landscape had changed so had Fraser.

In Edinburgh he'd seemed almost cheerful, but Elspeth had been able to see the effort he was having to put in to the façade. There had seemed little point mentioning it, though, when they both understood how complicated his feelings about this trip were. If he wanted to cover his real feelings with false chirpiness, then that was his prerogative. But as they had drawn closer and closer to his childhood home the pretence had fallen away, and now she could see the tension in his features. In the stiff line of his shoulders and his white-knuckled grip on the steering wheel.

'Are you okay?' she asked, not expecting anything more than the 'Fine' that he forced out through gritted teeth.

He wasn't exactly the 'talking about his feelings' type.

Especially, she kept reminding herself, as they were only friends. Despite the bump that was growing large enough to make her uncomfortable from time to time.

She rubbed her belly without thinking, and it was only when Fraser said, 'Everything okay in there?' that she realised that he was watching her. Or at least glancing over at her whenever an occasional straight section of road allowed.

'Aside from the dance party we're all fine,' she replied with a smile.

'Dance party?'

'The baby's usually pretty active this time of the evening.'

'Can I feel?'

Elspeth glanced at the twisting road ahead, pretty sure that she didn't want Fraser driving without both hands on the wheel. But before she had a chance to register what he was doing he had pulled over into a gateway leading down a dirt track and was looking at her with earnest longing on his face.

'Can I?'

Elspeth shrugged, trying to pretend that the thought of his hand on her body was something that only concerned her in her role as a mother. Trying to block out the memories of any other time his hand had stroked the soft, naked skin of her belly. This was it. This was who they were to each other now. Co-parents of this life growing—and apparently somersaulting—inside her.

'Sure.' Elspeth heard how steady her voice was and was quietly impressed with her composure.

She didn't exactly feel steady inside. But it didn't help her or Fraser for him to know that. She hitched up her T-shirt—she'd had to give in and buy some maternity tops the week before—and waited for the touch of his hand.

Though the car had warmed up, when Fraser's hand brushed against her skin his fingers were like ice. She yelped and he pulled away, his face a picture of concern.

'Did I hurt you?' he asked.

'Of course not.' Elspeth smiled. 'I'm not that fragile. But your hands are freezing.'

She pulled his hand back and chafed it between her own, rubbing warmth into his fingers.

'Try just here,' she said, placing his hand low on her belly, where the low-cut waistband of her jeans met bare skin. 'It'll still be cold enough to make the baby jump.'

They sat in silence as they waited, their breath starting to steam up the windows. As the minutes went past, and baby kept them waiting, Elspeth pulled the blanket around her again, concealing Fraser's hand beneath. They had both scooted sideways in their seats, to try and bridge the space between them over the car's central console, but after a few minutes Elspeth's back started to ache.

She stretched up, trying to ease out the knot in her spine without dislodging Fraser's hand. She knew that it was always when she took her hand away that the baby would decide to kick up a storm.

'Sure you're okay?' Fraser asked, and this time she was touched rather than amused by his expression.

It was protective, fiercely so, but also tender. Above all, it was intimate. It was a look that told her that they were bound together by this baby, whether they liked it or not. That, as much as they didn't know about each other yet, they were going to be tied together for a lifetime.

'Come here.'

Fraser wound his free arm around her back and pulled

her closer to him, turning her slightly so that her back rested against his front. For a moment she stiffened, knowing that being so close to him was a bad idea. It was bad for her self-control, bad for keeping her fantasies at bay. But it felt so right just now, in this minute, as they shared the moment.

She relaxed into him, sliding her hand on top of his where it still rested on her belly. She couldn't feel anything from baby—none of the little flutters or rolls she was slowly getting used to. Instead she could just feel Fraser. The slight scratch of his fingertips against her skin. The caress of his thumb as it started to drift back and forth across her belly. The heat of his breath against her neck, stirring her hair, warming her far more than she should expect from simple body heat.

His arms wrapped tighter around her and his lips tickled the sensitive skin behind her ear as they brushed against her skin. Not a kiss. Not quite—not yet. Without letting herself think too much about it, she let her head drop to one side, giving him more room, more temptation. As his lips finally pressed against her in a hot, moist kiss she felt a jolt low down in her belly, and it was only when Fraser exclaimed behind her that she realised that the baby had finally kicked.

'Oh, my goodness!' Fraser said, a laugh in his voice. 'Was that it? Was that the baby?'

'Well, it wasn't me,' Elspeth said, also laughing, relieved that they had been interrupted before either of them had done something they couldn't take back.

The interruption had chased the heated atmosphere out of the car and replaced it with something less dangerous as their focus centred entirely on the baby.

'Will it do it again?' Fraser asked.

'Probably—give her a minute.'

'Her?' Fraser looked at her with curiosity. 'I thought you weren't finding out.'

'I haven't. It's just habit,' Elspeth explained with a smile and a shrug. 'I have to call her something.'

'It's really real, isn't it?' Fraser said, with something close to wonder in his voice. 'We're really having a baby. *This* baby.'

'We really are,' Elspeth said, resting back in her seat and pulling the blanket tighter. 'Are you okay?' she asked eventually, when Fraser's silence stretched out.

'I am. I just can't quite believe it, you know? You, and the bairn and going home…'

Elspeth reached for his hand, knowing what a concession she'd just got, with Fraser acknowledging his nerves about where they were going.

'I know. I know it's all sudden, and it's all hard. But we're a team.' She squeezed his hand and the baby kicked again, right into Fraser's palm. 'All three of us.'

Fraser smiled and removed his hand, shifting back so he was sitting properly behind the wheel. 'Then I should probably drive us all there and get it over and done with.'

He resumed his grip on the wheel, but the smile that had reached his eyes when he had felt the baby kick was still there, still curling up the corners of his lips too.

That almost-kiss had been nothing, Elspeth told herself. It had just been them sharing a baby milestone, forcing them into the sort of everyday intimacy that expectant couples shared. They had forgotten themselves momentarily, forgotten that the normal rules didn't apply for them. It had made them confuse having feelings for the baby for feelings for each other.

It didn't have to mean anything. It definitely didn't

mean that they had to do or say anything. It was best forgotten about.

As the single track road they had been following for a few miles gave way to a gravel driveway Elspeth got her first proper look at the castle. She'd tried to find an image of it online before they had left, but the public highway ended miles from the castle itself, and the satellite pictures had offered up only a grainy bird's eye view.

The car swept around a bend in the driveway, the row of pine trees broke, and Elspeth got her first understanding of what this life was going to mean for her baby.

The ruins of an old castle sat atop a steep grassy bank in front of a small loch, most of the stones fallen, but a few arches and windows intact. With a nearly full moon reflecting off the water, creating dramatic shadows, Elspeth could only imagine the grandeur of the building in its heyday. And between the car and the ruins sat Castle Ballanross in its second incarnation, with its grey stone, round towers and steeple-like turrets. A burn skirted the farthest corner of the castle, and she wound her window down to hear the gentle burble of water over cobbles.

She tried to imagine a young Fraser here, running around the grounds. It was difficult to see this place as a home. Hard to see it as anything other than a tourist attraction or a relic from the past. She glanced over at Fraser to see how he was taking being back. But his face only showed the same tension that had been present since they'd passed the Cairngorms.

Fraser stopped the car and a door in the tower closest to them opened inwards, silhouetting a figure in the light that spilt from inside. Fraser didn't make any move to open the door, and that was enough for her to know that the man who had opened the door must be his father. She didn't know anything, know any*one* else who could stop Fraser in his tracks like that.

Just as she was wondering whether she would have to say something, Fraser heaved out a sigh and reached for the handle. He paused for a second and looked over at her.

'Look, if this gets ugly, I'm sorry.'

Elspeth took hold of the hand that was still on the steering wheel.

'Don't forget: we're a team. I've got your back.'

Fraser laughed, breaking the tension in the car. 'You make it sound like a duel, or something. I promise it won't come to that.'

Elspeth smiled. 'Good to hear. Now, get your backside out of the car. I'm freezing.'

He laughed again, and Elspeth relaxed just a fraction. Maybe this wouldn't be so bad, after all.

CHAPTER EIGHT

FRASER WALKED TOWARDS the door, his eyes fixed on his father. It had been a decade and a half since he had last seen him, but he could still recognise him just by his silhouette. He felt a spark of annoyance towards himself at that. How much of this man was still a part of him, even after Fraser had tried to pretend for fifteen years that he didn't exist?

Fraser shook his head as he walked closer. How were they meant to do this? He wasn't sure that it was possible to rebuild a relationship that had long-ago burnt out and gone cold. Would his father even want to? He'd had every opportunity over the past fifteen years to get in touch. To try and restart their relationship. And he hadn't tried—not even once.

He thought about the baby Elspeth was carrying, the little flutter of life that he had felt in the car on the way here. That was why he was doing this. Because that child had a place here, on this land, the place where Fraser had always felt anchored. Whole.

Whole.

He couldn't remember when it had started to feel normal to have such a huge part of himself missing. But as he looked around, took in the buildings and landscapes and sounds and smells of his childhood, he realised that he had been living with an enormous part of himself absent for longer than he could remember. And as he looked over to the door and saw his father standing there he was reminded of the reason.

This was his father's fault.

Yes, Fraser was the one who had walked away and refused to look back. But he never would have done that if his father hadn't torn his family apart. Hadn't humiliated his mother by abandoning her for another woman. If he hadn't been blinded by lust and infatuation and mistaken that for love. The sort of love that he and his mother had offered unquestioningly until his father had thrown it back in their faces.

He reached his dad and stuck out a hand in a gesture of greeting. He was the one who had arranged this reunion, and it was going to be on his terms. He would make sure his father understood that.

'Fraser,' his father said, with a waver in his voice.

'Father.'

Fraser noticed that his own voice was deeper than his father's, and that he'd managed to keep it unquestionably solid. He wouldn't give even a hint that he felt anything other than entirely unmoved about this reunion.

This was about the baby. Making sure that his child would have the place in the world it would be born to. That his child wouldn't feel the emptiness Fraser had struggled to fill since he was a teenager. His child belonged here—in this castle, on this land. That was why he was back. The fact that it meant a rapprochement with his dad wasn't relevant to this meeting.

'And will you introduce me to your friend?' his dad asked, his eyeline passing over Fraser's shoulder to where

Elspeth was climbing down from the car, her bump hidden in the shadows and folds of her coat.

He hadn't mentioned the baby to his father. In the end he hadn't known how to. He had just told him on the phone that he wanted to come up to the castle and talk.

Would he have guessed? If he had, he would probably be expecting that they were at least in a relationship, if not preparing to get married.

A knot in his stomach reminded him that he had known all along that it wasn't fair to drop Elspeth into this. That he should have explained the situation to his dad before bringing her up here. She was being dropped into the middle of a family drama, and the fact that he hadn't told his dad about the nature of their relationship was only going to make things worse.

He took a deep breath. It was too late to have regrets now. Elspeth was here with him and he couldn't make himself want to change anything about that. He'd take anything to distract himself from the enormity of being back here. Of going back on his promise to himself that he would never see his father again.

'Father, this is Elspeth,' Fraser said, placing an arm around her waist as she drew near to him.

He knew that it wasn't going to help with the mixed signals, but he wanted her near. Wanted the child within her body near, to remind him why he was doing this. To remind him of his responsibilities to the next generation of his family, the reason why he was here.

'Elspeth, this is Malcolm.'

Elspeth held out a hand and shook Malcolm's with a smile. 'Pleasure to meet you,' she said. 'Thank you for having me in your home.'

'You're very welcome,' he replied, with a curious look towards her middle. 'I'm glad to have you both here.'

Fraser felt anger rising within him. Because his father *did* look pleased. More than pleased. He looked delighted, if a little confused, and Fraser could guess at what he was thinking. He was thinking that this meant a rapprochement, an improvement in relations with his only son. He thought that he was being forgiven.

Well, he could go on thinking that for as long as he wanted. It wasn't going to make it happen. As soon as they were settled inside he would tell his father about the baby and explain that that was the only reason they were here. He would nip any expectations of reconciliation and forgiveness in the bud.

'Well, come in from the cold, both of ye,' Malcolm said after another awkward moment. 'There's a fire in the study—or the kitchen will be warm.'

'The study will be fine,' Fraser said, rejecting instinctively the idea of them all sitting around the range in the kitchen, scene of childhood lunches, hot chocolate and warm bread straight from the oven. The more formal study in the family apartments would be quite sufficient for making introductions and explanations. Then he and Elspeth could get to bed, and at least day one of this trip would be over.

Tomorrow he planned to be out through the door at dawn, looking over Ballanross. Making peace with his long absence and soaking up enough of the air to keep him going until the next time he had to come back.

He moved his hand from around Elspeth's waist, sensing the stiffness and awkwardness in her body. But he couldn't let her go entirely. When he moved his arm away he felt adrift, so he reached for her hand, hoping for an anchor. She laced her fingers between his and squeezed, and he let out a breath of relief that in her he had a friend and an ally.

But that was all he could think of her as. All he should expect from her. If he thought back to that moment that they had shared in the car, a moment that had promised so much more than friendship, he…

He couldn't. It was too confusing. Too distracting. He was grateful for her support in seeing his father for the first time in fifteen years, but he mustn't let himself be distracted by their attraction to one another. There were enough emotions, enough ghosts, flying around this castle without confusing one another by trying to make this relationship something that it could never be.

They followed Malcolm down a chilly corridor—so much colder than Fraser remembered from his childhood. Then, the grand formal rooms had been cold, but the small number of rooms where the family had really lived, where they'd spent their days—carpeted, centrally heated and free of cobwebs—had felt cosy.

In his father's study, a small fire burned in the grate, but even with the flames dancing in front of him Fraser could feel the chill in the room. He tried not to take it as an omen. He should have warned Elspeth to pack extra layers. He wasn't sure that a city girl like her could even conceive of the chill of a Highland castle in winter.

Or maybe he had just gone soft, he thought to himself, shivering again.

'Sorry about the cold,' Malcolm said, adding a couple of logs to the fire. 'I've had it burning in here all day, but this place takes weeks to warm up if it gets cold. Well, you remember…' he said, trying to meet Fraser's eyes.

No, Fraser thought. *You don't get to do that. You don't*

get to call on our shared history and pretend that nothing has happened. You don't get to dip into my past and bring it into the present at will.

It was only as his anger subsided that he started to process his father's words. Weeks to warm up? Why wasn't the central heating on? And if that wasn't enough to keep the place warm why wasn't he burning a fire in here every day?

He looked around the study and found it much as he remembered it from fifteen years ago. His father's old desk was laden with papers, and the same antique armchairs stood by the fire.

But the upholstery was worn through, showing the stuffing underneath. He didn't know what had happened in the intervening years, but he remembered the furniture in here gleaming, proudly withstanding the decay that had claimed most pieces of that vintage. But now there was dust everywhere, knocks and rings showing on the wood and the smell of damp in the air. It was clear that standards had slipped considerably.

He shook his head, resisting the urge to interfere in the upkeep of the estate. It wasn't his responsibility. Not anymore. Not yet.

When they were all seated by the fire his father looked at them both expectantly, and at last Fraser dropped Elspeth's hand. It was hardly worth the gesture; his father would have jumped to conclusions already. And he missed the warmth of her. The reassurance. The feeling that they were in this as a team. But it was done now.

'Father, my friend Elspeth and I are expecting a baby.' He emphasised '*friend*', hoping that it would get rid of the need for further explanations.

His father's smile beamed from every feature, travelling from his mouth to his eyes, and taking in every line and crag of his skin in between.

'Well, that's wonderful news…'

Questions remained unspoken but hung in the room around him. *And…? And we're getting married… And we're an item…*

And it was none of his business, Fraser thought. He had long ago given up the right to ask those sorts of questions. They were here for the baby—not because he owed his father anything.

'I'd like Ballanross to be a part of the baby's life from the start. That's why we're here.'

That was what was important here. His child's land and legacy. His family's responsibility to the people who relied on the estate for their livelihoods. The privileges and responsibilities that his son or daughter would one day inherit.

'Well, I'm very pleased to see you,' Malcolm said, not seeming the least bit put out that Fraser had just told him that he hadn't come here to see *him*. 'And to hear your news. That's wonderful. When is the baby due?'

Malcolm's placatory words made Fraser even more angry. How could he act as if nothing was wrong? As if he *hadn't* destroyed their family and kept Fraser away from his home for fifteen years? As if Fraser *hadn't* spent the whole of his adult life hating him?

Before he realised what he was doing he had pushed to his feet and balled his hands into fists to stop them doing something that he would regret. The rage that he had bottled up for fifteen years was making a break for it, and he couldn't let that happen. He couldn't lose control of his emotions like that. He knew better. Knew better than his father ever had.

He took one more look at Malcolm and felt such anger that he knew he had to walk away. He strode from the room, his feet marching ahead under their own volition, carrying him towards his childhood bedroom.

As he pushed open the door he realised that nothing had been changed in here since the day he had left. The few books he'd forgotten to pack had been tidied from the floor. The bed had been stripped. But there were still posters on the wall, a few old toys on the shelves. He dropped down onto the bed, feeling like the angry teenager he had been the last time he was in this room.

Elspeth took a deep breath before knocking on the door. Malcolm had directed her to Fraser's old bedroom—his best guess as to where he might have gone when he had stormed off. She had known from the start that this visit was going to be difficult for them all—Fraser most of all. But she hadn't expected it to be quite so dramatic quite so early on.

Fraser hadn't been kidding when he'd said that things were bad between him and his dad.

For a minute she'd wondered whether they'd made a big mistake, coming all the way up here just to reignite a family feud. But then the baby had given her a sharp kick—a timely reminder that she didn't want any bad feeling in this family, *her* family now. She wanted her baby born into love and peace and harmony, however hippy that might sound. And, while it might be a bit optimistic hoping that Fraser and his father would be all warm hugs and bonhomie by the end of the weekend, it didn't seem unreasonable to think that they might at least be civil to one another.

She knocked and turned the handle, and found Fraser

sitting on an antique panelled bed hung with heavy navy and gold drapes, looking not a little lost.

He stood as she walked in and rubbed the back of his neck. 'How did you find me?'

'Your dad thought you might be up here.'

Elspeth's instinct was to reach out to him, offer comfort. Pull him into her arms. But she knew that if she did that there would be much more than comfort between them. They had proved that in the car on the way up here. Any physical contact between them was a bad idea. They couldn't be trusted to keep things innocent.

'Your dad gave me directions,' she carried on, trying to shake the memories of what had happened earlier. 'Should have drawn me a map. I'll never find my way back.'

Fraser gave a smile, more in recognition of her attempt to lighten the mood than at her humour.

'I shouldn't have walked out,' Fraser said.

Not quite an apology, she noticed. In the circumstances, she could understand, but that didn't mean she was going to let him get away with it.

'And you shouldn't have left me sitting there. I said I'd be your wingman, not your cleanup crew.'

Another smile, less forced this time.

'I know. You're a hero. I shouldn't have walked out like that.'

Elspeth smiled. Knowing that he'd been an idiot didn't get him off the hook either. She dropped to sit on his bed, stretching out her back and taking in her surroundings. The posters on the wall, the figures on the shelves.

'Is this just how you left it?' she asked, to break the silence.

'Aye.' Fraser nodded. 'It's a little tidier now. But this was me at fifteen.'

'Does it feel strange?' Elspeth asked, realising what an intimate thing it was, to walk into a room and see someone's childhood. 'To come back and find it like this?'

Fraser shrugged. 'I don't know. I assume you still have your childhood room, if you're living with your mum. Is that weird?'

'Yes, honestly, it is sometimes.'

She might as well tell the truth. Living with her mum when she was in her thirties was never going to be ideal. But she didn't have the luxury of another choice. Her mum and Sarah needed her to be there.

'But my room isn't a time capsule,' she went on, after sitting quietly for a few moments. 'Your dad could have changed things in here. Taken down the posters. Even if you were going to come back he had to know that you wouldn't need a teenager's bedroom any more.'

Fraser's face hardened into an expression that came out whenever they talked about his father. 'Probably he just didn't care. I doubt he's been in here since I left.'

'Looks pretty clean and tidy in here for a room that's not been touched for fifteen years.'

Fraser didn't have an answer for that. All right, she knew that generally a castle came with an army of staff to look after it, but there was no denying that this room was well-kept. Better kept, in fact, than the room they had been in earlier.

It looked as if she had given Fraser something to think about, because he had sat back on the bed and rested forward on his elbows, staring pensively at the floor.

Did he really think that? Elspeth wondered. That his

father didn't care about him? Because it had been clear to her from the moment she had seen Malcolm waiting in the doorway of the tower, nervous anticipation obvious in his posture, that Malcolm cared very deeply about his son. But if Fraser really thought that his father didn't love him, what had that done to him over the years? To the way he saw himself? To his relationships? No wonder he had been scared when she had told him about the baby. If he hadn't ever been able to count on this most important bond, no wonder he had never made another.

Not that it mattered to *her*, she reminded herself. Fraser's commitment issues weren't her problem and they weren't why she wasn't interested in a relationship with him. There was way more than that standing between them and a happy-ever-after. It was good to have the reminder, though. That it wasn't just her who didn't want this.

Even if Sarah was suddenly cured and Elspeth's responsibilities magically melted away and her time and emotional energy and love weren't pulling her in three different directions, Fraser was in no position to be in a relationship.

All they had to concentrate on was being the best parents they could be to this baby. And as far as she could see, Fraser wasn't going to be able to do that until he'd fully come to terms with the breakdown of his relationship with his father. And perhaps tried to make a new relationship with him.

Elspeth reached for Fraser's hand, remembering how much she'd liked the way he'd held it earlier. She'd liked the way it had felt to be anchored to him. Liked the way it had felt, knowing that he'd come to her for support.

She was his family now, she realised, and felt the reality of their situation sinking in yet another level. She was the mother of his child, and that meant they shared a bond that would last for ever. She couldn't escape from it, even if she wanted to.

She couldn't think how she'd find the capacity to care for someone else, and suddenly wondered what she was doing here, in the Highlands, digging herself deeper into family issues that had been impossible to fix long before *she* had had anything to do with Fraser.

She gasped in a short breath as the baby kicked her ribs and she rubbed against them absent-mindedly.

'Can I feel?' Fraser asked.

She remembered the atmosphere between them in the car. How a simple touch had escalated so quickly into something that she had been so sure neither one of them would want—until they hadn't been able to help themselves. But she *wanted* him to touch her. This was his child—they had agreed to parent together and this was a part of that. It was something that they should share.

She shrugged her shoulders, faking a nonchalance that she absolutely did not feel, and then held dead still, resisting any reaction to the feel of Fraser's touch on her skin. She held her breath for a few seconds, willing the baby to kick quickly. For once the baby co-operated and gave its father a quick tap on the hand, cueing a snort of laughter from Fraser.

'I can't get over how amazing that feels,' he said with another laugh, breaking the tension in the room. 'How do you concentrate on anything when you have a whole person in there, trying to get your attention?'

Elspeth smiled. 'She doesn't make it easy. But it started gradually and I guess I've got used to it.'

'I can't imagine *ever* getting used to it.'

The wonder in Fraser's voice was intoxicating, and it caught them up for another few minutes, as they quietly waited for the baby to kick again. But then real life started to creep back in, and Elspeth couldn't help but point out the obvious.

'Well, she's not going to be in there for ever.'

Fraser withdrew his hand and coughed awkwardly. 'I guess not. I can't believe it's going so quickly. A few more months and everything's going to change.'

She made an effort to smile, but couldn't help feeling a twinge of anxiety. Not everything was going to change. Much of her life would stay the same. Her work. Her career. Her caring responsibilities. They weren't all going to fade away just because she had this enormous new challenge coming. They were all going to be just as demanding as ever.

Something of what she was thinking must have shown on her face, because Fraser took her hand back into his and gave it a squeeze.

'It's all right to be scared. But we're in this together.'

Sure they were. The baby part of it. But he wasn't the one who was going to have to fight to get his career back on track post-maternity leave. He wasn't the one who was going to have to call around for emergency cover when Sarah was sick. He wasn't going to be taking on the challenges that she already dealt with every day.

'Stop it,' he said gently. 'Whatever spiral you're heading down, I promise you we are going to make this work. Have you called home since we got here?' he asked, showing more insight than she'd realised he had.

'They're fine,' she said, reflexively tapping her phone through the fabric of her pocket, reminding herself that they could get hold of her if they needed to. 'I'm just not used to being away from home for more than a night.'

He pulled her down beside him on the bed as they both looked up to the ancient beams of the ceiling.

'I was surprised when you agreed to stay a few days,' Fraser admitted.

'I was being realistic about how much time you and your father might need,' Elspeth replied. 'And when you asked… I don't know. Objectively, three nights away didn't seem like that long. But now that we're here… I feel so far away. I feel helpless.'

Fraser squeezed her hand in support. 'But you know that your sister is safe. That your mum has the help she needs from the agency care assistants.'

'I know all that. I do. But… It's just hard to turn off the part of my brain that feels it should be doing something.'

'You *are* doing something,' Fraser said, letting go of her hand and rubbing the swell of her belly. 'You're growing this wee bairn, for a start.'

Elspeth let out something between a moan and a sigh at the feel of his touch on her tight skin. But being surrounded by Fraser's childhood things, both gazing upwards, not making eye contact, made the atmosphere quietly intimate rather than sexy.

'Mmm… And that's not getting any easier,' she admitted.

His palm traced circles over her skin, over their baby. 'How are you feeling?'

She let out a sigh. 'Tired, if I'm honest. And clumsy. And achy.'

She let out a squeak of protest as Fraser dropped her hand and pushed at her hip, rolling her on to her side with her back to him. His hands rested on her, applying gentle pressure, teasing knots from her neck and her shoulders, travelling down the length of her spine until they pressed hard into the small of her back.

'You should have said something,' Fraser said, his voice soft and close to her ear.

'I can't—'

'It's just a massage,' Fraser said, and she could hear the smile on his lips. 'This is something friends do for each other, right?'

She really wasn't sure about that. She'd never had a friend touch her like this before. Never felt so electric with a friend's hands stroking her. But then, she'd never had a baby with a friend either. She wasn't sure there was a rulebook for this sort of friendship. Certainly no one had given her one.

'Is it helping?'

She let out another long sigh, losing the ability to articulate.

Fraser laughed behind her, a warm little burst of breath on her neck. 'I'll take that as a yes,' he said, working his thumbs beside her spine until her body felt like jelly.

Then he lay back, and she followed, until they were both staring up at the ceiling once more.

'You know,' Fraser said, speaking softly, 'I think we make a good team.'

CHAPTER NINE

FRASER HAD LEFT her loose-limbed and relaxed at the door of an extravagantly decorated guest room with a kiss on the cheek and a pile of blankets spread on the feather eiderdown that topped the four-poster bed.

When she woke, pale sunlight was trying to make its way through the dust and condensation on the windows. She lifted her head from the pillows and goosebumps immediately broke out on her shoulders and arms. It was chilly in here. Forget that—it was downright freezing.

She pulled one of the blankets from the bed and wrapped it around her shoulders while she went and wrestled with the valve of the enormous and ancient radiator over by the windows.

She used the corner of the blanket to rub a clear patch in a pane of the glass and had her first proper glimpse of Ballanross in the daylight. The driveway that they had crunched across last night curved dramatically through the landscape, past the ruins of the old castle, which sat majestically on the top of the hillside. Snow was visible on the tops of the mountains to the west, and the loch was fishpond-calm behind the old castle. The pale sun was low in the sky to the east, trying valiantly to warm the picturesque Scottish scene—without much luck.

A door slammed somewhere below and Fraser strode purposefully out of the door, wrapped up in a heavy winter jacket and hiking boots, and peered up at the tallest tower. So much for being a team, Elspeth thought. He was leaving her alone with his father—*again*. She wasn't sure how he was meant to get anywhere with fixing this relationship if he was going to be out through the door at first light.

She checked the time on her phone—it was past nine already. She held on to the hope that Fraser and Malcolm had had a heart-to-heart over breakfast, but knew that it was unlikely.

Crossing over to her suitcase, she hunted out warm layers and thick hiking socks, and even considered for a moment going straight out to catch Fraser before he left. But then a jab in the ribs and a rumble in her stomach reminded her that she wasn't alone, and that the baby was demanding breakfast even if Elspeth thought there were more important things to be doing.

Trying to retrace her steps from the night before, she took a wrong turn and found herself in a grand hall adorned with suits of armour criss-crossed with cobwebs and an armoury's worth of weapons mounted on the wall. She spun in a slow circle, looking up, taking in the faded splendour of the castle, trying to imagine a childhood spent running through these hallways, amidst these riches, this history.

Would their child feel like the castle and the land was a part of them, as Fraser so obviously did? Or would she always feel the outsider? Feel the echo of the estrangement between Fraser and his father? Feel the city child, out of place in the country, like Elspeth did right now?

She turned sharply at the sound of footsteps behind

her, and smiled when she saw Malcolm walking towards her, carrying a cup of coffee that was steaming heavily in the chill of the room.

'Ah, good morning,' he said with a smile. 'I was wondering if I should bring you a cup, but then I saw ye come through this way and thought you might need directions. Let's go on back to the kitchen and I'll put the kettle on.'

She followed him through a warren of hallways until they reached the kitchen. A copper *batterie de cuisine* hung on the wall, covered with a layer of the dust she had seen everywhere else, and Malcolm went to fill the plastic kettle, yellowed slightly with age, that sat on a worktop.

'Will you have coffee or tea?' Malcolm asked as he fussed around finding a mug and some milk. 'You'll have to excuse the place. The housekeeper is only here three days a week, and there's really too much for her to manage. I do my best, but with a place this size you're never going to win.'

'I can imagine,' Elspeth said, and tried to hide the many, many questions she had about this. A housekeeper only three days a week? No wonder the place was looking tired. From what little Fraser had told her about his childhood here she had been expecting to find at least a few members of full-time staff, and more out in the grounds.

Not that she didn't think Malcolm could take care of himself, but a building like this needed specialist care. It was more than one person—*any* one person—could manage by themselves.

She made small talk as she drank her tea and ate a couple of slices of toast, and then took a deep breath, unsure what reaction she would get to her next question.

'Did you see Fraser this morning?'

'Mmmph...'

The sadness in the older man's expression tugged at her sympathy, and she knew that she had guessed right—Fraser had been out through the door without a word for his father this morning.

'Well, Fraser's not one for being kept still for long. He said something about taking a look at the north tower. Had a quick look outside and then came in and headed up the staircase.'

'I think I'll try and find him,' Elspeth said.

'Are you sure?'

'If you don't mind, of course,' she added, not wanting to be rude. 'I'll look for him inside first. And if he's not here I'll take a quick look outdoors.'

And hopefully she'd catch up with him and talk some sense into him, she added in her head. Remind him that they'd driven all the way up here so that Fraser could actually *talk* to his father, rather than put as much distance between them as possible at the earliest opportunity.

'Aye, well, if you can find him...' Malcolm added. 'But he could have taken one of the quad bikes. And—no offence, lass—I'm not letting you take one of those in your condition.'

Elspeth smiled, touched at his concern for her, even though she would have accused anyone other than her child's grandfather of blatant sexism.

'In any case I won't go far,' she promised, 'indoors or out. And if I don't bump into him, then I'll come back. Don't worry, I won't be hiking up a mountain alone.'

Malcolm nodded. 'I'll walk with you inside, if you like. I usually just keep to the family rooms. It'll be good for me to see the place through new eyes. And it'd be... good to walk with Fraser a while, if we find him.'

'Thank you,' Elspeth said, clocking his wistful expression, hearing the pain and longing in his voice. His love for his son was so palpable she couldn't believe that Fraser was refusing to see it. In her line of work she saw a lot of family politics. People who—under the great strain that ill-health put on families—turned on the ones they loved.

Occasionally she saw those families find a way back together. But she'd also seen estrangements that had festered until it was too late. She had seen loneliness that had become pathological, contributing to the misery of patients nearing the end of their lives. She wouldn't allow that to happen here. She wouldn't allow Fraser—that pigheaded man—to leave this place until he'd at least had a proper conversation with his father.

And she didn't care if that made her meddling and interfering. This was *her* family now, and that gave her every right to be involved.

She pulled on the fleece that she'd intended to wear outside, not realising that she would need it in the castle too. And as she left the kitchen with Malcolm she could feel a draught straight down the corridor. She stuffed her hands deep into her pockets, wondering whether it would be rude to put on her gloves and scarf too.

The further they walked around the castle, the clearer it became that it was falling into serious disrepair. The wind whistled through broken window panes, and there was a dampness in the air that spoke of long-set neglect.

Elspeth followed Malcolm down a long gallery that seemed to take them away from the inhabited part of the castle—away from carpets and radiators and home comforts, even the chilly and draughty kind. These rooms were imposing and echoing—lined with historical relics collecting dust. Where Malcolm's apartment was comfily shabby, these rooms were a testament to a grand way of living that had long since ceased to be practical.

They found Fraser in a small room high up in the north tower, inspecting another broken window pane— or was he looking out over the estate?

He turned as they crossed the threshold into the room. His expression shifted through surprise to anger in the split second it took for him to register Malcolm behind her.

'What are you doing up here?' he asked, the question clearly directed more at his father than at her.

'I wanted to see some more of the castle,' Elspeth said, feeling the tension in the room and wondering whether she had made a huge mistake. 'Malcolm offered to show me. We thought we might catch up with you.'

But she could see that he wasn't really listening to her answer. His eyes hadn't left his father when she'd spoken, and anger was clear in every line of his face.

'Look at the state of this place,' Fraser said, gesturing towards the window, knowing that he was letting his anger show.

How had his father let it come to this? It was hard to believe how badly the place had slipped into disrepair and decay in the years that Fraser had been gone.

'What's happened to it?' he asked, though he didn't really need to. His father had neglected it. He hadn't cared enough about it to take care of it.

His father shifted his feet, and Fraser felt sorry for him for a moment—before he remembered that he was angry with him.

'It takes a lot to keep this place running, Fraser. You know that.'

'Aye. I do,' Fraser replied. 'And I'd be ashamed of myself if the estates *I* managed looked like this.'

From behind his father, he saw Elspeth make a move towards him. For a split second Fraser could taste acid in his mouth as he imagined her walking across the floor. He could almost see the wood breaking apart beneath her feet, could see her falling through to the room below.

He moved faster than he'd known he could, and stopped her with a hand on her arm. 'Don't,' he said, aware that his voice was still tainted with anger, that he was speaking too harshly to her. 'The water has been coming in through the window and the roof. It's rotted the floorboards. It's not safe for you to be in here.'

The thought that something might have happened to her if she'd come up here before he'd pulled back the rug and seen the damage to the floor focussed his anger to a white-hot rage. If she had got hurt it would have been Malcolm's fault. Because of his neglect of this beautiful castle. Of the place where his family should be flourishing if he hadn't thrown it all away over a midlife lust for someone new and desirable.

The castle hadn't looked like this all those nights Fraser had dreamed of it. There had been no broken windows. No rotting joists. He dreaded to think what else he was going to find. How much time and money it was going to take to put it right.

It wasn't his responsibility yet, he tried to tell himself. Except it was.

If he wanted to come home here one day. If he wanted to raise a family here, he couldn't just leave it to rot away.

He had a responsibility to this place. And Ballanross clearly needed him.

He threw another angry look at his father. 'I can't believe you've let this happen.'

'Son, I don't want to argue with you.'

Son? Fraser crossed his arms. Malcolm had lost the right to use that word a long time ago.

'I'm not arguing,' Fraser pointed out. 'I'm asking a very simple question about why vital repairs haven't been done. I'm asking whether you even had a plan to stop this tower rotting straight through to the bare earth. When would you have stepped in? When would you have done something?'

'I had a plan. I have a plan for all the repairs. But they can't all be done at once.'

At once? Fraser thought. He hadn't seen a single thing that his father had done for this place. No doubt once the new wife had moved in there hadn't been time for thinking about floorboards.

His father had chosen his love-life over his responsibilities time and time again. It was clear that his stepmother hadn't cared for this place. He knew that she'd only lived here for two years, but there wasn't a single sign of her. His father had ruined their family for a relationship so insubstantial that it had already disappeared without a trace.

'You haven't done *anything*,' Fraser said. 'It has to start somewhere.'

'Right, lad. And who's going to pay for it?'

Fraser scrubbed his hands through his hair, either side of his head, trying to keep his temper in check. Trying not to lose it with his old man in front of Elspeth. But his father was testing every ounce of his reserve.

'Are you telling me there's no money?' He forced the words out through gritted teeth, the effort of not shouting them making them come out short and clipped. 'What's happened to it?'

Malcolm threw his hands up, but the helplessness of the gesture did nothing to calm Fraser.

'I'm telling you it's impossible to keep up,' Malcolm said. 'I've tried. I *am* trying. But this place soaks up every penny and then comes back asking for more.'

'We have an entire estate to support us. What's happening to all the rents? What about the investments?'

The money that Fraser had inherited and invested had been doing so well for so long he couldn't believe that the estate that had generated the capital in the first place could be struggling. If he'd known....

What would he have done differently? Forgiven his father and come home?

'I'm doing everything I can, Fraser,' Malcolm said. 'Isn't that enough?'

Fraser gestured towards the rotting floorboards. 'Apparently not.'

'Well, I'd love to hear your suggestions—because I've been doing this on my own for the past fifteen years and I'm out of ideas.'

How dared he throw that at him? Fraser thought. Make it *his* fault because he wasn't here? He'd wanted to be here. He'd wanted his father to choose *him*. But Malcolm hadn't. He had chosen some fickle attachment to a woman who hadn't stuck around.

It had been bad enough when Fraser had thought that it was only feelings that had got hurt. If he'd known that his father was going to sacrifice Ballanross on the altar of his doomed second marriage too, perhaps he'd have been back here years ago, giving him a piece of his mind. Making sure his children's legacy was protected.

Of *course* Fraser had suggestions. He had a whole list of them that he had started as they'd driven up here through the woodland and he'd started to get a sense that the place had been allowed to fall into the sort of state that he would never permit on an estate *he* was managing.

He hadn't seen the accounts, but he'd known even before his father had said anything that they would be as much of a mess as the castle was.

Could he fix it? A twinge of something like guilt pulled at his belly. This would never have happened if he had been here to take care of it. Instead there was an estate three hours' drive from here that was flourishing while his own home was rotting away.

But he would never have had to leave if his father hadn't chosen his new wife over him. This wasn't his fault. His father had been the adult at the time. This was all on *him*.

He remembered that Elspeth was standing beside him and turned to her.

'Let's go.'

He took her hand, vaguely aware that he was making a bad habit of doing that, and then snatched it back. His father's lust, kept unchecked, had led them here. He wasn't going to perpetuate the problem by making things complicated with Elspeth. Here was a reminder, as if he needed it, that indulging the intense desire he had for her wasn't going to get them anywhere. His father had gone down that path—and look where it had got them.

But Elspeth pulled his hand back, stopping him from storming down the staircase.

'Stop, Fraser. If you're running away from this you're not dragging me with you.'

'Leave it, Elspeth,' he said, still angry. 'You don't need to be involved in this.'

But she tugged at his arm, enough to stop him storming out. 'I do need to be involved. Last time I checked, you two hadn't made such a good job of working this out without me. Now, are we going to talk about this like adults?'

'I'm done talking,' Fraser said, turning for the door again.

'Well, I'm not,' Elspeth declared behind him. 'Malcolm, where's the best place for us to look at everything? The accounts and stuff? I'll help if I can.'

'Well…' Malcolm hesitated. 'If you want I can meet you in my study,' he said, his voice wavering a little. 'But I'm not sure what there is to be done.'

'I don't know how much help I'll be,' Elspeth replied, sounding more unperturbed. 'But I'm willing to try.'

Fraser met Elspeth's eyes and stared, waiting for her to read his silent message: *Keep out of this. I don't need you to interfere. I've got this under control.* But she stared back at him, steadfast, and he knew that she wasn't going to back down.

Fine. He should go through the accounts anyway. His father had been ignoring the problem for long enough—Fraser wasn't going to contribute to his neglect.

'Fine,' Fraser said aloud. 'I'll see you in there.'

He walked back up to the guest room where he had stayed last night and grabbed his laptop. He wasn't sure that he'd need it, but he needed the breather. Needed to be away from Elspeth and his father and let his anger subside.

He had been close to completely losing his temper, and he knew that giving in to those extreme emotions was going to get him nowhere. Since he had left the castle and his childhood behind he'd learnt that he had to keep his feelings in check. Not let them get the better of him. It was impossible to make good decisions based on emotion.

He stood at the window of his room, looking out at the ruins of the old castle, the stones warming in the winter sun, the loch a shimmering silver-gold behind, breathing deep until he felt the muscles of his shoulders relaxing.

He had spent hours up there as a kid. Exploring the old building, trying to imagine the lives of the people who had lived there.

When he was calm again, and could think of the conversation that he had to go and have without clenching his fists, he turned away from the window and headed for the door.

CHAPTER TEN

WHEN FRASER REACHED the study, Elspeth was peering over Malcolm's shoulder at an ancient computer. Thankfully it wasn't the monster of a desktop that he remembered helping his father use before he had left home, but he could tell just by looking at it that it was a good five years past needing replacing. And then there were the papers, stacked on the desk, on the bookshelf, on the floor in front of the leather wingback chair positioned by a cold fireplace.

They must not have heard him over the roar of the old computer's fan, desperately trying to keep the machine from overheating and blowing up. So he leaned against the door frame and watched them for a moment.

Would this ever have been what he wanted? The woman carrying his child getting to know his father? If he hadn't left this place… If his father had never met someone else… If his childhood and everything that had followed hadn't been marked by the choice that his father had made. Would Malcolm still be the man that he remembered before that day? Would his father be a different person? Would he, Fraser, be changed?

He shook his head. There was no point thinking like

that. Those things couldn't be undone. They could never go back there.

They had to go forward. They had to try and make a new relationship. It could never be what it was. But he had missed his father. He could admit to himself now that every time he had thought about his home over the years, every time he had felt that emptiness inside him that he thought could be filled by coming home, he had been missing his dad.

But building something new would mean letting go of what had gone before. It would mean forgiveness. And suddenly Fraser knew that he wasn't ready. He couldn't forgive his father...yet. But, seeing him talking with Elspeth, it made him want to. Perhaps one day they could have a relationship again.

He took another step into the room and Elspeth and Malcolm must have heard him, because they both turned to look at him.

'Well, I'm glad you're here,' Elspeth said. 'I'll take brain surgery over *this*. And I say that as someone who has actually performed brain surgery.'

'I'm suitably impressed,' Fraser said with a smile, somewhat relieved to find that it was something he could still do. 'Let me have a look.'

He pushed another chair up to the desk and pulled the laptop towards him. 'Right, then, tell me what I'm looking at.'

His father scrolled through a few tabs and open programs. 'Well, there's the bank accounts, and the investment accounts. Here's my cash flow spreadsheet.'

'Who's the accountant? Still Taylor?'

'No, I had to let him go a few years back. I've been taking care of things myself.'

Fraser gave him a look out of the corner of his eye but resisted saying anything. If he and his father were going to rebuild their relationship one day he was going to have to stop taking cheap shots every time the opportunity presented itself.

He clicked through the windows that Malcolm had left open on the computer and was vaguely aware of the silence that was falling around the three of them as he scrolled through page after page of financial records, trying to resist coming to the conclusion that was becoming harder and harder to escape.

Ballanross was broke. Flat broke. Falling-down broke. His father hadn't been exaggerating. There simply wasn't any money. From what he could work out, it was all gone. Investments had been cashed in for repairs and debts, but with them had gone their income and so the cycle had begun. The situation had gone from bad to worse, and then to worse still, until now there was nothing left, and the mother of his child was walking over a rotting floor four storeys up.

He rubbed his hands through his hair, hoping for the figures to change in front of his eyes, to persuade him that circumstances weren't as bad as he was reading.

'Dad… This is…this is bad.'

'Mmmph.'

The hint of a smile in that one simple syllable made Fraser realise that he'd used the word 'Dad' for the first time since he'd been back. It had fallen from his lips without him thinking.

It was a start.

'What else do I need to know?' Fraser asked, trying to keep his mind on the numbers. On something that he could make sense of.

He was already coming up with ideas to increase their income. How they could use the incredible natural resources of Ballanross to attract visitors and businesses to the area. To halt the decay of the castle until they had the money they needed to make real improvements. He could see it in his mind. He could see the rooms gleaming as they did in his memory. He could see the woodlands properly managed and flourishing. He could see his child running through the halls as if they were a playground, like in his earliest memories.

'You know what? Never mind,' he said. 'We need to go back to basics. Let's look at outgoings first. Where's that bank statement?'

His father pulled it up on the computer and Fraser went through it again, more slowly this time. He asked questions occasionally, when it wasn't clear what an expense was, and made a few notes on the spreadsheet.

Until he got to a name he recognised and his blood ran cold.

'What is this?' Fraser asked. There was a metallic taste in his mouth, and he hoped that his father wasn't about to say what he was expecting.

His father hesitated for long enough for Fraser to know that he was right, even before he said, 'It's nothing important, Fraser. It's Louise, my…wife. My ex-wife. We're still friends, you see, and she needed to borrow some money for a few weeks. I said I'd loan it to her.'

Fraser could feel the blood rushing to his face as his hands tightened into fists. He fought the reaction down, trying to keep his emotions under control. 'You're lending money to the woman you chose over me while our home is falling down around you? What's *wrong* with you?'

'Ach, Fraser, it's not like that. It's a small loan. If you let me explain…'

Explain? What could he possibly say that would explain this? He didn't want to know that his father was still in touch with his ex-wife. He didn't want to see her name or be reminded that she existed. His father had sacrificed everything for her, for a marriage that had lasted only two years. A flash-in-the-pan relationship that had cost Fraser his family as he knew it.

To know that his dad was still in touch with her, when he himself hadn't spoken to him for so long… He didn't know why that hurt so badly, given that he was the one who had walked away.

He rose to his feet, thinking that perhaps movement would help. That he would be able to walk off this restlessness, settle his heartbeat and find some calm. But instead, as he thought more about how his father had chosen *her*, that other woman, he could feel himself growing more and more angry. Emotions that had been long buried were forcing their way out, pushing him closer and closer to losing control. Tension ripped up through his core, stiffening his shoulders, moving back down to his arms and his fists, and he knew that he was closer than he had ever been to losing control of his feelings.

He headed for the door. Needing to be outside. Needing to escape that toxic atmosphere and get himself back in control. He charged out of the front door out into the grounds and strode across the gravel without a thought to the cold or to the direction he was walking.

Elspeth took the hat, scarf and mittens that Malcolm had pulled for her out of the cupboard by the door and thanked the Scottish weather gods for the weak sun and clear sky. She waved goodbye to Malcolm and headed out of the door and away from the sun, taking the bridge over the burn, and walking down the gravel path that led to the castle ruins and the loch, her shadow stretching far ahead of her. The sun caught on the face of the old stones, which seemed to glow a warm, creamy grey in the soft light.

She couldn't see Fraser yet, but much of the ruins was hidden in shadow, so she walked on.

The look on his face when he had argued with his father... It had been like a window into the deepest depths of his hurt. As if every doubt and fear that he had held over the whole of his life had re-emerged at once. She had seen the anger crash over him like a wave, and then seen the fear in his face as a response.

He had not walked out of that room because of the anger. He had been afraid. Of what, though? Of what he might say to his father? Of what he might hear? Or was he simply afraid of the feeling itself, overwhelmed by an emotion he wasn't equipped to deal with?

Perhaps she would learn something more about him up here, seeing the place he sought out when he needed to be grounded. Even if he wasn't there she needed to see it, now that Malcolm had told her it meant so much to Fraser. She wanted to know him. To understand him. Because he was the father of her child, she told herself.

But the thought rang false. Like when she glanced at an X-ray and knew there was something wrong before she'd had time to work out what it was.

Her feelings for Fraser had nothing to do with the baby.

She tried to unpick that sensation—the unease of having a thought, a feeling, lurking in her subconscious, just out of reach. If the way she felt about Fraser had nothing to do with him being the father of her child... Then it was *him*.

As soon as she articulated the thought to herself she knew that it was true.

From the first time that she had seen Fraser at Janet's wedding she had wanted him. That hadn't stopped just because of the circumstances that they now found themselves in. She couldn't stop responding to him, remembering the way that she had responded to his body, just because she knew that a relationship with him would never work. She had feelings for him. She admitted it at last.

But that didn't mean she was going to act on those feelings. It didn't mean she was suddenly released from her responsibilities and free to be with him. She'd already proved that she couldn't be in a relationship. Alex had made her choose where her priorities lay, and she had chosen her family. There was no reason the universe would suddenly bend its rules just because she was attracted to Fraser.

The path she was following twisted through a small copse of trees and Elspeth shivered, pulling the hat lower over her ears and the scarf tighter around her neck. When she emerged into the sunshine again she could see a figure up by the ruins, walking slowly along one of the fallen walls, jumping from stone to stone where the grass had grown in—nature reclaiming the site for its own.

She would have known it was Fraser even if Malcolm hadn't told her he would probably be there. She wondered when she had committed it to memory—the shape of his body, the way he moved, how he carried himself.

Had it been that night, when for hours he had been

the silhouette between her and the soft glow of a lamp in the corner? When she had traced the contours of his body with her hands and grasped them with her limbs, imprinting the shape of him on her, the feel of his skin, until she knew just where to touch, how to move to elicit a moan or a groan.

She could bring to mind in a fraction of a second the softness of his hair against her breasts, the roughness of his hands as they skimmed down her arms, making her shiver with anticipation. But as she put one foot in front of the other, bringing her closer and closer to where he sat on a collapsed heap of masonry, she knew that she had to concentrate on the reason they had come up to Ballanross rather than on her own feelings.

Fraser had been so angry back in Malcolm's study that she had been half expecting to find him pummelling something with his fists. But it looked as if he had walked off the worst of his mood. She knew that she should talk to him about what had just happened, but she didn't even know where to start. It didn't matter how much she wanted her baby born into a loving, harmonious family—she didn't know how to fix this, how to make them a family. She didn't know how to stop thinking about their night together. She didn't know how she could live with Fraser in her life without thinking of what might have been between them. Without wondering what it would feel like to be touched by him, kissed by him again.

With her eyes fixed on Fraser, she lost sight of her footing, and before she realised what was happening she had caught her toes on a piece of stone hidden among the grass and toppled forward. She let out a squeak of alarm but managed to right herself with nothing but her pride a little dented. She could only hope that Fraser hadn't seen her. She wasn't exactly sure what she was going to say to him, but this wasn't exactly the entrance that she wanted to make.

She brushed imaginary dirt from her jacket—she hadn't been anywhere near hitting the ground—and took a moment to regain her dignity. When she looked up Fraser was just a couple of feet away, standing on the remains of a stone wall, his face grey.

'What?' Elspeth asked, feeling the colour drain from her own face as she took in Fraser's expression.

'I thought…'

He jumped down from the wall and strode across to her. Before she realised what was happening he had pulled her into his arms. She allowed herself to relax, to breathe him in just for a second, before remembering that she had just been reminding herself that he was off-limits. She pushed him away, and it took some strength, given his vice-like grip around her.

'Fraser, what are you doing?'

He took a deep breath—composing himself, she guessed.

'I heard a noise and I looked over and you were falling,' he said by way of explanation. Taking a step back from her now that she had disentangled herself, he started to look a little sheepish. 'I started running as soon as I saw, but I knew I wouldn't be able to get to you before you hit the ground.'

Elspeth drew her eyebrows together. 'I didn't hit the ground. It was just a little stumble.'

'But you *could* have done.'

The words burst from Fraser with unexpected force, and Elspeth guessed that he still wasn't quite in control of himself.

She forced herself to be kind, reminding herself that he had come out here full of emotions about his father that he clearly hadn't been able to handle. Reminding herself as well that he didn't have the day-to-day experience of being pregnant. Or medical training. She could see from his face that he had been genuinely scared that the baby would be hurt.

She reached out a hand and rubbed his arm in a way that she hoped would come across as comforting, rather than anything more intimate. 'I'm fine and the baby's fine. I promise. I'm sorry you were worried.'

Fraser took another deep breath, and Elspeth watched as the colour returned to his face and the expression of terror faded. And then, the drama done with, unease began to creep in as she remembered that she still hadn't quite worked out what she was going to say to Fraser when she got up here. Her somewhat melodramatic entrance onto the scene hadn't made things any less awkward.

'How did you know I was up here?' Fraser asked, and Elspeth was grateful for a question she at least knew the answer to.

'Your dad,' she said simply.

The word 'Malcolm' had been on the tip of her tongue, but at the last minute she'd changed her mind. He *was* Fraser's father, whether Fraser liked to think or speak of him that way or not. There was no point in them coming all this way if they weren't going to get to the bottom of what had happened. But if she had learnt anything from working with her patients, it was that sometimes approaching a problem sideways was more effective than hitting it head-on with a hammer. Maybe if she gave him time and opportunity Fraser would open up to her without the need for her to interrogate him.

'He said that you liked to come up here when you were a boy. He thought you might be here.'

'I love this place,' Fraser said simply, sidestepping the issue of his father. 'I always have. It was a fun playground when I was a kid.'

'I can imagine,' Elspeth said, trying to.

She looked around, looked up at the empty spaces where windows must once have kept out the wind and the rain. At dark doorways and tiny chambers that had long ago lost their walls. At nooks and crevices that had once hidden secrets and long-finished lives. She brushed a hand against a stone wall, wondering who had touched it before her. Whose lives had played out in this room. How many babies had been born and children raised here.

It was starting to hit her, she realised, why it was so important for Fraser to bring her here, for him to think of his child here. He and his family had been a part of this place for so long that it was impossible to think of them as separate. They belonged together. And understanding that made her understand how pained Fraser must be to have been so long away from this place. How much his father must have hurt him for him to stay away from so long. She had not given herself an easy task.

'Will you show me round?' she asked, hoping that her plan of giving him space and time to talk would take effect.

She'd charged up here after him because she'd been so worried about that look on his face when he'd walked out. It had been disgust and disappointment and fear, all roiling together and fighting for supremacy. But he wasn't ready to talk now. He was jumpy and sensitive and he needed to do whatever it was he did to take himself off high alert.

Fraser nodded. 'Sure.'

He climbed up to the bank where he had been standing when she had first seen him and held out a hand to help her up. He kept hold of her hand as they walked to a long stretch of great archways.

'This was the great hall. See there? That's the space where the fireplace would have been.' Stones marked out a space the size of a decent-sized kitchen on the floor. 'That would have kept the whole hall warm. And in the early days it would have been where food was cooked, ale was warmed. It was the most important place in the whole castle. Everyone lived in this room. There was no such thing as privacy as we understand it. Eating together, sleeping together…'

She could imagine what else they had all been doing in the same room, and she didn't need him to say it. In fact, she needed him *not* to say it. To be able to keep her mind as far away from sex as possible.

Elspeth spun around, her eyes tracing a sweeping arc from the flat stones on the ground in front of her up to the jagged stones at the top of the tallest tower, and back to Fraser beside her. He was looking directly at her and her gaze met his, locked with it, and she found she couldn't break it.

But she had to.

She moved her feet first, turning away from him, hoping that she'd have the strength to look away. But he caught her hand, wouldn't let her break that connection. She knew that she must be imagining the heat she could feel in her palm. The temperature was still barely above freezing, and she was wearing mittens so padded that her hands barely felt as if they belonged to her.

'I wanted you to see,' Fraser said. 'I needed you to know why this place is important.'

'It's okay,' Elspeth said soothingly, sensing something frantic, urgent, below the surface. 'I understand.'

This wasn't what she had meant. When she'd wanted him to relax she hadn't meant for him to relax into *this*. She'd come up here to talk to him about his father, and now here he was looking at her with an intensity that she knew was dangerous.

He reached for her other hand and pulled her closer. She could see the hurt in his eyes. Could see the toll that confronting things with his father was taking on him. She was sure that under the surface of this confident, sexy, close to irresistible man of thirty was a fifteen-year-old boy who was still reeling from his father leaving him.

But when his hand brushed her cheek she knew it was the man touching her, not the boy. And when he leaned in close, so that his breath was warm on her icy lips, she didn't—couldn't—care what was motivating this. Her heart was pounding with anticipation and her hands were already reaching for him when, with a sigh, his lips finally found hers.

He moved slowly at first, and she wondered—with what small part of her brain was actually functioning—whether he thought she was going to startle and bolt. God, she wished she had the strength to do that. She might think—*know*, even—that this was a bad idea, but his mouth was hot and sure and so incredibly sexy that there was no way she was ever going to want him to stop.

She wished she was wearing fewer clothes. She felt a pull deep down in her belly as Fraser's arms wrapped around her waist, lifting her up to him, and she was desperate for the feel of his skin. To get closer. To climb inside him. She pulled off a glove and grabbed a handful of his hair, crushing her body against his, desperately pushing away every reason why this was a bad idea.

Fraser's breath was coming shorter now, and her heart was pounding almost painfully in her chest. Oh, this was intoxicating. *He* was intoxicating. She remembered the first time, at the wedding, up against that tree that had pulled at her dress and grazed her skin, and how she had been so tempted to just take him right there. How did he *do* this to her?

Just as she thought that this might be it—she might never be able to stop and would die kissing this man—Fraser broke away, dragging in air as if he had just climbed a mountain.

'God, Elspeth, I don't know—'

'Don't you dare,' Elspeth said quickly, trying to catch her breath, trying to stop real life from invading the moment and making her regret it. 'Whatever you were about to say, don't. Say it later, if you have to, but don't…not just now.'

She leaned her forehead against his chest, grateful for the difference in height that meant she didn't have to look him in the eye, that meant she could gather her thoughts and her dignity without him being able to see. She couldn't even summon up any embarrassment for the way she'd responded to him. Why should she, when he'd responded as passionately as she had?

Eventually she looked up, and Fraser gave her a smile that made her want to tear his clothes off and then her own, frostbite be damned.

'Shall we walk, then?' he asked, reaching for her hand again.

She didn't have an answer. Couldn't fathom where this kiss left them now. So she walked along with him, and the knowledge that that kiss was something they couldn't take back slowly sank in. She had reacted and thought and kissed all in the moment, completely ignorant of the life-changing decision they had just made.

They couldn't forget this. Whatever happened now, she had shown him exactly what she felt for him and she couldn't take it back. They could make whatever sensible grown-up decisions they liked, but she had just proved that.

The rational part of her brain told her that some of the tension between her and Fraser should have dissipated with that kiss. He was frustrated; she was worked up. They had just been getting something out of their systems. *Yeah, right.* She knew, and she knew Fraser knew, that they had just proved that didn't work. Ignoring this hadn't made it go away. And a kiss hadn't made it go away either. Which meant…what? They were stuck with it? With each other?

For a tiny breath of a moment, she allowed herself to imagine it. That this could work. That Alex had been wrong when he had told her she was incapable of having a relationship. Perhaps she and Fraser could take this fragile new thing and protect it and nurture it until it became… She didn't know what. But until it became *something.* Something strong. Something that would sustain her rather than drain her.

'I should apologise to my father,' Fraser said, as they walked back through the long shadows of the castle ruins.

'I think it would be a good idea. And then maybe the

two of you should talk. That's what we came up here for, after all.'

'I know. I'm just still so…so angry with him.'

Elspeth squeezed his hand, knowing how hard it was for him to talk about this. How vulnerable he was making himself just by having this conversation. 'You've been angry for fifteen years,' she reminded him. 'Has it helped?'

He shook his head. 'It's not easy.'

Well, there was no point arguing with that.

'I've never expected it would be,' she said. 'You've done something incredibly brave by coming here. But do you want a relationship with him again? Do you regret losing so much time?'

Fraser nodded. 'I think you know I do.'

'Then don't lose any more,' she suggested.

She saw the words sink in. Saw that Fraser was considering them. She smiled. Fraser was letting her in. It had to be worth something that they were working through this together. It gave her hope.

'What can be done about the estate?' she asked, knowing that this was always going to be a sticking point between Fraser and Malcolm.

'I'm not sure,' Fraser said, shaking his head. 'I have cash I can invest—though I wish I'd known about this before I bought the Edinburgh apartment. Even then, though, I won't have as much as it will need. Any amount of money runs out eventually, unless you can find a way to provide an income.'

'So what's to be done?' Elspeth asked.

'This place needs money coming in. There are some things I've tried on other estates that might work. If Malcolm is willing. We need the forests better managed—

the timber should be bringing in money, but they're not sustainable as they are. And then we need to get more tourists up here: sporting weekends, outdoor activities, maybe even consider opening up the castle a few days a year. Convert some of the outbuildings into luxury holiday homes. There are estates similar to this one that are thriving. But it's going to be a lot of work to turn it around.'

'Are you going to help him?' she asked, and then wondered selfishly for a moment what it would mean to her if he was. Would he want to be up here full-time? Hours away from where she and the baby would be living?

Fraser nodded. 'I haven't got a choice. I have to do it if I ever want to live here again. If I don't want it sold off before the wee one is old enough to remember it.'

They crossed the driveway and entered the tower door into the family apartments, heading for the kitchen first, and warming themselves by the range while they waited for the kettle to boil.

With a hot drink as a peace offering, they knocked on the study door and found Malcolm still poring over the spreadsheets.

Fraser pulled up a chair beside his father while Elspeth took an armchair by the fire, which Malcolm had built up while they had been gone.

As she watched Fraser and his father tiptoe towards a truce her mind drifted back to the kiss that they had shared. If she closed her eyes she could still feel it. Feel the rasp of Fraser's stubble and the chill of his fingertips when he had touched her face. Next to the fire, she felt her body warming again, felt the pull towards sleep that had come so easily since she had been pregnant.

CHAPTER ELEVEN

FRASER GLANCED BEHIND him and saw that Elspeth's eyes had closed and she had given in to sleep. Some wingman *she* was, he thought with an affectionate smile.

He and his father had started talking about the finances again, picking up where they had left off before Fraser had walked out. But it didn't matter where he looked. All he could see was *her* name. All he wanted was an explanation.

He took a deep breath, knowing what he had to say. 'I'm sorry for leaving the way I did before. I was surprised to see that you had given Louise money, but that's no excuse.'

'Aye, well, thank you for the apology. That means a lot,' Malcolm said, leaning back in his chair with a thoughtful expression on his face. 'Reckon it's about time that we talked about her, though, son. It's been a long time.'

This time Fraser didn't bite back at the word 'son'. There was no point denying who they were to each other. And, whatever had happened since, Malcolm had been his dad, been there for him every day of the first fifteen years of his life. That earned him some rights.

'I don't understand why you're giving her money,' Fraser said, sticking to the present, not ready to fall into the past just yet. 'You can't still be financially responsible for her. You've been divorced for ten years.'

Malcolm nodded thoughtfully. 'You're right, and it's not a regular thing. But she needed to borrow a little money and I wanted to help.'

'Our home is falling down around you and you're sending *her* money?' Fraser tried to keep the anger from his voice, but he could tell from Malcolm's expression that he hadn't quite managed it.

He shrugged. 'It's only a few hundred pounds; I couldn't see what difference it would make to things here. And it's a loan. As apologies go, son, this isn't the best I've heard.'

Fraser took a deep breath, tried to control his temper so that they could actually get to the end of this conversation. Elspeth was right. Leaving so much unsaid over the years had done nothing but make him unhappy. Finishing this was going to be hard. But at least he was trying something different. Now that he could see how his anger had been eating at him all this time he wanted it gone.

'So…you're still friends, then? You and Louise? When we heard that you were divorced… I don't know. I assumed it had ended as badly as it had with Mum.'

Malcolm winced, and Fraser could see the pain and regret in his expression.

'I never meant to hurt your mother, Fraser. I wish you could believe that. Back when I met Louise and thought that I was falling in love with her I didn't want to lie to your mother, so I told her I thought we should separate. If I'd known then what I was doing…how much it would hurt her…that I would lose you…' Malcolm shook his head, looking tired. Sad. 'Love's a confusing thing,

Fraser. And sometimes it makes us do—say—things we regret.'

Malcolm glanced over to where Elspeth was sleeping by the fire and Fraser wondered what he thought of their relationship. How much he had guessed about the feelings that were running between them. Well, if his father knew what was going on, Fraser would be glad of the information. Because he wasn't sure that he and Elspeth were doing such a great job between them of figuring their relationship out.

'You were only married two years,' Fraser said, accusing. 'You threw away everything that you and Mum had for something that didn't even last.'

Malcolm rubbed at his hair and sighed. 'Aye. It's easy to see that now. But at the time…'

'At the time you were only thinking about one thing.'

'Fraser…' His father's voice trailed off as he shook his head. 'That's not what happened. When I met Louise I fell in love with her. I'm sorry if it hurts you to hear that. I didn't want to lie to your mother, and so I told her what I was feeling. Louise and I were happy for a short time, but…but sometimes that's not enough. I was sad for a very long time after you left. It's hard for a relationship to survive that.'

'You chose *her*,' Fraser said, the words tearing at his throat.

It was the thought that had haunted him for so many years. The fact that he hadn't been good enough for his father. That he hadn't been enough. That his father hadn't chosen *him*.

'I didn't know at the time, Fraser, that that was what I was choosing. I know that's what you threatened, but I thought you would come round. That if I gave you space you would change your mind. I didn't know what to do. I always wanted you to come home, but I didn't know how to talk to you.'

Malcolm leaned forward, but Fraser moved away on instinct, needing to keep some distance. Everything his father was saying… It was making him question everything he'd thought he'd known about his past. About himself.

'You moved Louise in here when I was barely out of the door.'

Fraser held up his hands in defeat. 'You were a child, Fraser, and so angry. I didn't know what to do.'

'I just wanted you to choose *me*!' Fraser exclaimed, and then glanced across to make sure that he hadn't woken Elspeth. 'I wanted me and Mum to be more important than she was. I wanted our life together, what you had with us, to be more important than what you thought you might have with her.'

His father sank into his chair. 'If I'd known, son, that I wouldn't see you for so long, that you really meant it, I wouldn't have done it. I would do anything to go back and make a different choice.'

Fraser looked into his father's face and for the first time felt ashamed. He saw that he had brought as much pain to his father as he had felt himself over the years. If either one of them had compromised perhaps they both could have been spared some pain.

'It's not too late,' Malcolm said, reading the mood and placing a hand over Fraser's. 'There's a new life on the way and I hope—'

Malcolm's voice cracked, and Fraser swallowed down an answering lump in his throat.

'I hope that this is the start of something. I would so

love to get to know you again, Fraser. To meet my grand-
child and watch him grow up.'

'Aye,' Fraser said eventually, not trusting himself with
a longer word. After several deep breaths he lifted his
head and looked his father in the eye. 'I'd like that too,'
he said, with a small nod that sealed the matter.

CHAPTER TWELVE

'Do you—?'

'Should we—?'

Elspeth laughed nervously, feeling the doorknob cool and smooth beneath her hand as she started again. 'I think we should probably talk about what happened earlier,' she said.

After she had woken alone in the study and gone to find Fraser and Malcolm, Elspeth had been astonished to discover them at the table in the kitchen, papers strewn between them and an animated conversation in flow. She had wondered if she'd woken in some sort of parallel universe. But the two men had been full of plans, looking to the future of Ballanross.

They had all spent a lively afternoon around that table, playing with different ideas, making suggestions for new business ventures. And it had only been as they'd left the kitchen late in the evening that there had been space to think, never mind talk about the kiss that had happened earlier.

As she had turned the brass knob on her bedroom door she'd paused, knowing in that moment that she absolutely did not want to sleep on it alone. To let whatever had captured them that morning dissipate overnight or become too big to talk about. She'd opened her mouth to speak, only Fraser had too.

Now she took a deep breath, deciding to be brave, and to say what she had been thinking all day: 'I think we need to talk about what happened earlier. We're meant to be just friends, Fraser. I can't be in a relationship—not with all the other responsibilities in my life. But all the time we're either snapping at each other or—'

'Kissing each other?'

She tried to hide her smile, not wanting Fraser to know how the memory of that kiss lit her up from the inside.

'Or trying really hard not to.'

He snorted, gave a little huff of laughter. 'Hmmph, thanks for the ego-boost.'

She opened the door behind her and glanced back over her shoulder as she crossed the threshold to make sure that Fraser had read her invitation and followed.

Elspeth pulled the heavy velvet curtains before sitting down on the stiff upholstered bench in front of the window. 'I'm clearly not doing a great job.'

'I'm glad you stopped trying,' Fraser replied as he joined her.

'Who said I stopped?'

She ducked her head as he stared at her, not wanting him to know how she was feeling. It had been hard enough to resist him when her memories from the wedding were faded and dog-eared and starting to feel as if they could have happened to someone else. The memory of this morning was so sharp and Technicolor that her mind could have her back in the moment faster than she could blink.

'That helps,' he said, brushing one hand across her cheek. 'If everything that happened this morning was while you were *trying* to resist me I'd like to see what happens when you really let yourself go.'

She couldn't help the smile turning up the corners of her lips, and she gave him a look to remind him that he knew exactly what happened when she let down her guard with him. The widening of his eyes and the slight flush to his skin let her know that she'd hit her mark.

She felt herself leaning in to him, drawn to him as if she had no control over her own body. But she couldn't let that distract her—again. She pulled herself back into line. She wasn't just some slave to her hormones. She was going to be a mother: she had to get her life in order. She moved away, leaving Fraser with his lips moistened and fire in his eyes.

'Don't be sensible,' he said, reading her perfectly.

'We have to be,' she replied, glancing down at her bump, knowing that he would understand what she was thinking. He was developing an uncanny knack for that. 'We're meant to be talking.'

'I don't want to talk. I want to—'

She touched his lips with the tips of her fingers, stopping the words before they could be said.

'Don't say it. If you say it I might change my mind. We've been pretending we can will these feelings to disappear. We've done a terrible job, so we need a new plan.'

Fraser leaned away from her slightly. From the thoughtful look on his face, he seemed to be assessing how serious she was about this. Could he be playful and kiss her—or was this talk non-negotiable.

'Does there always have to be a plan?' he asked.

'Yes!'

Fraser visibly started at the bite in her tone, but to his credit didn't push her on it. Well, at least she'd answered his unspoken question, as well as the one he'd asked out loud. There was to be no kissing on the agenda until they'd talked about what happened earlier.

'Okay,' he said, speaking softly and slowly, as if trying to calm a skittish horse. 'Then how about this for a plan?'

He cupped her cheek, his hand moving as slowly as his words, and just as she was about to push him away he paused and flicked his gaze up to her eyes from her mouth. But he didn't kiss her. Didn't cross the invisible line that she had drawn between them.

'I think about this all day,' he said. 'It's exhausting trying to deny it. To deny myself.'

Elspeth heaved in a deep breath, sending it down to her fingertips to stop them grabbing at him—to her mouth, to stop it begging him to deliver on what that look had just promised.

'It doesn't leave me time or energy for anything else. Maybe if we stopped fighting. Maybe if we…'

She thought he was going to do it—to lean in and complete this kiss. He was going to make their bed and she would enjoy lying in it.

But he just rested his forehead against hers. 'Maybe, if we weren't putting so much effort into fighting so damn hard, things would work themselves out.'

'But…' Elspeth started to say. She had so many sensible objections that she didn't even know where to start. She couldn't be in a relationship. There was too much at stake. If she were distracted by Fraser and something happened to Sarah she would never be able to forgive herself.

'I know… I know,' Fraser said, lifting her hand back to his lips for a gentle kiss. 'There's a million reasons why this might not work. Why it would make more sense for us to resist. But I can't help feeling that if I weren't expending so much energy *resisting* you every second of the day, maybe we'd find the answer to making this work. Could that be our plan? We stop fighting against what we want and see what happens.'

What if he was right? She was thinking about him all day anyway—when she was at work, when she was with Sarah, when she was in the car, when she should be sleeping. Thinking about how she was going to resist him. Thinking about that night after the wedding. Thinking about all the reasons why this was a bad idea. If all that went away, would she have *more* time for everything else in her life, rather than less?

'Watchful waiting…' Elspeth said thoughtfully.

Fraser frowned. 'What?'

At last she met his eyes. 'It's doctor-speak for wait and see. For observing how something progresses before you decide whether you need to intervene or not.'

Fraser nodded, reflecting her smile back at her. He was still so close she could feel his breath on her lips. Still not taking that choice from her.

'Watchful waiting,' he echoed. 'I like the sound of that. Though the waiting part sounds a lot like what we've been doing already.'

A surge of heat started in the pit of her belly and spread up over her chest, until she was sure her cheeks were flaming. 'I can't wait for you much longer, I don't think,' she said, being honest at last. 'I'm not sure I've got the strength.'

He gave her a look that burned and melted her at the same time, like a candle, puddling wax around its own flame.

'You're the strongest woman I—'

She pressed her lips against his and it lit her up as it had the last time, the first time, every time she had kissed him. But with the urgency of knowing she shouldn't be doing this gone, she felt something else in his kiss, a sweetness, a tenderness that had been drowned out before. Or, she wondered, maybe this was new. Maybe this was deeper.

With her eyes closed, she brought her hand to his face, rubbed her thumb against the fullness of his bottom lip, rediscovering the contours of his mouth, taking the time to relearn every line.

The night of the wedding, and in the dreams she had had since, he was a silhouetted shape in the half-light. He was the desire and the urgency that had made her lose her inhibitions and led her into trouble. Now the urgency had gone, had been replaced with something richer. She didn't need to consume this experience in one sitting, knowing that she wouldn't have another chance. She could take her time over this. Indulge every curiosity. She could stop and enjoy every moment with each of her senses. And she intended to.

'Enjoying yourself?' Fraser asked, as her explorations continued.

'Mmm...' Elsepth replied as she trailed kisses along his jaw, pressed her lips to the soft, sensitive skin behind his ear.

His lips dropped to her collarbone, nudging aside the fabric of her sweater, sending a shock of desire right through her. His cold hands on her waist made her jump, and she pulled away.

'What's the hurry?' she asked, acting innocent.

Fraser held his hands up in supplication. 'If you want to be in charge...'

He leaned back and turned his head, pulling her on top of him so she could carry on where she'd left off—except he'd clearly forgotten the football-sized bump between them, and she let out an *oomph* as she landed on him and the breath was squeezed from her.

Fraser lifted his head in alarm, propping himself up on his elbows. 'Did I hurt you? Are you okay?'

'I'm fine,' Elspeth said, pushing him back on the bench seat, lowering herself gently until she was lying on top of him. 'Things have changed a wee bit since we were last here. That's all.'

He ran his hands over her bump and smiled at her appreciatively.

'You look beautiful,' he said, pulling her face down for another kiss with one hand. The other still rested possessively on her belly. 'And you feel incredible. All full and tight and about to burst. It's been impossible to ignore how sexy you are like this.'

She laughed, kissing him back. 'The hormones must have gone to your head. But I'll take it.' She resumed her explorations, and this time didn't protest as his hands found their way under her clothes and over her skin.

There was no light around the edges of the curtains when Elspeth's phone rang the next morning. That didn't mean much in the Highlands in winter—it could be nine in the morning or three in the afternoon. So she glanced at the time on her phone as she picked it up—five in the morning.

She felt a frisson of dread familiar to anyone living with chronic illness and disability in their lives when a phone rang in the middle of the night. Her mother's name was on the screen. Elspeth swallowed her fear down, not wanting her mother to hear that she was worried.

'Mum? Everything okay?' she asked in a whisper, not wanting to wake Fraser, snoring softly beside her.

Elspeth held her breath as her mum spoke. She had fallen in the shower and had to call an ambulance. She was in A&E now, which meant that the respite carer they'd booked was at home with Sarah, unsupervised.

'I'll come home right away,' Elspeth said, calculating driving times in her head. 'Don't worry. I'll be back in a few hours.'

She ignored her mum's protests—because what else could she do? She wasn't going to risk having someone underqualified and inexperienced taking care of Sarah when she could be back there herself in a few hours, making sure that everything was done exactly as it needed to be.

A *hmmmph* beside her in the bed let her know that Fraser was awake and unhappy about it. One of his hands curved around her hip, but she pushed it away. This wouldn't have happened if she hadn't come up here with him, she thought to herself. She wouldn't be sitting here wondering what might happen to Sarah if the agency had sent someone inexperienced, imagining all the worst-case scenarios that haunted her late at night when she thought about strangers looking after her sister.

She crept from under the blankets, hoping Fraser would fall back to sleep before remembering that she didn't have her car here and she'd need him to drive her home.

'What's going on?' he asked, lifting himself on to one elbow and eyeing her suspiciously as she flicked on a light and started throwing things into her suitcase.

'Elspeth?' he said, trepidation in his voice. 'Are ye going somewhere?'

'There's an emergency at home,' she said, without looking round. 'I've got to go and take care of my sister. I'm sorry. I know we meant to stay longer. Perhaps I could take the car and—'

Fraser sat up properly, pushing the hair out of his eyes, still not looking one hundred per cent awake.

'No, I'll drive you, Elspeth. Of course I will. Is Sarah okay? Your mum?'

'Mum's had a fall. She's in A&E waiting for X-rays—which means Sarah's home alone with the carer.'

'I'm sorry about your mum. But is there no one else who can help out? Someone closer?'

That's just what Alex would say.

The thought appeared in her brain before she could stop it.

'I really have to go, Fraser. I know it's not what we planned, but that's just the way it is.'

Fraser glanced around the room, trying to guess from the light—or lack of it—what time it was. From the grit in his eyes and the ache in his muscles he guessed that it wasn't much later than when they had finally fallen asleep.

'It's not about what we planned, Elspeth,' he said, trying to catch up with what was happening, trying to stave off the fear that she was about to walk out on him. 'It was an innocent question. I'm trying to understand what's going on.'

She stopped packing and stood still for a moment. 'Look, I know you're not used to this. But this is how it is with my family—my life. Sometimes I have to drop everything and just go.'

She was moving round the room purposefully, pulling on clothes, throwing others sharply into her suitcase. It was clear that she was leaving. Had she given him a moment's consideration or was she just going to lift his keys and go?

'This is exactly what I was worried about, coming up here. This is exactly why I've said all along that this won't work.'

'And would you be running so fast if it wasn't for last night?' he asked, knowing that he was entering dangerous waters. Last night they had found such a fragile balance…she had taken such a risk by giving in to what she wanted. What they *both* wanted. Was she regretting it now?

'What's that supposed to mean?' Elspeth asked, but it was clear from the way she refused to meet his eyes that she knew.

'Exactly what you think it means,' he said, his voice growing cold as the fear that she was walking away from him sank in. 'This would be a very convenient exit route if you regret what happened last night. If you've changed your mind about watchful waiting and want to take action instead.'

'If I had been at home last night none of this would have happened,' Elspeth said plainly, finally meeting his gaze with a stony expression.

Fraser rose from the bed and came over to her, bringing the thick bedspread with him and wrapping it around them both. 'Everything's going to be okay,' he said, kissing her on the lips and praying that she would respond.

She softened a little and warmed under his touch, her

mouth moving gently against his as he pulled her closer, holding on tight.

But as he deepened the kiss she pushed him away. 'We should go,' she said when they broke apart, her expression cold.

When she had kissed him, the fear had receded a little, but it was rushing back now. 'When do you need to leave?' he asked.

Elspeth glanced at her phone, checking the time. 'As soon as we can.'

She breathed a sigh of relief when he nodded.

He sat on the bed for another few moments, watching Elspeth pack. What had happened in this room while he had been sleeping? He'd closed his eyes late last night—early this morning?—with Elspeth breathing warm and soft on his chest and her bump pressing gently against his hip. And he had woken to an empty bed and the beginnings of the relationship they'd worked so hard for looking more fragile than ever.

He knocked on his father's bedroom door, his bags in his hand, and explained what was happening, and then they were crunching across the driveway, trying to get some heat into the car, chase the ice from the windows.

He glanced across at her as he drove, watched her withdraw into silence, and he wanted to pull her into his arms. Everything seemed so much simpler when he was touching her.

He reached for her hand and gripped it tight, trying to show her how much he wanted this to work. 'It'll be okay, you know,' he said, trying to start up the conversation that had gone cold back in her bedroom.

'You don't know that,' she said, her voice devoid of emotion. 'You *can't* know that. You don't understand.'

He didn't know what to say to that. Didn't know how to reach her now she had decided to shut him out. No, he didn't understand her—because she wouldn't let him in. He wanted to know her. Wanted to be a part of her life, a part of her family. But *she* needed to want that too. He couldn't support her if she wouldn't let him.

Finally they pulled up outside the home that she shared with her mother and her sister and he turned to look at her. Wondering if, at last, she would find some explanation for what was happening between them. Give him some hope that this wasn't going the direction he feared.

She had pushed him hard this weekend, forcing him to face up to the decisions—the mistakes—he had made in his life. And he'd worked hard to reach a point where he could picture himself with someone. Moving towards those big, scary feelings that had always had him running scared in the past.

And now what? Was she going to prove that he had been right all along? That he would have been better never getting involved with her?

'Thank you for driving me back,' she said, as if she were reading from a script, and reached for the door handle.

Fraser sighed, opened his own door, and then pulled her bags from the back of the car and brought them round to where she was standing on the pavement, digging through her handbag for her keys.

He dropped the bags at her feet, and before she could protest cupped a hand around her cheek.

'Please,' he said. 'Don't decide anything now. Don't go into your head and make this go away. I'll stop by tonight and we can talk.'

She hesitated, but he pressed a gentle kiss to her cheek.

'Remember this,' he instructed, his voice low, his breath on her ear, unable to drag himself away from her. 'Remember last night. Remember what we are to each other when we are together like this. This feeling—it's important. Don't give up on it yet.'

She closed her eyes and took a deep breath, and for a moment Fraser thought she would turn him down. Again. Instead she tensed her shoulders. Looked up and met his gaze.

'Okay. Let's talk tonight.'

CHAPTER THIRTEEN

ELSPETH SAT IN the quiet house, her hand resting on her bump, trying to take stock of the last twenty-four hours. When they'd driven up to the Highlands such a short time ago she had been so sure that a relationship with Fraser—with anyone—was nothing short of impossible. Then, last night, it had seemed inevitable.

But she had watched the sun rise as they had clocked up the miles this morning and her certainty, her faith in her decision had faltered. Now she was sitting here knowing that when Fraser returned she would break their relationship off, and feeling unsure of how she would live with herself when the deed was done.

As soon as they'd got back, Elspeth had jumped straight in with Sarah's daily routine—taking the splints off Sarah's hands and legs, teasing out her tight muscles with gentle wiggles and hard stretches that made her wince.

Elspeth had soothed Sarah through it, as she always did. She knew exactly how hard she could press and pull, which fingers would be most painful to straighten, when Sarah would need a break to catch her breath, with an understanding and an intimacy that an agency carer could never reproduce.

Now she had helped Sarah to shower and dress, brushed her hair and vacuumed her wheelchair, Elspeth still needed to keep busy. She'd hoped she could spend an hour chatting with her sister, but Sarah needed to study and had asked Elspeth to leave her in peace.

Fraser had asked her not to make any rash decisions, but what else could she do? The one night she'd decided to take a risk she had been called home for an emergency. She couldn't have asked for a clearer sign about the viability of their relationship.

She could hear what Alex would have said as clearly as if he were back in this house with her—*You choose them over me every time*. Of course she did. Because the risks if she made a different choice were unacceptably high. When Sarah had been born Elspeth had sat by her cot for months, willing her to get better, to come home. She never wanted to feel so helpless again, and if that meant she had to sacrifice her own relationships to be there for her sister, it would be worth it.

That last argument with Alex, when she had chosen her family for the last time and broken off their engagement, it had been such a relief. Alex had pushed her and pushed her to choose. Every time she'd had to cancel a date or cut short a holiday he'd rolled his eyes and she'd seen his judgement. And when he'd told her that he wouldn't move in with her mum and her sister she'd known they didn't have a future.

She didn't want to do that again. Didn't want to watch the novelty fade from a relationship, see love sour because she couldn't give what her partner was demanding from her.

She could tell herself that it would be different with Fraser. That he wasn't Alex. That he wouldn't expect her to choose, as Alex had. She *could* tell herself that—if she didn't already know that Fraser was the sort of uncompromising man who had been issuing ultimatums since he was a teenager.

When his dad hadn't been prepared to drop everything else because Fraser had demanded it, he hadn't spoken to him for fifteen years. This wasn't a man who was going to be happy settling for the small part of herself that she had to offer. It would be better for him to find someone who could give him the undivided love he wanted and deserved.

Elspeth cupped her hands around her belly. She loved her mum and Sarah more than she could say. And she knew she was going to love her baby with a fierce, limitless passion. She simply couldn't see how she could love Fraser like that too.

Except her heart hurt as if she did already. As if she loved him with her whole heart, with no room for anyone else. As if she'd be left cold and empty if she had to give him up.

She thought of a future of polite exchanges as they handed the baby over every other weekend. Of calling to pass on information about doctor's appointments or school reports. And then she thought how much worse it would be if *he* broke it off instead. If she loved all these people and made it work and then had Fraser tell her that she wasn't doing it well enough. As Alex had done. If he told her that the part of herself she was offering just wasn't enough for him. It would break her heart, she knew. In a way that couldn't be fixed.

When Fraser's knock on the door sounded that evening, after her mum had gone to bed to rest after her long day at the hospital and her sister had returned to her room after dinner to study, Elspeth had made up her mind and firmed her resolve. She opened the door and braced herself for the sight of him, knowing that her body would react, trying to get it in line before she did something she couldn't take back.

She spotted the flowers in his hand and shook her head, smiling slightly at the sweet gesture. Another reminder of what a man she was giving up.

'Fraser, you shouldn't have...' she started, her voice trailing off.

He leaned in and planted a kiss on her cheek. 'I didn't,' he replied, mirroring her smile. 'They're for your mum. I wanted to make a good impression, under the circumstances...'

'The circumstances being you impregnating me before you'd been properly introduced to my family?' she said with a raised eyebrow. 'I didn't realise they did flowers for that.'

Fraser smiled. 'You should see the poem in the card.'

She smiled back despite herself, despite knowing what she had to do, and stood aside to let him in.

'Come through to the kitchen. I'll find a vase for them.'

She stood and fussed with the flowers, hoping that somehow something would happen to make this easier. That she would wake up with it magically having been done for her. But as Fraser tried to catch her eye—to connect with her—she knew that she wasn't that lucky. She was going to have to live through every tortuous moment of this.

'Did everything go okay today?' Fraser asked. 'With your mum at the hospital?'

'Mmm...' Elspeth replied, building up her courage.

She couldn't engage in small talk. If she did that it would be too easy to be pulled back from what she knew she had to do. To chicken out.

'Fraser, I'm sorry, but I can't do this. We can't be together. It's never going to work. I have too many responsibilities, and it's only going to be worse when the baby gets here. We should just end it now, before we get any further in.'

Fraser nodded slowly, and she could practically see the machinations of his thinking as he tried to choose words that would make her change her mind.

'How have things changed since last night?' he asked eventually.

She leant back against the worktop, her weight pressing through her palms as she closed her eyes and fought the memories.

'Everything has changed since then.'

Fraser took a step towards her. 'I don't see how.'

'What happened this morning—'

'Has happened a hundred times before,' Fraser interrupted her. 'You told me that. And it'll probably happen a hundred times again. You knew that when we went to bed together last night.'

She threw her hands up. 'Yes, but—'

He thought he understood, but he didn't. He didn't know the strain that it put on a relationship. He hadn't lived through it already. She had. She knew where this was going before it had even got started.

'But what?' Fraser asked, maddeningly calm in his refusal to understand her or believe her.

'But I forgot,' she said, hoping that he wouldn't see the truth. That she'd known and remembered every reason why it might not work but none of that had seemed as important as the fact that she loved him.

She'd watched Fraser and his father put to rest fifteen years of pain and hurt and recrimination. And she'd thought, *I want that. If I love him enough, maybe I can have that.* But she'd forgotten that his problems stemmed from the past. Her problems were right now. They were happening today. And loving him, seeing him ready to love, didn't change *her* circumstances, however much she wanted it to be true.

'Maybe I just gave in,' she said. Not wanting him to guess how she really felt. 'Or I was kidding myself that I could do this. That I could be enough. But I can't. There's not enough of me to go around, Fraser.'

'Not enough? Elspeth, you're making so many assumptions here. You're telling me I can't have something I haven't even asked for. All I want is to talk about this. Why won't you do that?'

'Because I've talked this thing to death, Fraser. I've talked and talked and talked and the grand conclusion is that I can't do both. I can't be the daughter and sister that I need to be—*I want* to be—and be a good enough girlfriend as well.'

Fraser narrowed his eyes as he looked at her. 'You've talked about it with who? Because you haven't talked about it with *me*. And I'd have thought my opinion should count for something.'

She hesitated, but Fraser fixed her with a glare and wouldn't back down.

She shrugged in resignation. She might as well tell him. 'With Alex—my ex.'

'The one who called off the wedding?'

'*I* called off the wedding,' she said. The distinction was important.

Silence fell over the kitchen as she waited for her words to sink in.

'Why?'

Fraser said it in a way that she knew meant he wasn't going to take any bull. He would know if she was lying to him. If she wasn't being completely honest. And, really, he might as well know. This would be the final nail in the coffin of this relationship—if she could even call it that before it had really got started. There was no way he'd want her after this.

'Because he always wanted more than I could give. The part of my life that he occupied was never enough for him. He was insisting that after the wedding we would get our own place. My mum and sister said they were fine with it, but the closer it got, the less I wanted to leave. I *like* being here with them. I *like* it that if there's an emergency in the middle of the night I'm here to deal with it. I *like* it that my sister knows whether I need comfort carbs or a massive bowl of ice cream based on nothing more than the tone of my voice. But Alex wouldn't budge. He said if we were going to be married it was time to get our own place. I had to choose.'

She saw the realisation hit Fraser in stages, slowly sinking in. She'd been given an ultimatum. She'd made the choice he'd wanted his father to make. She'd do it again if she had to, and she wouldn't choose Fraser. He was second choice—again. Or that was how he would see it.

'I'm sorry, Fraser. It won't work. We were crazy to think that it could. I'm sorry.'

'You apologised already. Save it.'

Anger spiked in her. He was acting as if this was a *free* choice. It wasn't. Who would *choose* to feel this way?

'What would you have me do, Fraser? Should I choose you? Should I let my mother and Sarah and my patients fend for themselves while I go up to Ballanross and soothe your ego? You gave your dad an ultimatum and you've been punishing him for fifteen years for choosing love over his family. This is an impossible situation.'

'I'm not asking you to choose,' Fraser said, his voice raised and his tone frustrated. 'The opposite. I'm asking you to try and do both. To find space in your life for me. To make room for me.'

'I did that before and—'

'But not with *me*! So it didn't work out before. Why does that mean it won't work this time? I'm not Alex. I'm not asking you for more than you can give. I'm standing here telling you that I'll take anything you're willing to give me, and you're telling me that you're not even going to try.'

She shook her head. This pig-headed man was just refusing to get this. Out of spite. Out of… She didn't know why he was refusing to understand something so simple.

'I'm sorry, Fraser, but we both know you're the kind of guy who hands out ultimatums. You did it to your father and you'll do it to me. And I just can't go through that again.'

'Why are you so convinced that I'm the same as your ex? Can't you accept that I'm different? That *we* will be different? That the choices in front of you are different this time? I understand your being scared. What I don't understand is why you're not even willing to try.'

Well, at least she knew the answer to that one. 'Because trying is exhausting, Fraser. And I can't do it any more. It's just not worth it.'

CHAPTER FOURTEEN

HE WASN'T WORTH IT.

She'd given him the answer that he'd dreaded hearing since they had started this journey. Well, he didn't know much about her experiences with men and relationships, but he knew that he'd had a lot of women over the years and not one of them had made him question the way he was living his life. And then he'd met her. He might not be worth fighting for, but she was—and he wasn't giving up yet.

There was something special between them. Something rare and precious. There had to be. It was something he didn't want to lose. And if she didn't feel that way too she wouldn't have gone to bed with him last night.

He took a couple of steps towards her, until he was standing close enough to touch her if she'd let him, one foot either side of hers. She didn't move—not towards him or away—and he could read the indecision on her face. She wanted this. She wanted him. But she wasn't going to let that be enough.

He placed a hand beside one of hers on the edge of the worktop and with the knuckles of his other hand gently stroked her cheek. He moved slowly, not wanting to spook her. Not wanting to push her to do anything she didn't want to. He pulled her towards him, resting his forehead against hers.

'This is different,' he said, hoping above all that he was right about this one thing. Hoping that she felt something when they touched that she hadn't felt before. He was betting everything on it. 'Did it feel like this before?' he asked, letting his body sink towards her, his stomach pressing on her bump, feeling their baby growing there between them. 'With him? Or is this different? Am *I* different?'

Elspeth sighed. He felt the breath leave her body in a long, resigned wave, and for a moment he thought that was it. He was wrong. This wasn't different for her. But then she turned her cheek into his hand—just a fraction. A movement so subtle he might have missed it if he hadn't been desperately looking for any sign that she was still with him on this.

'It's not going to work, Fraser.'

'That's not what I asked.' Fraser allowed himself a tiny glimmer of hope that this wasn't a hard no, that she had evaded rather than answered his question. 'I asked if I'm different.'

She paused again, and tensed slightly beneath him.

'You are,' she conceded, glancing up and briefly meeting his gaze.

'And you *feel* different,' Fraser prompted, building on her concession, moving her towards what he was sure was true. 'You feel different from how you felt with Alex.'

She held her breath and he could practically *hear* her looking for the get-out. For a way of denying what they were both realising had to be true.

'Yes.'

The word was barely more than a breath, but to Fraser it was everything. It was hope. It was life. It was all he needed to know to keep going. She had pushed him and pushed him to face up to his past, to address the problems with his father that he had carried into every adult relationship he had ever made. And now he was going to do the same for her. He was going to make her see that she could do this. She *could* be enough. She could be everything she needed to be to her family, and whatever was left for her to offer him he would take it.

'Then we're going to try.' His voice rang with the certainty that he felt. 'This isn't the same. You don't have to be the person you were when you were with Alex. I'm not asking you to tear yourself in different directions. All I'm asking—*all* I'm asking—is that you don't write this off.'

He softened his hand and stroked her cheek with his thumb, trying with everything he had not to rush her. To give her time to think. To stop himself from breaching those last few centimetres between his lips and hers. To give her space to come to him when she was ready.

'I can't live at Ballanross,' she said, and he pulled back, surprised.

Of all the responses he'd thought she might give, that one had never occurred to him.

'I can't even live in your new apartment.'

'I never asked you to,' he reminded her.

'But I couldn't. I won't. And you would want to. Not now, perhaps. But eventually you'll want to go back to Ballanross.'

How many hypotheticals was she going to run through? How many times was she going to assume the worst of him? This relationship was never going to move forward if she couldn't see that this wasn't her last relationship. That he wasn't Alex.

'I'd like to spend time there, yes. If that's something that we can do,' Fraser said, keeping his cool even as Elspeth was losing hers. 'And there's plenty of room for your mum and your sister, if we ever want to live there. If that's what we all choose. But I don't need to.'

He realised the truth of what he was saying as the words left his mouth. 'I would choose *you*, Elspeth, if it came to it.'

The realisation that he meant it hit him like a truck. All these years he'd dreamed of going back to his home. All this time the castle had loomed large in his memory. But it had only been a symbol of what he had lost. Of what he was missing. It had never been about the castle. And he wasn't going to choose a symbol over the woman he loved. He would be wherever she was. For ever. If she would let him.

'I'm not asking—' Elspeth started to say.

He cut her off, because she didn't need to say it. 'I know you're not. Because you're not the sort of idiot who gives ultimatums to the people you love. But it's true anyway. I can live with never going back there. But I couldn't live without you. Without our baby. I want us to be a family—together—and I'll do that in the city if that's what it takes to make you agree. To make you happy.'

What would make her happy?

She couldn't remember the last time she'd asked herself that question. The last time she had made a free choice rather than weighing up all the opposing forces in her life and trying to pick the least bad option.

But Fraser was asking something different. He wasn't

asking what she *didn't* want. He wasn't asking her what the lesser of all the evils was. He was asking her, as no one had done for a really long time, what she *wanted*.

And there could only be one answer. She wanted him. She wanted him in her life, in her family, in her bed. She wanted him any way she could get him, and she wanted him now. But that didn't mean she could have him.

'Elspeth? I hope you're not about to do something stupid!' Sarah shouted from the other side of the kitchen door.

Elspeth shook her head in dismay. How long had she been there listening?

'Did no one ever tell you it's rude to eavesdrop?' Elspeth shouted back, leaning against the counter and letting out a sigh. She walked over and opened the door, stepping out of the way before Sarah could catch her toes with her powered wheelchair.

'You must have forgotten to teach me that one. Now, is there a good reason why you're not jumping on him?' Sarah asked with a raised eyebrow. 'I mean given how in love with him you are and everything.' She turned to Fraser. 'Don't let her tell you that she needs to look after us. I've been telling her for years that she needs to get over it.'

'In love with me, are you?' Fraser asked, looking from Sarah to Elspeth, raising his eyebrows.

Elspeth bristled, and decided the safest thing to do was to ignore the question. Safer to stick to the practical considerations—they came with easy answers. Talking about moving out and it actually being a viable possibility were two very different things. Something her sister didn't seem to grasp.

'*Getting over it* is easier said than done.' Elspeth busied herself filling the kettle and flicking the switch, needing something to do with her hands, somewhere to look other than at Fraser. 'Especially as you do actually *need* me here, Sarah.'

'Well, I'm going to move out when I finish college anyway,' Sarah said. 'You'll have loads more free time then.'

Fraser drew his eyebrows together in surprise as he looked over at Sarah. 'Sounds exciting,' he said. 'Elspeth didn't mention that.'

But Elspeth was shaking her head. She had been through this with Sarah so many times before. It just wasn't realistic for her to live alone. Sure, there were other people in Sarah's position who managed, but she didn't want her sister to just *manage*. She wanted her to have the best care. That meant Elspeth doing as much of it as possible herself. And that only worked if they were living together.

'You can't do that, Sarah. We've been through all this already.'

'Don't tell me I can't. I can employ a team of assistants and carers. Plenty of people do it. I'm not having you martyr yourself for me.'

Elspeth poured hot water into the teapot and then slammed it down on the counter, harder than she'd intended. 'I'm not martyring myself. I *want* to take care of you.'

'But that's not what Sarah wants,' Fraser said, glancing from one sister to the other. 'I think we need to talk about that. About why you're trying to keep your sister dependent on you.'

'You never stop,' Sarah added. 'Even when it's making you miserable.'

'Caring for you doesn't make me *miserable*, Sarah. How could you think that?'

Tears prickled at the back of Elspeth's eyes at the idea that Sarah could think that. She *loved* looking after her sister. And as for what Fraser had said—he couldn't possibly understand the relationship between her and Sarah. This wasn't his call to make, however much he might like to feel in control of the situation.

'Maybe it's not making you miserable,' Fraser conceded, 'but it's stopping you from giving our relationship a chance.'

Sarah smiled at Fraser. 'Did I mention that I really like this guy, Elspeth? He's right. Being apart from Fraser is making you miserable. And you *do* know, don't you, that if I move out I'm not going to suddenly drop dead?'

Fraser pulled up a chair and sat at the table. 'Look, we don't need to make any decisions about this now. If we all want to live together, we can make that happen. Sarah, if you want to live on your own I'm sure we will support you.'

Elspeth looked from one to the other, wondering when they had decided to gang up on her.

'Are you telling me that I'm making it all up?' Elspeth asked seriously. 'That I've *imagined* that I've needed to do everything I have? Because you don't remember, Sarah, what it was like when you were born. When I was terrified every day that you might die. When I had to remind Mum to eat because the only thing she could think about was getting you through the day.'

Elspeth brought the tea over to the table, and Sarah reached out to touch her hand.

'Of course you haven't made it up. You know Mum and I couldn't have managed without you. But we want you to be happy. If we'd known that the way things are makes you think you can't have your own life too we'd *never* have let it go on this long. Is this why you and Alex broke up?'

Sarah glanced at Fraser, obviously worried that she was oversharing in front of the new guy.

'I know about Alex,' Fraser said, his expression making it clear that he wasn't a fan.

'Well, that's good.' Sarah nodded approvingly. 'But, Elspeth, if you think that you split up because you didn't want to move out, then you've missed something important. You split up because he wasn't prepared to have this conversation with you. Fraser's not doing too badly so far…'

Elspeth could feel Fraser's eyes on her, trying to judge her reaction.

'Anyway,' Sarah said at last, 'if you put my tea in my bottle I'll leave you two to it. Oh, and Mum and I have booked a carer for the morning. So don't you *dare* use me as an excuse not to… Well… You get the idea.'

And with that parting shot Sarah left the room, leaving a heavy silence in her wake.

'Your sister wants to move out?' Fraser said, breaking the silence. 'You never told me that.'

Elspeth shook her head. There was a good reason for that. 'No, because it's not happening.'

'How does *that* work?'

Fraser came to stand in front of her and her whole body hummed with the awareness of knowing she could just reach out and touch him.

'Surely if she's an adult she gets to decide for herself.'

'Or maybe she should listen to her *doctor* sister when she tells her it's not a great idea.'

Fraser crossed his arms and narrowed his eyes. 'You don't *want* her to be independent?'

'Of course I do! I bend over backwards helping her to be independent. I don't want her to—'

She stopped herself, suddenly aware that the sentence had nearly got away from her.

'Finish the sentence,' Fraser prompted her gently. 'Come on—we were getting somewhere. You don't want her to…what?'

'I don't want her to *die*,' Elspeth said, her voice breaking.

'And is that likely to happen?' Fraser asked gently. 'If Sarah's care comes from somewhere else—like she says she wants? Does that make it more likely? Because *she* said that's not going to happen. Is she wrong?'

Her objective doctor brain provided the answer. 'No, she isn't.'

'Then why is it so hard to let her go?' he asked gently.

Elspeth thought about it for a second. Considered dodging the question. But she had been carrying this around for so long. Trying to make sense of her life. Trying to make the best of it. But it hadn't made her happy. It wasn't making Sarah happy. It wasn't going to make Fraser happy either. Maybe it was time that she started telling the truth.

'Because I've been scared that she might die for as long as I can remember. Since I was a little girl and she was born and there was nothing I could do except sit by her and hope that she wouldn't. I studied hard and I went to uni and I became a doctor because I didn't want to feel helpless. And now I can *do* something about it.'

The thought of living without her sister was unbearably painful. The thought of sitting and doing nothing was almost as bad.

'And what do you think would happen if you stopped?'

'I don't know,' she said. She had already voiced her darkest fear. And it didn't lose any of its power just because her objective brain knew it was unlikely. 'Do you think I'm completely irrational?'

Fraser shook his head and reached for her hand. 'I think you love your sister and you've spent your whole life putting her first. But now she's grown up I think she wants to take care of herself.'

'I don't know if I can just...stop caring. Stop being afraid.'

He squeezed her fingers, caught her eye and smiled. 'Well, then, it's a good job you don't have to do it by yourself. We'll work it out between us. *All* of us. In our own time.'

Elspeth brushed away a tear with the back of her hand.

'I asked you earlier what you want. You never gave me an answer,' he reminded her.

She reached up on her tiptoes, aware of her bump between them as she wrapped her arms around his neck and pulled him down to her, finally breaching those millimetres between their lips that had been driving her insane, making it impossible for her to think straight.

He let her come to him, true to his word, letting her lead, not demanding more from her than she was giving. But there was a time and a place for being restrained, and right now she wanted the Fraser who had pinned her wrists and made her moan the night they had met. She pressed harder against him, letting her fingers tighten slightly in his hair.

'God, Fraser,' she said between kisses. 'Of course I want *you*. You know I do.'

Another kiss and her hand was tangling in his hair. The other hand was exploring his shoulders. His back. Pulling at his shirt and diving for the skin beneath.

'I don't know how this is going to work…' she said suddenly, feeling a shot of reality start a slow puncture in their bubble.

'Stop thinking,' Fraser demanded, angling his head to deepen their kiss.

The heat of his tongue in her mouth sent a shot of desire straight through her belly, and the feel of his hands exploring her waist, her breasts, her bottom, had her wishing she had somewhere to take him that didn't share a flimsy plasterboard wall with her mother or her sister.

That thought acted like a pitcher of iced water to the back of the neck and she pushed Fraser away slightly, gasping for breath as she tried to collect her thoughts.

'Rethinking the whole living together thing?' Fraser asked with a wry smile, equally breathless, reading her thoughts faster than she could form them.

'For tonight. Definitely. After that…'

'After that we'll figure it out. I can't promise you easy answers, Elspeth. But I promise you that I'll be here. I promise you that we will do this together. We'll find something that works for all of us.'

She rested her head against his chest and smiled as his hands came round to her belly, rubbing, encouraging, until he was rewarded with a kick.

Fraser cupped her chin, tipped her face up to his for a light kiss on the lips.

'I love you,' Fraser said, his gaze locked on hers. 'And I want you every day. I don't care that this is the scariest thing I've ever done—I'm not going to run from it. I believe we can do this. I believe *you* can do this. And any time you doubt that, doubt us, I'm going to be here to remind you that we love each other enough to make this work.'

She didn't doubt him for a second—she couldn't when the truth of his words was written in every smiling line around his eyes. She stood with that feeling for a moment—the knowledge that they were in this together, the warm satisfaction of knowing that someone loved her as passionately as she knew Fraser did. That everything they would face, they would face together. Her heart was now part of something bigger than her. Something bigger than either of them.

She let the words settle into the quiet of the kitchen.

'I love you too,' she said at last. 'And I'm not just saying that because you did. I'm saying it because I can't live without you, Fraser. I want you in my life for ever. I want us to belong to each other for ever.'

Fraser pressed his lips against hers again and the kiss was sweet this time, rather than holding the fire they had shared before. Sealing the promises they had just made to each other. When he pulled away he was smiling, but she sensed a nervous anticipation in him as he reached for where he had left his jacket on the counter and pulled out a small leather box.

'Well, then, I'd better give you this,' Fraser said, lifting the lid to reveal a delicate platinum band with a channel of diamonds set smoothly into the metal.

Elspeth took the box from him, her mouth open in surprise as she looked from the ring up to Fraser's face.

'I was going to break up with you,' she said, a ghost of a smile on her lips.

'I know. And if you'd told me that you didn't love me and you didn't want to be with me you'd have never known that this existed.'

'But you thought you might be able to talk me round?'

'I hoped,' he said, pulling her tight against him. 'I hoped like I swear I have never hoped before that I wouldn't have to. That I was right to trust in what I feel. That I was right to think that you love me, and that what we share will be strong enough to survive this.'

'You have a lot of faith in me. In us.'

He nodded. 'I have faith in you. And I have faith that I know how to make you happy.'

'You know that I come as a package deal? Do you really want to move in here?'

He shrugged. 'I would do it in a heartbeat if you asked. *Are* you asking?'

'Are *you* asking?' Elspeth said, her face breaking out into a grin. 'Diamond rings usually come with a question.'

He laughed, tucking a lock of hair behind her ear and taking the ring back from her.

'You're right. I'm doing this all wrong.'

Keeping hold of her hand, he dropped to one knee in front of her.

'Elspeth, I have wanted you every day for the last six months, and I will love you every day for the rest of my life. Will you please put me out of my misery and agree to be my wife?'

She looked down into the face of the man she loved and saw all the possibilities for their future in his hopeful gaze. 'I will, Fraser. I love you and I'll be your wife tomorrow if I can.'

She pulled him up by the hands until he was standing in front of her, then wound her arms round his neck and pulled him in close.

Fraser laughed, the deep, rich timbre of his mirth muffled by her hair. 'I'm more than tempted to take you up on that, but I trust that you're not going to change your mind. Anyway, now this wee bairn is so close…' he smoothed a gentle hand around her bump '…I'd quite like to share the day with him, or her. What do you think?'

'I think that sounds perfect,' Elspeth replied, her face buried in his neck. 'I think that sounds like everything I've ever wanted.'

EPILOGUE

As Elspeth rapped her knuckles on the black front door, the sunlight caught the pretty row of diamonds on the third finger of her left hand and she smiled, wondering if she would ever get used to seeing them there. If she would ever glance at them and not be reminded of that evening in her mum's kitchen, when she had realised that despite all her best efforts to sabotage things Fraser loved her, and he wasn't going to let her go. That, despite years of telling herself that she couldn't have everything that she wanted, she was getting all that and more.

She dropped her hand back to her side and Fraser's fingers curled through hers with an intimacy that was nowhere close to losing its thrill.

The door opened in front of them and Sarah was waiting for them in the hallway, beaming with happiness and pride. 'Come in!' she said. 'Where is she? Where's my niece?'

Elspeth glanced across at the car seat Fraser was carrying beside him and was almost overwhelmed by tears at the sight of her baby daughter, tucked up in a blanket and snoring gently.

'She's so beautiful,' Sarah said, mirroring Elspeth's smile, causing more tears to well up. 'Come through to the living room—I'm desperate to cuddle her.'

'I'm to warn you that there are severe penalties for waking a sleeping baby,' Fraser said, in a voice of mock seriousness.

'That's an auntie's prerogative, surely?' Sarah fired back, pulling her chair up beside the sofa where Fraser had left the car seat in order to get a better look at the baby. 'Does she have a name yet?'

Elspeth glanced at Fraser. 'We're thinking maybe… Isabel. But we haven't set our minds yet.'

'Plenty of time to get to know her,' Fraser said, smiling at Elspeth and then beaming at his daughter.

It was something else she would never tire of, she realised, that expression. The pure joy and pride and love when he looked at their baby. It was everything she had dreamed of since she had found out that she was pregnant. Before she had even thought to dream of him for herself.

The baby snuffled, grunted and pursed her lips, and Fraser, Elspeth and Sarah all laughed quietly.

'I guess that's my cue to get comfy on the sofa,' Elspeth said, scooping the baby up and latching her on for a feed. 'You said on the phone you needed Fraser to do you a favour? You should get him while you can. We're thinking of going up to Ballanross for a few weeks, making the most of my maternity leave and spending some time there.'

'I think I'm going to like having a brother-in-law,' Sarah said. 'He volunteers for DIY and he brings a castle into the family. I'll like him even better when I get to see Ballanross for myself. How's the building work going?'

'Slowly,' Fraser said, his face serious for a moment. 'But we're doing it right. We're rebuilding the estate from top to bottom, and eventually we'll be self-sufficient again. By the time this wee one is old enough to remember,' he said, and smiled across at the baby, 'it'll be just how I knew it.'

Elspeth squeezed his hand, watching the interaction between her fiancée and her sister, seeing how they were supporting each other and feeling a warm glow of happiness.

Fraser had played an invaluable part in getting Sarah's apartment ready. It had taken a lot of planning, and a leap of faith and confidence, but Sarah had been determined to move into a flat on her own, and Elspeth had finally seen that it was up to her to support her sister's dreams—not get in the way. And now she was here, and she could see the pride on Sarah's face as she showed them round her new flat, showed them the changes that had been made since she had first moved in a couple of weeks ago.

Which was why Elspeth was curious about what Sarah needed Fraser for. They'd had a team of builders in here to make sure the flat was perfectly adapted for Sarah and her carers. She'd thought it had all been taken care of already. But if her sister needed a favour, and Fraser was happy to help out, then who was she to interfere?

She pulled a cushion from the other end of the sofa and tucked it under her arm, looking down and watching the baby's perfect round cheeks wobble as she fed.

Fraser returned, carrying a very large box and with a smile on his face. Sarah was just behind him.

She pointed at the large blank space above the TV. 'Right, you and I are going to direct, Elspeth, and Fraser is going to do the heavy lifting.'

'Okay...' Elspeth said, as if she had an idea what her sister was talking about.

She'd found, over the years, that it was often just easier

to go along with Sarah when she had one of her grand plans. Now she'd realised that her sister was perfectly capable of making her own decisions about where to live, she couldn't really dispute what she planned to do now she was all moved in.

'Where do you think we should hang this one?'

From the box Fraser pulled out a framed photo of Elspeth, Sarah and their mum, and held it against the wall.

Elspeth beamed—she'd had no idea that Sarah had been planning this. 'It's lovely,' she said with a broad grin. 'Centre of the fireplace, surely? Pride of place.'

Sarah agreed, so Fraser propped the frame against the wall and went back to the box.

He pulled out another picture—this one of Elspeth and Sarah, wrapped in a tight hug. Elspeth felt another wave of tears well up and knew she was fighting a losing battle. She smiled at her sister, who was watching her indulgently.

'And the last one?' Sarah said, gesturing for Fraser to get on with it, clearly still excited.

Fraser pulled out the final picture, and Elspeth gasped. It was her and Fraser and the baby, just hours after she had been born, still shell-shocked and dazed in the hospital.

'I want you all right here on my wall,' Sarah said. 'Just because I wanted to move out it doesn't mean I'm not going to miss you.'

Elspeth passed the now-sleeping baby to Fraser and squeezed her sister into a hug. 'I miss you too. But I'm so proud of you,' she added. 'I've always known that you could do this. I'm so sorry that I wasn't brave enough to let you do it sooner.'

'You got there in the end,' Sarah said with a smile.

'And you brought these two along with you, so I guess it was worth it.'

Elspeth glanced from Sarah to Fraser and then down to the baby, who was still fast asleep in his arms, and couldn't imagine any greater pleasure than this. Knowing that the people she loved most in the world were happy, safe, secure. Grateful and full of wonder that they had all been courageous enough to trust that their love for one another would be enough to make this a reality...to make them a family.

* * * * *

THE COLONELS' TEXAS PROMISE

CARO CARSON

This book was written with fond memories
of the two friends who each told me they were
going to marry me if they hadn't found anyone else
by the time they were thirtysomething.

But…

This book is dedicated to Richard, my husband,
who decided to marry me the day he met me.

Chapter One

"Attention to orders."

The military personnel in the conference room came to their feet. Major Juliet Grayson was already standing at attention, as was her new commanding officer, who stood at her right. On her left stood the most wonderful person on earth: her son. Matthew was eleven years old and halfway through sixth grade, but he still looked boyish and acted goofy—most of the time. Not today.

Today, her little boy was trying to fill a man's shoes. Juliet's husband should have been here, standing at her left, ready to pin her new rank onto her uniform at this promotion ceremony. He was somewhere else. With someone else. Which was why he was her *ex*-husband.

"...special trust and confidence in the patriotism, valor, fidelity and abilities of Juliet E. Grayson."

Fidelity. At least the US Army appreciated that quality.

"...she is therefore promoted to the rank of lieutenant colonel on this date by order of the Secretary of the Army."

There was polite applause in the conference room and genuine smiles. Promotions were happy occasions, even when the person being promoted had only been assigned to the unit for a couple of weeks. Juliet hadn't yet moved into a permanent house here at Fort Hood, Texas, but the conference room was still filled with at least two dozen well-wishers, including her commanding officer, several senior noncommissioned officers, and a few of their civilian spouses. The spouses had come to welcome Juliet's spouse, of course, but she didn't have one. She hoped they would make a fuss over her son. Matthew had insisted on wearing a necktie.

Her son might be dressed as an adult, but he was still kid-sized. Juliet bent down so he could unclip her shoulder board from the blue suit jacket of her service uniform. The rank insignia for a major, a gold oak leaf cluster embroidered onto the epaulet, was now a thing of the past. Matthew had her new shoulder board in his fist. Juliet suddenly wished they'd practiced the clipping and unclipping at home. He was just a child, and every adult in the room was focused on him; he might get flustered. His life had been rough enough without subjecting him to another potentially embarrassing situation. She should have thought of the possibility, should have shielded him from at least one small hurt, although she'd failed to shield him from the big hurt of divorce.

But after a moment of awkwardness when Matthew didn't know what to do with the old shoulder board—Juliet simply held out her palm, so he could place it in her hand—he clipped on the new shoulder board with its higher rank, an insignia of silver oak leaves. Juliet was prouder of Matthew for the dignified way he was participating in this ceremony than she was with herself for being promoted. She winked at him, then stood so that her commanding officer could pin the new rank on her other shoulder.

Just like that, she was a lieutenant colonel.

It had only taken a few minutes…plus sixteen years of active-duty service. Sixteen years ago, she'd graduated from college, changed from her cap and gown into her brand-new army uniform, then raised her right hand and made a promise to defend the Constitution.

Sixteen years ago, she'd bid farewell to her tight-knit circle of college friends before taking her diploma and

herself to her first duty station. Most of her friends had
stayed in the city to start new careers. Two had stayed at
the university to begin master's degree programs. Out of
their little gang of eight, only she and Evan Stephens had
made a military commitment, volunteering their lives in
the service of their country.

Evan Stephens. Blue-eyed, athletic, lover of beer and
baseball and blondes, not necessarily in that order. Juliet
was not a blonde. She and Evan—and the six others in
their circle—were just friends and had been just friends
since their sophomore year.

Sixteen years ago, she and Evan had gotten behind the
steering wheels of their separate cars and left the campus
for separate army posts, he to Missouri for the Military
Police Corps, she to Arizona for Military Intelligence. But
the night before graduation, after her parents had gone
back to their hotel to sleep, Juliet had run into Evan on
the college green. Under a full moon, they'd talked about
their futures, just the two of them.

Their parents were proud of them, and she and Evan
were excited to don their new uniforms, which shone with
the single gold bar of a second lieutenant on each shoulder, but by that fountain in the moonlight, they'd dropped
their ROTC cadet bravado and gotten real.

Do you think we'll be stationed at posts we don't want?

*Do you think we'll miss Christmas with our families
next year?*

Do you think we'll see combat?

Do you think we'll die?

These were concerns that didn't come with the civilian
careers their friends had chosen. More and more students
had gathered on the central green, milling about in the
moonlight. Then one student had gotten down on bended
knee as he held up a little ring box to an excited girl. Or
rather, a woman. They were adults now.

Juliet and Evan's questions had taken a different turn. Evan had wondered why any civilian woman with a successful career would want to marry him and be dragged from post to post. She'd have to restart her professional life every few years, going back to handing out résumés and going to job interviews with each move. Juliet had wondered if any man would be willing to be left behind to take care of their babies on his own while she was deployed. A civilian spouse was pretty much guaranteed to face time as a single parent during the military spouse's inevitable deployment or hardship tour.

I'm probably killing my chance of finding Mr. Right anyway, just by serving in the army. Military women have double the divorce rates of military men. Did you read that article?

Yeah, real nice of Colonel Hodges to post that crap.

Students from the college of music had shown up at the green with their violins and cellos for an impromptu jam session. Juliet and Evan had carried on the rest of their conversation as they'd danced with the crowd to stringed versions of current hit songs.

Slow songs.

They'd danced as a couple.

I don't know why I'm worried about divorce, she'd said. *I'd have to get married first, but I scare guys off just by being in ROTC.*

You don't scare me.

She hadn't laughed. Evan hadn't said it as a joke. His hands had felt strong and warm on her waist. She'd been dancing with her hands linked casually behind his neck. At his words—*You don't scare me*—she'd looked up at him and realized how well she knew his handsome face after three years of shared cafeteria pizzas, study sessions at the library, Frisbee games right here on this green. She was going to miss it. She was going to miss *him*.

She was holding on too tightly.

She'd looked away. *You're so lucky, Evan. You can wait until you retire and then get married and have your kids. Why can't you?*

Because we'll be, like, forty-one years old at retirement. We'll be colonels. Colonels are old. You're a guy. You can have babies at forty-one, but it's not likely I can.

Don't be so sad. You're worrying too much. Men are going to line up to marry you. You're twenty-one and completely gorgeous—

She'd looked at him, startled. He'd caught the edge of one of his flip-flops on the grass and tightened his hands on her waist, but his voice had sounded very steady. *I'll marry you when you're a retired old colonel. I promise.*

And then he'd kissed her. She hadn't known, hadn't guessed, hadn't given a thought to how warm his mouth would be. How soft his lips would be when the rest of his body was so hard. Hard shoulders she clung to. Hard thigh muscles her legs brushed against.

He'd ended the kiss, and this time, he'd been the one who looked away.

Her heart had pounded because this was wrong, all wrong. She was graduating. She was being sent to her first duty station, far away from his. He was her friend, and she should tease him like he was her brother, but she didn't feel like teasing him. She felt like kissing him again, on the grass by the fountain, under the moon.

It would mess up all her plans. It would be absurd to start a new relationship mere hours before they were leaving one another to begin careers at posts that were thousands and thousands of miles apart.

They'd danced some more instead. As long as the violins had played, they'd danced. *This is it. Goodbye to Evan, goodbye to all of my friends, to this green and this college and this life.*

Her heart had kept pounding and the future had suddenly seemed more scary than bright. This was the last night she'd live in a city she chose. The last year she'd be certain she'd be home for Christmas. When would she see all of her friends again? When would she see Evan again?

She'd broken the silence. *Why should I marry you as a retired colonel? I'll be too old to have children by then.*

He had laughed at that and gone one rank lower. *Lieutenant colonel, then. We'll be thirty-five or thirty-six, right? Plenty of time for making babies. If we're both still single when we get promoted to lieutenant colonel, we'll marry each other.*

His laughter had chased away some of her fears. His promise, as silly as it was, had given her a fixed point of certainty in the vast, unknowable future. She'd let go of him and stepped back, but she'd held out her pinkie finger in the moonlight.

Evan had only scowled at her hand. *Dudes don't do pinkie promises. You have my word.*

Dude, she'd mimicked him. *Pinkie promise, or I won't believe you.*

He'd hooked her finger with his own and repeated his promise. *If we're both still single when we get promoted to lieutenant colonel, we'll marry each other.*

"Lieutenant Colonel Grayson, would you like to say a few words?"

Juliet thanked everyone for coming. She thanked her son for being there, and she joked that perhaps the promise of cake had been of equal enticement to the promise of skipping a half day of school. She cut the sheet cake with a tasseled sword her new unit kept on the wall for just such occasions, cutting neat square after neat square, but all the while, her heart was pounding like a college girl's at midnight.

Juliet knew Evan had already been promoted to lieutenant colonel. The army published promotion lists that were avidly read throughout the military, so she'd seen his name when he'd been promoted below the zone, one year early.

She hadn't seen Evan in person for years, not since a chance meeting on an airfield in Afghanistan that had lasted less than a minute. Before that, there'd been an alumni tailgate at a homecoming football game. She'd had a toddler-aged Matthew in her arms then, and she'd still had hope that her husband would grow into his role as husband and father, still hoped he'd become a more reliable man.

Juliet watched Matthew now, a preteen who was eating cake with the gusto of a little kid. He'd carried his plate over to a group of men in uniform and stood right in the middle of them as he ate forkfuls of frosting. He always gravitated to men in any situation, proof to Juliet that he needed a man in his life. Her father and brother lived too far away to fill in the gap left by her ex-husband. Matthew had no one to serve as a role model beyond a coach he might interact with for a few hours each week during Little League T-ball season, or a teacher he might have for one hourly class each semester.

Matthew looked so very young, despite his necktie, as he craned his neck back to watch the men as they talked over him. While he ate black and white cake layers, his eyes followed their conversation like it was a ping-pong match. Did the men remind him of his father? Or was he so fascinated because they were nothing like his father? Maybe he gravitated toward the authority and stability that uniforms represented, although it was because she herself wore a uniform that Matthew had just been plunged, yet again, into a new school in a new town in a new state. He might turn out fine despite his unstable childhood, or he might be scarred for life.

Matthew's future was so uncertain, so unknowable—

which meant hers was, too. She was so tired of facing down the unknown alone.

When Matthew caught her staring at him, she mustered up a smile, but she was thinking ahead to her plans for the immediate future. For this afternoon. After the cake, after she drove Matthew back to school, Juliet had somewhere to go.

Along with the promotion lists, Juliet had read that Evan Stephens was a battalion commander now, a position of great responsibility. Evan had been a reliable friend back in the day, and now the US Army clearly depended on him as one of their most reliable officers. The battalion Evan had been entrusted with was headquartered right here at Fort Hood. As of two weeks ago, so was she.

It was time to let Lieutenant Colonel Stephens know that she was now Lieutenant Colonel Grayson.

And single.

Just like he was.

Evan sat at his desk, busy with paperwork, bored out of his mind.

He flipped to the last page of the police blotter and initialed it. He was the commander of a military police battalion, a unit nearly 600 soldiers strong. The buck stopped here, on his desk. So did the police blotter.

Actually, the battalion had 589 personnel today. Evan always knew exactly how many lives he was responsible for.

He tossed the blotter into the outbox on his desk. Reading the blotter wasn't strictly one of his duties. The MP station sent it directly to Evan's commander, who was the Provost Marshal of Fort Hood and the commander of the 89th Military Police Brigade. Colonel Oscar Reed signed off on it, and then *his* boss—the commanding general of III Corps—was sent a copy. But if Evan's boss and his boss's boss read the blotter, then Evan read the blotter. He was never surprised, never blindsided, not when he could prevent it.

It was rare for one of his MPs to make the blotter as either a perpetrator or victim, but it happened. If the brigade commander called him for more details, Evan always knew to whom and what he was referring, and he'd already taken corrective action. No surprises. No blindsides.

Being proactive had made him a good platoon leader. A better company commander. A great operations officer. His file was full of glowing evaluations from superiors who appreciated an officer who stayed ahead of problems and stopped them before they started. Evan had been promoted below the zone because of it, not only selected for lieutenant colonel, but promoted earlier than 90 percent of the other officers who had also made the cut. That had not been a surprise, either.

Evan sat back from his executive desk, a piece of burnished wood furniture that the army only provided for its upper echelon of officers. His career to this point had been conducted from sturdier, uglier, government-issued desks of metal and Formica. He turned his chair so he could look out the second-story window at the Texas landscape outside. Even his chair was executive-level now. This was it: the big time. Battalion commander. One of the most-prized, high-speed, low-drag positions in the US Army.

He was bored as hell.

If he were a platoon leader fresh out of school or even a company commander in his midtwenties, he would leave his office and go check on his soldiers. Like practically every soldier in the army, he wore his camouflage uniform with his coyote-brown leather combat boots daily, so he was always ready to jump into a situation. Boots on the ground: that was the best way to gauge a unit's preparedness. He'd go to the motor pool and walk the lines of the hundreds of vehicles that were his responsibility.

But he was a battalion commander now. The only difference between his uniform and everyone else's was the embroidered oak leaf cluster at the center of his chest, but that was a big difference. If he showed up at the chain-link gate to the motor pool, there'd be a flurry of activity. His motor pool officer would drop what she was doing and come out to escort him, a matter of military courtesy as well as her pride. The motor pool was Chief Braman's domain. Nobody, not even her commander, roamed around her turf without her knowing what was going on.

The first sergeants of every company would appear within minutes, jogging over from their company headquarters. If Evan spotted anything out of line, the NCOs would get it fixed immediately—and chew out the soldier who had let it slip in the first place.

A simple walk through the motor pool might make Evan feel less restless, but it would pull too many people away from their day unnecessarily. He should and did conduct inspections of the battalion's equipment without notice, but he didn't jerk his people around just to alleviate his own boredom.

Evan turned his chair back around and continued doing paperwork in his combat uniform.

Three short knocks on the open office door were followed by Sergeant Hadithi entering silently to collect everything from the outbox. He deposited more papers in the inbox. Evan nodded; the sergeant briskly left to go back to his desk, the metal-and-Formica kind, one of several in the administrative office that acted as a buffer to Evan's inner, more executive office.

A few minutes later, he heard the sudden creaks of chairs and the squeaks of wheels that meant his administrative staff had all come to their feet. Someone of a fairly high rank must have walked in. How ironic—maybe his brigade commander was pulling a pop inspection on *him*. He'd wanted something to relieve the tedium of this day, hadn't he?

Evan checked his watch. Still not quite three o'clock. Would this day never end? He tossed his pen on his desk and waited.

Sergeant Hadithi reappeared. Three more knocks—but this time, the sergeant didn't cross the threshold. "Sir, there is a Lieutenant Colonel Grayson here to see you."

Evan drew a blank. "Colonel who?"

"Grayson, sir."

Grayson. Good God, Juliet Grayson from college? It had to be. Just like that, out of the blue, Evan's day rocketed from mind-numbing to adrenaline-inducing.

The sergeant pushed the door open wide and flattened himself against it.

Juliet Grayson walked in.

She was wearing the blue service uniform with its knee-length skirt and black pumps, her hair smoothed back into a military bun. The medals and ribbons and badges she'd earned were displayed in precise rows on her dark blue jacket, attesting to a career in the profession of arms that had been as demanding as his. She was no longer a carefree college student with golden-brown hair that fell freely to the middle of her back.

He still would have recognized her in an instant. She was still tall, still energetic, still full of purpose—

Still beautiful.

Still another man's wife.

"Hello, Evan." She turned to the sergeant and dismissed him with a nod. "Thank you."

Sergeant Hadithi backed out of the room, closing the door behind himself. It shut with a quiet *snick*, the only sound in the room as Juliet crossed the carpet to Evan's desk. He'd never seen her walk in high heels before, had he? Sharp as hell. *Sexy* as hell.

She set her hat on the corner of his desk as he began to stand, but then she leaned forward and planted her fist squarely in the center of his desk. She opened her hand and stepped back, leaving a shiny pin on his desk, a silver oak leaf insignia.

He sat back down.

"I was promoted today."

That was all she said.

It was all she needed to say. The memories he'd spent so many years deliberately repressing broke free. The fountain, the moonlight, the promise—and now here she was.

He'd never been more surprised in his life.

one

Chapter Two

Evan kept his eyes on the silver oak leaf insignia.

The memories came crashing to the forefront of his mind for the first time in…seven years?

Yes, seven years since he'd last seen her. Seven years since he'd buried his emotions for the last time. It had been a chance meeting, a crossing of paths at an airfield in Afghanistan. He'd been arriving; she'd been leaving. They'd almost walked past one another, both captains at the time, both loaded down with combat gear. A passing glance, a double take, a step away from his unit to shake hands, to grip her shoulder—only a minute available to ask an intense question.

How have you been?

Better now, she'd said, and he'd had a moment of insane happiness thinking she meant she was better now that she'd run into him. But she'd nodded toward the waiting jet and the long line of soldiers boarding it. *That's my ride home. I'll see my son in twenty hours. Twenty! I can't wait.*

Her son. Of course. When Evan had last seen her at a tailgate party at their alma mater's football stadium, she'd been carrying a toddler on her hip. She'd looked crazy in love with her child, laughing at his determined little face when his chubby hand made a grab for her hamburger. It was the moment Evan had realized what he wanted in life.

It was the moment he'd realized he was too late.

After the game, her husband—also an alumnus of their

college, a guy who'd played baseball with Evan—had chosen to leave his wife and baby at the class reunion hotel while he went out with the single men in their group. No surprise there; Evan had known that guy's habits too well after a couple of seasons traveling from university to university together on the varsity baseball team. That night, Evan had watched Juliet's husband have one too many drinks, have one too many dances with women who weren't Juliet, and he'd stepped in. *Go home and appreciate what you've got—or another man will.*

Evan had spent the two years between the alumni tailgate and Afghanistan doing his best to forget Juliet and her husband and her baby, but as he'd faced her on that airfield, he'd wanted to know if her husband had grown up and settled down. If they were still married.

He'd had to shout over the idling jet engines to ask a more socially acceptable question that would still give him the information he wanted. *Is your husband still on active duty?*

A quick shake of her head. *No, he got out of the army last year. Good timing. He's been able to stay home with the baby. Actually, my son is four now, not a baby. Crazy how time flies, isn't it?*

They'd looked at one another from under the brims of their Kevlar helmets. Evan had told himself he was happy for her. She was married with a child—exactly the life she'd once been afraid she'd never have because of her military commitment.

Evan had squeezed her shoulder one last time and let go. *See? I told you not to worry. I knew you'd marry a guy who would take care of your children while you were deployed.*

Evan had spent the rest of his year in Afghanistan pummeling his emotions into submission. Juliet, his college buddy, was happy. She was married, and there was nothing he could do about it. He wouldn't lust after a married woman. He wouldn't pine for a woman who was building a life with someone else. He hadn't been smart enough to pursue her while he'd had the chance. It was over and done. She was the one who'd gotten away. End of story.

Except now she was standing here in his office at Fort Hood, telling him she'd been promoted to lieutenant colonel.

Her voice broke the silence as he continued to stare at the pin. "Don't you remember dancing with me the night before graduation?"

Of course he remembered. Every word. *Pinkie promise, or it doesn't count.*

"We're both lieutenant colonels now," she said. Her voice had not changed in seven years, not in sixteen. "Crazy how time flies, isn't it?"

Their eyes met.

He felt something like anger. The seal on his memories had been broken. The emotions she was resurrecting were both painfully fresh and achingly familiar.

"I'm single," he said, "but you're not."

"Divorced. He moved out for the last time three years ago. We've been divorced for two."

Good God. All these years…trying to forget her, determined not to think about her. He hadn't heard about the divorce because he hadn't kept in touch with anyone from their old circle. It was easier to move on that way.

Except he hadn't really moved on to anything. To anyone.

"Is divorced not the same thing as single?" she asked, and for the first time, her voice wavered. She dropped her gaze. Now she was the one staring at the silver rank of a lieutenant colonel. Her eyelashes were dark, feminine, alluring even as they hid her eyes from him.

After another moment of silence, she reached for the silver pin.

Evan closed his hand over the pin first. "That's not the important question, Juliet. The real question is, shall we do this in the courthouse or a church?"

He couldn't be serious.

Evan Stephens couldn't be agreeing to honor their pact so easily. Why should he?

Suddenly, Juliet felt foolish for coming here to challenge him to keep it. It was a ridiculous promise. They'd practically been children at the time. They'd even sealed it by linking their pinkie fingers together.

Evan came to his feet. He was a battalion commander, and he looked every inch the military warrior. He couldn't have gotten taller, but he seemed taller anyway. He was a little bigger, a little broader in the shoulders, and a lot more fierce in his camouflage than he'd been in shorts and flip-flops on a college green.

Her mouth felt dry.

She had things to say to him. To explain to him. The reason she wanted to gauge his willingness to honor their college pact. The gut feeling she had that he was the father her son needed.

Instead, she was mute as she watched him walk around his desk to stand before her, right before her, just close enough that she felt alarmed, and she took an involuntary step backward.

"Courthouse," she said, her voice husky but still the voice of an officer. Decisive.

"You've already thought this through." He took a step forward. "I'm fine with a judge instead of a minister, but what's your reasoning?"

This is happening. This is really happening. And he was so very…real. Not a memory. Definitely not a senior in college. She'd grown into herself over the years, physically, losing the last of that lingering teen lankiness—but she hadn't thought about the fact that Evan would have, too. He was all grown up, fully an adult, and damn, but a man in his midthirties was a man in his prime.

She cleared her dry throat. "The courthouse would be quicker."

She was in high heels, but he still had to bend his head down an inch to bring his mouth to her ear. They might have been slow dancing, as close as he was to her, but he didn't touch her with anything but his voice.

"Are we in a rush? How many children are we going to have before we retire?"

He remembered. He'd chosen the rank of lieutenant colonel because she would still be young enough...

She remembered, and he did, too, and it made something in her chest feel suddenly weightless.

But that wasn't why she was here. Weightlessness wasn't welcome. It only made her feel wobbly. This was supposed to be about Matthew.

"I already did that part," she said. "I have a child."

Evan touched her then, setting his hands on her waist lightly, but it gave her a little stability, a little strength. His eyes were really as blue as she'd remembered, a pure shade of blue that had left dozens of girls sighing in the bleachers at their college's baseball stadium. She'd teased him for it, time and again.

Now those blue eyes were looking at her with something like...tenderness? Affection? Like he knew her. It had been so long since a man had looked at her so *personally*. Not as a subordinate or a superior. Not as a daughter or mother or commander or staff officer.

"I have—"

"A little boy named Matthew. I remember. Cute child." The corners of Evan's eyes crinkled just the slightest bit, a small smile at whatever he remembered about Matthew. "Did you have any more children after him?"

"No." She supposed that was a reasonable question. It had been, gosh, seven years since that chance meeting in Afghanistan, when she'd mentioned going home to her son. But the question unnerved her, exposing how little Evan knew about her life. How could he have accepted her proposal as if he'd marry her no matter what, when he didn't know anything about her? He hadn't known she was divorced until two minutes ago. He didn't know how many children she had. He hadn't kept tabs on her.

She didn't feel so weightless now. "Just Matthew. But I have full custody."

"Rob never sees him?"

It was startling to hear her ex-husband's name said so casually by someone else. For the past three years, if Rob had come up in conversation at all, it had been only as "Matthew's father." Polite, careful questions from new teachers: *And will Matthew's father be coming to the school play?*

"He has visitation rights," she told Evan. "He just doesn't use them."

Her polite smile was automatic. *Matthew's father lives out of state. However, my neighbor has agreed to be my designated caregiver if I'm unreachable in an emergency.* For three years, her answers had been so polite, so practical.

"I'm sorry," Evan said.

The teachers never said that. Sorry for her son? Sorry for her? For Rob? Evan didn't explain himself further.

She explained herself instead, calmly—but her heart was pounding so hard, he ought to be able to hear it. "That means you'd be living with a child if we…if we went to the courthouse."

"You still don't scare me, Juliet." He touched her face with the back of his hand, a light run of his knuckles from her cheek to just above her ear, before he leaned in again to speak softly into the ear he'd just barely caressed. "Children don't scare me, either."

"That's because you've never lived with one." But she couldn't keep carrying off this calm conversation. She couldn't pretend it was normal to be in Evan Stephens's office on a Friday in February, discussing living together as a couple.

She moved away from his hand on her waist and paced a step or two before turning to face him. She let go of her dignity and her military bearing, threw her hands up and huffed out a sigh. "This is insanity. I can't believe we're even talking about following up on an old promise right now."

At that, he half laughed as he half sat on the edge of his desk. "*You* can't believe it?"

For the first time, she managed a smile and wrinkled her nose apologetically. "I guess you weren't expecting me to pop in this afternoon. Sorry."

"I hope you're not sorry. That you'll never be sorry."

She didn't laugh. He hadn't been kidding. Again.

"You don't have to honor an impulsive college promise," she said, giving him chance after chance to take the easy way out. He could give her a smile, a friendly *good to see you again*, and tell her he had to get back to work.

"But you must have wondered if I would honor it," he said. "You didn't come find me after all these years to tell me to say no. Is 'no' what you wanted to hear me say, or just what you expected me to say?"

"I came to hear you say… I don't know what I expected. I didn't think you'd be…"

"A man of my word?"

"It was a silly pinkie promise, Evan. Nothing more."

She said it, but she didn't believe it. Their promise had meant something. In the back of her mind, this day had always been there. As long as Evan stayed single, there'd always been this alternate future on the horizon. She'd needed that fantasy future, some years more than others, so at every reunion, every get-together with anyone from their circle, she'd asked casual questions. *Have you heard from Evan Stephens? What's he up to these days? Not married, still?*

The army was a small world. She and Evan had never been stationed together before, but on every post, she'd run into people who knew Captain Stephens or Major Stephens or Lieutenant Colonel Stephens. His rank progressed, but he was always single. Never married.

She hadn't thought to ask about a child. He sounded so confident, saying children didn't scare him, as if he knew what parenthood was all about. A man didn't have to be married to have a child. Had there been an accidental pregnancy in his past?

Perhaps an intentional one. He could have been half of a couple who'd wanted to have a child but had no intention of ever marrying. He could have met a woman he thought would make a good mother for his child, and they might have decided to…to conceive a baby.

Her flash of jealousy was unjustified, considering the existence of Matthew, but she felt it all the same.

"Do *you* have a child?" she asked.

Evan shook his head. She couldn't decipher the serious look in his eyes, but since he never took his gaze off her face, she had to mask her irrational relief.

"I knew you'd never married," she said, "but I didn't think to ask if you'd had any children."

"You asked people about me?" The smile that was really just a crinkle at the corner of his eyes reappeared. That was easy enough to interpret: he was pleased.

"I had to. I couldn't expect a married man to care if I'd been promoted to lieutenant colonel today."

"No, of course not." He pushed away from his desk and

walked back into her personal space, still studying her. Then he raised his hand to touch her, and she held her breath, braced this time for that light brush along her cheek. After all, there was nowhere else he could touch her. Her jacket covered her arms to her wrists. Her black tab-tie held her white dress shirt closed at her throat. She was safe in her uniform.

She was not. He placed his whole palm on the side of her neck, warming her tight throat with the heat of his hand, holding her still as he bent his head and kissed her.

It was the college green all over again. The night air, the string music. The impossibly soft mouth of a very hard man. She might have made a sound, an unintentional *mmm* of delicious recognition, like that first bite of homemade food after months of army rations, or it might have sounded like a whimper at just how overwhelming it was to taste the real thing after years of trying to remember a flavor.

He spoke over her lips. "The courthouse it is, then."

This close, she could feel what she couldn't see. Under that easy confidence, his heart was pounding, too.

"You think this is a good idea?" She'd meant to state it as a fact, but her tone of voice had taken on a girlish kind of wonder.

"I do. I have no intention of waiting another sixteen years for the next kiss."

He kissed her again, and she lost herself in that midnight feeling. Kissing him felt so very intimate. No tongues, no tasting—but oh, his mouth felt so sensual against hers.

She'd had her arms around his neck back then. Today, her suit was too constricting, but she wouldn't have reached up to throw her arms around him anyway. They no longer saw one another day after day, semester after semester, so although he still seemed familiar, they lacked that casual familiarity. But she felt weightless and wobbly, so she held on to him, a hand on each of his upper arms. His body warmth carried through the camouflage fabric. The flex of his biceps felt insanely sexy as he moved to cup her face in two hands.

His fingertips were warm and gentle along her jawline, while the bulge of his arm muscle felt like steel. She breathed in at the contrasting sensations, parting her lips, and then he was tasting her, and she was tasting him. The instant rush of arousal—a throb, a wanting, a contraction low in her belly—was so strong, it was almost painful.

This wasn't why she'd come. This wasn't the point. This wasn't supposed to be about feeling sexy or—hell—even remembering what sex was, or how they'd once talked about having babies together. No, this was about…something…

She dug her fingers into his biceps a little harder.

Something…making babies…

Matthew. Her son was the reason she was here.

Her gasp ended the kiss.

Evan Stephens, strong and terribly handsome, this more fierce version of the Evan she'd once known, *laughed* against her lips. "I can't tell you how glad I am that I am single on the day of your promotion."

She backed away in one jerky step. Evan let her go, lowering his hands in an almost lazy way to settle on his hips.

She forced herself to breathe slowly. She would *not* pant. She was in her thirties, she was a divorcée, she was the mother of a middle schooler, she was a lieutenant colonel, for crying out loud. She was not going to be flustered by a kiss, no matter how long it had been since she'd felt so aroused.

How long *had* it been?

An eternity.

Sex was like riding a bicycle, maybe. Once you knew how, you never forgot—but she hadn't come here to ride a bicycle.

"You should meet my son first."

"Yes, I should." Evan smiled, a real smile, a flash of

white teeth to go along with those sexy, smiling eyes. How many times had she seen him flash that cocky smile? Every time a cute blonde girl cheered for him at a baseball game.

Three knocks sounded at his office door. Evan had his back to it. He didn't stop smiling at her, didn't change the way he was standing with his hands on his hips, but he called out, "Enter."

The door opened. "Sir, the brigade S-3 is requesting to schedule a commanders' roundtable for Monday morning."

Evan looked over his shoulder at the sergeant. "Put it on my schedule." Then he reached for the patrol cap he had sitting on his desk, a sure sign that he was ready to leave the building. Everyone in uniform had to wear their cover—their hat—when outdoors. He handed Juliet her hat, its dark blue crown decorated with a gold eagle and the oak leaves of a field-grade officer. "What time is Matthew done with school? Does he have an aftercare program, or does he take a bus home?"

"I've been picking him up. We're still in temporary housing. We've been at the Holiday Inn for two weeks."

Evan shot her a look—she couldn't guess the meaning of that one, either—before he headed for the door. He nodded to his sergeant as he gestured for Juliet to precede him out the door. "I'll be out the rest of the afternoon, Sergeant Hadithi."

"Yes, sir. Good afternoon, ma'am."

"Good afternoon," Juliet replied by habit.

She left the office with Lieutenant Colonel Evan Stephens by her side, matching her step for step.

They were really going to do this.

Chapter Three

Evan followed Juliet down the stairs and out into the crisply cool and brightly sunny Texas afternoon.

He followed *Juliet*.

Juliet Grayson was here.

He'd kissed her, and everything was still *there*. Everything that he hadn't known how to handle at twenty-one. Everything he'd recognized too late at twenty-seven. Everything he'd tried to bury at twenty-nine. Everything he'd thought he'd never have in this lifetime.

Because I don't deserve to have her.

He shoved the guilt deep down, where it had been locked away with his memories of Juliet. Now he could allow the memories of Juliet, but he wanted to keep the guilt buried deep. Maybe he'd inadvertently pushed the wrong man her way, but he'd done the right thing and stayed out of their life once he'd heard Rob Jones had gotten her to the altar. Evan hadn't had anything to do with their divorce.

She'd gotten divorced anyway. She was free. Single. And she'd come to remind him of their marriage pact on the very day the conditions of that pact had come into play.

She'd come to do more than remind him.

You should meet my son first, she'd said, and he hadn't been able to contain his smile. *First*. Before the actual ceremony, she'd meant, as if it were a foregone conclusion that they would be married. She had come not to say hello, not to reminisce, but to fulfill the pact they'd made the night before their graduation.

He needed to touch her again, to feel her skin so he'd know this wasn't a miraculous mirage dredged up from subconscious dreams. He wanted to give her hand a squeeze of excitement or reassurance or something.

He could not. It would break regulations. There was no hand-holding between soldiers in the US Army, not even if they wore one another's wedding rings. If Evan were wearing the more formal blue service uniform and *if* it were after dark and *if* they were attending a social function, then he would be allowed to offer her his arm to escort her through the parking lot.

That wasn't the situation now. He was the battalion commander, being saluted by every single person they passed. She was being saluted as well, of course, since they were the same rank. He loved the way they both raised their right arms in sync and briefly touched the right corners of their brims to return the salutes. He loved the sound of her high heels on the concrete sidewalk. He loved the cool but sunny Texas winter weather. He loved every frigging thing about the whole frigging universe.

Juliet Grayson was here.

She stopped beside his vehicle. Since it was parked in a spot marked *Battalion Commander*, it was no surprise that she guessed which vehicle was his.

"A Corvette," she said with a little laugh.

The memory was so clear, it was incredible that he'd forgotten it until this second. He laughed, too, and imitated the frustrated lament of a college-age Juliet. "Why is such a sexy car always driven by somebody old enough to be my grandfather?"

She shrugged a shoulder as she traced one metal curve, but her lips twitched with mischief. "I was right, you know.

When I saw this car on my way into the building, I had a moment of worry that you were ready to retire to Florida."

"Not yet. Nor for a long while." He watched her feminine fingers sliding along his sports car. "We can enjoy this while we're still young."

Her fingers paused. That brief, familiar flash of Juliet's teasing smile disappeared, leaving something more polite, more distant. "Unfortunately, they haven't invented a Corvette with more than two seats. We'll have to use my car when we go anywhere together. Party of three, not two."

"Makes sense." But he would take her for a long drive, just the two of them, top down, engine purring. Soon.

"School lets out in forty-five minutes," she said.

He checked his watch, a simple reflex. The second hand swept in its circle. The minute hand had moved just a quarter of an hour since he'd last checked the time. Juliet had walked into his office fifteen minutes ago. It hit him hard: his life was never going to be the same from this moment on. In less than a quarter of an hour, everything had changed.

Was it possible for life to take a turn for the better so suddenly?

God knew it could turn bad in less time than that. A car accident could alter the course of a life in the second it took tires to screech and metal to crunch. An explosion could shatter the monotony of a base camp overseas. One minute, life was fine, and in the next, it would never be the same. He'd seen it happen enough times to enough people. They could pinpoint the exact moment their life had abruptly been set on a new path. Whether one of nightmares or prosthetic limbs, regrets or rehab, they hadn't been ready for the sharp turn. No one was ever ready.

Evan hadn't expected his life to take a sharp turn today for better or for worse. But as Juliet stood by his Corvette and told him about school schedules—spring sports teams had started practicing, but games didn't start for two weeks—he knew his life would never be the same again. He'd been a confirmed bachelor fifteen minutes ago; Juliet Grayson had set a silver insignia on his desk, and now he was going to be a husband and a father—or rather, a stepfather. A family man.

Finally.

The euphoria took him utterly by surprise.

"Juliet." Damn it—were his hands *shaking*? He clasped them behind his back, a soldier's stance, *parade rest*.

Juliet had fallen silent at the way he'd said her name.

He forced himself to relax. *At ease.*

She was waiting for him to say something else. How many times had he seen her look at him just like this? Waiting for him to help her haul somebody's parents' used couch up a flight of stairs. Waiting for him to pour some rum they were too young to have into her can of Coke at a party that wasn't supposed to be held in the dorm. Waiting for him to dance with her by a fountain on the green.

"What, Evan?"

I feel like I've been waiting my entire life for this minute.

He couldn't say that. He couldn't say anything. He could only look at her—he couldn't look *away* from her, a vibrant, vital woman who was about to become a vibrant, vital part of his life, a life that had just changed radically.

He forced himself to speak, even if emotion made his voice a little too rough, a little too low. "I forgot... I'd forgotten how you looked." *I forced myself not to think about it.*

"Oh."

"I'm saying this wrong. I didn't forget what you looked like," he admitted to her. To himself. "I forgot how it was. How good it was to have you as my friend. How good it *is* to have you here, standing right here. To watch your face as you talk. To hear your voice. It's—"

"I know what you mean. It's really different to see you

in 3-D after so many years of only having those old photos from college."

She'd looked at photos of him, for years.

He could not touch her. Not here. Not now. But soon.

She'd come to get him at his own office, a very Juliet move. When she wanted something, she'd always gone out and gotten it. And now she wanted him.

She could have him.

"I'm overwhelmed." His voice was still rough, but he was sure now what he meant to say. "I can't get enough of looking at you. I'm overwhelmed that I'm going to have such a very beautiful wife."

She closed her eyes. He watched her hand close into a fist on the roof of his Corvette, and then she spoke, although there was a note in her voice that didn't quite sound like any note he'd heard from her before. "Do you think this Corvette could get us to the courthouse and back in forty-five minutes?"

At that, he laughed—and stepped back from her. "Don't tempt me."

She looked at him then, and damn near blushed—no, she did blush, heat reddening her cheeks on this cool February day. This senior army officer, with her overseas stripes on her sleeve and her chest full of ribbons and medals, was blushing.

She kept her chin up and her eyes on him. Not a blush; she was flushed. That note in her voice hadn't sounded familiar because it held arousal, the anticipation of passion, and she'd never spoken to him that way in college. Everything in him tightened in response, but he was standing in his battalion's parking lot.

"I looked it up, and the courthouse is open until five," Juliet said, but despite any flush of desire, her tone had already changed. More practical, less passionate. "But they stop issuing marriage licenses at four thirty. We'd have to rush."

"You're serious."

"There's a three-day waiting period in Texas, but they'll waive it because we're active-duty military."

The caveman part of him wanted to rush her into the car and take her to the nearest judge to claim her as his, permanently, but he was too experienced, too well trained by the army to do anything but think coolly when emotions were running hot. Something was off. "What about your son?"

Her jaw clenched. Her fist clenched. "He's in a phase that can be… It might be just as easy to simply let Matthew know it's a done deal."

"You want to go to the courthouse with me and *then* pick up your son and introduce me as the man who just married his mother?"

"Yes." She dropped her hand, relief written all over her face. "Do you think we have time?"

"Juliet, that's insane."

"All of this is insane. I already said so in your office." She laughed.

He didn't. She'd forced that laugh.

It was her turn to check her watch. "If we took my car instead, we could go from the courthouse straight to the school. As long as there isn't a line at the county clerk's office, there might be enough time that way."

It was his turn to frown. He'd bet she had no idea how anxious she sounded. "It's been a long time since I was eleven, but I don't think I would have been too happy to be left out like that. You wanted me to meet him first. What changed while we walked from my office to my parking lot?"

She dropped her too-determined smile. "There's a chance that when you meet Matthew, you'll change your mind."

Not a chance. "I already told you kids don't scare me."

"Mine might. He was wonderful this morning, pinning on my rank. I just never know from day to day if I'll get the wonderful Matthew or…or not." Her frown was genuine, her next declaration emphatic. "It's just a phase."

"Are we talking about a phase like he's gotten into drugs or he's been sucked into a gang?"

"No, nothing like that. That was a very military police kind of thing to ask, by the way."

"It happens." *Eleven years old. What had it felt like to be eleven years old?*

"He can just be so difficult. Deliberately contrary." Juliet ducked her chin a bit and peeked up at him from under the brim of her hat. "He's been hard to live with, admittedly, but I'm certain it's just a—"

"A phase. I got that. So, we're talking about a kid whose dad doesn't come to see him and who got sent to live at a new post by the US Army. He's been living at the Holiday Inn for two weeks, and he had to change schools in the middle of the year. That kind of phase?"

She stilled, eyes wide like a deer caught in the headlights. A very beautiful deer with golden glints in her brown eyes, which he let himself remember for the first time in years how much he'd always admired. He'd noticed it one day in their junior year, when he'd made fun of her safety goggles in a chemistry lab. He'd never told her that he saw gold in her eyes.

"Are you sure you're not a parent?" she asked.

"You don't have to be a parent to realize that's a lot on a kid's plate. This is a bad idea. I don't want to make things harder for him." He opened the car door to get his sunglasses.

"You'd like him if you met him." She blurted out the words.

He snapped his attention back to those golden-brown eyes. The way she'd taken a step closer, the way her hands almost reached to stop him—did she think he was going to get in the Corvette and drive off without her? Was she afraid he'd drive off without her?

It was hard to imagine Juliet Grayson afraid of anything. Evan grabbed his sunglasses, shut the car door and silently cursed the impossibility of having this conversation in his battalion parking lot. In uniform. He wished he could hold her, hug her against his chest until some of the tension that was humming through her subsided.

"I think you would," she said more quietly.

He could only reassure her with his words. "I'm sure I'll like him. He's your kid."

"And Rob's."

"I know he is. I know Rob, and I know you were married to Rob. This isn't news to me." Evan felt a touch of relief that she wasn't afraid to bring up potentially difficult subjects. That was the Juliet he knew.

"It doesn't bother you?" she asked.

"No." An incredible lie, but now was not the time to confess how jealousy had nearly eaten him alive. "That has nothing to do with anything. When I said it's a bad idea, I meant it's a bad idea to spring a marriage on any child as a done deal. We can get married when the courthouse opens on Monday as easily as today. Matthew and I can meet under a little less pressure. You and I can spend the weekend catching up."

He wasn't going to say they'd spend the weekend getting to know each other, because they knew each other. They'd always known one another. Time had passed, and they'd had separate experiences during that time, but nothing had changed them. He was still Evan. She was still Juliet.

"You have a roundtable scheduled for Monday," she said. "I've only been at Fort Hood for two weeks. I can't show up Monday morning and ask for the day off. I can't ask for any day off next week."

"Next Friday afternoon, then, so we'll have the weekend afterward. I'll wear my blues to work. We'll go straight to the courthouse."

She clasped her hands behind her back—had they been shaking like his?—but she didn't nod or agree.

"Why today? Is there some legality I need to know about?" Evan tried to imagine what that could be. The army could be a minefield of legalities that affected soldiers' lives. "Are your household goods going to be put into long-term storage if you don't give them a delivery address today? Are your orders for Fort Hood going to be changed if you're not married?"

"I hadn't even thought of those things. Stop, or I'll have even more to worry about."

"Then why do you want to go to the judge right this minute?"

"Because you said…" The flush was back—no, a blush. This time, she looked embarrassed, not aroused. She turned away from him, just slightly, and fixed her gaze on the colorful sign in front of the building that was painted with the battalion's crest. The green shield depicted a gold gauntlet in a fist, enforcing order.

"Because I said what?" He watched her face as she put her thoughts in order.

"I've been in the army too long. For a minute there, I thought the best course of action would be to exploit my advantage. Strike while the iron is hot. Allow you no time to regroup after my ambush. If I let you stop and think about it, you might choose to retreat."

"Not a chance." He said it out loud this time.

"There's always a chance, but you should have that chance. And I shouldn't assume everything is a battle." She turned her face toward him once more. "Forget I tried to rush it. I'm sorry about that. Back to the original plan. You should meet my son first, before you decide anything."

She *was* afraid he was going to change his mind and leave without her. Juliet: afraid. Incredible.

"I already decided. If a week could make any man change his mind, then you shouldn't be with him anyway. You deserve better." *You know that*—but he choked back the words, because her brown eyes suddenly glittered not with gold, but with unshed tears.

She tugged the brim of her hat down a half inch.

Time had passed. They'd had separate experiences, for certain, and hers had included a man who had changed his mind and broken a promise, hadn't it? Rob Jones had been so much less than she deserved.

Evan shoved down the guilt. "Juliet, I won't change my mind."

"Twenty minutes ago, you didn't know I was divorced. You didn't know I was stationed at Fort Hood."

A sergeant passed behind Juliet. Evan returned his salute without taking his attention off Juliet. He looked her squarely in the eye, unafraid, as sober and serious as he'd ever been about anything in his life. "You and I are getting married because we've had sixteen years to think about it, and neither one of us has changed our mind."

They stared one another down for a moment.

The memories continued to bombard him, the times they'd gauged one another just like this, each holding their ground during debates over chemistry lab hypotheses or proper pizza toppings. In retrospect, he could see that their showdowns had been frequent but fearless, because they'd been so certain that their friendship wouldn't be changed by championing opposing views. They'd opposed each other on lab reports and pepperoni just for the heck of it sometimes, because it was always invigorating, often fun, and it had made the rest of their friends either groan or place bets on which one of them would concede the point.

Now here they were, debating how and when to get a marriage license. It felt natural.

Surrounded by the sights and sounds of his everyday life—the beige building, the battalion sign, the people in camouflage crossing the sidewalks—Evan was struck anew by the miracle of Juliet restored to his life, standing here, right before him, right in the middle of his ordinary world. He shook his head slowly and started to smile.

"Lieutenant Colonel Grayson, can we please get in your car and continue this conversation somewhere, anywhere, away from here? I can't touch you or hug you or have any kind of normal interaction with a woman I'm so damned happy to see, because we're standing outside my own headquarters."

"You're happy to see me?"

"Ecstatic."

"You want to hug me?"

"You have no idea."

"Hmm." She pressed her lips together skeptically, another expression he knew so well. It tugged at his heart. He hadn't thought about missing Juliet's expressions. Now that he didn't have to miss them any longer, each one was making him realize in how much denial he'd been all along.

She pulled out a car key from somewhere in the vicinity of her skirt waistband. "Being in a car isn't going to make us invisible, but I'm parked over there."

"Lead the way."

But she didn't move. "You made a valid point. It's been sixteen years. Next Friday will work."

"Yes, it will."

But she didn't smile. In fact, she'd barely smiled at all in the past twenty-something minutes. Juliet had always been smart and sharp and driven, but she'd also been joyful. He knew her expressions, and her smile had been the most frequent of them all. Even at the end of a deployment to Afghanistan, she'd smiled on that airfield. Had life dealt her so many negative experiences while they were apart that smiles were less frequent than skepticism? That talking about her current life required stoicism?

There'd been nothing stoic or skeptical in that kiss in his office.

She kissed like the Juliet he'd known, the woman who loved life. She'd been the ringleader, the friend who'd coaxed everyone else to go to new places, to taste new foods, even to wear crazy hats or face paint, just for fun.

He was a man who didn't like surprises in general, but to realize Juliet had lost her joy in life was the least welcome surprise of all. Evan assigned himself a new mission in life: to bring a little fun back into hers.

A lot of fun.

Exploit the advantage. Strike while the iron is hot. Give her no chance to retreat.

"We have some time before school's out. Let's go to your hotel room and get you out of that uniform."

Chapter Four

He couldn't be serious.

Evan Stephens couldn't be asking her for a quick afternoon tumble in a hotel room.

Could he?

Juliet turned to walk toward her car. Evan walked beside her—close beside her. He was serious about honoring their marriage pact. He might be serious about the hotel, too. Maybe a compatibility test of some sort.

"Is that a line?" she forced herself to ask. "Something like, 'Why don't you slip into something more comfortable?'"

He bumped her shoulder with his, barely, a subtle touch because there were eyes everywhere, but he chuckled openly. Such a deep, masculine sound of amusement. Her heart pounded, but then again, it hadn't stopped pounding since she'd walked into that headquarters building. When had Evan Stephens become such a…such a…such a *man*? A sexy man, not a brotherly buddy. A sexy, single man who oozed authority and athleticism. Women must fall all over him.

Of course they did. They always had, even when she'd thought of him as that brotherly buddy. Whole rows in the ballpark bleachers had been filled by sorority sisters enjoying the view as Evan Stephens stepped up to bat. Juliet had teased him about it, but she'd also been a little proud of him, pretty much in the same way the girls who had handsome brothers were proud. They enjoyed showing them off while simultaneously poking at them to keep them from getting vain. Back then, Juliet had felt so superior to those girls in the bleachers. After all, she could tease and joke with Evan anytime she wanted, without being a slobbering slave to hormones each time he'd stepped up to bat in those white baseball pants. Except—

Right now, when she pictured those ball games in her memory, she could only see how Evan had looked at home plate, poised with the bat over his shoulder, staring down the pitcher just before smashing a fast pitch over the fence. Home run—that smile he'd flashed at the stands as he jogged around the diamond, touching every base. Oh yes, Evan Stephens had never had trouble scoring…

"Something like that," he said. "I already know what a nice girl like you is doing in a place like this, but if you want to invite me up to see your etchings—"

"Not funny." She stopped abruptly and stabbed the unlock button on her key fob.

Evan whistled low at the car that had responded with a flash of lights to her button-jabbing. She'd bought the four-door sedan when it was already well used and had driven her child everywhere in it for years, adding tens of thousands of miles.

"The Mom Mobile," she said, by way of introduction. She had all the enthusiasm of a resigned Eeyore.

"A Lexus," Evan said. "Not exactly a sturdy minivan."

"It's very sturdy."

"It's red."

"It's got a good safety rating and a big trunk for hauling everything moms have to haul."

"Juliet." He crossed his arms over his chest, a move that was entirely too self-assured, too *macho*. "It's a red Lexus. It's luxurious. It's high performance."

"It's—"

"It's very you."

She heard everything he put in that compliment. It was

a come-on, a little too suggestive, a little too…Casanova. She'd called him that in college. They all had. *Mr. Casanova*, a teasing nickname their circle had given him for good reason. None of his girlfriends had lasted very long. Juliet's stomach knotted up as a feeling of dread crept through her. None of her husband's affairs had lasted very long, either, and in the end, neither had their marriage.

"The old me, you mean?"

Evan only knew Juliet-from-College.

She could barely remember that woman. "The truth is, I bought it when it already had seventy thousand miles on it, because it was affordable and practical. I've had it for two years."

"Two years. A divorce present to yourself?"

"No." She'd only been trying to pick up the pieces after Rob had traded in her car one day while she was at work. He'd taken off on a new Harley. She'd needed something reliable and reasonable, something available to buy immediately from a used car lot. But still…it *was* a red Lexus. She frowned at the shiny chrome wheels. "Maybe."

Had she been defiant? Reclaiming herself by buying something that was to her taste, for a change?

Not consciously. She'd only been staggered by betrayal, struggling to hang on to her last shred of dignity after being rejected in bed and displaced in her own husband's life—she and Matthew had both been displaced—for the third time.

Was she jumping from that frying pan into the fire with Mr. Casanova? The knots in her stomach pulled tighter. She put a little distance between them, walking toward the driver's side of the car.

"It looks like it's fun to drive," Evan said. "I'll let you drive mine if you let me drive yours."

Definite innuendo there. She rounded on him, catching him looking not at her car, but at her legs.

He had those blue eyes back on her face and an innocent smile on his face in a fraction of a second. "Some things never change. When we were all wearing shredded jeans, you were more comfortable in shorts and skirts. You still are, or you would have worn the trousers with your uniform today."

Women had the option of skirt or trousers with this uniform. Evan was right; she preferred the skirt. "If you know I prefer skirts, then you know I'm already comfortable. There's no reason to go to my hotel room. None."

His eyes narrowed just the tiniest bit. She wasn't fooling him. This man wasn't distracted by either the full military regalia of her uniform or by her talk of motherly concerns. He kept looking at her as if he knew her, and he knew she was being defensive, wound too tightly to handle a silly tease.

Not sorry. I need to keep some defenses.

This man had said *I'm overwhelmed* and had cut right through her hard-earned, clear-eyed grip on reality, had cut deeply enough to expose a young girl's fantasy. God, dear God, she knew better. She knew how fleeting infatuation was, yet she'd believed, wholeheartedly, in the fairy tale. Just for a few seconds, she'd felt like his beautiful future wife, one whom he kissed like she was precious, like she was desired. She'd wanted to capture that irrational joy in her hand by taking Prince Charming's hand and running with him to the courthouse, logic and practicality be damned.

Evan had called that impulse insane.

He'd been right.

Her insanity didn't faze him much; he remained unflappably friendly. "Why not change at the hotel? You'll be able to have more fun this afternoon in civilian clothes."

"Have fun?" It was the furthest thing from her mind. There was so much at stake here, everything that mattered in her life, every*one*. Meaning Matthew. Today was a big test, the biggest of tests.

Evan laughed at her confusion. "Yes, let's have some fun. You want Matthew to meet me. I'm not above stacking the deck in my favor by meeting him over ice cream."

Juliet blinked. She was thinking about sex and betrayal and hotels and courthouses and all her worries about her son, and Evan was thinking of ice cream.

"Or tacos? I think I was always hungry when I was eleven." Evan slid his sunglasses on, classic Ray-Ban aviators with mirrored lenses. "Tacos are sloppy. You might want to change first."

The way he wore those Ray-Bans short-circuited her brain. It was so unfair that he should have gotten sexier as he got older.

It was distracting her from her purpose today. She needed to think of Matthew, her too tender-hearted son, who was right this moment navigating the treacherous halls of a new middle school, absorbing the thousand small hurts that went with being the newest student. She needed to think about what would be best for him. She did not need to think about the panty-dropping hotness of a military commander in Ray-Bans.

"Matthew never turns down ice cream," she said.

Panty-dropping? Had she seriously just thought that? *Panty-dropping?* The term hadn't crossed her mind since graduation.

"Great. We can hit the hotel and the school and then head for an ice cream place that's just off post. I haven't been there, but they must be good. They're always busy."

"It's just…" She could see her reflection in his glasses, her sharp hat, her crisp white collar. She looked like a professional army officer. She needed to act like it. "Matthew's wearing a necktie. He wore it for my promotion ceremony, because he knew I'd be in my service uniform."

"He can take off his tie. You can't."

That was a simple truth. The uniform had to be worn

complete at all times. She couldn't undo her tab-tie or shrug off her jacket at an ice cream parlor. She gestured toward Evan's camouflage uniform, the ubiquitous ACUs, or Army Combat Uniform. "You're in something comfortable. It's just a plain Friday, isn't it? But if I were to get into civilian clothes, I'd feel awkward. Matthew would know that while he'd been working hard in class, all dressed up for my sake, I'd been kicking back at the hotel, unpacking my jeans. It doesn't seem fair to him."

She couldn't begin to read Evan's face. His Ray-Bans hid his eyes. His mouth gave nothing away. He might as well have been standing at attention, expressionless. No longer laughing. At least he wasn't frowning at her as if she was, once more, saying something insane.

She wasn't crazy. She was just a mother.

Same thing.

"I know you're probably thinking I'm attaching too much importance to a necktie, but it was more than a tie. He put a lot of effort into that tie. It was his idea. He wanted to look like a grown man this morning, and he did it all for me. A sign of—a sign of respect, I guess."

He'd been trying to be a man, like his absent father.

Rather than looking at her own reflection, she looked at Evan's throat, visible at the open collar of his combat uniform. Where the knot of a tie would be, his tan uniform T-shirt was visible. "It's going to be good for him to have you around. He'll be able to see how you wear a tie. We had a little trouble this morning, figuring out how to tie the knot." She fell silent, because she was afraid that she sounded like her world revolved around mundane minutiae.

It did. And she was asking this sexy, single man to restrict himself to her world. Some friend she was.

Evan uncrossed his arms. "All right. Let's stop by my house, and I'll put on my blues."

"You'll—" She caught her breath.

"The point is to have a little fun, not to make a child feel like he's dressed as the odd man out."

"Yes, exactly," she said on a rushed exhalation.

"Let's go." His eyes stayed masked by those mirrored lenses, but his mouth curved into a grin. "We'll all eat ice cream in our Sunday best, if that makes you and your son more comfortable."

How odd to be understood. Stranger still not to have to plead her case or resort to making a demand. Was this how things could be in a relationship? So much less stress.

She found it easier to take her next breath. "You know what? Matthew's an army brat, born and raised. He's not going to think twice about meeting an officer in ACUs. Why don't we just stay as we are and head to the school now? We'll beat about fifty other cars to the parent pickup line."

She could see Evan raise an eyebrow despite the sunglasses. He walked around her to open the door of her Lexus, as if he were a valet. "Please get behind the wheel. Please. I don't care if you turn this car toward the school or my house, the Holiday Inn or the Taj Mahal, but please get us out of this parking lot."

"Right. Sorry."

"Don't be." He shut the door once she was seated, walked around the hood while returning another salute from yet another soldier, then got in. He shut the door, and they were sealed into the interior together, the sounds from the rest of the world instantly silenced. She was acutely—absurdly— aware of his size and his presence. There was such a big difference between sitting in this closed space with a child and sitting with a man.

Naturally, there is. Get a grip.

She'd driven other men in this car, taking her sergeant to lunch or giving another officer a lift home. No big deal. She was around men all day, year after year, intelligent men, physically fit men, men in uniform. But they were all people she worked with. This man was not.

It made more of a difference than she would have guessed. She'd come to see her old college buddy, but now she had a man in her car who wanted her to slip into something more comfortable. This wasn't the old friend she'd come to see.

As she backed the car out of the space, Evan tossed his hat onto her dash. He'd done that with his baseball cap, too, when she'd given him a ride to their college's practice field. She could practically see his burgundy baseball cap where the camouflage patrol cap sat now. She sneaked a quick peek at his profile as she drove away from his headquarters, and her heart rate finally slowed. Baseball cap, patrol cap—he treated them the same. He wore them the same. This man was Evan. Still him.

She stopped at a red light and let go of the steering wheel to smooth one hand down her skirt. "Thank you."

"For what?"

For being Evan. "For being my friend. You were always my friend."

He raised his hand and she braced herself for another masculine touch on her throat or her cheek, but he was holding out his pinkie finger to her. She linked it with her own.

"I always will be," he said. "As long as we both shall live."

Since he wore the mirrored sunglasses, her eyes fell to his lips. Those lips had kissed her. Today.

"Everything is going to work out, Juliet, my friend. Let's get your son and go eat some ice cream. It's time to have a little fun."

Never had a child looked so miserable while sitting in front of a banana split.

"Your ice cream's melting, honey."

Evan watched Juliet prompting her son in a voice of pure

kindness and concern. Maternal love—this little grouchy guy was too young to appreciate it.

Juliet had that same cheerful, you're-the-best smile that had once blinded Evan at a reunion tailgate, but it was only the same on the surface. Back then, she'd practically been glowing from within. Today, her cheerfulness struck Evan as determined, like the laugh she'd forced when she'd said their plan was insane, but she'd wanted him to run with her to the courthouse right that minute anyway.

He almost wished he had. He kept catching her darting little glances his way as her son resisted her attempts to engage him. She didn't need to be so nervous; Evan wasn't going to *not* marry her just because her son was letting his ice cream melt.

Juliet could only get one-word answers from Matthew. How was school? *Good.* Did anyone say anything about your tie? *Teachers.* Did they like it? *Yeah.* Do you have any homework to do before Monday? *No.* This had been accompanied by a vigorous head shake, at least.

The only complete sentences had been spoken in the school parking lot, after Matthew had pushed his backpack into the back seat and climbed in after it. Juliet had introduced Evan as Colonel Stephens. Evan had turned around and Matthew had shaken his hand like a little adult. *Pleased to meet you. My name is Matthew Grayson-Jones.*

You can call me Evan.

You can call me Matthew.

Evan had nodded and turned back around, amused at being given permission to address Mr. Grayson-Jones as Matthew.

"Did you turn in the money for your baseball uniform?" Juliet asked. "I can't wait to see it."

"Yeah." Matthew darted another look at Evan. He knew something was up. Smart kid. Matthew's one-word answers were his way of playing his cards close to his chest—

even smarter, in Evan's opinion. He'd be suspicious of himself, too.

Enough was enough, though. Juliet wanted her son to enjoy the ice cream outing, that much was obvious, but she was forgetting to eat her own ice cream in the process. If they didn't all stop being so awkward, they'd end up sitting at three sides of this little square table with three melted sundaes in front of them.

This wasn't the kind of situation Evan normally found himself in, but he applied an old military adage: *Lead by example.*

Evan ate his ice cream.

He talked in complete sentences, too—to Juliet. "I can't believe you've been here for two weeks without letting me know. This whipped cream is amazing, by the way. It would be good in coffee."

Under the table, he tapped the toe of Juliet's shoe with his boot. *Play along.*

"Ah… I'm not usually one for anything sweet in my coffee." But she turned away from her son and sat squarely in front of her sundae. Evan enjoyed the picture she made, so prim and proper with her tightly closed collar and her pristine hair bun, her straight rows of ribbons a dignified contrast with the sloppy monstrosity of a sundae before her.

"Where were you stationed before Hood?" It was a genuine question for Juliet, but to Evan's surprise, Matthew answered.

"Fort Benning." Matthew poked at a banana slice with his finger.

Two whole words. It was a start.

"Benning." Evan shook his head at Juliet. "And you've been here two weeks? Why didn't you let me know sooner?"

She waited for the excess hot fudge to drip off her spoon before eating it, her eyes lowered to her ice cream, her lashes hiding those gold-flecked eyes from him. That look was just as alluring as when she'd stood at his desk and looked down at her insignia. He'd thought she was another man's wife then.

She was going to be *his* wife.

He waited as a fresh wave of wonder passed through him, a physical sensation. Then he leaned forward. "Did you really think two weeks would have made a difference?"

"I hadn't been promoted yet." She looked up from her sundae, directly into his eyes. "I didn't want to leave anything to chance."

She'd wanted him to say *yes*. She'd succeeded. As she stared him down across giant sundaes, she finally started to smile a genuine, Juliet smile, one that said she was the girl who'd gotten her way, the cat who'd gotten the cream.

God knew what his smile was saying, but he could feel himself smiling back, truly happy to see—

"Fort Benning is in Georgia," Matthew informed him.

Juliet looked down at her sundae once more. Evan sat back.

"Have you heard of it?" Matthew asked.

Evan tore his gaze from his future wife to look at her suddenly talkative child. "I was stationed there once."

"Oh." Matthew seemed disappointed.

"Not for very long. I went to Airborne school there." Evan tapped the embroidered black wings above his name tag. Juliet's were shiny silver on her service uniform.

"Yeah, my mom has those, too."

"I noticed."

"So does my dad. He said so." Matthew poked at the banana some more, this time with a spoon. "I don't remember, because I was a baby when he was a soldier. But he was a real soldier."

Nobody was enjoying a conversation about Airborne school. Evan hadn't meant to derail the boy's attempt to initiate a conversation about Fort Benning. "I went to Airborne school so long ago, I was an ROTC cadet. I had to live in the barracks, so I didn't see anything except that one little piece of the post. Did you live on post?"

"Yeah."

"See anything cool?"

Matthew studied him for a moment, his skepticism clear.

Evan ate another bite in silence as he waited for Matthew to decide whether or not this grown-up stranger really wanted to hear from him.

This grown-up really did. What did an eleven-year-old boy think was cool nowadays? If it had been ages since Evan had been an ROTC cadet, it had been even longer since he'd been eleven.

"There's a museum there." Matthew dredged his spoon through the whipped cream and took a bite.

Glory, hallelujah. "What kind? An art museum or a science museum?"

"It's about the infantry. There's a helicopter hanging from the roof. Remember that, Mom? And there are really, really old cannons." And with that, Matthew was off and running, describing a museum with an enthusiasm that matched the way he began slurping down spoonfuls of mostly melted ice cream between sentences.

Evan sat back and enjoyed the monologue. How could he not? All that enthusiasm and animation made Matthew look like a miniature, male version of Juliet. The actual Juliet, *his* Juliet, was listening to her son with such an expression of love on her face, it took Evan straight back to that tailgate party.

Evan had always thought of Juliet as attractive, but he'd never seen her in love before that tailgate. She'd been so in love with that baby. The sight of Juliet laughing at Matthew had made something in his heart, something in his whole pitiful soul, shift into a new place. The concept of having a wife and child had crystallized from an abstract idea—sure, he'd get married someday and have kids—to something real. That wife he'd have someday when he was older suddenly became someone he wanted now, because she was a woman he enjoyed being around, a woman who was so much more than attractive. A woman he *wanted*. Why would he want to wait another day for that?

Why hadn't he realized a wife could be fun and gorgeous? Marriage meant that fun and gorgeous woman loved him back, loved him so much that she'd want to have his baby—and she'd love the baby that was half him.

Evan had watched Juliet set her cheek on her baby's head when the little guy snuggled into the curve of her neck. *Everything that's worth having is right there.*

Evan had never recovered from the impact.

Rob Jones had been the most fortunate bastard on the planet, but he'd blown it and walked away. Evan hadn't missed the implication this afternoon when Juliet had said Rob had moved out *for the last time*. Rob had put Juliet through the wringer more than once. He was no longer a fortunate bastard. Just a bastard.

The guilt was harder and harder to shove down. Evan had been the reason Rob had been able to win Juliet. Evan had never recovered from that, either.

"Ms. Libling knew more stuff than the stuff that the museum put on those little signs." Matthew segued from his description of the museum to the teacher who had led his field trip there, then from the teacher to his school in general. Speaking more slowly, tapping his spoon, he mentioned the kids he'd traded some kind of cards and discs with, and then silence. No more words. No more tapping. Just a child who looked down at the table, dark lashes hiding his eyes.

Evan liked it when Juliet glanced down like that, because he knew that when she lifted her eyes again, they'd be fierce or laughing or anything else that reflected the way she'd decided to handle whatever had made her turn introspective.

With Matthew, Evan didn't like it at all. It just looked sad.

"Sounds like you liked Fort Benning," Evan said.

Matthew still didn't look up. "I had a lot of friends there."

But not here.

Evan could practically see Juliet's heart turn into a sad slush. His own heart melted a little, too. Kids were so vulnerable.

But being with a sixth grader was bringing back Evan's memories of being in sixth grade. He'd had so much pride that he was no longer in elementary school, so much anxiety because sixth graders weren't nearly as big as eighth graders. He certainly wouldn't have wanted a man pitying him, cooing over him in sympathy. God, no.

Evan was more than done with his ice cream. All that sugar and fat had gone past the point of deliciousness and into that zone of too much, too rich. He took another bite anyway, to keep the conversation casual. "Yeah, every time the army moves me, I have to leave my friends behind, too, and start over at the next place. I know I'll make more friends, though, because I do every time, but it's a pain in the neck for a while."

Matthew looked up at him, perplexed. "You have friends?"

"Of course."

"But you're a grown-up."

Evan ate another bite of ice cream to keep himself from laughing.

"Hey, grown-ups have friends," Juliet said in mock offense.

"You don't, Mom."

She almost faltered at her son's somber response. "Just like you have Bill and Ronny, I had Miss Teresa and Miss Catherine. Did you forget about them?"

"Those were *neighbors*."

"Neighbors can be friends." But Juliet had hesitated before answering.

Kids spoke the truth, or so everyone said. Evan wondered how many friends Juliet had made at Benning, or rather, how many she'd had time to make, since Rob had left everything on her shoulders.

Evan pushed his ice cream bowl away. "I'm her friend."

Matthew looked from his mother to Evan and back, plainly trying to decide if such a thing was possible.

"For real. I met her at school, same way you made your Fort Benning friends. Same way you'll be making your Fort Hood friends, sooner or later."

"You met at school? Airborne school?"

Evan smiled at the logic of that.

So did Juliet. "I met Evan before I was in the army. I was in college. He's a Masterson Musketeer, just like me… and Daddy. In fact, Evan was a good friend of Daddy's."

"Oh."

"They played baseball together, like you and Tim."

Evan bristled at the description of himself as a good friend of Rob's—they'd been teammates, nothing more—but Matthew's reaction was stronger. He'd been looking at Evan with the wide-open, curious eyes of a child, but with the next blink, those eyes narrowed in a keen sort of calculation, reassessing Evan now that he had this new piece of information.

From the positive, friendly way Juliet spoke to Matthew about *Daddy*, Evan guessed Matthew had been shielded from the truth of his father's actions. Juliet must have expected her son to think it was a point in Evan's favor to be associated with Rob. From the look in Matthew's eyes, Evan wasn't so sure.

I'm nothing like your father.

Judging from the hostility being directed Evan's way, Matthew sensed this—and maybe that was a strike against Evan.

Or maybe bringing up his father had made Matthew realize that Evan was sitting where his father should be.

Either way, that baby Juliet had loved so much would be living under Evan's roof soon. Matthew didn't know it yet, but he wasn't going to be happy about it at first. What he might never know was how much Evan wanted to do right by him and his mother, how awed Evan was by the bond between them.

But Evan knew.

He returned Matthew's gaze with neither hostility nor sympathy. *Go ahead and figure me out, kid. Test me. Get to the bottom of this. I'd do the same if I were you.*

Chapter Five

Juliet stopped her car at the exit of the ice cream parlor's parking lot. Where should she go from here?

She'd felt the change in the air just before they'd all thrown in their spoons and declared defeat. For a few minutes there, things had been going so well. Now she had a child frowning in the back seat and a man deep in thought beside her.

"I'll take you back to your car," she said to Evan, and turned the car toward post.

"What would you like to do for dinner?" he asked.

In the rearview mirror, Juliet saw Matthew go on alert, like a watchdog who heard a noise that was out of place.

"I'm so full, I can't think about dinner." It was a cowardly response, but it bought her a little time.

She felt the weight of Evan's gaze on her. Could she not fool him about anything? There was a definite drawback to being with someone who knew her so well.

Evan tipped his head toward the back seat. "I'll bet Matthew will be thinking about dinner soon enough. I think middle school was when my mom started calling me 'the bottomless pit.'"

"No, I'm full, too," Matthew said immediately. "Can we just go back to the hotel, Mom? Please?"

Matthew sounded whiny, which meant he was upset. "Sure, honey, but we have to take Evan back to his car first."

Matthew threw himself back into his seat in a huff.

She didn't take her eyes off the road. "That kind of thing won't get you what you want any faster, young man. Did you think we'd just leave Evan in the parking lot and let him walk home?"

She could feel Evan's gaze. She'd sounded like such a mother just then, hadn't she? Did Evan think she was a good mother? A pushover? Too strict? She was probably all of those from one day to the next. Maybe from one hour to the next. She hoped she got it right often enough that Matthew would turn out okay, despite…oh, everything. Everything she'd done wrong. Everything she was trying to fix.

She slowed to a stop at the post's main gate and took out her military ID to show the military police on guard.

"Good afternoon, ma'am." The MP on duty took her ID card and bent to look in her window to see who her passengers were. Every adult had to have a photo ID to get on post, not just the driver, but Evan hadn't moved to get his ID out of his wallet.

The MP did a little double take. "Colonel Stephens, sir. Good afternoon."

Evan acknowledged him. "Afternoon."

Ah, of course. Evan commanded the MP battalion. They must all know him by sight. The guard handed back her ID with alacrity and waved them through with a crisp salute.

It was like being with a celebrity. Should she find that sexy? She did—more feelings she hadn't bargained on feeling.

She sighed. So far, nothing this day had gone like she'd expected.

"What were you expecting," Evan asked, "for us to do tonight?"

That was an alarming little bit of mind reading. "Matthew and I have a little routine. The hotel has a fridge and a microwave, but we're out of frozen dinners at the moment." She craned her neck to see her slouching son in the rearview mirror. "What do you say, Matty? Subs again? Pizza? Or should we go to the PX and get another frozen lasagna to nuke?"

"I don't care."

Juliet was just about to sigh again when Evan set his hand on her seat's headrest, an easy reach for him. She could feel the heat of his hand behind her ear, sense the strength of him, this man in command of hundreds—

"Really, Juliet?"

She swallowed. "Really what?"

"You walked into my office two and a half hours ago. Your plan was to just…" He glanced toward Matthew and kept his voice even and polite, but he wasn't happy with the situation. "To collect on a promise and call it a day? See you next week at the courthouse? Go home and eat lasagna for two, not three?"

Great. Now both of the guys in the car were scowling at her.

She didn't have any brilliant plan from this point on. She braked as the next stoplight turned red. Red light after red light—she knew where she wanted to end up, but there didn't seem to be any way to drive there smoothly.

If that wasn't a metaphor for her life, she didn't know what was. She knew where she wanted to end up—happily married, raising a happy family—but damn if she knew how to get there. She'd tried the swept-off-her-feet-by-infatuation route with Rob, but that had been a dead end. Relying on an old friendship with Evan had seemed like a better path, but this road wasn't going anywhere she'd expected, either.

Evan wanted to know what she'd expected to do for *dinner* tonight. Dinner? She wouldn't have been surprised if she'd gotten to Fort Hood and found out that Evan Stephens had forgotten all about their pinkie promise.

But he hadn't.

"We have a lot to discuss," Evan said. "I'd think dinner together would be a given." This was said in a tone of voice that probably meant Evan's staff needed to pay attention because he was about to lay out his plans. It would be sexy in an authoritative kind of way if it wasn't directed at her, but since it was, Colonel Grayson didn't need any orders from Colonel Stephens, thank you very much.

Great, what a lovely family we make, all three of us scowling in unison.

She kept her eyes on the red light. "I realize we have a lot to discuss. I also realize that you have a life that didn't include me until two and a half hours ago. It's Friday. I *expected* that you might already have plans for tonight, if I was even able to see you today. When I went to your office, I only *half* expected you to be there. You could have been out on a field exercise for the next two weeks or on a vacation cruise in the Bahamas."

The light turned green. Good, because she was just getting revved up. "You seem to think I should have plans for everything from this point on, but you'll have to excuse me for not being that presumptuous. It's not like I know a lot of men who would drop everything without any notice just because I showed up."

"Now you do."

"And it's not like—" His words sank in. "I do?"

"You do."

Another hard pang hit her, this time in her heart.

He ran his thumb over an inch of her bared neck, a subtle move Matthew couldn't see. "There's no one I'd rather have dinner with. Nothing I'd rather be doing than spending time with you."

It took her breath away. All of it did. *I'm overwhelmed—* kissing her in his office—*such a beautiful wife*—dropping everything for her.

What had she expected? Not any of this, not in her wildest dreams.

"Pizza." Matthew's voice was loud and clear, zinging her attention from Evan to him. "I want pizza. In our room, Mom."

Juliet heard what her son didn't say: *Without this strange man I've never met before.*

She barely knew this man, either. He was a far cry from the college sophomore who'd pulled off a sweat-soaked T-shirt, twirled it into a rope, snapped it at her butt and made her spill her beer. Instead, he wore the uniform of a lieutenant colonel, looked her in the eye and told her he'd drop everything for her.

She couldn't do the same, not with Matthew as her priority. Expecting her child to immediately include Evan in their routine was too much, not when his whole life had already been turned upside down by the army's orders that she move to Fort Hood, but orders were orders. They'd had to pack up and move.

Liar. It wasn't the army's idea. You knew you were being promoted. You knew where Evan was, and you requested Fort Hood. You pulled a few strings, called a few friends at the Pentagon. You knew...

She was grateful for the next red light. She needed to close her eyes for a moment, just a few seconds, because she needed to remember how to breathe.

She felt two hundred pounds of man shifting in the seat next to her as Evan turned to address her son. His hand stayed, warm, just behind her head.

"Pizza's good, but have you had the really good Texas food yet?"

"What's Texas food?"

"Barbecue, but not the sticky sauce kind. Have you heard of brisket?"

Matthew must have shaken his head no.

"You don't want to miss out. Brisket is beef they cook over wood fires for an entire day. You can feel the heat coming off these huge pits of red-hot coals. I know one place where you can't sit near the pits because they give off so much heat."

Juliet opened her eyes. The light turned green. She drove.

"Sometimes the pit masters ask customers to bring them logs from the woodpile. They'll hold up two or three fingers if they need two or three logs, and then people jump up from their picnic tables to grab 'em and bring them over. Of course, it's usually kids who beat everyone to it, older kids, because adults are too slow and little kids can't carry heavy wood. But the kids who help have to drop off the wood next to the pit and get back fast, because of the heat of the fire."

Juliet cracked her window open a few inches and breathed in the cool winter air of the Texas post she hadn't come to by accident. February's early dusk was approaching, but her mood was brightening with each glimpse of her son's face in the rearview mirror. Matthew was waging a mighty struggle to stay aloof. Ice cream and red-hot firepits? Evan sure knew how to tempt an eleven-year-old boy.

She parked in the parking space to the left of Evan's. His car was the only one left in the row.

The Corvette was too much for her son to withstand. His frosty disinterest went up in smoke. "Is that your *car*?"

"It is."

Matthew scrambled out of the back seat, nearly banging his door into the Corvette, which gave Juliet a heart attack. Evan didn't seem to notice the close call. He got out in a more leisurely manner, reaching into his pocket and pulling out his keys. Juliet needed to get out, too, so she could see Matthew. Over the roof of her car, she kept an eye on the top of Matthew's head.

Evan hit the unlock button on his key fob. "Go ahead,

Matthew. Sit behind the steering wheel, if you want. See how it feels."

"Evan, no," she protested.

Matthew wasn't going to wait for his mother to talk Evan out of it. He opened the Corvette's door—fortunately, Evan was a human blockade to keep the Corvette's door from dinging hers—and jumped in. Evan closed the door as Matthew jerked the steering wheel from side to side while sliding off the seat to see if he could mash the gas pedal.

"Evan…no."

"At least one of you Graysons appreciates it." He snorted in disgust. "A grandpa car."

"You realize that you look as old as a grandpa to him, right?"

"Juliet?"

"What?"

"Get back in the car." He started to get back in his side.

"Why?"

He stopped midmotion. "We need to talk."

"Right this second?" She was afraid to get back in that private space with just him.

"Yes."

"Why?" Maybe she was stalling because she *wanted* to get back in that private space with him.

"Because I said so. Isn't that what a grandpa would say?"

"You're not my grandpa."

He opened his mouth to fire back, but then he started to laugh. "It's like riding a bicycle, isn't it?"

Riding a bicycle. When he'd kissed her, she'd thought the same thing about sex.

"Wh-what is?"

"Teasing each other like this. Arguing for the hell of it, to see who'll win." He grinned at her. "You win. I'm not your parent. But I *am* going to be your husband, so, Juliet, my little turtledove, please get back in your car so we can talk about expectations, my sweet baby doll."

She got back in the car.

He shut the door. Without a seat belt to restrain him, he faced her, one forearm leaning on the center armrest, invading her personal space within this private space.

She could feel her heart pounding again. Rather than look at Evan, she peered over his shoulder, trying to see Matthew through the car windows.

"He's fine."

She did look at Evan then, to give him the sour look he deserved. "Your Corvette won't be."

One corner of his mouth turned up. His blue eyes were turning darker in the dusk. "I really missed you."

She couldn't look away.

"Nothing's changed." His deep voice was soft, quiet in the small space.

Everything's changed.

"It's been two and a half hours since I said I wanted to get out of this parking lot, so I could touch and kiss the woman I'm so damned happy to see, and we're still here."

"Hug." But she was looking at his lips. "You said 'hug' this afternoon."

"I meant kiss."

Before she realized she should retreat, his palm was gentle against her jaw as his thumb traced her bottom lip lightly, deliberately. That same hard contraction of desire hit her, low and intense. The near-pain of it made her words a little desperate. "We're still being watched."

Evan's thumb paused. Slowly, he turned his head to look over his shoulder at Matthew in the Corvette. He turned back to her. "Nope."

"I thought—I thought you wanted to talk about—about expectations."

"Nope."

She wet her lips, a nervous move, but her tongue flicked against Evan's thumb, a fleeting taste of warm-rough-salt. Evan closed his eyes. A full second passed, and then he leaned in and placed his lips where his thumb had been.

It was a beautiful kiss, a charming prince bestowing a blessing on a woman asleep.

Then Evan began to wake her. He kissed her again, her lower lip. And again, the left corner of her mouth. She felt him breathe in, felt his hand sliding to the softness under her jaw, lifting her face. He kissed her, his mouth fully on hers, a firmer pressure. Her lips clung to his for an extra moment as he lifted his head away just long enough for her to breathe in, too, the air between them warm, intimate. Her hands shifted a little uselessly, brushing against camouflage and leather upholstery.

"I can't—we can't just make out in a car."

"We can. We are." Evan traced the edge of her ear with the pad of his thumb. "Were you never a teenager?"

"You're thirty-seven." She spoke against the warm skin of his jaw. "Thirty-seven, and—"

"And I learned how to kiss in a car when I was seventeen. That's twenty years to get it right." He kissed her face as he spoke, gentle kisses here, harder ones there. "Twenty years, just so I could get this one moment right." Sweet kisses here, a passionate taste of her skin there. "Just for this kiss with this woman in this car. Right now."

That was the end of the preliminaries. Her mouth was taken by a man who knew how to kiss. He drew her into him like she was something desirable, someone he absolutely must have. The taste of him, the texture of him was exactly right.

It made her want to cry, because it made her feel too much. Emotional closeness went hand in hand with physical closeness for her, but the physical pull wouldn't last. Passion never did. And it made her angry, suddenly, that he would kiss her so perfectly when it couldn't last. What did it prove?

She could make him want her, too. She could kiss him and leave him weak, if that was all he wanted. A moment of mindless abandon? Easy. Meaningless.

She kissed him without caution, tasting, breathing, nudging him to a slightly different angle, exploring deeply.

Evan broke away, breathing hard, but she heard his soft curse. He pressed his forehead into hers, eyes closed. "Juliet, Juliet."

Oh, God. This was Evan. What was she trying to prove here?

"I'm sorry," she whispered.

"Sorry? Two weeks, Juliet. You've been here for two weeks. You *should* be sorry. We could have been doing this for two weeks."

She smiled a little. It was a compliment. It was nice to be wanted, but she knew she wouldn't always be exciting and new. This pleasure wasn't worth the inevitable pain. She sat back a bit, which only gave her a better view of Evan's face, his eyes closed, his mouth set as if… She didn't know what.

What did she know about men and passion? Rob had always seemed turned on by her, too, but she'd learned the hard way that she wasn't as exciting as another woman. Or two. Or three. Sex and emotions were two separate things. She got them confused too easily. "I'm sorry. I'm not really good at, uh, these things."

Evan made a sound, not a laugh, exactly, but a sound of disbelief. "You're really insane."

"Not about this."

He looked up at that, but his eyes flickered as he spotted something behind her. "If my motor pool officer wasn't coming down the walk right now, I'd prove you wrong. Why the hell is Chief working this late?" He sat up straighter, but his breathing was still that of a man who had…expectations.

Don't expect too much. I'm not exactly irreplaceable in bed.

She tried to warn him. "It was just a kiss."

"One kiss with you is worth ten entire nights with any other woman."

It hadn't been a joke, but she had to laugh or else the misery would kill her. "Nothing I do is worth ten nights in bed with some other woman. I know that for a fact."

"Are you kidding? That was incredible." Those blue eyes were serious.

"Don't." She jerked her gaze from him to look out the windshield. "Just don't. I know exactly how I stack up, compared to other women." *Don't make me spell it out.*

"How can you think—?"

"*Evan.* I know how I compare, damn it."

His silence said too much.

She glared at the steering wheel. Her knuckles were white. "We'll be fine. Just keep your expectations realistic, not—not ten-nights'-worth type of stuff. Let's leave it at that." *Don't make me remember.*

"How could you not…?" Evan sat back, all the way back. He shook his head slowly, rolling it against the leather of his headrest, an inch to the left, to the right. "That bastard."

She didn't need to spell it out, then.

Of course, Evan would guess why Rob Jones had left her. Of course—but it was still humiliating to have anyone know her husband had strayed. *Strayed.* Like he'd drifted outside the line of a bike lane as they'd pedaled along on a Sunday afternoon ride. Rob hadn't strayed; he'd screwed other women. Often.

She was dimly aware of someone walking past the hood of her car, stopping abruptly just before the Corvette, Evan raising a hand in greeting, the person moving on. She saw it all without seeing it.

Wake up. Stop wallowing in your memories. You have responsibilities. A child.

She looked out Evan's window. "I think Matthew's getting bored over there. We should go."

Evan didn't even look. He just picked up his key fob and pressed a button. Music began playing in the Corvette, muted through the car windows. Matthew's little whoop of delight carried more clearly.

"You didn't have to do that."

"For God's sake, Juliet, give me a minute here."

"To do what? Oh." She was not going to blush, she was not going to blush...

"To catch my breath." Evan looked into the Corvette for a moment, then put his head back and laughed a little disbelieving laugh. "I'm in no condition to go anywhere *emotionally.* You've stirred up every emotion, every single one, I swear, since you walked into my office, Lieutenant Colonel Grayson. Every emotion."

"That was not what I expected."

"That makes one of us. I always knew if you came back into my life, all hell would break loose in here." He rubbed his chest.

"I'm sorry." She looked straight ahead, pretending she wasn't aware that he was studying her.

"You apologize a lot. That's new."

"I didn't mean to cause you turmoil. That seems to be the natural state of my life, though. Parenthood will do that to you."

Matthew was worth it, but he was her child and she couldn't imagine life without him.

Evan had just met him. They weren't related, nor did they have an eleven-year history. Evan really was a friend, someone she cared about, and here she was, expecting him to take on too much—and so, for the dozenth time, she tried to give him a chance to bow out gracefully. "Look, preexisting children were never part of the bargain. I understand if you want to reconsider—"

But Evan had burst into laughter. "Preexisting children. Good one."

"Well, it's true."

"I said you stirred up every emotion. That includes things like happiness. Anticipation. We always had fun together. That's the one thing you don't seem to expect."

"Fun?"

"Yes. You said you don't know what to expect from this point, so let me tell you what I expect."

He put his hand on her seat's headrest again. When she turned to look at him, she realized how easy it would be to simply rest her cheek against his hand. She didn't. But she could have, and he…he wouldn't have minded.

"I expect us to enjoy dinner together," he said. "I expect that you and I will enjoy some truly delicious food, and I expect your son will get a splinter on at least one hand from hauling hickory wood and having the time of his life. I expect us to laugh at something we don't know right now will be funny, but it will crack us up. And after we laugh together, when you and Matthew go back to your hotel and I go back to my house, we'll all fall asleep in our beds remembering it. And I expect you to do all of this in comfortable civilian clothes. You cannot eat brisket and corn on the cob in a service uniform."

"Says who?"

"Cowboys. It's their food, and they don't eat in suits and ties." He tugged on his lapel with his free hand. "And I can't be out on the town after 1900 hours in ACUs, and before you ask, smart aleck, the post commander says so. The policy is in your welcome packet. So why don't you let me drive your Lexus back to my house?"

She started to object, but Evan held up his keys.

"While you make your son's day and drive him back to the hotel in my Corvette. I'll change and meet you at your hotel, and then you know what to expect next."

"What?"

"Fun."

Juliet lay in the dark, staring at the ceiling of her hotel room, reliving every minute of the evening, of three people having a uniquely Texan dinner experience.

She'd forgotten.

Life could be fun.

Men could be fun.

A *date* could be fun.

But she, Juliet…

She was not fun.

She was a good person. She loved her child. She took care of her soldiers. She knew how to be loyal, how to put others first, how to take command when placed in command. But in a situation where she was supposed to relax and enjoy herself, it took effort to go through the expected motions: grin, chuckle, say politely pleasant things.

She was not fun.

Evan was. He smiled. He laughed. He pretended to race her son to a stack of hickory logs and overacted like a cartoon character when he got beat by an eleven-year-old.

Evan deserved a woman who wouldn't drag him down. Who wouldn't expect him to raise another man's son. Who didn't have to pay another man *alimony*, because she'd been so very, very stupid.

She hadn't warned Evan that she had to pay alimony. She'd have to tell him. She'd have to tell him everything.

The worst thing was, she'd be able to sit down with the man and explain court decisions and obligations without faltering. But to sit down with the man and explain what she thought of fun food made her feel like an alien attempting to assimilate with the native life forms. *The banana pudding is delicious. I had no idea it was so popular in Texas. How funny, to think of macho rodeo riders loving a kid's dessert.*

The tears rolled from the corners of her eyes, down her temples, into her hair.

What if I'd married Evan eleven years ago?

Then Matthew wouldn't exist.

She wiped her nightgown sleeve over her eyes. One day with Evan had made her realize how terrible it was of her to call in this chit, to hold a man to a sixteen-year-old pact. It was terrible, because Evan was wonderful.

They'd been a match once, not lovers, but a matched pair of friends who'd valued the same things, who'd approached life with the same attitude. She'd hoped they would be again, but she was not…she was no longer…

Fun.

Oh, Evan. I forgot that life was supposed to be fun.

Tomorrow, he wanted to take Matthew and her somewhere special. Somewhere they could relax, he'd said, some place Matthew might like, because Evan wasn't done stacking the deck in his favor.

Tacos, then.

She'd tell him tomorrow, after she choked down a taco to be polite, that he was too kind and such a good friend, but that she realized how different their lives had become. They were no longer the same people who'd been friends in college. He deserved better than a divorced mother with a deadbeat ex. She'd let him go. After all, their pact hadn't been signed in blood.

It had only been a pinkie promise.

Chapter Six

"No way."

Juliet's son said exactly what she was thinking, except she was thinking *no way*, as in *that is not possible*, while Matthew was saying it in a voice of amazement, like he'd gotten a gift ten times better than he'd been expecting: *No waaay*.

"Six Flags? Today?" Matthew turned to her, as excited as a puppy. "I'm tall enough for the really good roller coasters now, aren't I, Mom? The big ones?"

Juliet stood in the Holiday Inn parking lot and tried to be the voice of reason. "I don't know what the height requirements are, honey. I'm not sure this is a good idea for today."

They were in the middle of a move. She was in the middle of a huge, life-changing decision. She had priorities, issues that needed to be settled. Yet Evan had just set her up to be the bad guy if she refused to go along with his plan, and a very old feeling of being the only adult in the situation settled into her chest unpleasantly. "We have a lot of things going on."

"Oh, *maaan…*"

"Fifty-four inches tall," Evan said. "Just for a few of the rides. A couple at fifty-two inches. The rest are forty-something."

"How tall am I, Mom?"

"I'm not sure." Juliet frowned at Evan. "How do you know all this?"

"I checked first. There are lots of coasters. We'll ride whatever we fit."

"Yes! Let's go, Mom."

"For Pete's sake, give me a minute here," she said.

Evan squelched a bark of laughter.

She rolled her eyes. "To *catch my breath*. I don't even know how far it is to Six Flags. It's not close, is it?"

"There are two within driving distance from Fort Hood."

Matthew gasped. "Two! No waaaay."

Evan winked—at her son, not at her. "Fiesta Texas in San Antonio and Six Flags near Dallas. Today is opening day for the year at both of them. Fort Hood's in the middle, more or less. We can be at either one in just a couple of hours."

"Awesome."

"Tell me about it." Evan held out his palm and Matthew smacked him a hard high five.

"Two against one. Not fair." But Juliet's protest lacked any *oomph*, not when Matthew actually, finally thought something about their new post was awesome. Still, Evan should never had made such a suggestion without checking with her first.

"Let's make it three against nobody." Evan's attention was back on her, those ice blue eyes looking at her with unmistakable warmth. She'd been expecting to see triumph—but that would have been Rob. "You love a good coaster, Juliet. You always have. Nobody has to do anything else today, right?"

"I thought we were just going to get some tacos for lunch." *I have to tell you about alimony and Rob and all kinds of negative things.*

"We'll get tacos on the way." Evan looked sternly at

her son. "You weren't joking when you said you had no homework this weekend, were you?"

"No, sir."

"Just Evan, not sir. You don't work for me."

When Matthew looked her way, Juliet nodded her agreement, again, that he could call Evan by his first name. In a military town, it was no big deal for children to address adults by their proper ranks, *Captain Smith, Sergeant Thompson, Mr. Cooper,* but Juliet understood instinctively that Evan didn't want to have a child who lived in his house addressing him as *Colonel Stephens.*

If they lived in the same house. They had so much to discuss…

"I don't have any homework, Mom."

"We're still talking about a very long day." Then again, it might take a very long day for Matthew to get comfortable enough to call Evan *Evan.* She did want to see if they could get along, didn't she? Wasn't that the most important thing?

Evan shrugged. "Three hours to get there, eight hours to ride awesome coasters, three hours back. We'll be home by midnight."

"This is going to be great." Matthew thought the whole idea was so fantastic, he couldn't imagine any reason they might not go. "I love coasters!"

"How did I know Juliet Grayson's kid would love coasters?" Evan put his hand on Matthew's shoulder and looked from her boy to her, as pleased as he could be with himself.

It struck her: *He's trying to make me happy.*

She had to wrap her mind around the novelty of it. He wanted her to be happy, and he'd remembered that she loved amusement parks, once upon a time. This wasn't a power struggle. This wasn't a disregard for her parental authority. This wasn't Rob; this was Evan.

She dug in her small purse for the hotel room key and

held it out to Matthew. "We'll be there after the sun goes down, so you need to get your jacket. And mine. The blue one. And grab—"

Matthew had already snatched the key from her hand and taken off at a run to go back into their hotel.

"—a couple of bottles of water, too," she shouted after him. She didn't quite look back at Evan. "That ought to save us ten bucks. Theme parks are so expensive."

Evan stepped up behind her and did that thing again, setting his hands lightly on her waist. It was somehow even more intimate when he was behind her, bending his head to speak into her ear. "This is my treat. Good morning, by the way." He pushed her loose hair away from her temple with his own cheek, then kissed her lightly near the corner of her eye.

"You don't have to do that," she said.

"I love your hair down. Having it up all the time in uniform makes it seem all the more exotic when it's down."

That was a Casanova line if she'd ever heard one. She turned around and put a little space between them. "Nice line, but you've only seen my hair up for less than a day. I was talking about the tickets. You don't have to pay for our tickets."

"I suggested the date. I'll pay for the date." There was the slightest hint of steel in his voice.

"This isn't going to be cheap. You shouldn't have to pay for two extra people. It's more like an outing when there's a kid along, not like a date."

"Juliet, don't. Just—don't."

"Don't what?"

"Don't pretend this isn't a date. It is. And don't pretend this is going to break the bank or empty my wallet. I've been a bachelor my whole career. I've got the sports car and the newest TV and the best gaming systems, because I don't have much else to spend money on."

He closed the space between them and put his hands on her waist again. Why did he do that so often? He'd only touched her so intimately that one time, on the college green...

He gave her waist a little squeeze. "Since I'm a bachelor on a lieutenant colonel's salary, and since you know exactly how much that is, I can't even impress you by buying you ice cream and souvenirs. That won't stop me from trying. I'm not only paying for the tickets, I'm paying for the super tickets that let us skip lines."

"That's not necessary."

"It is. I hate standing in lines when I don't have to."

"You'll spoil Matthew."

"Good. I want to spoil you, but I'll start with your son."

She raised an eyebrow at that. "You'll regret that. You don't spoil the child when you have to live with the child." Then she could've bitten her tongue out. It came back to her now. She'd decided last night that she'd lay out all the concerns he needed to consider before making a commitment. Here she was, teasing him back, when she should be serious.

But Evan was the one who got more serious. "I've regretted worse things."

The man kissed so very skillfully. Persuasively. He kissed her lightly, softly. With a light lap of his tongue, he coaxed her lips to part on a little breath, and he invaded her mouth gently, nothing crude, nothing that said he wanted this kiss to lead straight to sex. He kissed her as if he enjoyed kissing.

Kissing just for kissing's sake...

Evan's hands were cupping her face, his fingers in her hair, when a car engine started and she remembered where she was.

She covered his wrist with her hand. "Matthew will be back any second."

Evan let his gaze roam over her cheeks, chin, forehead before he let go of her face. He didn't back up one inch.

She didn't move, either, because her legs had turned to jelly.

She didn't like it. She'd come to Fort Hood for a purpose, and it hadn't included losing her mind while being kissed by Casanova in his office or in his car or in the parking lot of her transient lodging.

"You never kissed me like that," she said, hearing the resentment in her voice. "Before. In college."

That familiar blue gaze dropped to her mouth one more time. "Like I said, I've had far worse regrets."

Then he stepped back and turned away. Matthew came pounding up to them at a run, and Evan switched from serious to smiling. "Got the jackets, Matthew? All right. Let's go have some fun."

The Fireball coaster was designed to send its train full of passengers around a loop. Just one loop—over and over and over.

The riders were seated two by two. It was clear to Evan that Matthew would sit with his mother. The child had made sure to stand between Evan and his mother for twenty minutes in the winding line, so he sure as hell wasn't going to let Evan sit with his mother once it was their turn. Sadder still, he wasn't going to sit with Evan.

Evan was in the disconcerting position of being a thirty-seven-year-old military officer who wished a middle-school boy would include him at the hypothetical cafeteria table where the cool kids sat.

Hey, I'm cool. Sit with me on this coaster. Did you know I fought in a war? I'm in charge of, like, hundreds of real soldiers. Can I sit at the cafeteria table with you?

Not happening. Not today.

Matthew kept his mother's hand in a death grip as he

climbed into the coaster car, pulling her with him. Evan resigned himself to the bench behind theirs, sitting back to back with them, shoulder harnesses and a foot of hard, molded plastic between them, shutting him out.

He'd underestimated the impact of the adrenaline rush, however, on how expansive Matthew would be after the ride.

"That was awesome. Wasn't that the best? The best!"

Evan enjoyed Matthew's enthusiasm. He was a fun kid when he forgot to keep his guard up.

"I could hear you yelling 'hair,'" Evan said. "What happened to your hair?"

"Mom's hair! Show him, Mom. Do what your hair did when we were hanging upside down."

"You mean this?" Juliet dug her hands in her hair and then lifted it straight up into the air. Matthew thought it was hysterical. Evan thought Juliet looked beautiful—silly, smiling, carefree. It might be only a temporary post-coaster high, but Evan loved to see it. It was a vast improvement over the grimly determined woman from yesterday.

"Where to next?"

Juliet let go of her hair and shook it back in the Texas sunshine. "How about bumper cars?"

"Yeah, cool!" Matthew said.

"Here's the map. Lead on." Juliet fell back to walk next to Evan, which made him feel as excited as a sixth grader himself, one who'd gotten the pretty girl to stand next to him in the cafeteria line. Pretty and smart, too. Evan admired the way she'd been letting Matthew learn how to orient himself and navigate with a map, letting him lead the adults, boosting his confidence without seeming to be doing anything at all except having fun.

Hadn't he once bragged to Rob about what a good mother she'd be? He'd been puffing on a cigar and pretending he liked to sip port. *Gentlemen, please. We're talk-*

ing about the future mother of my children. I'm not going to have ugly children. Not stupid ones, either.

Juliet spoke to him in a voice meant only for his ears as they followed in Matthew's wake. "I need to stay right-side up and on the ground for a ride or two. I hate to admit defeat, but my stomach isn't what it used to be."

Evan buried the guilt. "Say it ain't so. You never met a thrill ride you didn't like."

"I still like them, but now I get motion sick sometimes, ever since I had a baby. I don't know why pregnancy has weird side effects like that, but things never are quite the same."

"Really?" Evan was fascinated. He'd never heard that pregnancy could make a woman become permanently susceptible to something like motion sickness. "Side effects like what?"

She didn't answer for a few steps, and Evan realized he'd made a misstep himself, asking about something that probably got really personal, really fast. Before he could try to change the subject, Juliet cleared her throat and did an admirable job of sounding like she wasn't embarrassed. "Oh, you know. Stretch marks. Other things. I have a friend who swears her breasts got smaller."

For the love of— Was he supposed to not look at Juliet's chest now?

He didn't. He was an adult. He didn't look.

Until Juliet waved her hand toward her own sunny yellow knit shirt. "But me, well… I didn't get breast implants after college or anything, in case you wondered. I got bigger when I was pregnant and stayed that way."

He didn't stumble, he didn't stare, he didn't giggle like an embarrassed schoolboy—outwardly. He did all that and more inside. As a matter of fact, he *hadn't* been wondering anything like that in the last twenty-four hours, because he hadn't checked out her breasts, not when she'd been wearing military regalia yesterday afternoon and a denim jacket last night. *Jeez, Juliet, give me a minute here...*

"Are you blushing? Why, Evan Stephens, you are blushing. Hey, you're the one who asked the question."

He couldn't keep it together. He half laughed, looked away, rubbed the back of his neck.

Juliet's laughter was worth his embarrassment. "Sorry."

He'd like to swoop her off her feet or tickle her, something to get a little revenge, but he'd gotten the distinct feeling that she was trying to stick to the *this is my friend Evan* narrative with her son today.

Fine. It was effortless to slip into their old friendship as they walked along. "No, you're not sorry one bit, but you're cute and I like you anyway."

"Aww, that's sweet, coming from a blushing man. Let's see, what else does pregnancy affect?"

"Forget I asked. You're enjoying this too much."

"Would you expect hair to change? A woman in my last unit had her hair turn completely gray. No joke. It was crazy."

He touched her hair without thinking, then changed the caress to a friendly tug. "Not you. Yours is darker now, though."

"Not the baby's fault. It started getting darker years before I was pregnant." She was silent for a step or two. "No longer dirty blond. Sorry. I know you usually prefer your women blonde."

Stop apologizing. "Shows what you know. There's gold in your hair when the sun's hitting it, and I wouldn't care if there wasn't."

Her smile lingered, but she was gazing at nothing, far away from him.

"My favorite look is just the way you look, Juliet. I said it yesterday, and I'm saying it today, and I'll say it again tomorrow. I am so damned happy to see you, and you are

very beautiful. All of you. Head to toe." He let his gaze
drop to her chest rather obviously. "And everywhere in
between, now that you've pointed it out."

That snapped her out of that distant stare. "Stephens!"

"Mom! You're too slow. Come *on*." Matthew back-
tracked to grab his mother's hand and pull her along.

Just as she skipped into a jog, she reached back and
grabbed Evan's hand. He jogged to keep up with her, his
happiness almost complete.

Almost.

When Juliet had said he preferred blondes, he'd remembered, for the first time in the last twenty-four hours, one
blonde in particular. Linda was the meteorologist on the
local television station, easy on the eye as she pointed
at weather maps during the evening news. They'd been
dating—and spending Saturday nights together when she
didn't have to do the 11:00 p.m. news and he wasn't out
on field exercises—but she was not someone he'd made
any promises to. It went without saying that Linda was
now the woman he *had been* dating. Juliet was everything.

But Linda deserved a face-to-face goodbye. He'd break
up with her once she returned to the States. She was currently on assignment in a third-world country that had
been devastated by a storm. She said her station got better
ratings when she gave her weather updates with toppled
palm trees behind her. Even if he could reach her by text,
he wouldn't do that to a woman. Got married. Won't be
seeing you. Hope your trip is going well.

Juliet squeezed his hand as they came to a stop at the
entrance to the bumper cars. Her cheeks were pink from
the jog in the crisp air, the V-neck of her yellow shirt revealing the rise and fall of her rapid breath. *Vibrant and
vital*, he'd thought yesterday, the best part of his life from
now on. It was still incredible to him that, after years of

convincing himself she was out of reach, she was standing right here, holding his hand.

Nothing would stop him from marrying Juliet.

And then, the week after that, he'd break up with his girlfriend when she returned to the States.

Simple.

Chapter Seven

"I'm tapping out. Two rounds were enough for me."

Juliet unfastened her seat belt and shimmied her way out of an orange bumper car.

Evan was grateful for reasons that had nothing to do with a woman shimmying. His knees had been smashed against the dash of his blue bumper car long enough. If Juliet was out, he was out.

"But, Mom, there's no line. We can keep our cars and do it again."

"You go ahead, honey. You're plenty old enough to ride alone. I'll wait by the exit. Ride as many times as you want."

Evan didn't have a cute shimmy like Juliet, but he managed to unfold his six-foot-plus frame from the blue car that was definitely built for a smaller human. Or one with better knees. The army was hell on knees, just like most professional sports.

"You, too?" Matthew sounded dismayed. His black car was parked next to Evan's, since he'd just smashed into Evan when the electricity had died, and the ride had ended abruptly.

"Me, too." Evan put his palm on top of Matthew's head and pretended to use him as a crutch as he balanced on one foot and got his other leg free. "Give 'em hellll…heck for me."

He messed up Matthew's hair as the kid laughed at him.

What could be funnier at age eleven than an adult trying to salvage an accidental cuss? Evan headed for the exit.

Juliet was waiting for him, laughing at him, too. She backed against the swinging gate and pushed it open. He threw his arm around her shoulders and took her with him as he walked out.

"I think he likes you, Grandpa."

"Then my knees didn't make that sacrifice in vain." Behind them, the distinctive buzz of electricity preceded the screech of rubber bumpers on a slick floor. He steered Juliet to a landscaped spot a few yards away. "So, when are we going to tell him?"

Her smile faded. "I don't know."

Evan leaned back against the waist-high wrought-iron fencing that kept the crowd off the grass. He draped their unnecessary jackets over the railing. The late afternoon was still warm from a whole day of sunny skies.

"You should come over tomorrow." He pulled Juliet to stand between his knees, living the dream of every teenage boy at the park who wished his crush would let him do the same. "See the house. We can let him know that he'll be moving in. He can choose his bedroom. I've got three empty ones."

"Wow." Juliet had a little worry line between her eyebrows.

"I know, the quarters are way too big for one service member. It was the smallest thing that post housing offered in the neighborhood." He didn't have to explain to her that neighborhoods on any army post were essentially assigned according to rank. Field-grade officers were given same-sized houses on the same set of streets. "Key personnel are supposed to live on post, so I had to take what they offered. I'm tagged as key personnel."

"Sure," she said in an absentminded way. "Battalion commander."

Evan tried to read her change in mood. "I can put in for an exception. There's no compelling reason it wouldn't be granted. It's not like we ever get snowed in by blizzards in Central Texas. We could buy a new house anywhere you like."

Juliet bit her lip.

"Near any school you want Matthew to attend. What would you like? Say the word. We'll do it."

"You don't have to spoil me."

"I think I do." *Someone should have been spoiling you for years.*

"It's just me. Juliet Grayson, the girl who is forcing you to keep a pact you made when you were twenty-one."

"You're not forcing me to do anything, Juliet Grayson, except forcing me to show more restraint than I want to on a perfect Saturday. I've been doing my best all day to pretend I'm just your friend." He hooked one thumb through a belt loop of her jeans to keep her close. With his other hand, he captured her hand and brought it to his lips.

"Oh…"

He smiled against the back of her hand. He knew the sound of a woman who was melting. Why hadn't he tried to make Juliet melt years ago?

Because she was married to someone else, thanks to you.

"You're right," she said. "I don't want to force you to do anything. Instead of riding coasters today, I thought we'd talk through some serious issues. Seriously."

"This is serious. This is family togetherness time. Bonding with my future stepson while pulling some Gs together." Without taking his eyes off her face, he kissed the back of her hand again, then paused. "That sentence was supposed to put a smile on your face, not make you look quite so horrified."

"Before we tell Matthew anything about future housing, we have to be sure this is really going to happen. He's had a lot of promises broken in the last few years. I don't want to tell him one thing today and something different by Friday."

"I'm a sure thing, Juliet. Friday is going to happen."

"You can't say that, you really can't."

"I'm a sure thing, Juliet." But he didn't laugh, because he wasn't joking.

"We haven't talked about…things."

"For example?"

"Things like finances."

"I'm pretty sure we know each other's salary, Colonel Grayson. Anyone can look at the army pay scale and see how much a lieutenant colonel gets per paycheck."

"*For example*, my paycheck gets garnished." She had that Juliet expression on her face, the one that meant she was resolved to broach something difficult. "I have to pay alimony to Rob."

"What?" He wanted to laugh it off. He wanted to believe it was a joke, a test, a tease.

She looked at him like she was refusing to flinch no matter what kind of punch might clip her chin next.

"Doesn't Rob have to pay you child support?"

"No."

"But he doesn't see Matthew. Ever. Three hundred and sixty-five days a year, you pay for all the food and housing and clothing? Transportation. Medical." He knew the breakdown after years of dealing with the child support issues of soldiers under his command. "Why doesn't Rob have to contribute?"

"His lawyer was better than mine."

He flinched. She might stand there stoically, but he felt sick. So damned sorry she'd had to deal with legal battles. So damned sorry she'd had to fight such a selfish son of a—

"Mom! Can I go again? The man said I could, but the

rule is that I have to get out and go back around to the entrance after three turns."

Juliet forced her mouth to curve in a smile before she faced her son. "Of course. I'll be here whenever you get sick of having your teeth rattled."

"I'm never going to get sick of it." Matthew was off, sneakers pounding on the asphalt, unzipped jacket flapping in the air, completely unaware that his mother was so deeply unhappy, because she didn't let her child see it. She bore everything on her shoulders as a single mother, picking up the slack for her ex-husband, that goddamned, lazy—

She squeezed his hand. "Say something."

"That son of a bitch. Rob lawyered up, did he?"

"Like you wouldn't believe," she said.

"I'd believe it. I can tell already, we're going to need a drink if we're going to get into serious things. Come with me. I'm buying."

"Thanks, but I told Matthew I'd wait here. Plus, you know, my stomach's not in great shape after that death-loop thing. And it's not five o'clock anywhere."

"We've definitely gotten old if we can't drink before five on a Saturday."

"I just think with Matthew here—"

"I'm kidding you." Evan stood and turned her around, then pointed over her shoulder, which gave him a great chance to feel her warmth against his chest. *She's here, right here, where I can keep her safe from Rob. She isn't going to have such a hard life anymore.* "I meant a slushie. Nonalcoholic, fluorescent frozen sugar. The stand is right over there. You can wait here, and I'll bring you one, so you won't miss Matthew if he decides his teeth have been rattled enough."

"I'll get brain freeze."

"Can't hurt worse than having to rehash your ex's legal crap."

"The pain won't last as long, at any rate."

It was a sarcastic joke, but at least it was a joke. "Pick a color. Looks like there's red, blue, orange, green. What flavor is blue? That's just wrong."

"I'll take a blue, please."

He pulled her into a hug as he stood behind her, something he'd probably done dozens of times at school. "I think we're riding that bicycle again."

She ducked her chin, almost bashful. "Definitely not."

"No? Then we're done arguing about slushies. What color should I get Matthew?"

He felt her go still. Then she turned around in his arms and looked at him as if she was about to say something.

He waited a long second. "What is it?"

"It's just…" Her eyes looked a little too bright. He cursed Rob for being so awful that the thought of him made Juliet tear up on a day that was full of coasters and bumper cars and slushies.

Juliet suddenly let go of his arms. She concentrated on smoothing out the sleeve she'd wrinkled, patting it into place. "It's just sweet that you don't forget about Matthew."

"That's it? I get points for not buying two slushies when we're a party of three?"

"It's not as common as you'd think. Generally, if a man buys my child a treat, he's pretty transparently trying to get into my pants."

And your old pal Evan isn't?

"I see," Evan managed to say. Was he supposed to insist he had no intention of getting into her pants? He wouldn't have used that terminology, but…

"It's not like I've dated much since the divorce. Babysitters are hard to find and more expensive than you might think. But it's been my experience that guys assume I'll arrange a babysitter, even for a daytime date. Even for an amusement park."

"I'm getting a kick out of doing this with an eleven-year-old. If he wasn't here, I would never have remembered that I used to run from ride to ride when I was his age. I would have walked right past the bumper cars and not even ridden them, like some boring adult."

That's the truth, and it has nothing to do with getting into your pants.

"That's what you truly think?" She looked at him with something a little too close to amazement in her expression.

It shouldn't be so hard for her to believe. "Matthew's definitely a plus, not a minus."

He hadn't expected the full-body hug that followed, but suddenly, he had Juliet's arms around him, her warmth pressed against his chest. She even rested her head on his shoulder, her hair—darker than college, but just as soft—brushing the underside of his jaw.

Evan brought his arms around her and held her as he looked at the colorful slushie stand and listened to the snapping electricity and screeching rubber of the bumper cars. Life was rarely so perfect.

"It's so good to have a friend again," she murmured.

"Things will be easier now," he said. "Serious things. Everything."

Her sigh was silent, but he felt it as he held her. "Marrying you won't change anything. I'll still have to pay Rob the same amount every month."

"Marrying me will change everything," he countered, as easily as riding a bike. "You'll have someone to curse with you every time you see that money going to him. We can chase down each payday with a shot of tequila. It'll give us something to look forward to each month."

She laughed. Maybe it was more of a snort than a laugh, but he'd take it.

It was the most natural thing in the world to kiss her. She needed kissing. She needed reassuring, but as he cupped the back of her head in his hand, as he admired her face and those eyes that were a touch too sad, just as he leaned in to place a kiss on that beloved mouth, he caught sight of Matthew out of the corner of his eye.

Too late. He was already kissing Juliet. Her mouth was soft, willing and welcoming, and he felt that sense of rightness pass through him, as he had every kiss before.

He kept the kiss very brief, then moved to kiss her forehead, buying himself a moment before breaking it to her. "Try not to jolt out of my arms like you've done anything wrong, but we've just been busted."

"What?"

He smiled into her gold-flecked eyes, then looked past her to a child who had those same eyes. "How'd it go, Matthew? Done with the bumper cars?"

There'd been no line for the slushies a moment ago. Now, of course, ten people were ahead of them.

Juliet had handled Matthew's shocked silence after the kiss by brightly suggesting it was time for a slushie. She should have looked at the line first. Ahead of them, teenagers talked over each other nonstop. Behind them, small children spoke with treble voices and the lisp that appeared when front teeth went missing. The teens had tired parents. The little lispers had grandparents who encouraged every sentence with a delighted *how about that?* The contrast to her awkwardly silent party of three was intensely uncomfortable.

She felt uncomfortable, at least. Evan looked as calm and confident as always, and Matthew... Well, if looks could kill, she'd be a goner.

She tried to deflect his laser beam stare toward the row of slowly turning slushie machines. "Have you picked a color yet?"

Silence.

"Evan has never had blue. Can you believe that?"

"I thought he was your friend," Matthew said, as if Evan weren't standing right there.

"He is." *I will stay calm and factual and try not to look guilty.*

"I don't kiss my friends." Matthew turned his glare on Evan. "That would be disgusting."

One of the teenage girls looked back at them and giggled.

Evan only shrugged. "That depends on which friend you kissed. Some would be more disgusting than others."

Both teenage girls looked back this time—and kept looking. At Evan.

He's too old for you, girls. But Evan had always had that certain something that made women look twice.

The sun was starting to set, its golden beams slanted at an angle that made her squint. "By the time we get to order, it might be too cold for a slushie. The sun is going down fast." She put her jacket on.

"You're supposed to kiss Daddy, not *him*. I remember you kissing Daddy."

So much for her attempt to change the subject. The grandma looked their way. Granny did a little double take and checked out Evan. *Can't blame me for kissing him, can you?*

"Daddy and I are divorced," she said firmly. She kept the statement short and clear so that Matthew couldn't misunderstand it—and maybe so any of Evan's eavesdropping fan club wouldn't think she was some kind of Jezebel.

Evan shrugged into his leather bomber jacket, pulled those silvered aviator glasses out of his pocket and slid them on. The teenage girl who'd turned away was immediately elbowed by her friend. She looked back, looked at her friend, and they made OMG faces at each other. Then their mom looked to see why they'd gone so quiet. She stared, too.

Matthew's youthful voice wavered. "You're divorced forever?"

In a flash, all her focus was on Matthew. What a question! "Oh, honey. Yes, divorce is permanent. We've talked about it, many times."

"But Daddy doesn't kiss anybody else."

Daddy never stopped kissing other people.

It hurt. She didn't love Rob at all, not anymore, but it still hurt. Her son's blind loyalty was age-appropriate for him, but painful for her.

"Maybe Daddy does, maybe he doesn't. It doesn't matter either way, because we are divorced."

She couldn't look at Evan. He knew Rob too well, and he'd already guessed too much.

Juliet smoothed down Matthew's hair, but she only got one stroke in before he squirmed away. Apparently, a man ruffling his hair at the bumper cars was funny. A mother smoothing it was not acceptable.

Matthew still looked both indignant and bewildered. "So, are you allowed to kiss anybody you want?"

"I suppose I could, but I don't go around kissing just anybody." She put her arm around Matthew's shoulders and gave him a little squeeze and a shake. "Come on, Matty. You know I don't."

"You kissed *him*." Apparently, Matthew couldn't look at Evan, either.

"Yes, I did." Juliet sorted through a dozen things she could add to that short sentence, but she didn't say any of them. Maybe it was the reminders about Rob. Maybe it was the slushie-line audience. Maybe she was just an adult who didn't need to justify her actions to the world, not even to her eleven-year-old son, but whatever it was, she was done with the subject.

"I did," she repeated, then pointedly looked toward the rainbow array of churning slushie machines. "I'm getting the green slushie. What color do you want?"

Only after the teenagers ahead of them were finished with their order did Matthew answer. "Green."

Evan ordered three greens and handed them out. "We can drink them on the way to the next ride."

"Which is...?" Juliet asked as she sucked some fluorescent green ice up the straw.

Evan looked at Matthew and waited for a moment, but Matthew wasn't going to contribute. He was too busy scowling at the world, including the slushie in his hand.

Evan addressed Juliet instead, with a wry twist to his kissable mouth. "There's Boomerang. Pandemonium. Spinsanity. I think they all sound about right, don't you?"

Juliet grinned despite the straw in her mouth. "I do."

Chapter Eight

"I hate hamburgers."

"Matthew Grayson-Jones, that is a lie."

"I don't want to go to Evan's house."

At least that wasn't a lie. Juliet headed her car toward Evan's house. They'd gotten home from the amusement park just after midnight, as Evan had planned. Today, he'd invited them to his house, also as he'd planned. Her own plans, however, were freaking out her son more than she'd…planned.

She tried to say something positive after a morning of negatives from Matthew. "It will be nice to have real food cooked at a house instead of eating more microwaved stuff in our hotel room."

"We could get McDonald's."

"Honey, we've had McDonald's at least twenty times this month already. Ten times on the drive from Georgia, at least." The light ahead turned yellow. She drove through it. "Besides, maybe you'll like Evan's house."

"Who cares what his house looks like?"

"I want to see his house, and I want to eat some home-made food."

"Are you going to kiss him again?"

"I don't know." She hadn't expected the sight of a man kissing her to be so traumatic for Matthew.

"All we ever do is stuff with Evan, Evan, Evan. We see him every single day."

"We've seen him twice."

"And *today*," Matthew whined.

"Okay, thrice."

Matthew usually loved exotic words like *thrice*, but he refused to be cajoled in any way out of his bad mood.

Juliet tapped the steering wheel with one finger as they waited for the next light. The whole purpose of coming to Fort Hood was to give Matthew a better life, a better family, a better male role model. She'd always liked Evan so much, she'd been certain Matthew would like him, too. Matthew usually stuck like glue to the man in any situation, whether it was her father or cousin, his coach or a teacher. She could have predicted that he'd stand near the men while he ate his cake after her promotion.

But if Matthew didn't like Evan, and if they didn't get along, then there was no reason for her to force any of the three of them to go through with her plan.

Except you would have a partner and a friend. A man who can really kiss...

If her first marriage had taught her anything, it was that kisses could be meaningless.

This was about family. About Matthew. And if that wasn't going to work, then she should stop this marriage pact madness.

"Come on in."

"Hi," Juliet said. She gave Matthew's shoulder a quick squeeze.

"Hi," Matthew muttered.

Juliet had tucked two bottles under her arm. "We brought you some drinks. This is a good red wine, but it's not expensive. Feel free to enjoy it with a burger. Or, if you prefer, this is a very, very good beer."

"Yes, it is." Evan took the bottles from her. The beer was almost as big as the wine bottle, sealed with a cork in the Trappist monk style. Any money she'd saved on the wine she must have spent on the beer.

He approved. They made such a good couple.

"We have a favorite nonalcoholic option, too." She squeezed her son's shoulder one more time.

Matthew stuck out his lower lip as he stuck out the cardboard six-pack carrier he'd been holding. It was filled with what looked like brown beer bottles.

Evan took that, too. "Thanks. You're a little young to be a beer aficionado, aren't you?"

"It's root beer," he said, then mumbled, "Really good kind."

"Great. Come on in."

Damn if Evan didn't feel *nervous* as they walked into his house. There wasn't a fancy foyer, just stairs to the second story. They basically walked right into the living room. He tried to see it through their eyes. This level had wood flooring, a considerable upgrade from most post housing he'd lived in. He led them through to the kitchen, which had upgraded appliances and countertops as well. It was good to live on the same street with a general and a few brigade commanders; the houses were the army's version of executive-level.

He watched Juliet's face. He could read her expressions so well, couldn't he? Well, he could tell she was nervous, too.

"First impression?" he asked casually, as he set the beer in the fridge.

"This is so much nicer than our house at Benning, isn't it, Matthew?"

Matthew was not exactly enthusiastic about a kitchen. Evan could remember being bored out of his middle-school mind while adults discussed things like carpeting and double-paned windows.

Matthew stayed silent. *I feel you, kid.*

Evan kept up the conversation. "It's nicer than any housing I've had, too. I didn't put up much of a fight when they said this was the only one immediately available in their inventory, but I'm the only person on the street that doesn't have kids living in his house. The school bus picks up at least a dozen kids for the middle school." *There are kids for you to play with, Matthew.*

"We saw some kids playing basketball in one of the driveways when we drove in," Juliet said. "Matthew recognized one of them. From which class was it? Math or earth science?"

"Earth science," Matthew muttered.

Evan took out one of the root beers and held up a bottle opener with a raised eyebrow at Matthew, universal guy code for *do you want one?*

He opened the bottle and slid it across the counter to Matthew, Wild-West-saloon style. Matthew caught it like a pro. His smile was fleeting, but at least there'd been a smile.

"Do you want to see the rest of the house?"

"No." Matthew was determined to be stubborn.

"Juliet, do you want to see the house?"

"Maybe in a minute?"

That kind of wishy-washy statement was as uncharacteristic as her frequent apologies. Juliet was worried about something. Probably her son.

Matthew lived with a mother who loved him completely, but she'd dragged him from Georgia to Texas, and then she'd kissed someone who wasn't Daddy yesterday. Matthew was acting sullen and stubborn, but Evan guessed that was just how a sixth grader expressed anxiety.

Juliet tried again. "Honey, wouldn't you like to see—?"

Matthew cut her off. "Can we leave now?"

On the other hand, Matthew might just be acting like a jerk.

"That was rude, and you know it." Juliet spoke through clenched teeth.

Evan looked between mother and son and realized the tension was between them, not with him. At some point between leaving them at the hotel last night and opening the door to them today, Juliet and Matthew had had a falling-out.

He probably should stay out of it. He wasn't a parent. Juliet had eleven years of experience dealing with Matthew. Evan had less than forty-eight hours.

"Leave now to go do what?" he asked.

He couldn't stay out of it. No part of the past sixteen years as a leader had prepared him to stand and do nothing while problems sat in front of him, simmering. Besides, Evan had known he was going to be tested sooner rather than later.

Matthew gave him a ferocious frown but stayed silent. *I'm not your enemy, but let the battle begin.*

"You've got no homework. You already checked out a major theme park yesterday. It's going to be time for dinner soon enough. You've gotta eat, and I've got burgers you can put on the grill and cook however you like them, but instead, you want to leave. You must have something very cool to do."

"No."

A one-word answer. Still, it was an improvement over the silent glare, so Evan stayed on that path, because if Matthew wasn't happy, Juliet wasn't happy. Evan would consider this battle won when Matthew was as happy as Evan could make him. Somehow.

"What would be cool to do?" Evan began the process of uncorking the wine to cover the awkwardness of Matthew's silence. "When you had a Sunday free at Benning, what did you like to do?"

"Nothing."

"You'll like Fort Hood better, then. There are things to do here."

That earned him another frown. "I had things at Benning. I *have* things. Lots of things. Video games."

Oh, son, you are mine now. "Which video games?"

"*Minecraft. Lego Batman.* Stuff."

"I like *Minecraft.* All of the Legos are good. Juliet, you want a glass?"

"You like them?" Matthew asked.

"I think I could use a glass." Juliet matched his nonchalant tone, but the start of a smile touched her expression. She knew what Evan was up to.

He made a production out of pouring two glasses as he answered Matthew. "*Lego Avengers* is the newest one I've got. Do you play *Minecraft* on Xbox or PlayStation?"

Matthew just gaped at him, as if he'd never heard an adult speak those words.

"Or do you have the PC version?" Evan asked.

"I got an Xbox for Christmas, but it's still with our household goods." Matthew easily spouted military-speak like *household goods*, a true army brat, born and bred.

"Since you're not interested in seeing the house, help yourself to my Xbox. It's in the living room. Look for a small black box to the left of the TV that lets you select which input you want. I think it's set to PlayStation right now, so just switch it to Xbox, unless you want to try playing *Minecraft* on PlayStation. See if you like the controller better."

"You have them *both*?"

"Holler if you can't get it fired up."

"Cool." Matthew grabbed his root beer and made to bolt out of the kitchen, but Juliet caught him by the sleeve.

"Drink," she said. As Matthew put his bottle back on the counter, Juliet explained to Evan. "Drinks stay in the kitchen."

Evan started to say, *It's fine if he drinks it on the couch*, but he stopped himself. Juliet obviously had house rules, and this was going to be her house. He watched Matthew leave, glad to see some of the enthusiasm he'd had for the coasters returning. The enthusiasm was for Evan's gaming systems, not for Evan, but it was a start.

Juliet's wineglass still sat on the counter. Evan gave it a gentle clink with his. "Tough morning?"

"He's not adjusting well."

"Which means what? What happened this morning?"

"Our transient lodging is suddenly exactly where he wants to be. He refused to… Well, we just had a temper tantrum."

"*We* did? You did, too? Or was it just him?"

Juliet spun the stem of her glass. "I'm being serious."

"So am I. I assume tantrums include yelling. If you yelled this morning, too, then maybe you're feeling bad about it. I don't know how it works, honestly, so I'm asking."

"He refused to get dressed so that we could come here. I told him he was going to look really silly in pajamas, because we were going to stop at the Class Six store on the way to get some nice drinks." She flashed a look at Evan. "He knows I'll plunk his little butt in the car in his pajamas. He got dressed."

Ah, Juliet. You're so you. Evan tried to remain gravely parental. "The opposite of him voluntarily wearing a tie to impress you."

"Yes, exactly so."

"Like living with Dr. Jekyll and Mr. Hyde."

She studied the swirling red wine in her glass. "It's not as amusing as you make it sound."

"When we tell him today that this is his new house, that will help. Once he can have his things delivered and settle into his own bedroom, it'll be easier on him. He'll get into a routine."

Juliet stopped spinning her glass.

Evan realized he'd just told a mother how her son would react, as if he knew her child better than she did. "At least, that's what I think. What I hope."

"I think he's not adjusting to the idea of me having a friend, especially one I'm suddenly seeing every day. Maybe we shouldn't tell him anything today. He needs a little more time."

"Friday will be here before you know it. You've got to— *we've* got to let him know so he'll have time to adjust to the idea. You can't leave this to the last minute." *Can you?*

"Maybe we should wait until Thursday evening. If he's still in this mood…" She started swirling her glass again. "We can just go to the courthouse while he's at school. Maybe that would be better for him, or at least less embarrassing for me. I don't want to deal with a tantrum at the courthouse."

Evan studied her profile, beautiful Juliet, back in his life with lines of strain on her face. He could defer to her judgment about this, but would that make her happier?

All the responsibility for the decision would be on her shoulders. Evan would be no better than Rob by leaving everything up to her all the time.

They were going to be a team, starting now. "I think Matthew should be at the courthouse, regardless. Anything that's a big event in your life is a big event in his."

She nodded slowly. "It will change his life. It's only right that Matthew should be there for the—the courthouse. For the judge and the legalities. He should see what's involved."

Even felt a cold prickle of unease. "Like a field trip?"

"The formality of a government proceeding is something he understands, since he's grown up in the military."

"The wedding."

"What?"

"Your child should be there for the *wedding*. I don't think we need to resort to euphemisms like 'courthouse' and 'legalities.' 'Government proceeding' is downright clinical. We're talking about our wedding." He set his wine down and took her hands.

"Juliet," he began, but holding hands wasn't good enough. He drew her to him, dropping one of her hands to slide his arm around her waist. She moved into his arms as gracefully as she had when they'd danced under the moon. "It's our wedding. It doesn't have to be in a church with two hundred guests. You don't have to wear a white dress, and we don't have to spend a year planning it, but it will be our wedding."

She closed her eyes briefly, then blinked at him. "Wow. Sorry. It's just…when you say it like that…"

He waited.

"It's so real."

"Yeah," he said as gently as he could. "It's so real."

With the soothing theme music of *Minecraft* in the background, he kissed his bride.

"And please, don't be sorry. I don't want you to ever be sorry."

Chapter Nine

Their *wedding.*

Juliet followed Evan up the stairs as her mind reeled. *My wedding is this Friday.*

She'd only been thinking in terms of pacts. Deals. This driving need to secure something, to take control of some piece of her future. She'd been slowly sinking at Fort Benning during the three years she'd spent picking up the pieces. She was sick of being praised for being valiant and self-sacrificing for the sake of her child, as if it was acceptable to the whole world that her life sucked and she was only able to give Matthew enough time and attention to get by. There had to be a better life out there for her. She was missing something.

Or someone.

Evan had made lieutenant colonel below the zone, a year earlier than she had. During that year, she'd watched Matthew sinking, too. There was only so long even a child could keep their faith, and Juliet believed Matthew had started to admit to himself that his father was never coming back.

You're better off without him, Juliet had wanted to say, but Matthew couldn't know that, not unless he had a better father to compare Rob to. Juliet knew she was better off without Rob, because she knew there were better men out there. One in particular, and he was not at Fort Benning. She'd formally put in a request for Fort Hood.

She'd taken a calculated risk to find out if Evan remembered their pact, because it would mean stability for her son. Support for herself. She'd thought of practicalities.

But Evan had said *our wedding*, and suddenly she'd thought of hearts and flowers and promises, pretty gowns, optimism…romance.

She didn't feel like a bride. Not once as she'd managed all the army regulations to get her relocation and promotion in sync, not once as she'd imagined living with Evan, had she thought anything so girlishly glamorous as *I'll be a bride*.

They'd reached the top of the stairs. They were standing in a little hall. She heard Evan's voice, but her brain swirled with white lace and promises. Did she want them? Should she want them? Was it bad that she'd forgotten them?

"This is the first bedroom. Since it's the closest to the front door, I've been keeping some sports equipment here. The garage is like an oven most of the year. You can't keep leather baseballs and gloves in an oven."

Our wedding.

She followed him into the room like an automaton. Sports equipment was separated into piles along the bedroom's longest wall. The sight triggered a memory that broke through the haze. Evan had piled his baseball gear just like this in one corner of his dorm room, glove always draped over the end of the bat. He'd tossed everything else except his hard plastic batting helmet. That was placed right-side up every time, just as it sat now. Evan didn't want the top all scratched up. She was going to be the bride of a man she knew so well.

She held his hand as they left that room and went to the next.

"I have a spare bed in this one for guests, but we can move it. How many beds do you have coming?"

She cleared her throat. This was familiar ground. Household goods, permanent addresses. She'd thought this type of thing through. "Just two. Matthew's twin and my queen."

They walked together into the third bedroom, which was completely empty. The carpet had been vacuumed in a symmetrical pattern of lines. Juliet stopped just inside the door. "I hate to leave footprints in here. It's so clean and neat. Your entire house is so clean and neat. It would be a lot harder to keep it like this if you had two more people living here." *Warning, my friend. You can still back out.*

"I can't keep it this nice with just me living in it. Yesterday, while we were riding roller coasters, there may have been an entire team of maids in here."

"Yesterday? You didn't even know I was going to barge into your life Friday afternoon. How did you get a cleaning service lined up for Saturday morning?"

"A few phone calls, a neighbor with a key to let them in. I wanted you to be impressed with your new house. Did it work?"

He'd gone to so much trouble for his bride. "The house is really nice."

"I'll carry you over the doorstep on Friday."

It was so sweet. A wedding, a bride carried over a threshold, that first flush of infatuation. She'd give him her heart and feel so happy, bluebirds might as well flutter around her.

"And this is the master bedroom." Evan turned on the lights. A king-size bed dominated the room, its wood headboard modern and masculine. They would spend their wedding night in that bed, making love.

It was all so real now.

But it wouldn't last. He'd tell her she was beautiful and special, and he wouldn't be able to keep his hands off her. They'd have sex nearly every night for a month, and she'd believe it was true love that would last forever, but it was only sex. She'd be a little less beautiful as the months went on. Then, finally, she'd find out she wasn't special at all.

And it would kill her.

"I don't know about this," she said, sounding all breathy and shy, like the virgin bride she was not.

"About what?"

"I had so many things to take into consideration. I didn't really think about that part of the equation." She tried to shake off that haze of white lace and romantic expectations. There was a good reason she'd avoided bridal hopes this time around.

"Juliet, what's wrong? What equation?"

Get your act together. You knew this was going to be a factor. You can handle it. You've learned your lesson. It's not love. It's just sex.

But she was going to need time to keep the two separate, because with Evan, a long history of friendship and trust had to be taken into account. *Friends with benefits.* Other people slept with their friends and stayed just friends. They didn't fall in love. She could do it. She just needed a little time.

"I don't know that I can just move into your house and your—your bedroom, just like that. I have a hold on a house just two streets over. I could sign a nine-month lease. We don't have to rush."

"You picked out another house?"

"I needed a contingency plan. I didn't want Matthew to have to keep living out of a suitcase any longer than necessary. If you'd said no, then I was moving into a permanent residence this week anyway. I had to think of Matthew's needs."

"But I said yes."

She studied his bed a moment. "Matthew and I could each have our own bedroom here."

"No."

"At least at the beginning. At least for a few months. This is about being a family. I don't want to add distractions. Maybe after a few months…" She made the mistake of looking into her friend's achingly familiar, wonderfully unchanged, blue eyes. *Maybe after a few months, I'll be able to have sex with you without falling madly in love with you.*

He was studying her intently. "How do you see that arrangement playing out? Matthew gets all comfortable with us being housemates who live in our little bedrooms all in a row, and then one day Mommy just ups and moves into my bedroom? Or do you imagine that I'm going to sneak into your room at night and leave before Matthew wakes, until the day we get caught?"

"Like I said, I didn't really think about it. I'm focused on a stable family for Matthew."

"Matthew, again."

"Matthew, always. He has no one else."

"Neither do you."

"I'm an adult. He's a child. That's the difference."

"Families aren't built on marital celibacy. We're getting married and we're sharing a bed. That's a normal family, and that's what you want for Matthew, and that's what matters most. Isn't it?"

She couldn't bear the hard look on his face, the way his eyes narrowed as he looked at her with something too close to anger.

"Isn't it? This whole marriage is for Matthew's benefit, *isn't it*?"

"It's about us as a family. Three of us."

Silence fell. Her whole world was in the balance as she watched him gauging her, weighing her. Something in those blue eyes flickered.

"Yes. This marriage will begin a new family of three." Then his arm was around her waist, pulling her close as if he had the right. "But from the very beginning, you've been half of every kiss. Can you remember them? Go back, way back, to school. It started with kisses on the cheek, too many to count, too quick in passing, just friends. Good luck on the test, thanks for the ride, don't be late for the game."

A million kisses. A familiarity she hadn't fully appreciated until he was stationed thousands of miles away.

"But when it comes to real kisses, you and me, mouth on mouth, those you can count, Juliet."

He held her so close, they could have kissed. Instead, he looked into her eyes. "There was the first one, the kiss the night before our graduation. It was a farewell, or an awakening. A promise made. A promise we're keeping."

With every word, the chemistry between them built. She wasn't sure how. He only held her to him with one arm as he spoke, but his height or his size or the absolute authority in the way he spoke made her so very aware of the physicality of him, the reality of a man made of muscle and sinew, flesh and blood, a beating heart.

"Then the kiss in my office, your return to me. Everything was still there. Everything. The kiss in the hotel parking lot the next morning, just to be sure I hadn't dreamed you. At the amusement park later, relaxed and sweet. Patient, because we knew more private kisses were in our future. Are in our future."

She could hardly breathe. He held her, but she felt like he was laying her on his bed, undressing her, exposing her.

"A moment of selfish desire, that kiss in the front seat of your car. I didn't want to stop. I couldn't breathe, I wanted you so badly. You remember each one of those kisses, Juliet. You were half of every single one. This is going to be a real marriage. Celibacy won't be part of it, not from the very first day."

He finally kissed her, bending her back over his arm,

making her feel secure rather than unbalanced, as skill-ful as ever. His other hand traveled down her body in one sure stroke from her throat to her breast to her waist, as if he knew her body already, as if they were lovers who'd already shared every touch there was to share. She wanted it, every word, every kiss, every touch. She craved it, she loved it, she loved him, so much—

Too much.

I can't. Not again.

She pushed away and turned her back, frantic to get her bearings. She was standing in a friend's army quar-ters on a Sunday afternoon. She was wearing jeans and a sweater and comfy loafers. There was nothing magical to this, nothing mystical. Two adults who liked one another could have sex, could *enjoy* sex, without losing their heads and their hearts. As long as she didn't fall back into wish-ing for a fairy-tale love, it wouldn't hurt again when the passion faded and the love disappeared with it.

She took a deep breath and straightened her shoulders.

"You made a good point. We won't have separate beds. I'll—I'll do my best." She looked at the bed instead of him. "I'm just not very good at this."

"You said that before." In her peripheral vision, she saw him hold his arms out, palms up, baffled. "I don't know what that means. Are we talking about something... medical?"

That startled her into looking at him. "Nothing like that."

Tell him. You owe him.

"I'm not good at the whole friends with benefits thing. I think friendship is better without sex. And sex shouldn't get confused with friendship. Or kill it."

He was quiet again, trying to figure her out, she just knew it.

"Honest," she said. "That's it."

"I guess it's a good thing we're not going to be friends with benefits, then."

"We're not?"

Did she sound disappointed? Probably, because Evan's lips quirked in a bit of a smile.

"We're not. We've never been friends with benefits, and we're not going to start now. We're going to be husband and wife." He took her in his arms again and kissed her, their sixth—seventh?—real kiss. She'd lost count.

He read her mind. "We're going to kiss so many times, we'll lose count, because you aren't going to be a friend I shack up with now and then. You are going to be my wife, whom I live with and sleep with and kiss every day. My one and only."

The sadness swamped her. Yes, that was what they'd go to the courthouse and say. *My one and only, forsaking all others*—and it would be true for a little while. When it ended, she'd be ready this time. She would be on guard.

She wanted to tell Evan that they needed to be careful not to destroy their friendship, so they would still have something for the long term, but Matthew came up the stairs, calling her name.

"Mom? Where'd you go?"

As she stepped into the hall, she glanced at Evan one more time. He was watching her with an expression she rarely saw on his face. He looked sad.

So maybe she didn't need to explain anything to him at all.

Evan had always known Rob would make a lousy husband for any woman.

He would never forgive himself for letting Rob become a lousy husband for Juliet.

He'd known she was marrying a man who wasn't good enough for her, but he hadn't known, hadn't really understood, just how much damage a lousy husband could leave behind.

Evan smacked the lever of the kitchen faucet and shook the water off his hands. As he punched the ground beef into hamburger patties, he looked out the kitchen window to his backyard. Juliet was throwing a Frisbee to her son.

Just looking at her made Evan's heart bleed. It had been even worse for her than he'd imagined, when he'd let himself imagine her life at all.

Rob had cost Juliet money, soaking her for a shocking amount of alimony, unconscionable when he was an employable, able-bodied man who'd cheated on his wife multiple times.

Evan threw the patties onto a platter, raw meat hitting the stoneware with force.

Rob had cost Juliet friendships, too, by leaving every responsibility on her shoulders so she had no time or energy left to make friends. Her son couldn't remember her ever going out with a friend. She'd forgotten how to have fun, because she hadn't had the time or opportunity to have fun.

Worst of all, this incredibly appealing, physically fit woman tossing a Frisbee in his yard doubted her own inherit sexiness. She didn't trust herself. Her body responded to his touch, but her instinct was to keep her distance. Was that Rob's fault as well?

It had to be, because Juliet had liked sex before she'd married Rob.

How the hell do I know that?

Juliet leaped to make a one-handed catch, a sliver of her bare waist showing as her sweater rode up with the reach, and the memories came quickly: Juliet dancing at a party in a dress that bared her middle, a dress she wore with confidence. Juliet in the hallway after class, talking to a guy she thought was cute, flirting like a champ. Evan could picture her laughing at juvenile jokes about sex positions or props. He could remember her telling bad jokes herself.

One morning, he'd caught her making the so-called walk of shame. He'd been going out for a run, stretching first on the steps to the seniors-only dorm. She'd been coming toward him on the sidewalk, head down, wearing a little black dress at seven in the morning, barefoot. Her fancy shoes had been in her right hand, just one more instance where he'd never actually seen her walk in high heels, not until she'd walked into his office forty-eight hours ago.

That morning, he'd relished the chance to tease her. "Good morning, Miss Grayson."

She'd looked up, startled and guilty as hell. Hair a mess. Makeup smudged. "Oh. Evan. Hi. Uh, you're going out for a run?"

"Nice morning for it. You're out for a walk, too?"

"Yes. I'm done now. Just heading back to my room."

He'd kept his tongue firmly in cheek. "Shoes hurting your feet after your workout?"

"Oh. Uh, they're Tana's."

"I see."

"So, I'm just carrying them back to the dorm for her, because…"

"Because?"

"Because I borrowed them. Last night. It's morning, so I have to return them, and…am I fooling you at all?"

"You are stone-cold busted."

She'd dissolved into giggles, and he'd laughed at her and with her, both. He'd hopped off the steps to start his run. She'd given him a shove off the sidewalk when he passed her.

He'd just turned around, jogging backward. "By the way, nice dress. Really."

The memory made him want to smile. It was odd that the thought of Juliet with Rob destroyed him, but the memory of Juliet carrying her high heels after a night with her college boyfriend didn't.

He picked up the platter of raw hamburgers and headed out to his patio and the grill he'd spent his money on, because he hadn't had a family to buy park tickets and slushies for.

Juliet carrying her high heels...

The only emotion that stirred in his chest was affection. Maybe he didn't feel jealous now because he hadn't felt jealous then. That morning had been in the fall of their senior year. They'd been friends, so he'd felt no more jealousy than he would have felt for any of his other friends, for Connor or Wayne or Tana sleeping over at someone else's place, someone they liked, someone they wanted to be with.

He hadn't felt possessive toward Juliet then. Not yet. Not until that night in May, when he'd realized he was going to lose her to the United States Army, and he'd wondered why he'd never kissed her before.

Evan set the platter down and fired up the grill. The important point was that Juliet hadn't thought she was bad in bed, that was for sure. Not until she'd been married to Rob.

Evan's fault. Rob was Evan's fault. The guilt was going to kill him.

But first, he was going to make sure Juliet remembered how to have fun.

In bed.

Chapter Ten

After the burgers and before the s'mores, Evan saw more of the damage Rob had left in his wake.

Juliet wasn't the only one who'd learned to shield herself. So had Matthew. The best mother in the world still couldn't fill the hole an uncaring father left. The evening was revealing glimpse after glimpse of that hole.

It was too cold to sit outside after the sun went down, but Evan owned an outdoor space heater, a stainless-steel tower that was a foot taller than he was. He'd lit its central flame, which shot up a glass tube, providing an arresting visual effect as well as radiant heat.

"No waaay," Matthew had said.

"Impressive." Juliet had laughed at him. "Heating the outdoors. Such an ultimate dude thing to buy."

He'd winked at her. "Man toys."

Matthew had said, "Yeah, we don't have one." *Because we don't have a man.*

Was that his childish rationale? They didn't have a man toy because they didn't have a man?

Evan had decided he was reading too much into it. Then Matthew had patted the metal tower. "This would be a good present for my dad. He'd want one for Christmas. Did you get it for Christmas?"

That damned hole sucked all kinds of happiness away from that boy, even the pleasure of an eye-catching flame.

Evan was certain now that Juliet was hoping he'd be

able to fill that hole, while the two of them played friends with benefits. He could see that her experience with Rob was shaping part of the equation. She was afraid the sex would become lovemaking. She was scared to fall in love.

Evan didn't like it, but it made sense to him, knowing what a bastard she'd married. The part that didn't make sense was how Juliet had come to the conclusion that Evan would make a good substitute father. They'd had so little contact since college. What had he done as a nineteen- and twenty-year-old that translated to father material in her mind?

He added another log to the iron firepit he used in the winter. Between the heater and the firepit, he'd turned his patio into a place where a man could look at a fire, sit and think. Tonight, it was a place where a man could make s'mores with a kid who gave him a lot to think about and no peace to think it in.

Maybe Juliet thought of Evan as a potential father because he'd said, *Kids don't scare me.* He'd said it on that college green, and he'd said it again in his office. It was true.

Juliet had said, *That's because you've never lived with one*, which was probably even more true.

The one he was going to live with accidentally set his marshmallow on fire. He blew it out more quickly than he had the first time he'd burned one.

"That's still good to eat," Evan said. "You're getting better at this."

"I don't like them burned."

Evan held out his graham cracker. "I do. Slap it here."

Another marshmallow was speared and began its transformation to charcoaled near-inedibility.

Evan sat back and devoured the s'more. "So what else do you like to do besides video games and grilling?"

Matthew had enjoyed the grilling. Evan had let him flip

the burgers. Only one had landed on the patio—and then the trash—a small sacrifice to teach a kid a new skill. Matthew had forgotten to pout for an entire half hour.

That half hour was up, and so was Matthew's guard. He didn't answer Evan.

Juliet answered for him as she continued to skip the graham crackers and the chocolate to eat one perfectly toasted marshmallow after another. "Matthew is on his school's baseball team. They've had their first three practices."

"I hate baseball," Matthew said.

"You loved baseball at Fort Benning."

"That was T-ball. It was dumb, baby stuff. That's why Dad didn't come to the games."

There was that hole again. *Rob, you bastard.*

"I don't think that's why, honey. He moved to Nevada. It's too far to drive." As Juliet began toasting another marshmallow, she and Evan exchanged a look, a silent acknowledgment that they both knew Rob wouldn't have made the time for a T-ball game regardless of where he lived. Matthew's conclusion about his father's absence was actually correct, but how was Juliet supposed to tell him so? Nevada sounded better than complete disinterest.

Evan was done toasting marshmallows. He sat back in his Adirondack chair and used his marshmallow stick to take a few one-handed baseball swings, liking the sound as the stick swiped the air. "So, what are they playing in sixth grade if it's not T-ball? Coach pitch?"

That was the next step, if memory served. The players were too young to pitch accurately, so the team's adult coach stood on the mound and gave his or her players the easiest pitches possible.

"No, I'm playing real baseball. Real pitchers from the other team try to strike you out, like the major leagues. It's how adults do it."

Evan nodded. "That makes the game very different."

"I mean, maybe Dad wouldn't be bored at a real pitching game. You're going to tell him where we live now, right, Mom? Can you tell him I'm not playing baby T-ball anymore?"

Juliet's voice was very calm and even. "I'll send the information to the bank when we get a permanent address."

"And you'll tell him about the baseball?"

"I can try, but I can't promise he'll get the message, and I can't promise he'll come to Texas if he does."

Evan used his stick to tap the arm of Juliet's chair lightly. *I'm here. I'm getting all this. I see the problem.*

Matthew tried to blow out the fire on his marshmallow, but that one had burned too quickly to be saved. It plopped on the patio. "Sorry."

"It doesn't hurt concrete," Evan said.

"You have to make him get my message, Mom." Matthew put another marshmallow on his stick and glared at Juliet, which had to hurt her. "Make the bank give him my message."

Evan sat forward. "You're old enough to know it's not your mom's fault if your dad doesn't visit. It's not your fault, either. Your dad is an adult and you are a kid, so whether or not he decides to come to Texas isn't something you can make happen. You can't force an adult to do something, even if you think it would be great."

Matthew just watched his next marshmallow go up in flames. This time, he didn't make any attempt to save it. It plopped into the firepit. "Dad wouldn't see me play if he came, anyway. I'll be on the bench, because I suck. I only played the stupid baby leagues at Benning, and everyone here has already done coach pitch."

Evan studied Matthew's self-pitying pout in the firelight. "Sounds like you suck because you haven't practiced enough."

"Evan!"

He tapped Juliet's chair and sent her a reassuring wink. Juliet was a good mama bear—nobody could say her baby sucked—but in this case, Evan hoped she'd give him a chance to reach Matthew.

"Here's the thing about baseball. Whatever level your skills are at today, you can improve them if you practice. If you suck at batting, but you keep going to batting practice, you won't suck as much. If you can only throw a ball ten yards, and you practice throwing balls every single day, you'll be able to throw farther than ten yards, guaranteed."

"Pete Gomez can throw it from left field all the way to home plate."

"What's Pete Gomez have to do with whether or not you can throw a ball ten yards?"

"He gets to play every game. The other kids told me." Matthew was still feeling sorry for himself.

"Sounds like the coach is putting players where he thinks they'll help the team win."

"The coach is his dad."

There was that hole again. Evan steeled himself to sound unaffected. "I can't help you make another player suck, but I can take you out to practice your catching and throwing. You can't make another player suck, either, but you can control how much you work on your own skills."

"I'll get better than Pete?"

"Who cares? You'll get better than you are now."

Matthew perked up a little. "Okay, yeah. And since you and my dad are friends, you can tell him when I get good."

"We were on the same team, but that was sixteen years ago. We never run into each other." Evan wished Juliet had never said he and Rob were friends. That little untruth was going to come back and bite him.

Juliet tried again. "Honey, your father still lives in Nevada, no matter what kind of baseball you play or how good you get at it. Nevada is still very far away."

The disappointment on a child's face was too easy to read, too pitiful to see. Evan rubbed his chest. It wasn't just Juliet who stirred up every emotion. The two of them— *jeez*.

Evan wanted to cut through Matthew's useless desire to please an absentee dad. It gave Rob too much control over him. "Let's just assume your dad won't show up this season."

Mother and son looked at him, startled. He turned to get out another graham cracker and chocolate bar, keeping the vibe casual, so Matthew wouldn't put his guard back up. Between the s'mores and the sundaes, he was going to gain ten pounds trying to talk to this child.

"If you knew for sure he wasn't coming, would you still want to play?" Evan paused to give that question a moment to sink in. The candy bar wrapper made a pleasant crinkling sound as he opened it. "I like the sound the ball makes when it hits a glove. Walking out on that diamond should give you a feeling of anticipation, like standing in line for a roller coaster. You dig your cleats into that orange clay by home plate, ready to bat, and it feels a little scary, right? Exciting, too. If you like that feeling, then you should play this season, no matter who sits in the stands. But if putting on a glove or sitting with your team in the dugout sounds boring, then we should check out things you might like better. It's your call."

Matthew and Juliet watched the fire. Evan watched them. He'd done it again, wading into a situation as if he knew the child, while the real parent was sitting right beside him. He'd just given someone else's son permission to quit a sport.

That little speech had come easily, probably because he'd given it a dozen times to privates who were deciding whether to reenlist after their initial two-year commitment to the army was up. It was a question he'd first heard his platoon sergeant ask a soldier in their platoon, back when Evan was a brand-new lieutenant. *I know a two-thousand-dollar reenlistment bonus sounds like a lot, but if that wasn't being offered, would you still want to be a soldier?*

It was good advice, time-tested advice—and it took Rob out of the equation.

Matthew's marshmallow caught fire again. Evan leaned forward with his graham cracker and chocolate. "Put it here."

"It's on fire."

"I know."

Matthew set the blackened marshmallow on the chocolate, and Evan used the second graham cracker to scrape it off the stick, smother the flames and turn it into a sandwich, a million-calorie, messy sandwich of pure sugar.

He'd already eaten two. He handed it to Matthew, as if that had been the plan all along.

Matthew took a huge bite and had barely swallowed it before he made his announcement. "I like baseball a lot. I'm going to stay on the team."

More emotions, warm emotions, surfaced. "That sounds like a good decision. How hard do you want to work to get better at it than you are now? If someone offers to give you extra practice time, are you going to take it?"

"You mean you?"

"I mean me."

Matthew scrutinized him. *Looking for loopholes, kid? There's no trickery here.*

"Okay. I'll practice with you."

"We'll play some catch in the street tomorrow, before dinner." With that, he'd also settled the question of whether or not they'd be having dinner together again. He hauled himself out of the deep chair and stretched, feeling like he'd just hit a home run. "Next question. I'm going to get some wine and sit out here and talk to your mom. Do you want to stay and listen, or would you rather play *Lego Avengers*?"

"Avengers." Matthew jumped out of his chair and beat Evan to the sliding glass door, opening it with sticky hands that left marshmallow goo on the glass.

The smudged, child-sized handprint was half the size of his hand. It gave Evan pause. He'd wanted to be a family man, hadn't he? He'd dreamed of it for years, ever since that tailgate. That handprint was proof that his impossible wish had come true. *My wife. My child.* Maybe it was messier than he'd expected, but it was real.

For the second day in a row, Evan appreciated one of life's perfect moments.

He stepped into the house and called for Matthew in the living room. "Hey, Matthew. Wash those hands before you touch my game controllers."

He almost laughed. He'd sounded like such a dad just then.

Evan walked into the kitchen to get a glass of wine for his bride.

"That was very devious of you."

Juliet took both wineglasses from Evan, then waited as he pulled his chair close to hers. "You got him to take ownership of his baseball season, you got him to agree to spend quality time with his mother's evil kissing-friend, and you got him here for dinner tomorrow night before he could remember to object."

Evan's smile seemed a little reserved.

"It was a triple play," she said.

He took a breath as if he was going to say something, but he hesitated, then said, "I'm happy to help."

Juliet wondered what he hadn't said.

They sat back in their chairs. The fire crackled. The space heater hissed quietly. Through the glass door, the sound effects of a video game were mercifully muted.

"I'm happy to help whether we're married or not," Evan said. "You don't have to marry me to have me spend time with Matthew, okay?"

Her world went silent, except for the pounding of her heart.

"What are you saying?" But he'd spoken plainly. They didn't need to be married. He'd gotten a taste of Matthew's phase. He'd seen Juliet in full motherhood mode. Now marriage wasn't so necessary, after all.

"I'm saying I'd spend time with Matthew even if you didn't want to sleep in my bed, to be blunt about it. I want that to be clear between us."

What had she missed over s'mores? Too much talk about Rob? That would be enough to make any potential second husband have second thoughts.

"Are you—? Do you—?" She couldn't breathe. This was her fault, all her fault. It had nothing to do with Matthew's fixation on Rob; Evan had just said he'd help Matthew no matter what. It was about *her.*

She'd freaked out by his king-size bed. Evan didn't think she would be any good in bed, or he didn't think she wanted to have sex with him at all.

He was backing off.

"Are you volunteering to be Matthew's coach or something?"

"I suppose I could, if they were shorthanded."

She'd ruined everything. He was going to mentor her son, but he didn't need to be married to her. *But I want so very badly to be married to him.*

"That's not what Matthew needs." She didn't recognize her own voice—neither did Evan. He was looking at her in surprise. "He needs you. All the time, for a million different reasons. He needs to live with you, so I can see you every day. I don't think I could stand it if you were only his coach. I want so much more with you." *Oh, God.*

What am I saying? "With him. I want so much…with you and him. And me."

"Juliet? Hey—"

"I wanted—I wanted *us*. I wanted us to be a family." Her lungs couldn't seem to inhale.

"Yes, I know. I know—*Juliet*." Evan caught her wine-glass before she knew it had slipped from her fingers, able to do so because he was crouched on his haunches in front of her. When had he moved from his chair?

She was freaking out again. She covered her face with her hands.

"Shh, Juliet. It's okay. We're going to be a family, yes. Definitely, yes. Come here." He tugged on her wrists as he stood. "Come here."

I'm sorry I'm so scared. I'm not like Juliet-from-College anymore.

But Evan was using her wrists to draw her arms around his waist. Then he folded her in a bear hug.

It had been sixteen years since she'd had one of Evan's bear hugs. It felt like some kind of Pavlovian response, a forgotten reflex, but she shuddered as a sense of safety flooded through her, quieting even more nerves than she'd known were jangling. She burrowed into him. She could breathe again.

"I'm an idiot, Juliet. I just said something that had the exact opposite effect of what I was trying to say. I wanted to tell you that I wasn't marrying you because of Matthew."

"He's my baby. He's a good kid. Why wouldn't you marry me because of my baby?"

"I wouldn't. I would." He squashed her tightly. "I don't mean I'm not marrying you. You said yesterday that when men are nice to Matthew, it means they are trying to get into your pants. Those were your exact words. Do you remember?"

She nodded into the side of his throat.

"Okay, so when I said I was happy to help with Matthew whether we were married or not, I meant that I didn't want you to think the only reason I was offering to play catch or make s'mores was because you were agreeing to sleep with me. I'm not pretending that I'm interested in him because I want to get into your pants. I'm interested in him because I'm interested in him."

She scowled, even as she pressed her cheek into the bulk of his shoulder muscle. "That's not what you said. You said you weren't marrying me because of him. You wanted that to be very clear. Those were your exact words."

"I know. I hope this turns into something we can laugh about at some point."

He kissed her forehead like he was her friend, her brotherly buddy. "I wanted to make it clear that it works both ways. I don't want you to sleep with me because you think that's the reason I'm helping out with Matthew. I don't want... I don't want to be *paid* that way."

"I wasn't thinking that. Honest."

"I have this friend. He and his wife barely tolerate each other, but he said they stay together for the sake of their child. It sounds miserable. Maybe that works for some people, but I don't want to be married just to keep two adults in one house for a child."

"I tried it. For Matthew's sake, I stayed with Rob even after I knew that he was never going to be a good husband. I can't—" She couldn't help the sudden tears in her eyes, but she refused to sob over her ex-husband. "I can't do that again."

"And yet, you said this was all about Matthew. So be careful. I don't want you to do that again, either."

She rested against him, soaking up his attention and his warmth and everything that was Evan Stephens. She loved...this feeling. It had nothing to do with her child.

She wanted to keep this feeling forever. She wanted to keep Evan forever.

"I meant I can't go through a divorce again. When I divorced Rob, I lost a guy who'd let me down. Our relationship was a series of pleasant dates that seemed to be growing into something more, so I married him. When I divorced him, that was what I lost, just this one person I'd dated and spun hopeful romantic fantasies about.

"He'd never been my friend for years, never friends with every one of my friends. I'd never relied on him for anything except perfect dates at perfect little places. He'd never fought with me, either, not once about anything before we married. He hadn't been *important* to me before we started dating. But you, Evan, *you*—" Her breath hitched. "If I divorced you, I'd lose everything. I couldn't do it."

Evan was quiet for a long time. She kept her face smooshed against his shoulder, her forehead pressed against his throat.

Eventually, he dropped another kiss on top of her head. "Well, that's convenient. I have no intention of getting divorced, either. So, let's get married. We'll sleep together for reasons that have absolutely nothing to do with a sixth grader."

She did look up at that. "What kind of reason?"

"How about because it will be fun?"

"Fun?"

"Because it's going to feel good?" His smile started slowly, more of a twinkle in his eye. "Maybe because we've secretly wondered, for a longer time than we'd ever admit to each other, just how good it would feel together."

"Oh."

He captured that *oh* in a swift kiss. "Or, maybe, we should sleep together because we're old enough now that we *know* it will feel insanely good to sleep together."

Then he didn't have to capture her answer with a kiss, because she kissed him first, luxuriating in the freedom to kiss him like a lover, not a friend. She could kiss this gorgeous, strong, blue-eyed man as lustfully as she wanted, for as long as she desired.

Or until the sliding glass door opened behind her.

"*Mom!* Are you guys *kissing* again?"

Chapter Eleven

Sunday night had ended in something of a debacle.

A sixth grader's fury was no small thing, which Evan had been humbled to learn. Juliet had nerves of steel. He'd admired them, he'd admired *her*, as she'd managed to get a muttered *thank you for the s'mores* from her child as they left, because *we thank people for their hospitality and it doesn't matter who they kiss you still owe them the courtesy and Evan made you s'mores so stop acting like they were poison, for Pete's sake.* Then she'd marched her child to her car. That had been the end of that. Evening over.

Evan hadn't known whether to laugh or cry.

Monday morning began with the roundtable led by Evan's commander, Colonel Oscar Reed, the brigade commander and Provost Marshal. Since Colonel Reed was running the meeting, Evan indulged in a bit of daydreaming, looking around the table and wondering if any of these officers could have handled a sixth grader's tantrum as well as his future wife had.

Captain Tom Cross, one of the four company commanders under Evan's command, had recently announced that his wife was expecting a baby. They'd only been married a year or so, and this baby would be their first. They still had eleven long years to go before they could compete with Juliet in the parenting Olympics.

Perhaps Major Aiden Nord, Evan's operations officer, could have survived. He had twin girls, but they were only preschoolers. Still, there were two of them, which might total up to one sixth-grade boy.

"If that's everything, ladies and gentlemen, we can wrap this up," Colonel Reed said, finally.

That was Evan's cue. "Sir, I do have one more thing."

"Go ahead."

Nothing to be nervous about.

"It's an announcement. I'm engaged." Evan cleared his throat. "To be married."

Smooth—as if there were any other kind of engagement announcement.

The shock only lasted a second. Then congratulations came at him from around the table.

Colonel Reed sat back in his chair. "Well, well, well. I have to say, this is a surprise. A man stays single as long as you have, and you have to figure he's escaped the ball and chain for life. When is the happy occasion?"

"This Friday."

Colonel Reed didn't hide his surprise. "This has been in the works a while, then. Did I miss Linda's ring at the Valentine's Day ball? You should have announced it there."

Well, crap. Evan had brought Linda to the brigade's annual ball just two weeks ago. Everyone had met her. Everyone had felt like they already knew her, too, since she appeared on their televisions every evening.

"Congratulations," Aiden Nord said. "She's really something. Bet they'll show a clip of your ceremony on the news. They showed the sportscaster's proposal."

"I'm not marrying Linda."

That got a moment of silence. No one was getting up and leaving, Evan noticed. This was getting too juicy, and a roomful of military commanders loved getting the inside scoop on anything that was happening. In other words, they loved gossip.

Major Nord apologized. "I just assumed, sir, since the ball was so recent—"

"I understand. Linda is a very nice woman. She just wasn't...the one."

"So, if it's not the weather girl, who is the one?" Colonel Reed asked, making air quotes when he said *the one*.

"Lieutenant Colonel Juliet Grayson. Military Intelligence. She just PCSed to Fort Hood a couple of weeks ago." He wasn't smiling like a schoolboy, was he? No—but he probably had some dopey grin on his face.

"An officer, eh? And she didn't mind her fiancé taking the weather girl to the ball while she was unpacking moving boxes?" Colonel Reed was as nosy as hell. He was also one of the best men Evan had served with.

"I didn't know she'd arrived at Hood yet, sir."

More murmurs. That had sounded bad.

"We weren't engaged then." He paused, then figured *what the hell*, and flashed a bit of his cocky, college-star, home-run smirk. "She didn't ask me until last Friday."

The whole table loved that. So did Evan. Juliet had come and gotten him. That was going to make him grin for the rest of his life.

"Better and better," Colonel Reed said. "This is the best darned gossip since— Actually, now that I look around, you all are a bunch of sappy romantics. Let's see... Stephens has only a week from the engagement to the wedding. How about you, Major Nord? You can top that, can't you?"

"I'm still engaged, sir. No wedding date yet."

Colonel Reed waved his hand impatiently. "Yes, yes, but there was something in there..."

"I met India and proposed to her seven days later."

"That was it."

Down the table, Tom Cross coughed into his hand. "Amateurs."

Everyone laughed at that. Tom had met and married his wife the same day—in Vegas.

Colonel Reed wasn't done with Evan yet. "What's your story? How long did it take you to pop the question, or should I say, how long did it take your fiancée to pop the question to you?"

"She didn't have to ask me on Friday, to be wholly accurate. I did propose first. I knew her for three years in college, so it took me three years before I asked her to marry me on the night before our graduation. Last Friday, she walked into my office and said yes."

And with that truth bomb dropped, Evan gathered up his papers and left the boardroom, grinning so hard, he gave up and called it a smile.

Monday evening was as perfect as any family could want.

Matthew's grudge against Evan for kissing his mother a second time—the horror—didn't last long once they started throwing the baseball in the street in front of Evan's house. Before the first toss, Evan had adjusted the laces on Matthew's glove, which had earned him points, and then he'd put on his own well-worn glove, which Matthew thought was even more cool. Evan had let him choose one of his ball caps to wear, to keep the setting sun out of their eyes. He was trying to give Matthew a sense of control when his world had changed beyond his control. Maybe choosing a ball cap was trivial, but it didn't hurt to try.

For half an hour, they threw the ball to one another. Evan demonstrated the proper form, like placing a hand over the ball the second it hit the glove, so it wouldn't bounce out. Matthew really liked that one. He told Evan he'd dropped two balls last week, so the coach had moved him from second base to the outfield.

Evan demonstrated how to shrug it off. "So, we'll work

on catching fly balls this week. That's what you'll need to be able to catch as an outfielder."

"We can do that?"

"Yep. We'll start with a tennis ball, because it can be easy to get hit in the face when you're beginning."

"I know, right? It's scary when the ball just falls out of the sky onto you."

Baseball was followed by spaghetti and meatballs, and that was followed by all three of them playing a Lego video game together. The game required them to work together as a team to get their characters through an obstacle course. When they made it to the end, after nearly an hour of shrieking and laughing and calling out instructions to each other—*Jump off the ledge! Just jump!*—they all sat back on the couch, exhausted.

Matthew was in the middle. Juliet looked at Evan over her son's head. He knew exactly what she was thinking, so he nodded in approval. The timing would never get better.

Juliet smoothed down a piece of Matthew's hair. "Honey, I have some really big news to tell you."

And that was the end of the perfect family evening. Monday ended much the same as Sunday had, with Matthew's fury a palpable thing and Juliet's nerves of steel allowing her to stay calm as she marched her son out to her car.

Evan hoped Tuesday night would end differently.

Just how long did a phase last, anyway?

Evan left his headquarters as early as he thought he decently could.

He was the boss. He could leave whenever he wanted, but he was rarely the first to leave.

He was also a family man now. Evan was anxious to be home when Juliet got off work and came over with Matthew, so they'd have time to throw the baseball again before dark. It might help after the drama that had followed their big news.

I have to live with him for the rest of my life? Matthew had wailed. But that had been Monday. This was Tuesday.

Once Evan got home and changed into some track pants to play catch, it became very obvious, very quickly, that one day had not cooled down Matthew's emotions one degree.

Evan knew this, because the little skunk was trying to bean him with a baseball.

Fortunately, Matthew couldn't throw worth a damn. He was throwing with all the force he could muster, though, and if a ball went wild, somebody's car might get dinged.

Evan threw the ball to Matthew, using just enough force that Matthew could handle the impact when the ball hit his glove. The ball hit his glove because Evan threw with the kind of accuracy one developed by playing ball from childhood through intercollegiate championships.

Evan tapped his chest. "Right here, Matt. This is where you're aiming."

Matthew hurled the ball, letting his eyes close as he grunted with effort. The ball went far to Evan's left. It took every bit of speed, every bit of muscle memory Evan had, to make that catch before the ball hit his neighbor's car. He made the catch. He still had the skill, but he got no satisfaction from using it tonight.

He held the ball in his hand, then tossed it back into his own glove, where it landed with that satisfying *thunk*. Tossed it. Caught it. He turned back to look at Matthew, gauging him while he kept tossing the ball, catching it, letting the sound soothe him as he decided how to handle a miserable boy who was testing him past an acceptable limit. Physical harm was out of bounds. Always.

Toss, *thunk*. Toss, *thunk*.

Matthew shifted from foot to foot until the anticipation got to him. "Aren't you going to throw it?"

Evan assumed a correct throwing stance. "Hold out

your glove. Keep your arm straight out to the side. That's it. I'm going to throw full force. Keep that arm out, so if you can't catch the ball, it won't knock you over."

"Wait. What?" Matthew started to drop his arm. Held it out again, confused. "You're going to do what?"

Evan dropped his stance and walked in a little closer. Not too close. He wasn't trying to tower over Matthew and make him feel helpless. "You don't want me to throw the ball at you as hard as I can?"

Matthew shook his head *no* immediately. He kept his arm straight out to the side, the glove as far away from his body as he could get it.

"Then what makes you think I want you to throw the ball at *me* as hard as you can?"

"You're big. It's not like I can hurt you."

"Sure you can." *You already have. You won't let me sit at the cool kids' table with you.* "I've got a nose that can get broken, same as anyone of any size. If you don't hurt me, then you might hurt that car over there. I don't think General Snow will appreciate it."

Matthew dropped his arm. He looked at the toe of his sneaker as he kicked at the street.

"We're out here to get better at baseball, maybe even enjoy ourselves a little before it gets dark and you have to go in to start your homework. This out-of-control clown act wastes our time, so here's the deal. You know that you can't control an adult. We talked about that yesterday. You can't make me stay out here and teach you, right?"

Matthew nodded silently at the street.

"It works both ways. I can't force you to stand out here and catch a ball, either, can I?"

That stopped Matthew's toe-scuffing for a moment.

"So, we each have to make a decision. Go inside now, or stay and practice. My decision is that I want to play catch with you. What's your decision?"

Matthew looked up at him warily. "Play catch."

Two whole words. Evan felt ridiculously relieved. The emotions these Graysons were churning up...*jeez.*

"All right. Keep your eyes open this time and concentrate on your target. What's always your target, every throw?"

"My teammate's chest."

"Correct." Evan rubbed his chest. "You hit me right here, kid. Right here."

Chapter Twelve

"Because I said so."

Juliet sent her son back to the living room to finish his homework now that supper was over. He stomped away with mutiny in his eyes.

She looked down at the sink, at the white suds that hid her hands, as she listened to Matthew's stomping end with the scrape of a chair. He'd sat back down at the table then. She kept her hands in the water.

"I am so sorry."

Beside her, Evan paused in the middle of drying a frying pan. "I don't think the dishes are going to forgive you. You've been scrubbing with a vengeance."

She couldn't laugh. She wanted to, but that just wasn't how life worked. "I was apologizing to you. Evan, I'm so—"

"You really need to stop apologizing. You keep saying you're sorry when you haven't done anything wrong." He said it lightly as he spun the dish towel like pizza dough and caught it. "You're too slow. I'm drying faster than you're washing."

Juliet was glad that the floor plan of the house was a little outdated, not truly an open concept design. The kitchen was mostly walled off from the living room. They could talk without Matthew eavesdropping or glaring them down.

Matthew, of course, was the topic. "I'm sorry you have to put up with my son's attitude. I knew better. I should have waited until he was in a better frame of mind before introducing you, so you two wouldn't start off on the wrong foot. I knew I should have waited."

"Waited to do what?"

"Waited to let you know I'd come to Fort Hood, that I'd been promoted, because…" She looked up at him.

He blinked at her innocently.

She knew that innocent face. The pest was *teasing* her. Honestly, it was like being nineteen again.

"Are you seriously going to make me spell it out?" She gave a knife a quick, soapy swipe, rinsed it and tossed it into the drain board.

Evan smiled at being caught, the same sexy and charming smile he'd always had. Maybe sexier, because he wasn't nineteen. No longer Mr. Casanova. He was this man with responsibilities—and the shoulders to carry them. She watched the muscles of his shoulders move as he picked up the knife and began drying it.

He took his time. "The deal was 'when you get promoted to lieutenant colonel.' It wasn't 'when you get promoted unless you have a preteen in the middle of a tough phase.'"

"Preexisting children." She'd made him laugh with that term.

"Preexisting children do not nullify the pact." He seemed so relaxed as he put the knife away, as if the last time he'd done dishes with her had been yesterday instead of a lifetime ago, after a party at Tana's new off-campus apartment. Falling back into their old rhythm of washing and drying and talking was as easy as riding a bicyc— No. She wasn't going to go there.

"Cheer up," Evan said. "Tonight's dinner was not that tragic. I'm fine with giving Matthew some space to get his sulk on. He'll come around when he gets bored of pouting in silence all by himself."

She washed a wineglass and thought that over. It was

simple, but it was probably true. Somehow, Evan had gotten not only sexier but wiser. The wiser part just made him sexier.

"That's a good point." Since this sexy Evan was still Evan, she could tease him back. "I don't know if you are a genius at parenting, or if you're just too dumb and inexperienced to know what's what."

"Do I get to choose which one?"

"No. Don't even think about snapping that dish towel at my butt."

He looked startled. "How did you know? What is that, some kind of motherhood spider sense? Is it one of those pregnancy side effects?"

"If I told you, my motherhood license would be revoked, and I'd be kicked out of the club."

He was all smiles, so pleased with her. If he wasn't careful, she'd get addicted to that approval and start making wisecracks to him all the time. It felt really, really good to hang out with someone and not stress about every little thing.

She was washing the second wineglass when Evan swooped in and kissed her, quick. "You're a great mom, you know. You really are. I'm surprised you didn't have a second child."

She froze, just for a second, as the stress descended once more, the realities of life that couldn't be laughed away. But she tried. "That's just the way things worked out, I guess."

"You guess, huh?" Evan leaned back against the sink, facing her, making it impossible to hide her face as she squeezed the sponge tightly under the white suds. "Remember when you thought we should sit around and talk about serious things instead of riding roller coasters? This is a serious thing. Why didn't you have a second child? You were married for nine years."

"He left after eight."

"Eight years, then, and you loved being a mom."

"How would you know that?"

"The tailgate, remember? Matthew was a baby. Even when you were wrestling with a stroller to get it into your car, you kind of glowed with this happiness. You looked so good with a baby in your arms."

He knocked her out with these statements. *Such a beautiful wife, you're a great mom, you glowed with happiness.* Knocked her out and made her heart hurt at the same time, because it felt like he was seeing a different woman than she really was, as if he saw some better version of her.

She rinsed the wineglass and had to reach behind him to set it in the drain board. "That's a nice thing to say."

"That's a nice way to not answer the question."

"Okay. We talked about it. Rob got out of the service after four years, so Matthew was three. Instead of starting a new career, Rob was all excited to have another baby. He could be a stay-at-home dad, taking care of a preschooler and a baby. I didn't have a good feeling about it, but if anyone should be open to switching gender stereotypes, it should be a female army officer, right? Nobody would think twice if a man was an army officer and his wife stayed home full-time with two little kids. Nobody would expect the wife to work, so why should I expect Rob to work?"

Evan made no attempt to keep drying dishes. His teasing smile had turned into a concerned, brooding sort of face.

"But then I got deployed. Afghanistan. It seemed like a blessing that Rob would be able to care for Matthew full-time."

"You seemed very happy on that airstrip to be going home to your husband and son. You were going to see your son in twenty hours."

"You remember that?"

"Every word."

She stirred the suds a little. "We landed and deplaned and formed up in our units to march into the hangar where the families were waiting. Signs and balloons and kids everywhere, filling up that hangar. You could feel the energy practically explode when we were given the order to fall out and everyone raced off to find their families." She fell silent, dropping the story.

Evan picked it up. "It's incredible, isn't it? My sister tackled me when I came back. I had no idea she would be there. She lived in another state and everything. She looked just so good to me. So good to see a familiar face."

"I remember her—oh, my gosh." She seized on the distraction. "I haven't told my parents about Friday yet. You have to tell your sister and your parents. I think my parents are going to be angry I didn't give them any notice. What do you think yours will say?"

"Mine will fall over dead from shock. Then they'll be very happy that I'm finally settling down—that's how they'll put it—and then when I tell them I'm settling down with my friend Juliet from Masterson, they'll be even happier. They liked you at school."

"Too bad you're going to kill them with shock, then."

She got her reward for being a smart aleck, that flash of Evan's boyish grin, but it didn't last. He picked up his dish towel, picked up one of her hands from the water and started drying her fingers off. He looked at her hand as he worked, thoughtful but a little sad, the way he'd looked when she'd walked out of the master bedroom after telling him she'd try not to let sex destroy their friendship.

"Why didn't you have a second child?" he asked, quietly persistent.

"I waited in the hangar, but they weren't there. Rob wasn't there, so Matthew wasn't there. I looked for a long time, until everyone else was all paired off and grouped up.

I thought maybe they'd gotten caught in traffic. I waited a long time. I wanted my baby."

Evan took her other hand and started drying it, too. He was calm, only he wasn't. The muscles in his arms seemed more defined. His chest, his neck—every muscle tensed, ready for action, but he just leaned back against the sink and tossed the dish towel on the counter.

"Where were they?"

"Rob had dropped the baby off with his mother. She lived in another state. Then he'd taken off for eight weeks, a spontaneous cross-country trip to deal with his emotions, supposedly. I took leave as soon as I could, so I could drive to his mom's house and get Matthew. When Rob showed up again, we went to family counseling. I was told I had to understand that there is so much pressure on the stateside families during deployments. I had to expect our family dynamic to be different after being away for a year. I hung in there. Things got better."

Evan crossed his arms over his chest, looking as deadly serious as a man could look. "Don't even think about trying to change the subject."

"I—I wasn't going to."

"You were."

He was right. She'd been about to dust her hands off and head out of the kitchen. "What is that, some kind of motherhood spider sense that rubbed off on you? Am I contagious?"

He smiled a little. "Why didn't you have a second child?"

She kept it light, kept it quick. "We decided to start trying. So, you know, there goes the birth control, and so, you know…when you catch your husband cheating and you've been having unprotected sex with him, then you have to go to the doctor and get tested for everything he might have picked up and passed on to you."

Evan winced.

"Everything was negative. I hadn't gotten pregnant, and I hadn't gotten any diseases, either. I survived that round of Russian roulette. Whew. Close one." But she couldn't laugh, because she'd felt like she really had dodged a bullet.

"How old was Matthew?"

"He was five and a half. You're going to explode, aren't you?"

"Have I ever told you how much I hate Rob Jones?"

"I'm being serious."

"So am I."

She poked at his pectoral muscle, rock hard with tension. "You should shake out your arms or something. It's okay."

"It's okay?" He did explode then, shoving away from the sink to cross the room, which only took one pace, so he turned around and scrubbed his hands over his face and then over his short hair. "It's okay. Five and a half years old—so you stayed with Rob another two years? Three?"

It might have been longer, if Rob hadn't left, but she wouldn't tell Evan that. She felt stupid enough. "He was my son's father. I agreed to couples' counseling. He screwed another woman after that, and I got to sit next to him on a couch and be told I was partly to blame."

Evan cussed like a soldier.

"Failure to align our goals. Bad communication. Marriage takes two. We failed together, and we could repair it together. Yada, yada, yada. It was my job to meet him halfway and fix our marriage after he screwed a girl he met at a barbecue that I couldn't attend because our son was running a fever."

She bit her lip and looked away from Evan. "I was more skeptical of the advice that time, but I'd made a vow for better or worse. My one great certainty was that Matthew adored him. Divorcing Rob would hurt Matthew. How could I hurt my baby?"

It was as if she'd popped a giant bubble of tension. The

anger dissipated in an instant, and she was suddenly enveloped in Evan's bear hug.

"I could have had another baby when Matthew was six. Rob would've been fine with it, and I would have known not to expect him to do any of the real baby care, but…"

"But?"

"My career was demanding. The timing was bad." In the safety of Evan's hug, she could whisper a terrible truth. "A part of me didn't think Rob deserved to have another perfect little human being worship him, not when he barely made room for Matthew in his day. I think—I think I was punishing Rob."

"Because he didn't deserve another baby, you didn't get to have another baby."

It sounded so final, as if that ship had sailed. She'd thought so, too, until she'd walked into Evan's office just days ago. *How many children are we going to have before we retire?*

She'd said she already did that part, and he'd been fine with her answer. Which was a good thing, wasn't it? She wanted to get Matthew through some trying years, not add even more to juggle.

"Evan…?" *Do you still want to marry me if we don't have children?*

She couldn't ask. He might say no.

"Juliet…?" He gently imitated her, this man who was her friend.

Her friend. Having a child was the most rewarding thing she'd ever done. She couldn't deny her friend that chance. She forced herself to ask.

"I'm not sure I'm ready for another child. I'm thirty-seven, so I don't have a lot of time to be ready. It's not realistic to think I'd really be able to have more than one baby before I'm forty. Neither could you, if you married me. You shouldn't limit yourself like that. Unless you're…

I don't know. Sure? Sure that you can be unsure whether or not you'll ever have a child?"

Evan let go just enough so he could look at her. "If we never have *another* child, you'll still have given me one."

"Matthew?"

"Of course. He's a great child."

She felt weightless and wobbly. She had to make herself laugh, because she didn't want to melt into a puddle of tears. "I don't know about that. Matthew hasn't been much of a prize lately."

"It's just a phase," Evan said.

"I hope," she said. "I have to be honest and tell you I don't really know what a phase is. I've never had an eleven-year-old before."

"Me, neither."

"You're sure about this? You'll feel like you got to be a father if, *if*, we don't have a baby?"

"I get to play baseball and ride roller coasters and have my authority challenged daily. If that isn't fatherhood, what is?"

I love you.

She loved the way his arms held her like a shield against the stress that was always pecking at her.

I love you, and I'm dragging you down. I have so much baggage.

But she rested her cheek on his shoulder, because she didn't want to let go.

The quiet was broken by the stomping of a child barging into the kitchen. Matthew made a sound of strangled indignation. Juliet peeked in time to see him throw up his hands in disgust and stomp back out of the kitchen.

"Oops," she said.

Evan sighed. "I definitely feel like a parent."

Chapter Thirteen

Hugging was apparently as heinous as kissing.

Juliet had rolled her eyes at Matthew. She'd winked at Evan, they'd shared a laugh, and then she'd once more managed to get Matthew and his homework in the car without further fuss.

This time, Evan had watched it go down with different eyes. He stopped being impressed and amused by Juliet's nerves of steel and looked a little harder as she faced a temper tantrum.

Juliet was barely hanging on.

She'd seemed so confident on Friday, walking into his office in her service uniform. The woman had her act together, her plans and contingency plans in order. She'd already chosen quarters for herself and had been ready to sign a lease, had Evan let her down.

She'd expected to be let down.

Why would she expect anything else? Time and again, she'd been through that pain.

It was all his fault.

The painful events in her life had hit her one after another, like dominoes falling. The cheating husband who'd abandoned her child while she was overseas, the second tries that ended in more cheating. The son who pleaded for her to make his father behave properly, the judge who ordered her to support her ex's laziness, all of it was on Evan's shoulders.

Evan had pushed that first domino.

He walked out to his patio. He didn't light the firepit. He didn't fire up the tower heater. Instead, he sat in the dark and lit a single cigar, taking a few shallow puffs to get the burn going.

He couldn't push aside the guilt any longer.

He studied the ash glowing on the end of his cigar, and he remembered.

The wedding party had been huge, eight bridesmaids, a weeklong destination wedding. The groom had been the baseball team's pitcher in college, a guy named Terry. His eight groomsmen had been the other eight starters of the team that had won the championship their senior year, including Evan, who'd played first base. Evan had been twenty-four. They all had been. Twenty-four and masters of the universe, kings of all they surveyed.

The bachelor party had moved from a swanky bar to a pool hall, everyone drunk enough to switch to cheap pool hall booze gladly.

The groom was being all grown-up, though. Instead of something cheap, Terry had produced a bootleg box of Cuban cigars and bottles of port. Evan and the rest had made manly noises of approval, as if they were experts on port and cigars at twenty-four. The groom had made an emotional speech and gotten all teary-eyed. Evan and the other true bachelors had been relieved when it was over. Someone had made a toast to Terry's future fertility, and they'd all drunk their port.

Port was gross. Evan drank it anyway. It was expensive and sophisticated.

Their former catcher became glum. "I suppose we'll all get tied down, sooner or later. Resistance is futile. I'm going to call dibs on one before all the good-looking women are gone."

The second baseman tried to lighten things up as he

lit his cigar. "Yeah? In that case, I call dibs on the blonde Evan brought this weekend. She got a twin?" He passed the butane torch to Evan.

Evan lit his cigar and took a few puffs, letting the smoke only flavor his mouth for a second before blowing it out. The cigar needed to develop a deep burn. These were just shallow puffs, to get it going. *Shallow, like my women.*

Shallow Issue Blondes. His friend Juliet had called his girlfriends that in college. No—that made no sense. He took another sip of port.

Standard Issue Blondes, that was it.

Juliet. What a smart aleck. Always fun. He'd hoped she'd be here for the wedding, but she wasn't. He'd have to catch her at homecoming in the fall.

His favorite smart aleck was wrong anyway. Evan knew their names. He'd brought Christie to this week's wedding festivities. Christie Brinkley. No—Christie Bartley. Bartles?

Christie *What's-her-name*?

He'd studied the ash forming on the end of his cigar.

Juliet *Grayson*.

The second baseman clapped him on the back, making the ash drop to the floor.

"I'm not marrying Christie." Evan took a deep drag on the very fine cigar, holding the smoke in his lungs this time. He wasn't a smoker, so the nicotine hit him hard. He was still drunk, but suddenly alert.

Third base jumped in. "Damn, Stephens. She's a knockout. If she's not wife material, who is?"

Juliet Grayson. Her name made his brain hum like a live wire. He could suddenly recall every detail of her face, perfectly clearly. Clearly perfect—Juliet had been clearly perfect. Violins on the college green—he'd kissed her. Why had he never kissed her before that? They had a pact, though. A fallback plan. An ace in his pocket.

A pinkie promise.

Evan had smiled smugly. "All in good time. Haven't gotten to her in the lineup yet."

Rob Jones, who'd literally been out in left field their whole season, had never been able to tolerate it when anyone else got too much admiration. "You guys are buying this? Suckers. Stephens doesn't have a lineup of potential wives."

"Ah, Robbie, my friend." Evan blew out the smoke, a deep, satisfying exhalation. "There's no list for the wife potential. You only need one. Got that already squared away, gentlemen. She'll be ready for the altar when I'm ready." He chomped the cigar between his teeth on one side as he chalked his pool cue. "If I'm ever ready. Not likely." He threw a comical look toward the groom. "No offense."

Everyone laughed, except Rob. "You're full of it, Stephens. You're not the stud you pretend you are."

"Whoa, there." The catcher tried to put his hand on Rob's shoulder to calm him down—and missed. "Whoa. Crap."

"It's supposed to be a party," Terry said with a smile— and an undertone of warning.

Rob shook off the groom's restraining hand. "Right. A party. We're here to shoot some pool, so let's do this, Stephens. You and me. A friendly game."

There was no one Evan wanted to play against less, but he was in it now.

The pool table was readied, and Evan lined up his shot. Just as he was drawing back the stick, Robbie called his name.

What an ass. Thinks he'll mess up my game.

"Who's this woman that's willing to wait for you to decide you're in the mood to get married? Name her, or I don't believe it. None of us do."

Evan took his shot. The sound of pool balls ricocheting off one another was satisfying. Two sank in pockets.

"What's wrong, Robbie? Just because you can't keep a girl longer than a week, you think a guy like me can't?"

"A guy like you." Rob snorted. "The guy who struck out and lost us the championship."

"That was four years ago. Kid stuff. It's time to man up."

But Rob's snide remark hit Evan where it hurt, right in the ego. He'd ended their junior year as the player who'd struck out in the bottom of the ninth, the final out that had ended the championship game with a loss.

He'd learned a lot of lessons from that, like how it didn't matter that two other guys had struck out before him, because he was the one who'd struck out last. The infamy belonged to him, fair or not. He'd learned how to keep his head up, how to keep practicing, how to keep his faith in himself—how to step up to bat the next year and do better. His senior year, he'd been the player who'd hit the RBI that had won the whole enchilada.

He put those lessons to use in the army now. He encouraged the soldiers of his platoon to have the same response to setbacks. His biggest failure had made him a better leader.

A winner.

Screw Rob. He was a loser, and he always would be.

Evan sank the orange ball in the corner pocket. The cigar was making him frigging dizzy. It was a miracle he'd sunk that shot.

But he had.

"See, while you're still clinging to old glory on the baseball diamond, I've already been promoted to first lieutenant. Why do I have a woman lined up to marry me and you don't? Because no woman is going to marry a guy she has to support. Do you know how much a dozen roses costs? What about a mortgage? Insurance? You want a wife? You need a real career."

"Join the army?" Rob all but spit the words. "Be like

you and a bunch of eighteen-year-olds trying to stay out of jail?"

Evan bent over the table, lined up his next shot, then looked up at Rob. "You got a better career going?" Without taking his eyes off Rob, he struck the cue ball and sank the shot.

Everyone around the table reacted like they were at a comedy roast, and Evan had just delivered a killing zinger.

He had. The guys all knew Rob flitted from project to project, pursuing business ideas that were little more than scams. He wanted to make a quick buck without having a boss to answer to, but he was failing. Rob didn't answer to authority well.

First Lieutenant Evan Stephens could take an order, and he could give one. He was the platoon leader of thirty soldiers, which meant he was personally responsible for thirty lives. It was a sacred duty, one he'd been sworn to. Not something to laugh over at a bachelor party. Not even something to brag about.

He eyed Rob through a curl of smoke. "You wouldn't make it through basic training. You're scoffing at eighteen-year-olds who did. They succeeded. They're part of something bigger than themselves."

Now Evan was the one getting the warning pat on the shoulder from the catcher. "Don't get so heavy, either one of you. This is a wedding. We're talking about women."

The groom, who probably liked the idea of someone else on the old team tying the knot, pressed Evan. "Who is this woman that the legendary Evan Stephens will deign to marry? This paragon of women? This…dare I say it? This unicorn?"

More guys weighed in. "If she'll wait indefinitely, she's not a unicorn. She's a dog."

Evan sipped his port. "Gentlemen, please. We're talking about the future mother of my children. I'm not going to have ugly children. Not stupid ones, either."

"I think Rob might be right. I think you're making this up."

"I think you've forgotten quality women exist." Evan raised his glass in a little toast. "Women like Juliet Grayson."

The murmurs of approval went around the room. Someone whistled.

"You've got one problem, Stephens. She's a brunette."

"She's not brunette. She's dirty blonde." Since he had the cigar in his hand, he wiggled his eyebrows like Groucho Marx. "Emphasis on the *dirty*."

Everyone laughed, except Rob, who was still glaring at him like he hated him.

Evan kept a smile on his face while his gut began to churn. What the hell was he doing? He made Juliet sound like she was a nympho. "Kidding, guys. Kidding. Juliet and I are only friends."

It was time to change the subject, but when he asked the third baseman about his new job, Rob cut him off. "Wasn't Juliet in ROTC? Is she stationed with you?"

"Fort Huachuca is a thousand miles away from my post." He walked away from Rob, rounding the table to line up his next shot. "That's why you need money. If you can buy plane tickets, distance won't matter. Hell, it'll help. A woman with wife potential will be impressed you spent your money and your time to see her. You have to make the effort."

Evan ought to do that. Fly to Juliet's place for a weekend. Not to impress her, not to date her, but just to pal around with the smart aleck for laughs.

"She's got the same career you do," Rob said. "She doesn't need your money."

Evan didn't hit the next shot well. The ball ricocheted badly, but it hit another ball into the pocket instead. As long as Evan sank a ball with every shot, Rob would never get a turn.

Evan kept going. "There's more to pocketing a wife than

having a job. You've gotta show them you've got father-hood potential, too."

A couple of guys groaned.

"I didn't say you had to like it, gentlemen. I just said you had to do it. You've got to show them you're daddy mate-rial if you want them to think you're husband material."

"How do you do that?"

Evan hadn't actually done that. He'd just told Juliet he was willing to have kids someday, when they were over the hill. Past thirty-five. Geezers.

He puffed on his cigar, buying time.

"Borrow a baby?" one guy suggested. The rest laughed, except Evan, because he was in midinhalation, and Rob, because he was a jerk.

"Buy her a kitten?"

Evan pointed his cigar at that guy. "That's actually a good one."

"It's perfect," the catcher said with enthusiasm. Maybe he had someone in mind already. "I can buy her a kitten."

"It would have to be a puppy for Juliet." Evan took aim at the last ball on the table. "She's allergic to cats."

He hit the ball, a perfect strike that sank the last ball in the side pocket.

Game over.

"Sorry, Rob. You didn't get to take a shot, did you? Play the next guy. I've got a cigar to finish."

That had been that.

The domino had been pushed. At homecoming that fall, Evan had been astonished to learn that Rob Jones had en-listed in the army. Evan had been sickened to learn that the reason Juliet wasn't at homecoming was because she'd gone to Rob's basic training graduation instead. Rob wasn't good enough for Juliet. Surely, she'd see that.

Months later, when he'd heard that Rob and Juliet had gotten married, he'd punched a hole in a wall. He'd gotten his hand in a cast and he'd paid for the drywall repair, but it would take another three years before Evan would see Juliet laughing at a hamburger-stealing toddler, and he'd realize the life he'd ruined had been his own. Not hers.

But he'd been wrong about that.

He'd fallen out of touch with Juliet after Afghanistan intentionally. She'd seemed happy on that airstrip, happy to go home to Rob and her four-year-old. For that one moment in time, her life had seemed good, so Evan had cut off everything there, wanting to believe that pushing that domino hadn't really hurt her, after all.

At the time, he'd told himself that he couldn't have her, so he couldn't think about her. But the truth was, he hadn't wanted to know if she was struggling as Rob's wife, because then Evan would have had to accept the blame. That made him more than a bad friend. That made him a coward.

Evan stubbed out his cigar and tossed it into the cold firepit. He hated his old, arrogant boasts. He hated the way he'd underestimated Rob, and it had nothing to do with his pride or his manhood or any other foolishness. He hated it because it had resulted in years of pain for Juliet.

He was going to fix this.

Everything he'd taken from her, he was going to give back. She was going to have a faithful husband. She was going to have a happy son. The things she didn't realize she'd lost, he would give back as well, like days spent having fun, free time to develop her own friends and her own interests. He wanted to put the joy back in sex, and give her—God, yes—that second child she'd denied herself.

And he was going to pray that she never, ever found out he was the one who had taken all those things from her in the first place.

Chapter Fourteen

"Grab your fishing pole. We'll walk the rest of the way to the dock."

Matthew trudged along, complaining all the way. "I didn't want to come. I told you that. I told my mom that."

His tone bordered on insolent, but Evan focused on the telltale tremor that sounded more fearful than hostile. It was Wednesday, and the first time the two of them had done anything alone. Matthew knew the man he'd never heard of a week ago was going to be his stepfather, and he was as keyed up as if that man was taking him to jail instead of an empty dock on a pond.

Earlier in his MP career, when he'd taken patrol, Evan had taken enough men to jail to know that the more powerless they felt, the more they tried to bait officers into arguments. Their emotional maturity could quickly regress to schoolyard level. Evan had kept himself above it by addressing insolent criminals as if they were rational adults. It had always helped defuse the situation. Evan hoped it would help him deal with a pouting, angry, frightened eleven-year-old.

"Why aren't we playing catch?" Matthew complained. "I thought we were going to play catch."

"We did, Monday and Tuesday. You practiced at school today, so we can do something different this evening."

"But why are you making me fish?"

Because it's Wednesday, and I'm marrying Juliet on

Friday, and before that happens, you and I are going to come to an understanding. Your mother is sad, and you are sad, and it's Rob's fault, but mine, too. I'm going to fix everything I can fix.

Evan sat on the end of the dock, letting his feet hang freely over the edge. The water level was far enough below them, he could leave his shoes on.

Matthew sat, too. "If you didn't want to practice, then I could've played Avengers instead of doing this. There's nothing out here."

Evan looked at the still water of the little pond, at the wild brush on the opposite bank, the golden cast to the sunset. There was a beauty to it, but when he was eleven, he would have thought this was nothing, too.

Evan kept his tone matter-of-fact. "I thought this might be fun."

"What if I don't think sitting on a dock is fun?"

Evan shrugged. "Then you won't have fun. But by the time we're done, you'll know how to bait a hook and cast a line. Good skills for a boy to know."

"I don't want you to teach me boy stuff. I don't want to learn boy stuff."

"Why not?" Evan tore a slice of white bread in half and handed him one piece. "Here, mash this into a ball."

"My dad said kiddie time was over."

There was that hole again.

"Dad said it was time to…to man up."

Man up. Matthew even said it with that derogatory inflection that means one guy thinks the other guy *isn't* man enough. When had Rob said such a stupid thing to his own son?

Evan demonstrated how to bait the hook. "You stick the hook right in the middle of the ball. Mash it some more, so it doesn't fall off the hook as soon as it hits the water."

Matthew did it, imitating Evan with hands that were

half his size. He was still a child, so his hands were a little clumsy as they attempted a new task.

Man up. Rob hadn't contacted Matthew in three years, so that conversation had to have been at least three years ago. Matthew could have been no more than eight. His fingers had to have been even smaller then, even less co-ordinated. Rob had told a child that he needed to stop being a child.

Evan could think of no appropriate response, so cast his line, a sharp throw, a flick of the wrist. "Like this."

Matthew did a fair job imitating him. Evan wound up some slack, and then he waited. Waited for Matthew to say more. Waited for the right words to come to him. Did anybody know the right words to say to a child whose father had told him his childhood was over?

"Dad said there has to be a man in the house, and since he was leaving and didn't know when he was coming back, I was it."

Since he was leaving. This was how Rob had left Matthew? His parting words had been to order an eight-year-old boy to pick up the slack for him.

Rob wasn't here. If Evan let himself get upset, Matthew would mistakenly think he was upset with him. Evan wound his reel once, calmly.

"I can't keep doing baby things, because he said Mom needs a man in her life."

"Well, she has one now, doesn't she?"

Matthew went absolutely still beside him.

Evan reeled in his line slowly. "I'm thirty-seven years old. That makes me a grown man. Your mom is a pretty kick-butt kind of woman, but if she needs a man for any-thing, I've got it." *It's not your burden to bear, little guy. Let me carry it.*

He glanced at Matthew out of the corner of his eye.

That earnest face was scrunched up in concentration as he stared at Evan, not the water.

Evan checked the bait on his hook unnecessarily. "Here's the thing. I didn't get to be thirty-seven without being eleven first. There's stuff you have to handle at every age. You don't have to handle the grown-man stuff anymore, because I'm here, but you do have to focus on being eleven. There's a ton of schoolwork to handle. Math, English, history—"

"Earth science."

"Earth science. You've got a commitment to a baseball team. I'm going to ask you to help me take out the trash every Tuesday. Plus, you have to get to know people at your new school and the other kids who live in our neighborhood. Figure out who is a friend. Figure out who is not."

"And I have to load *and* unload the dishwasher."

Evan squinted at the reflection of the sunset's colors on the water. He nodded in what he hoped was a sage manner. "There you go. You handle all the things you're supposed to handle as a sixth grader, and I'll handle all the things expected of thirty-seven-year-old men. Deal?"

Matthew thought it over, smart kid that he was. Looking for loopholes, probably. Trying to figure out if there was a catch. After a small eternity, he turned away from Evan to squint at the water, too. "Deal."

If Evan grinned a little bit, it was only bittersweet. *Man up.* This kid shouldn't have had such an oversize expectation, such an impossibly adult burden, put on him in the first place.

"I still don't want you to marry my mom, you know."

"I know." Evan flicked his wrist and sent the line flying over the water. Satisfied with the red bobber's place in the water, he leaned back on the railing and turned toward Matthew, giving him his full attention.

Matthew glared with all his eleven-year-old fury at the

water, but he was undoubtedly nervous about what Evan might say next. Matthew's statement hadn't been polite, but it took a kind of bravery to tell a thirty-seven-year-old man that his mom was off-limits. He was Juliet's son in every way.

Yet another emotion caught Evan by surprise. *Tenderness* was probably the best word for it. Affection. A desire to help this child navigate his own bubbling cauldron of emotions.

Evan let the tenderness settle into place as he studied Matthew's profile. He looked so much like Juliet, not just in the color of his eyes or the shape of his chin, but in the way that chin was being held at a bit of a stubborn angle, looking determined. Or, perhaps, that chin was simply braced for life to throw another punch at it. Evan wanted to fix that.

"I'll tell you why I'm marrying your mom." He took a moment to put it in terms for a boy to understand. "I've known your mom for a long, long time. She was one of my best friends in college. I missed her a lot when the army sent us to different posts after graduation. I missed her so much, I didn't want to think about it. Now she's moved here, and she wants to marry me."

Probably for the wrong reasons. Probably to help raise her son, although, watching Matthew and his fishing pole right now, it felt like a good reason.

"If she wants to marry me, then I'm definitely going to marry her. We'll get to live together that way, and I won't have to miss her anymore, for the rest of our lives."

Matthew was silent for another small eternity. Evan marked the time with short flicks of his wrist, making the end of his pole swish like an orchestra conductor's baton. The bobber bounced on the surface of the water.

Matthew swished his pole. "I don't get to decide anything. It's all grown-ups doing what they want to do."

"True. Eleven-year-olds aren't supposed to decide marriages. I think your mom is deciding to do what will make her the happiest. That's her call to make, not yours. If she's happy, though, it will make you a little bit happier, too, don't you think?"

That might have been too complicated. Matthew's brow was furrowed in deep concentration.

The golden sunset had ended, leaving only the gray light before dark fell. It was going to get cold, fast.

"Looks like it's time to go in." Evan started winding in his line. "I do have a question for you, though. Even if you're not very excited about this wedding, would you stand up with us at the courthouse on Friday?"

"I have to go. Mom said so."

"Right. But I'm asking you to stand up with us. The bride and groom usually have friends or family standing next to them when they take their vows. Bridesmaids and groomsmen, right?"

Matthew nodded.

"We're keeping it low-key, just us in front of the judge. There are benches in the courtroom where you can sit, but it would be nice to have someone stand up with us. You're the most important person in your mom's life, so it would mean the most if that person was you. I'll be in my service uniform, so you would have to wear a tie. It'll be a lot like a promotion ceremony."

"I stood next to my mom for her promotion ceremony. I did one of the shoulder boards."

"She told me. She was bragging about you." Evan caught the hook with his hand. "Hold it like this. You just take the bait off and throw it in the water. Let the fish have it. They outsmarted us today."

Matthew threw the soggy bread in the water. "Okay. I'll stand up with you guys."

"Thanks. I appreciate it." Evan showed Matthew how

to secure his hook to his rod and reel, and then they both stood and started walking off the dock.

"That's it?" Matthew asked. "We're done fishing?"

"That's it."

"We didn't catch anything."

"That's how fishing goes a lot of the time."

"Nothing happened."

Evan gave him a pat on his shoulder, one guy to another. "Yep. Nothing happened."

This is not a rehearsal dinner.

Juliet looked around the lakeside restaurant. The water looked black in the night outside the windows, but inside, the space was warm with candlelight. A single long-stemmed rose had been waiting for her at her place setting, tied with a white bow, surrounded with white baby's breath.

Thoughtful—but not a bride's bouquet, because they were just going to the courthouse tomorrow. She and an old friend were going to formalize an old pact and move in together. There was nothing to rehearse.

She touched the petals lightly. "Thank you."

"You're welcome." Evan looked sinfully handsome in the candlelight. No groom had ever looked more masculine, more capable of keeping a bride safe and secure. If she looked into his eyes too long, thoughts of hearts and flowers and white lace distracted her from the reality of their arrangement. It was one-sided, and all in her favor, but she'd given Evan so many chances to back out, and he hadn't.

The reality was that this arrangement would make them a party of three, not two. Even if tonight was just the two of them at a romantic restaurant, the third person was on her mind. "Matthew hasn't stomped around since you went fishing yesterday. He asked me where his tie was, because he needs to wear it tomorrow. You're a miracle worker."

"Your definition of a miracle is a little off."

"You found a babysitter for this evening."

"That's not a miracle, either."

"How many times have you tried to book a babysitter on short notice? It's a miracle." She made a face at him. "Or beginner's luck."

"General Snow's daughter lives right across the street. She's happy to come over and get paid for playing video games with Matthew."

"Your quarters are really in the ideal location, then." She laughed.

He didn't. "Something's worrying you."

Evan reached across the small table and set his hand on top of hers, stilling it. She looked down to see that she'd picked the tiny white flowers off the baby's breath. They were scattered over her place setting, leaving the needle-thin stems denuded.

She hadn't even realized she was doing it. "I've ruined it."

"Don't worry about tomorrow. I'm not going to let you down. I'm going to be at that courthouse, all dressed up in my service uniform. It's possible you won't show. But I will."

"I know." She *did* know. She'd looked into a man's eyes and been lied to, but she looked into Evan's eyes, and she believed him. "I'm not afraid you'll stand me up. I won't stand you up, either. Friends don't do that to friends."

He squeezed her hand and let go. "Glad to hear it. You're being a little skittish. It's got me concerned."

"Skittish?" She felt a little pique of indignation. Nobody described Colonel Grayson as skittish. Matthew's divorced-but-successful mother was not skittish.

Evan made a point of looking at her flower-strewn place setting. "Skittish."

She couldn't argue the point.

"If you're sure about the wedding, then are you nervous about after the wedding? This is your last night at the Holiday Inn."

"We already talked about that." Tomorrow night, they would sleep together, for reasons that had nothing to do with their party of three. They were going to sleep together because they'd always wondered how good it would feel. Evan had said so on the patio.

He'd been right, of course. She'd wondered about it, and she was wondering about it right now, every time she looked at him. His dress shirt was unbuttoned at the throat. Tomorrow night, she'd unbutton it all the way, taking her time, tasting the skin she exposed. She'd dreamed about that often enough.

She could go crazy physically; she only had to keep her emotions under control. She couldn't let all those orgasmic endorphins fool her into thinking they were in love.

Love never even came up in their conversations, which was for the best. They were getting married because they were friends. He thought she'd make a good wife. She thought he'd make a good husband. They'd had sixteen years to think about it, as he'd pointed out, so why not marry each other? They'd have a good relationship. It was enough.

It had to be enough, because Evan didn't love her. If this marriage had been about romance, he would have told her. There would have been hearts and promises and flowers.

She toyed with the baby's breath some more. Flowers—he'd just given her flowers, hadn't he?

The waiter moved her flower and set down a glass of champagne. The discussion of the appetizers, the chef's special, the wine list were all a relief to Juliet. She studied her menu in silence when the waiter left.

Evan closed his casually. "I'm getting the filet. Were you this nervous the night before you married Rob?"

She cleared her throat. "Nice try, slipping that question in there to catch me off guard. I don't think that question is considered good etiquette. When it's a second marriage, I think everyone pretends the first one didn't exist."

"My bride is nervous as hell. I want to know if she's as scared to marry me as she was to marry Rob."

"I wasn't scared to marry Rob."

Evan was silent.

"I'm sorry. I shouldn't have said that. I've hurt you."

"You've shocked me. You weren't nervous about marrying Rob?"

The disbelief in his voice echoed her own feelings when she looked back. Why hadn't she been nervous? Why hadn't she seen the signs that she was taking a big risk by marrying Rob Jones?

"I should have been, but that's in hindsight. I've told you so many terrible things about Rob, you must wonder why I married him in the first place. Why didn't I see the red flags?" She folded her hands in her lap and looked out the window at the blackness. "I'll never understand it. You knew me then, Evan. Wasn't I the kind of person who would have seen any red flags?"

"You're being too hard on yourself. You were young. Twenty-four. He was good-looking."

"Hormones?" She laughed a little at the idea that it had boiled down to that. "I wasn't that young. Something about him reminded me of you, though. Probably the baseball thing. Maybe that made me too comfortable when we first ran into each other."

"How did you meet?"

"I recognized him from Masterson. He was on your team, so we must have run into each other at college. It wasn't really our first meeting."

"You know what I mean."

"I was at a bookstore in the town outside Fort Huachuca. Looked up and there he was, browsing in the same aisle, a total coincidence. He looked familiar—the baseball thing again."

"I was *not* his friend on the team. I wish you had remembered that." Evan sounded angry.

She looked at him sharply. He'd told her she was being too hard on herself, and now he was telling her what she'd done wrong.

"As a matter of fact, I did remember that. So did he. He was embarrassed about the way he'd goofed off in college. He regretted letting his teammates down. He even told me about showing up to a game drunk and how you guys gave him the butt-chewing he deserved. It impressed me that he had this self-awareness. He was getting his life together. He'd been to a wedding of someone on your team, and it had made him realize what mattered in life. Love. Family."

Evan just stared at her, shaking his head.

"I know." She felt the need to defend herself. "I was skeptical, too. He'd come to Huachuca as a programmer for a defense contractor. It was a short-term project. When it ended, he decided to join the army, too. He wanted to be part of something bigger than himself. I admired the way he was taking concrete steps to turn his life around, but I wasn't a total sucker. I wanted to know he had the ability to stick with something when times got tough. I waited until he finished basic training before…ah, before really letting myself fall for him."

Which meant before she'd had sex with him. Evan didn't need to know that much.

"That was very smart of you."

"Don't be too proud of me. I still married the guy. He must have spent a lot of money just flying back to see me on weekends while he was away at his advanced training course, but he said I was the kind of girl you marry, and he didn't want to lose me. Then one day, he showed up on my doorstep with a dozen roses in his hand and a puppy, this adorable little beagle puppy under his arm— What? Are you okay?"

Evan had put his elbow on the table and dropped his head into his hand.

"I shouldn't tell you this story. I have a hard time forgiving myself. I feel like a fool. But honestly, every time I go back over it, I still can't see the red flags. He carried through on his military commitment. He never even glanced at another woman when he was with me. He loved his dog. He spent his money and all his free time to fly in to see me. What did I miss?"

Evan raised his head and reached across the table to hold both her hands. "You didn't miss anything."

"I wanted to be married and have a baby, and here came this guy who said he wanted the same things. I must not have wanted to see anything else."

"You were only going after what you wanted, which is a very Juliet thing to do. You swung for the fences. With all your heart and soul, you swung for the fences."

"I struck out. Game over."

He gripped her hands more tightly. "Yes, that game is over. It's a new game now. Fresh uniform, fresh season. You're up to bat again, and you're a better player now, more experienced. Swing for the fences again."

She was sitting here, leaning into Evan, spilling her heart out, holding his hands, soaking up every bit of sympathy and approval he dished out, and he said *swing for the fences again*?

He might as well have dumped a bucket of ice water on her. Did he not understand that the fence, the ultimate goal, was true love, romantic love, the kind from fairy tales? The kind that made people do stupid things and ruin their lives?

The kind she felt for him.

The kind he didn't feel for her. He loved her, his long-time pal. But he didn't *love* her. Did he even realize he'd just told her to put her heart back on the chopping block while she tried to have the kind of marriage they were specifically not trying to have?

She sat back and picked up her champagne glass. She looked at him over the rim, unable to place the expression on his face. What was up with Evan?

A waiter stepped in quickly, put a plate in the middle of the table, mumbled, "Your scallops," and took off like those scallops were about to explode.

She and Evan looked at each other in surprise.

"How long do you think he was standing there?" he asked.

"You mean, how long was he sweating it out, watching his customers have this intense conversation, praying that we'd let go of our hands so he could put his appetizer down and get the hell away from the drama?"

"Yeah. That."

They looked at each other another second, then burst into laughter—which, given the elegant restaurant setting, meant they sat there sniggering and snickering and trying not to be too loud.

It felt good. She really liked Evan, and if she could just focus on how good it was to be around her friend and keep her fairy-tale fantasies in check, everything might be okay.

She stabbed a scallop. "Rob wanted you to be in the wedding party, you know."

"I'll bet he did." Evan sounded super sarcastic. Or bitter. Or something.

"I told him no. I didn't tell him why."

"Why did you say no?"

"Because of this pact we had. Don't you think it would have been sort of rude to have you stand with us at the altar to watch me nullify the pact?"

"Ah. That. Yes. When I heard you got married, I was... upset."

"You were? I thought it was kind of obvious that the pact couldn't hold. There was no way I was waiting until I was thirty-seven to be married. That sounded like waiting until I was one hundred and seven. I was sure there was no way you would make it to thirty-seven without being married, either. You'd have this fabulous blonde wife, and there was no way I'd be the stupid old maid who had expected otherwise. You had so many girlfriends, I knew you would fall for at least one of them."

"Nope."

"Never?"

He ate a scallop.

She forgot about the food. "Why not?"

In the silence that followed, she knew what she wanted the answer to be, because she still wished fairy tales could come true.

Evan just made a dismissive gesture with his fork. "Are you still nervous about marrying me tomorrow?"

"Very," she whispered. She wished for fairy tales, because she was already in love with him.

He set down his fork immediately and took her hand again. "Don't be. I promise you, this marriage is going to be nothing like your last one. I will never cheat on you."

"I'm ignoring every red flag." *I'm already in love with you. You don't love me back. You're not even looking for it. This is going to be disastrous.*

"What red flags? This is nothing like last time. How long did you know Rob?"

"Before I married him? Six months. It took him a couple of years to break his promise and cheat on me for the first time."

Evan leaned in, speaking with an urgency that she found thrilling. "How long have you known me? It's been sixteen years, and we're still keeping this pact. We knew each other for three years before that in college. We practically lived together in the dorms. That's nineteen years. I haven't broken a promise to you in nineteen years."

She felt the hope rising.

"So tomorrow, when I stand before the judge and make a promise to you, remember that it's more than words. You have a track record with me. You can believe me, Juliet, when I say that I'm not the kind of man who cheats on his wife. I'm not the kind of man who would keep a girl-friend on the side."

It wasn't the same as love, but trust was significant. He wouldn't cheat on her. Her heart wouldn't shatter that way. She was never going to look through a credit card statement and find gifts for a girlfriend.

"I trust you," she said. They weren't the three little words of fairy tales, but they were three very, very important little words. "I trust you."

His smile was absolutely breathtaking. He squeezed her hand, hard. "Good. That's a start. It's safe to swing for the fences again. I won't let you down."

He let go of her hand, and they both leaned back a lit-tle. A waiter dropped a bread basket on their table, then darted away. Juliet looked at Evan, and they started snick-ering again.

The sommelier topped off their champagne glasses, then backed away, and a professionally dressed woman stepped in, perhaps the manager. Juliet barely glanced at her, but Evan stopped laughing.

"Evan?" the woman said. "It *is* you. I thought so. I got back early, and the station manager brought me here for a debrief. I was going to come by tonight afterward and surprise you. I know you hate surprises, but I thought you wouldn't mind."

Evan closed his eyes and kept them closed, a man saying a fervent prayer, or a child hoping everything would disappear.

"I'm not sure what's going on, sweetheart, but…" The woman brushed her hand over Juliet's rose. *"Surprise."*

Chapter Fifteen

"Linda."

Evan spoke the woman's name without opening his eyes.

"Are you just going to leave me standing here," the woman said with a tight smile, "while everyone stares at me?"

Juliet couldn't *not* stare, but she wasn't staring at the strikingly beautiful Linda. She felt mesmerized, incapable of moving, incapable of speaking, incapable of doing anything except staring at Evan.

Linda didn't wait for Evan to answer her. She turned around a chair from the empty table next to them and sat down, lightly and politely.

Evan opened his eyes and looked straight at Juliet. Only at Juliet. "I am so sorry."

Her heart shattered.

It felt so horridly familiar, that crushing of expectations. It felt exactly as it had years ago, when Rob had first looked like a man facing a firing squad as he'd also said *I am so sorry.*

Who is it this time? Juliet looked at the woman. Linda was someone people noticed, confident and attractive, fully made up with tons of wavy blond hair. She was exactly Evan Stephens's type.

Nothing's changed.

"Who are you?" Juliet asked, although she could guess why this woman was seating herself at their table like she owned Evan's time.

"I was going to ask *you* that." Linda turned away from Juliet, back to Evan, not panicking.

Juliet knew that feeling: not panicking. Those minutes where one didn't panic, because there must be a sane excuse.

"What have I just surprised myself into, Evan? Who is your dinner companion?" Linda was exceptionally poised, professionally so, like a model or a spokesperson or an actress. Evan had always preferred blondes, but never bimbos, after all.

Juliet practically felt it when Evan dragged those blue eyes away from her and looked at Linda for the first time—the first time Juliet had seen him look at Linda, for he'd clearly looked at her many times before. There was a difference in how people looked at one another when they were strangers compared to the way the gaze settled on the face of someone they knew well.

It was the *tell* when Rob lied. He'd fake a pleasant greeting when he was introduced to a lover in public. *Nice to meet you. What did you say your name was again?* Juliet had always known. *He already knows her.*

Evan was looking hard at Linda now. There was no welcome on his face, not one iota of happiness to see her, but she wasn't his enemy. He looked concerned. "I had no intention of you finding anything out by surprise. When you returned from Haiti, I was going to contact you and speak to you in person."

"What are you saying?" She was still not panicking, but she turned to Juliet. "Who *are* you?"

"Linda." Evan said her name firmly, to draw her attention back to himself, so that Juliet wouldn't become her target. In a surreal kind of way, Juliet appreciated the effort. It was courteous of him. Chivalrous, really. Rob certainly hadn't tried to stop any girlfriend from screeching at Juliet.

Wasn't that what Evan had just promised her? *This marriage is going to be nothing like your last one.*

"Who is she, sweetheart?"

"This is an old friend of mine from college. Juliet Grayson."

Linda relaxed a fraction. She turned to Juliet, still wary. After all, there were flowers involved. "I'm Linda Pettington, his girlfriend. I'm sure he's mentioned me. We've been together for so long. Half a year now. A little more."

This woman had the prior claim.

I am the other woman.

Juliet was the thing she hated most. She could hardly speak for the crushing sensation in her chest. "I didn't know. I wouldn't have— I'm so sorry."

Evan stopped her. "Don't be sorry." He laid his hand over hers. She was still gripping her fork, her knuckles white. "This is on me, Juliet, not you."

But Linda was panicking now, looking at Juliet as a stranger does, cataloging the appearance, storing information. "You're sorry for *what*?"

Juliet wanted to answer Linda, but the words wouldn't come. *I would never hurt you. I didn't know he was your man.*

"Linda," Evan said firmly once more, taking control of the situation. "It's a long story, and I know you're going to be shocked, but Juliet and I are getting married tomorrow."

"Married!"

All eyes in the restaurant turned their way.

"Married." She stood, all professional poise forgotten. The shock on her face was genuine. "How could you? I thought *we* were going to— Oh, Evan, how could you?"

As Linda fell apart, Juliet kept herself together by calling upon her military bearing, although she wore a pastel sweater dress. She sat as if she were standing at attention. Knees together, feet together, shoulders back, eyes front.

Most important of all, no expression on her face, a neutrality that was impervious to distractions—which didn't mean she wasn't aware of them.

She heard everything Linda said, every attempt Evan made to restore sanity. The tears began, and the maître d' approached to kindly offer to escort Linda elsewhere or to call her a cab, as if Evan had driven her here and had intended to dump her and leave her stranded.

No kindness was offered to Juliet. She'd never appreciated before how everyone must have been on her side when she was the person being cheated on. This time, she was the villain.

"You should go with her." Her voice sounded decisive, the voice of an officer, thank God.

"I'm not leaving you here." Evan spoke as firmly to her as he had to Linda, who stood over them, weeping.

"You two should go talk in private," Juliet said.

"We will. Not tonight."

The maître d' took that as his cue. "Miss Pettington, won't you come with me? We'll wait on the patio for a cab to arrive."

Her tears were real. "N-no, thank you. My station manager is h-here. He'll get me home."

"Then perhaps you would care to step onto the patio for a few moments to compose yourself. Please, right this way."

Evan rested his arms on the table and stared at the scallops in the resulting silence.

Juliet felt sorry for him. That was different, too. She'd never felt any sympathy for Rob during these scenes. Then again, Rob had tried to save his own hide and weasel out of any suggestion he was at fault. Evan had been courteous and compassionate and had claimed all the blame for himself. *This is on me, not you.*

"You should go speak to her, Evan. It's okay."

"It is not okay. I'm not leaving you at the table alone, with everyone staring at you." Evan looked at each table around them. Diners turned away and became engrossed with their own plates.

"I said it was okay." She put a little steel into her voice. "I've been through worse."

God knew what he saw in her face, because he closed his eyes once more, just for a moment, before addressing her with quiet, urgent words. "I'm not Rob. I am nothing like Rob. I would never—"

"And yet, you did. To her, if not to me."

"I am not Rob."

"But I have been her."

They both knew that heavy truth.

"She's wondering how she could have missed the signs. She's wondering why she isn't enough. You should do what you can to soften the blow. Please."

They stared at one another, neither blinking, a horridly serious version of the staring contests of their youth.

Abruptly, Evan pushed back his chair. "Do. Not. Leave."

She sat alone, aware of all the looks being sent her way. The blatant curiosity didn't feel unusual. *Another scandal. Another time to be stared at.*

She looked out the window. The water was black, but just off to the right and a little below her spot, she saw Linda, alone on the patio decking, a man's jacket around her shoulders like a cape, although there was no other sign of the station manager she'd referred to.

A station manager? Television. That was why she looked familiar. Juliet had seen Linda on billboards that advertised the local news. Linda's professional poise was gone now, though, as she cried into the glass of red wine she clutched with both hands.

Evan joined her, looking businesslike and polished in his civilian clothes, tailored slacks and the dress shirt that was unbuttoned at his neck. He must have said Linda's name, because she suddenly spun around. She let Evan walk up to her, let him put his hand on her arm as he talked to her, a natural move of comfort between two people who had known each other well.

Juliet could hardly stand to watch. Half a year, this woman had had with him.

Linda took a step back and Juliet saw the heartbreak in her face, the kind she knew came when one realized her whole world had just changed. Juliet had been just as heartbroken to learn that Rob was having sex with someone else, a woman who'd come over to her house and screwed her husband while baby Matthew was there.

Evan had not done anything like that.

Linda must assume that Evan had been sleeping with Juliet for a long time, long enough for them to be marrying tomorrow. That hadn't happened, and Evan hadn't planned to keep seeing Linda once he was married. *When you returned from Haiti, I was going to contact you and speak to you in person.* Evan had explained that to her several times at this point.

As Linda ranted and raved, Juliet felt the tiniest bit of annoyance. The woman had the right to be upset, but Juliet had had the right to be *horrified* when she'd been in her position, because she'd had a wedding ring on her finger and a child in a stroller. She still hadn't indulged in this much public drama.

Linda had been dating a man and had thought they were exclusive—or rather, they had definitely been exclusive if Evan had told her they were. Evan wasn't the kind of man who cheated.

Kind of a bizarre thing to think, considering the scene she was watching.

When Linda raised her wineglass, Evan made no move to defend himself. The wine hit him in the face with a spectacular splash. Juliet heard murmurs from the other diners who had tables that were against the window, the sounds of people enjoying a show. Linda stormed away, disappearing from view.

Evan only tilted his head and gave it a single, strong shake, one attempt to keep some wine out of his eyes. He didn't wipe his sleeve over his eyes or take any other action. The wine had to be stinging his eyes. He was letting it.

He shouldn't.

Without questioning the impulse, Juliet picked up both of their napkins and walked toward the stairs that led out to the patio, aware that every eye in the restaurant was on her.

She could make the walk with cool dignity, not because of her military bearing, but because she knew the truth. *I am not a homewrecker.*

But that didn't mean she was any good at building a home, either.

The night air was colder than Juliet had braced herself for.

She crossed the deck to Evan anyway. He had his back to her, his hands braced on the railing as he looked out over the water. He didn't turn at the sound of her high heels as she walked.

"It's me. I brought you a napkin." She held one in front of him.

He moved to take it as if his arm were made of lead, but he wiped the wine from his eyes.

"I never even asked you if you were dating anyone." She looked at Evan's profile in the moonlight. "She's very beautiful."

Evan continued to look at the water impassively. "She said the same thing about you."

"She seemed like a serious girlfriend. A significant one."

"We were only dating. I don't break promises. She was out of the country on assignment and not due back until next week. I planned to invite her out for coffee and explain in person that I wouldn't be seeing her anymore."

"But we would have already been married."

"Yes, we would have." He did not look at her. "There was no way I was going to postpone our wedding so that I could wait until a woman I'd been dating returned to the country and found time in her schedule to have coffee with me."

Juliet had heard Linda's opinion on that. The whole restaurant had. "She seemed to think you were not only dating. She thought you were going to propose."

He exhaled heavily. "I didn't give Linda a reason to assume anything. I'd thought about it. I always think about it when I'm with someone, but…" He shook his head.

The jealousy hurt, but there was more than that. It gave her pain to realize how much she'd hurt her friend. She'd leveraged their friendship to make her life easier, but she'd derailed his.

She gave him a little push on the shoulder to make him face her. Then she wiped at the red wine on his shirt with her napkin. The wine had soaked through to his chest. She pressed the napkin against his chest, against hard muscle, a steady pressure to absorb as much wine as possible. It wouldn't be enough, of course. Wine stained. The shirt was ruined.

"If you were thinking about marrying her, you ought to continue to think about it. This isn't a reality TV show, where you have to choose someone by the end of the week. You have more than two contestants to choose from, too. You don't have to marry me or Linda. You can marry anybody you want."

"That's not how it works. Not for me." He placed his warm hand over her hand, keeping it pressed against the napkin, against his chest. Right over his heart. "I'm not ever going to marry anyone else."

"Because…why?"

"Because you walked back into my life, and everything changed."

"Don't let me ruin your life. Don't let me make you settle for a marriage without love. I didn't do well with the happily-ever-after fairy tale, but you could. You should marry for love. You can propose to Linda."

"No, I can't. Not once in sixteen years have I been able to get down on one knee. Linda was no different than the others. I thought about it, but I couldn't do it."

"Why not?"

"Because she wasn't you."

Juliet stood there with her hand pressed against his heart and frantically tried to wall off her own. *Don't make me wish for what we don't have.*

She shook her head. "The marriage pact wasn't like that. It was conditional. *If* we were still single. I married someone else. You knew you were free to marry someone else, too. It doesn't matter if it's not me."

"It matters."

Don't make me hope.

Evan sounded grim. "There was a reason that marriage pact seemed like such a good idea that night. There was a reason, but by the time I realized why, it was too late for me. Rob had already gotten what I wanted. You're right—I had no choice but to move on. But you were the standard, Juliet. I couldn't get down on bended knee for anyone less than you, and no woman has ever lived up to the bar you set when we were together."

"Together? We were only friends." She was so used to hurting, this tiny spark of hope hurt, too. "I never realized you thought of me that way at school."

"I didn't, either. But as the years went by, as relationships came and went, I knew. I've known for a long time now."

"You should have told me. I didn't know."

"You weren't supposed to know. You'd chosen to take a shot at happiness with another guy. Everyone who was at your wedding told me what a happy bride you were. Telling you I was jealous couldn't possibly have made you happy. I had to leave and let you live the life you wanted.

"I tried to stop using you as my standard. I even bought a ring for someone once. I told myself she was as good as it gets, but I couldn't make myself take a knee, even when you were someone else's wife. And I—I hated that. She was a great person, but you are the standard, and no one has ever, ever been like you. You think I can propose to Linda? I can't. For sixteen years, I've never been able to do this."

He let go of her hand and fell to one knee, landing hard on the wooden deck. It happened so suddenly, she still had her hand in the air where his chest had been.

She dropped the napkin. "Oh, Evan."

He was close against her, just as they'd been standing, his chest brushing her thigh. He simply stayed there, head bowed. She felt his body shake with a single sob— no, a laugh. He laughed quietly, shaking his head. "It's so damned easy. It's so damned easy to do when it's you."

He took her hand and pressed her palm against his cheek, a move that was so romantic, Juliet had no defense against it.

"Please, Juliet. I am so very tired of women who are not you. Please meet me at the courthouse tomorrow. Please marry me."

"Evan." His name was all she could manage.

"Does that mean yes or no?" It was not a flippant question. He asked it with his head bowed.

"I have to explain something to you before I can answer." She ran her fingers over his hair, although it was too short to need to be smoothed down. "You were right when you said I was scared tonight. I've been terrified, because I knew that I was going to sleep with you tomorrow night. I was afraid that while you were enjoying insanely good sex, I'd be convincing myself it meant more to you than it did. As it is, I can barely keep my heart safe from feeling all this love for you. Not friendship. I mean crazy, romantic love."

He rested his forehead against her thigh.

She thought she might cry. "If we were in bed, skin on skin, nothing between us…if you were inside me and making me feel wonderful… I'd lose the battle and all this love would break right through my shell and I'd probably do something foolish like blurt out 'I love you.' Then you would feel so awkward and you'd pity me, and it would ruin everything."

She sank down to perch on the knee that was raised, his strong thigh giving her a secure seat, and she put her arms around his neck.

"Before I can answer you, you have to answer me. Would that ruin everything? Because if it does, then I can't marry you. I know that the first time you take me to bed, I'll be a goner. I'm going to be so far in love with you, I'll never be able to turn back. If that bothers you, then you need to speak now or forever hold your peace."

Evan took her head in his hands and tilted her face to kiss her. His mouth was so skillful, her body wanted more, but it was the way his hands trembled in her hair that made her heart soar.

"There is one part of our plan I want to change," he said, kissing his way along her jaw.

"What part?"

His voice was a delicious baritone rumble in her ear. "I think the very first time I take you to bed should be tonight, not tomorrow. That way, when I meet the woman I love at the courthouse, she'll already love me back when I marry her." He kissed her one more time. "Do you think that's a good idea?"

"I do."

With his hands in her hair and her hand clutching a fist-ful of his wine-stained shirt, they laughed with each other on the patio by the lake, under the moon.

And then, because so few of life's moments were per-fect, Evan had to ask her another question. "Do you want to walk back through the restaurant and all those friendly diners to get to the parking lot?"

"Hell, no."

"Me, neither. I'll settle the bill tomorrow." Evan picked her up the way a groom would carry his bride over a threshold. He carried her to the end of the patio closest to the parking lot, climbed over the railing with her in his arms, carried her over the gravel of the lakeshore, then crossed the asphalt of the parking lot to set her down in the leather seat of his Corvette.

Before he closed her door, he hesitated. "Matthew."

Juliet bit her lip. "And the babysitter."

"I'm new to this, but we can't exactly go past them into my bedroom and lock the door, can we?"

"I have to take Matthew back to the Holiday Inn tonight. Our clothes are still there. His toothbrush, his pajamas, his books for school tomorrow."

"But Matthew's at my house right now, which means your room at the Holiday Inn is empty." He smiled at her. "The babysitter isn't expecting us back for another two hours."

"Do you think this Corvette can get us to the Holiday Inn and back in—?"

"Yes. From now on, the answer is always yes."

Chapter Sixteen

It was Friday afternoon.

Evan checked his watch. It was just now sixteen hundred hours—that meant 4:00 p.m.—and that meant he'd now been a married man for exactly one week.

It felt insanely good.

He was so damned happy to have Juliet back in his life. Evan had told Matthew the truth when they'd gone fishing. He'd missed Juliet, and he never wanted to miss her again.

He'd left out the fact that it had been his own fault. There was no reason for anyone to find out that he'd pushed that first domino that had kept them apart for so long.

Thank God he'd gotten this chance to give back to Juliet all the things he'd never meant to take. She had a faithful husband now, although only time would truly prove it to her. Evan would prove it year after year, happily. Making fun a priority, making friends—all of that was happening already, and Evan looked forward to sustaining that year after year, too.

They were already making friends with the other parents at the middle-school baseball diamond, light conversations among adults as they all leaned on the chain-link fence and waited for practice to end, so they could all get their kids back to their houses in time for dinner.

Evan exchanged nods of greeting with some of those new acquaintances as he made his way to the bleachers. This Friday afternoon, on the one-week anniversary of his wedding, Evan was going to sit on hard wooden bleachers and watch preteen boys attempt to play baseball, while his wife was at work.

He'd had to remind her she wasn't a single parent anymore when she'd been upset that she wouldn't be able to get out of the office in time for the start of the game. "I'll be there. I'll save your seat."

"Make sure Matty sees you, so that he'll know he has a parent in the stands, okay?"

That question had been an anniversary gift. Juliet knew—she'd known from the first, somehow, though he might never know how—that he wanted to be the father Matthew needed. She said little things like that parent-in-the-stands comment all the time, as if they were already a true family.

It would take Matthew longer, perhaps, but they were well on their way. He was still suspicious of Evan, but that was no surprise when he'd lived his entire life loving a father who had appeared and disappeared at his own whim. It might take years for Matthew to realize he now had a faithful father, just as it might for Juliet to accept that she had a faithful husband, but they'd get there.

The boys came jogging out of the dugout in a single file line, their new uniforms hanging a bit too loosely on their young bodies. All of the parents had laughingly admitted they'd ordered the uniforms a little large, so the children wouldn't outgrow them before the end of the season.

Matthew scanned the bleachers looking for his mother, naturally. Evan stood halfway and raised his arm. He was one man in uniform among so many parents in uniform, but Matthew spotted him and waved his arm back with all the enthusiasm of a puppy wagging its tail.

Evan sat back down and rubbed his chest. That wave made his day. It might not take years, after all, for that little hamburger-stealer to enjoy having a new father.

It was the bottom of the third inning before Evan saw Juliet. Parents had been arriving in a steady stream throughout the game, about half of them in uniform, but something about *that* woman in uniform caught his eye. She'd always caught his eye. Juliet preferred shorts and skirts, but she'd come straight from work in her camouflage and combat boots. She crossed the sidewalk toward him. Sharp as hell. Sexy as hell.

The most selfish thing he'd wanted to fix for her had been to put the joy back into sex. Mission accomplished—and lesson learned. Evan had been naive to think it was a matter of enjoying physical pleasure, although it did feel insanely good. The real joy came from being free to experience all the emotion he'd never felt so deeply before. It was humbling, how powerful it was to connect so intimately with the woman he loved so much. The words they whispered in bed came from their souls: *I'm here. I'm with you. I've got you. Let go. I love you.*

Last night, afterward, he'd been running his hand over her back as she drifted off to sleep. He'd been overwhelmed by how precious she was to him, how close he'd come to never having her, and he'd nearly said *I never meant to hurt you. Forgive me for Rob.*

That impulse had been dangerous. What Juliet didn't know needed to stay unknown. He couldn't fix anything if she didn't trust him.

She started stepping from bleacher to bleacher, working her way through the crowd up to his level. He reached down for her hand and hauled her up to his row, an appropriately soldierly move to give a teammate a hand up, since they were both in uniform. Before she turned away from him to sit, though, he murmured, "Well, hello, Mrs. Stephens."

She winked. "You mean, 'Good afternoon, Colonel Grayson.'" She settled onto the bleacher with a not-so-subtle bump of her hip against his shoulder. Sitting close but not touching, she cast a few furtive looks around them from under the brim of her patrol cap, and then she whispered, "Mrs. Stephens bought herself some new lingerie today on her lunch break, just FYI. Got it stuffed in my left cargo pocket. Wanna guess the color?"

Then the crack of a bat brought everyone in the stands to their feet, and all the parents for both teams cheered for someone's skinny little kid who was running his heart out to reach first base.

What a honeymoon.

The inning ended. The kids from the other team headed for their dugout to get ready to bat, while the kids from their team grabbed their gloves and hats to take the field.

"Is *edible* a color?" he asked pleasantly, at a normal volume. *Edible* wasn't a dirty word.

As Juliet kept an eye on the field, she casually unbuttoned the flap to the large cargo pocket on her uniform pants. Evan caught a peek of hot-pink silk for a nanosecond before she buttoned the camouflage pocket back up, cool as a cucumber. One second later, she grabbed his arm in excitement. "There's Matthew. Coach is putting him on the field. Oh, I'm so happy for him. Oh, my God, I'm so nervous."

Evan tried to keep up with the playmate to parent zigzag. He watched Matthew jog all the way out to left field, punching his fist into the pocket of his glove, breaking it in like Evan had shown him. If any of these pint-size players ever hit a ball hard enough to send it out to left field, Matthew might actually get to use that glove for something besides his fist. It wasn't likely, which was probably just as well. Matthew had taken a few tennis balls to the face this week as they'd practiced looking up to catch pop flies.

The crack of the bat brought all the parents in the stands to their feet again with a collective *oh* at the power of that hit. The ball sailed high into the sky. Pop fly—holy cow, that skinny kid from the opposing team had hit a pop fly to left field.

Matthew. The ball reached its zenith and started heading back down to earth. Matthew had to catch it to get an out. If he failed, the other team would have more than enough time to score.

Dear God, let him catch it, dear God, let him make the out...

Juliet grabbed his arm again—in terror.

Get under it, kid, don't take your eyes off it, don't get hit in the face...

Matthew caught it. Before it could bounce out of his glove, he remembered to smack his free hand over it and trap it.

"Out!" The volunteer umpire sounded like he was calling a major-league game.

Evan and Juliet collapsed onto the bench.

"He did it," she said in wonder.

Evan rubbed his chest. "I thought I was going to have a heart attack."

"Me, too. I can't believe he caught it. All that time you've spent throwing tennis balls up in the air paid off. You did it."

"He did it." And thank God, he'd done it. Matthew would've been crushed if he'd missed. Crushed.

But he hadn't missed. Evan pulled the brim of his patrol cap down. Way down. He covered his face with the cap.

"Are you okay?" Juliet asked.

"Mmm-hmm."

"Evan?"

"I'm trying not to cry, damn it." He sighed and put his patrol cap on straight. "It's easier to play in a championship game than it is to watch your kid play."

"You know what? When you're in dad mode, I love you

even more." She leaned closer and lowered her voice. "And you know what happens when I love you even more…"

He whispered in her ear, tilting his head so the cap's brim prevented anyone from doing any lipreading. "You want to have more sex? Love, sex. Sex, love. I can't keep track of which one leads to which one."

She covered her mouth with her hand and whispered behind her fingers. "Stop. I don't think we're supposed to engage in foreplay at a child's baseball game."

"You're the one with the pocket full of panties."

They were still laughing when the game was over as they waited by the fence for the coach to finish talking to the team. They stood side by side, a good foot apart, with their arms crossed over their chests like a couple of tough soldiers, but Evan figured they weren't fooling anybody. They couldn't keep their eyes off each other, but they hadn't broken any regulations about public displays of affection in uniform, so what more could they do? They were newlyweds.

The kids came flying around the fence to find their parents. Matthew made straight for his mother, shouting the whole way. "Did you see me? Did you see me?"

"That was such a great catch, honey." Juliet hugged him.

Matthew squirmed away and turned to Evan. "Did you see it? It was just like the tennis balls. It was coming at me, and I told myself it was just like a tennis ball, and I stayed under it just like you taught me."

"You did everything right. I was so proud of you."

"Yeah?" Matthew practically blushed at the compliment.

"Really proud."

"Thanks— Dad! *Dad!*"

Evan had a split-second of surprised happiness that Matthew was calling him *Dad*, before he realized Matthew was talking to someone behind him. *Dad* was not him.

Evan turned around.

Dad was… Dad.

"Rob," Juliet said under her breath. "Three years. Three damned years."

Matthew took off running and tackled Rob in a hug that would have made a tear come to Evan's eye, if he'd thought there was the slightest chance Rob might deserve such a hero's welcome.

He and Juliet barely needed to glance at one another before they began walking toward Rob and Matthew. They didn't speak; they both knew why Rob was here. Juliet was required to update Rob on his son's location and living situation, including members of her son's household. She'd had to send Evan's name and address with the alimony check.

They stopped close enough that Juliet could set her hand on Matthew's shoulder as he hung on to his dad. She stared down Rob like the adversary he was. "You should have let us know you were coming."

"Juliet Jones, looking good. I assume so, anyway. Hard to tell under all that camouflage." Rob moved to kiss her on the cheek, an awkward action with his son wrapped around his middle.

Juliet pulled away before he reached her.

Evan warned him off with a single word: "Don't."

Rob smiled. "Well, well, well. If it isn't my old pal, Evan Stephens. I didn't expect to see you here. Or did I? Not much of a surprise, really."

Evan knew two things immediately.

One: Rob had no idea how much his son worshipped him.

Two: Evan was going to find out exactly what would happen if Juliet ever learned that he'd been the cause of everything bad in her life. Rob had come to make sure of it.

So, make that three things: the honeymoon was over.

* * *

"Did you see me play, Dad?" Matthew asked for the fifth time, as he kept his arms locked around his father.

Juliet spoke through gritted teeth. "Rob. Your son is asking you a question." *Quit trying to stare down Evan. You can't.*

Rob was probably glad for the excuse to look away from Evan. He patted Matthew on the shoulder while backing up to disengage himself. "Yeah, I saw the game. Some of it. I couldn't find a parking space."

"Did you see the top of the fourth inning? I got an out. I caught a pop fly."

"Okay. Good. That's what you're supposed to do."

"Are you going to come to my games now?"

Juliet died a little inside. She knew the real answer to that, and she knew Rob would just string Matthew along and then disappear without ever giving him a straight answer.

"Well, hey." Rob's laugh sounded a little nervous. "I'm here now, aren't I?"

"Yeah!" Matthew threw his arms around him again and buried his face in Rob's middle.

Juliet felt sick. Matthew was going to be so hurt. The man he was hugging was going to abandon him again as surely as the sun rose, and she didn't know what to do about it. She hated that Rob was putting her son through this.

Evan put his arm around her shoulders. His arm was strong. He was strong, and he was on her side. She'd never been so grateful to have a uniform regulation broken in her life. His touch was just what she needed to keep from spiraling down into that awful, helpless feeling she'd felt around Rob so many times before.

Rob was pushing Matthew away again. "All right, now.

Enough of that. Let's get a look at you. You're a lot taller than last time I saw you."

"That's because I'm in sixth grade now. You're going to like my games. We have real pitchers."

"I don't know if I'd call them pitchers. There were enough wild pitches that every runner could've stolen home, even the fat kid."

Matthew blinked. "You mean Josh?"

"I don't know his name. None of you even tried. Steal home next time, for fu—for God's sake." Rob must have finally noticed Matthew's frown, because he stopped egging him on and patted his shoulder again, his one sign of affection so far. "But you did good. Good game."

"I would steal home if they would let me."

"If you're anything like me, you'll be great at it." Rob turned Matthew around to face her. He stayed behind Matthew with his hands on his shoulders, all fatherly and protective. "You should let our son try. Don't hold him back."

"No players are allowed to steal home in the middle-school leagues," Juliet explained in her best motherly tone. "And we don't describe our teammates as fat."

"Chunky, then. Whatever." He shook Matthew by the shoulders to get him in on the joke. "Fluffy."

Matthew smiled a little as his father laughed, but the confusion on his face was obvious. An adult was making fun of fat kids. Was that okay?

"How long are you going to be in town?" Evan asked.

"As long as I want to. What does it matter to you?"

Unemployed? Juliet wanted to ask snidely, but she wouldn't while Rob had Matthew in his clutches.

"I'm asking so we can set a visitation schedule." Evan nodded toward Matthew. "Matthew and Juliet and I need to get going, but if you intended to be around this weekend, we could arrange to meet you tomorrow or Sunday."

"Dad just got here. We can't leave."

"We have plans, honey." She was so thankful Evan had reminded Rob that they had a custody agreement. Rob couldn't just pop in whenever he felt like it.

Rob smiled at her, sickeningly sweet. "What do you say, JuJu? You, me and Matty, some ice cream? A little family time."

He was such a bastard, manipulating her by using Matthew. He knew she would seem like an evil witch if she said *no* now.

She said it. "No, thank you. Like Evan said, we'll need to set up a visitation schedule."

Matthew didn't understand the problem. "Dad and Evan are friends. We'll all eat ice cream. It will be fun."

Rob jumped on that. "Good idea. You can ride with me, Matty."

"No." She and Evan said it at the same time. The man couldn't just show up after three years and take off with her child in his car. It was a bad idea on every level.

Rob ignored her *no* and homed in on Evan's. "Are you telling me I can't drive my own kid in my own car?"

Evan looked as he had while they were washing dishes and she'd told him too much about Rob's infidelity. He looked perfectly calm, yet every muscle in his body looked perfectly tensed for action.

"You're on post. Children under twelve are not allowed in the front seat if the vehicle has a back seat, and they're required to use a booster under a certain weight."

"Or else what? The MPs will arrest me?" He made a show out of checking out Evan's uniform. "What are you now, the king of the MPs or something?"

"He's the battalion commander," Matthew said, happy to provide the facts to his father.

Rob's eyes widened a fraction.

Juliet felt a little rush of satisfaction. Rob had been enlisted for four years. He knew just how impressive Evan's position was. *He's a little more than you bargained on, you weasel.*

"Battalion commander. Well, aren't you just the big dog on campus?" Rob jerked his chin toward Evan's hand on her shoulder. "No wonder you feel free to grope your wife while you're in uniform."

Grope your wife? He did not just say that in front of Matthew, surely.

But he had. And Juliet had had enough.

"We're done here. Come on, Matthew." She stepped out of the safety of Evan's arm and took her son's arm.

"Nooo," he whined.

"Yes."

"Go with your mother. Your father and I are going to talk." Evan's order was given with all the authority of a military police battalion commander, that was for sure, because Matthew stopped whining and Rob let go of his shoulders without another word.

Juliet took her son by the hand and walked away, thinking, *I hate Rob, I hate Rob*, with every step. It was a familiar refrain.

Then her heart refused to repeat it any longer, because now she could say, *I love Evan, I love Evan*, instead.

She sat in the Lexus with Matthew and waited. She was, miraculously, not dealing with her ex-husband. Evan was doing so for her, because…

Because he loved her.

She smoothed her hands over the leather steering wheel, wondering at the sensation of having a partner in life. She wasn't having to face the world alone anymore, because she'd made a pinkie promise on a college green once upon a time.

She saw her fairy-tale prince walking toward her, all camouflage and silver aviator glasses—and felt a thrill that she was the princess who got to take all that off of him at night. She loved his heart and soul, but if that came wrapped in a layer of panty-dropping hotness, who was she to complain?

She rolled down her window.

"Everything okay?" she asked, a yes or no question because he wouldn't be able to say much while Matthew whined in the back seat.

"I wanted to eat ice cream with Daaad."

Evan ducked his head in the window a little way to speak to Matthew. "We're all going to eat ice cream together tomorrow, at our house, at two o'clock."

Then he kissed her, hard and swift, and walked away.

Juliet followed the Corvette all the way back to their castle.

Chapter Seventeen

"I'll be back in thirty minutes."

"Have a good run." Juliet sent Evan off with a kiss, then shut the front door. She knew he ran during the week for the army. He ran on Saturdays for himself.

When he got back, she might go for a run, too, just for the stress relief it would give her. In four hours, Rob Jones was going to be sitting at Evan's kitchen table. They were all going to eat bowls of ice cream, and Rob was going to prove he could be civilized and find topics of conversation that were appropriate for an eleven-year-old to hear. If he could not, then she was going to go back to court to have their custody arrangement reviewed. Considering the way Rob had disappeared from Matthew's life for three years, Rob couldn't expect things to go well for him.

Evan had done all of that for her, while she'd sat in her Lexus yesterday, falling more in love with him by the minute.

Matthew came downstairs. "How much longer until Dad gets here?"

"Not for four hours, honey. Still. Are you unpacking your books?" Their household goods had been delivered just the day before yesterday, so the house was currently a little crazy with two couches, two tables and two of just about everything wedged into one house. Today, she was just going to focus on unpacking the kitchen stuff.

"I'm going to be in the kitchen. Evan's out for a run."

Two songs on the radio later, she was waist deep in the white butcher paper she'd unwrapped from all her glassware, when a man's familiar voice scared her to death.

"Hi, JuJu."

She whirled around. "What are you doing here?"

"Two didn't work for me, after all. The hotel checkout time was ten, so I came over now. I wasn't going to sit in my car until two." He looked so smug, so sure of himself.

"Who let you in?"

"Our son. Who else?" He had his hands in the pockets of his jeans. "Relax, JuJu. Come on into the living room. I brought doughnuts." He turned around to leave, completely casual, utterly calm.

Why did she feel so alarmed?

"Evan will be back in a few minutes." She said it to his back.

He turned back and shook his head at her, as if she was some sort of crazy woman. "So what? You know what he'll see when he comes in? Matthew eating doughnuts with his mother and father."

Matthew was already in the living room. When she followed Rob in, she saw Matthew's face light up like a Christmas tree. Her poor boy. He wanted love so badly from a man whose ability to give it was stunted.

Rob knew how to pretend, though. He sat next to Matthew and ruffled his hair. He didn't have Evan's touch, a quick fluff and done. Rob really messed up Matthew's hair, too hard, and didn't stop until Matthew squirmed away. "Sorry, sorry. I forget kids today are wrapped in bubble wrap." He pretended to poke air bubbles all around Matthew but never laid a finger on him. "Ooh, can't touch you. Oh, no, I might hurt the pwecious wittle baby."

"Rob."

He patted Matthew's knee and handed him the doughnut box. "Just kidding. You're not a baby at all. Man, I can't get over how big you've gotten. It's amazing." Rob turned to Juliet. "It really is amazing."

It was the first sincere thing he'd said, and for just a flash, when the expression on his face was genuine, she could see the man he'd been when she'd first married him. Maybe Evan was right, and she should be easier on her twenty-four-year-old self for not seeing the red flags.

"He's grown two inches just this school year," she said.

"Sixth grade, right?" He ruffled Matthew's hair again. "When I was your age, I was raising hell."

"How did you raise hell?" Matthew asked.

"Let's not use that term. It will get Matthew in trouble at school."

Rob rolled his eyes at her correction and seemed to think Matthew ought to find that cool. "Moms. Am I right?"

"Right. Moms."

"When we raised *heck*, we left our mark, I'll tell you that much. Stole three stop signs one night. A screwdriver, a friend's shoulders to sit on, it was a piece of cake." He looked around the living room stuffed with extra furniture and moving boxes. "What did you do with my stop sign? Where is it?"

"I have no idea what you did with your stolen stop sign after we got divorced."

Rob sat back and stretched his arms along the back of the couch. "Enjoy yourself now, Matty, my man. Those were the good old days. We broke into the school and tore that place up. Spray painted everything. It took them a week to clean it all up. We emptied, like, three cans of spray paint on that crap hole. Never got caught."

Juliet stood. "Okay, Rob. I think that's enough. It's time for you to go. You may come back at two o'clock, if you like."

He rolled his eyes again. "Mother, may I?"

"Matthew, say goodbye and go back to unpacking your stuff in your bedroom, okay?"

"Relax, Juliet. You're acting like I'm some kind of monster. All I want is the chance to be part of my own family. Matthew is already so much like you, I can barely recognize myself in him. Now Evan's in the picture. Matty's going to turn into a little Evan instead of me. He's halfway there already, little Goody Two-shoes, teacher's pet, coach's favorite, a little offshoot of you two. You know other kids are going to hate him, right?"

Rob, you are an ass.

"Matthew, honey, please go upstairs to your room. This is an adult conversation for adults only."

"But, Mom…"

"Go."

She waited until his bedroom door shut with a slam. "You have visitation rights, Rob. You could use them. You could see Matthew every other weekend, if you wanted to."

"You expect me to move to Texas?"

"If you want to be in your son's life, then yes. I'm in the army. I can't leave Fort Hood. You don't have a job and you don't have a permanent address. Why not look for something in Central Texas? If Matthew is really your priority, you will."

"Just like old times. Telling me how I should act, how I should treat my son, what kind of job I should get. Give it a goddamn rest. No man could live with your constant criticism."

It *was* like old times. She could feel him baiting her into an argument. She wasn't going to go there. "We're talking about Matthew. I don't care what kind of job you get. You can keep living off your alimony. Use it to make your son happy. Live near him. Spend time with him."

"God, you're bossy. Work there, live here, spend your money on that. I don't need this." Rob was running with his train of thought now, getting louder and louder. "I don't need any of this. I give up. Go ahead and screw Evan every night." He shouted it loudly enough to carry up the stairs.

She kept her voice quiet. Her child did not need to hear any of this. "Get out of my house now."

"I'm here for Matthew. My son! You're keeping my boy from me."

"Keep your voice down."

"I still have rights, you know, at least until you and Evan go to a judge and try to take them away from me. I get every other weekend."

"Then this is the wrong weekend." She opened the front door.

Rob walked up a little too close to her, invading her personal space. "I forgot how hot you look when you're angry. I loved you, you know. We could have patched things up. We had a good run there for a few years, right? We could be that way again, but you decided to screw another man."

"He's my husband." Her voice broke on the word *husband*. "Quit trying to make it sound like I'm cheating on you."

"I forgive you. Come back to me."

The man was unhinged. How could she encourage him to reestablish any kind of relationship with Matthew? He could only confuse him with his bizarre, twisted logic.

"Get out."

Rob...smiled.

He ran one finger over her shoulder. "Make me."

Then he was no longer in front of her, but up against the door frame, arm twisted behind his back by Evan, who looked to her eyes like he'd come straight from heaven. He was hot and sweaty and furious, but he still hissed his words in a voice that would *not* carry up the stairs to a child's room.

"You touch my wife again, you come here and think

about laying a finger on her, and I will break your arm."
He yanked up on Rob's arm, and Rob grunted in pain.
"Are we clear?"

Rob's face was smooshed against the door frame, so
his words were mumbled. "You can't stop me from seeing my son."

"I wasn't trying to, but I've already called a lawyer.
We'll be renegotiating your custody rights and your goddamned alimony while we're at it." Evan pulled him away
from the door frame and pushed him over the threshold,
releasing him.

Rob staggered to regain his balance on their front steps.
"You're just pissed because I got her first."

"Get in your car."

Rob craned his neck around Evan to look at her. "You
didn't know that, did you? Your big hero here, he's the one
who turned me on to you. He told me you were wife material. He told me where to find you and how to get you, step
by step. You really thought I wanted to be part of something bigger than myself when I joined the army? You
think I liked being a frigging lowly-ass private while you
two were lording it over me with your big-ass officer pay-
checks? I bought you flowers on a damn private's salary,
but it was worth it, because it worked. A dozen roses, he
recommended. I'm still raking in the alimony from that
investment."

What was Rob ranting about?

Evan was deadly calm. "Get in your car, or I'll put you
in your car."

"The puppy was the best touch. Good thing he told me
you were allergic to cats. Wouldn't have been so romantic
if I'd given you a kitten."

Evan pulled the front door shut behind himself as he
walked outside and Rob scrabbled backward.

The silence was sudden. Juliet sat on the stairs. She was

shaking. Only now that it was over did she realize just how scared she'd been.

Poor Matthew. He must be terrified. She needed to go check on him, try to find out if he'd heard horrible words shouted at his mother. *Screw Evan every night. You're keeping my boy from me.*

There'd been other words, too. The laughable idea that Evan had told him to buy her roses. Where to find her? She watched her own hands tremble.

Then Evan walked in, shut the door and just stood there. She wanted to feel his arms around her in the worst way, so she stood on shaky legs and took one step toward him before she collapsed.

"I've got you. I've got you."

Evan's voice, Evan's arms around her.

She threw her arms around his neck, and she never wanted to let go. He was here, by some miracle, he was here—the man who had promised her, as violins played under a full moon, that he would be here right at this moment.

"Evan, I'm so sorry—"

"Don't you dare apologize for that ass—"

"Dad? Dad!" Matthew came thundering down the stairs.

"Oh, Matthew, honey." She kept one arm around Evan, but she reached out the other one to her son. "Come here, baby."

Evan was reaching out his arm, too. Two adults, reaching out to Matthew, *come in for a hug,* party of three, not two. Everything Juliet had wanted for her son.

"Where's Dad?" Matthew looked wildly from face to face to door.

"Honey—"

"Dad!" Matthew bolted for the door.

Evan caught him by the shirt without letting go of Juliet. "He left."

"I hate you. I hate you!" Matthew backed up and looked at her as she clung to Evan, the man who was keeping her from crumpling into a heap. "I hate both of you!"

He thundered up the stairs.

Juliet turned to Evan. With both arms around his neck once more, she cried—not for everything her son had lost, but for everything he was refusing to accept.

Matthew was sound asleep. He'd cried his way through the day, refusing comfort from the two people he blamed for his dad disappearing again. When two o'clock came and went with no sign of Rob, he'd cried harder. He left the room every time Evan walked in, and he refused to eat the spaghetti Juliet made for dinner. Little wonder that he'd finally fallen asleep while sitting up on the couch.

Evan had carried him upstairs as easily as if Matthew was a toddler.

Juliet checked on Matthew again. His face looked so young, even though he was tall enough for the big coasters now. She kissed his forehead and went downstairs.

Evan had been sitting on the patio ever since he'd tucked Matthew in. She went out to the patio and kissed him on the forehead, too, and sat down.

"Well," she said as the silence stretched on, "this sucks. Rob shows up for less than an hour, total, and now all three of us are unhappy."

Evan looked at her then, really looked at her. She was content to simply look back. The warm light from the house illuminated his face.

"Aren't you going to ask me, Juliet? The answer is yes. What he said was true. I'm the reason he courted you."

"You must have made me sound really terrific to inspire him to move to Fort Huachuca just to date me."

Evan frowned at her. "No, you did that just by being

you. I didn't have to tell him you were wife material. Every man who's ever met you knows that."

"Aw, thanks." She smiled.

Evan didn't. "I didn't mean to do you any harm."

"Harm?" she echoed, to be sure she'd heard correctly. Rob was the kind of guy who did harm. Not Evan. Never Evan.

"I was an arrogant fool. We were drinking and shooting pool, the whole team back together for this wedding. I was stupid, and you paid the price." He looked at her as if he were confessing a terrible crime. "I will never forgive myself for the pain I caused you."

"What did you do?" *I don't want to know. Don't tell me. Hush.*

"Everything he said I did. I told him you were at Fort Huachuca. I told him you wouldn't be impressed with his little quick-buck schemes. Everything. The dozen red roses. The puppy."

"You told him to buy me a puppy? Why would you do that?"

"Even the *attitude* he needed to have to impress you. I told him that."

"But you guys weren't even friends. Why would you give him all this advice?"

"I—I didn't *give* him advice. He just took it. He listened to me as I bragged, and he used it. It was a bachelor party. Everyone started talking about how they'd have to find someone to marry someday, and I said I already had the best woman all lined up. I didn't tell them about the pinkie promise. I just told them that you were going to be mine. Rob took it as a challenge."

"I still don't see why you feel so guilty. It was Rob who presented himself as someone he wasn't. You were just being you."

"A cocky, arrogant son of a bitch."

She smiled a little bit at that. "You were cocky in college, but you weren't a jerk. You weren't mean to people. That's why women flocked to you."

"I was arrogant. Stop letting me off the hook, Juliet."

"I don't know why you've put yourself on it."

"Don't you understand? I'm the reason there weren't any red flags. Me. I did that to you."

That silenced her. She'd berated herself for not seeing the red flags. She'd doubted her own judgment for years.

"I see." She was not panicking. There had to be a sane excuse. "But it was an accident. You were just bragging."

"The result was the same. The guilt is mine. I'm trying to fix it now."

"Fix it how?"

He was silent.

"By marrying me? You married me because you felt guilty? You felt obliged?" She pushed herself out of the deep Adirondack chair.

"I'll fix everything I can fix, but there is no way to give you back the years you lost with him. I'm so sorry."

"Those weren't your years."

"They were yours."

"Exactly. They aren't your years to fix or change or erase. I was young and finding my way through life and I made some bad decisions, but those were *my* years. *I* made that decision."

"He wouldn't have gone after you if I hadn't taunted him."

"Gone after me? He *charmed* me. I'm not the first woman to get charmed into something."

"He broke your heart. He cheated on you."

"Yes, he did, but that's not a good reason for *you* to marry me."

She paced the length of the patio, trying to think, not to freak. Rob had married her so that she'd provide him with a stable home base, so he could continue to go out and play. According to Evan, Rob had married her as some kind of dare or revenge. But if Evan had married her out of *guilt*, that was no better. She'd wanted love. She'd wanted Evan to love her back.

Which he did.

She stopped in front of Evan's chair and looked down at him. They'd been in these positions when he'd begged her to marry him. He'd dropped to one knee and told her there was no one else like her. It wasn't guilt. It was love.

"I wouldn't have married you if you only felt guilty. How did I miss the red flags this time around, with you?" she asked.

Evan shook his head, but before he could apologize again, she dropped to sit on his strong thigh. She put her arms around his neck.

"It's a trick question, Evan. I didn't miss the red flags this time, because there weren't any. You didn't marry me out of guilt. You married me because you love me. You do. I've had eight days of marriage to prove it. You said one kiss from me was worth ten nights with anyone else. Well, one day of marriage with you is worth a hundred years with anyone else. For eight hundred years, I've been loved by you. I want eight million more, so you've got to stop feeling guilty. You'll muck up my eight million years."

Evan was very still and very silent.

Juliet put her head on his shoulder. "Take your time. Think it through. But if you've been feeling guilty for twelve years, you need to remember we've loved each other as good friends for nineteen, and we're going to love each other every way we can think of for at least sixty more years into the future. So don't let the guilt take up more space than it deserves. I'll just sit here and kiss you while you think about it."

She did, kissing his cheek and the corner of his eye,

smoothing her fingers through his hair as she kissed her way down his throat. "Are you done thinking?"

"No."

"What are you still thinking about?"

"I was trying to figure out how someone as young and sexy as you are can also be so old and wise. I think I solved that one."

"What's the answer?"

"I think you are a miracle."

She didn't laugh, because he hadn't said it like a joke. "I love you, Evan."

"Like I said, a miracle." He sighed deeply, his chest rising and falling beneath her hand. "I was also thinking that we need one more miracle."

"For Matthew."

"Exactly. I don't know how to make things right for him."

"I've been thinking about it for the past three years. How do you make things right for a little boy who has a lousy father? I decided the only thing I could do was keep loving him while I prayed for a miracle for him. And here you are."

He hugged her tight. "I'm just the guy who teaches him how to catch baseballs and who keeps kissing his mother, which isn't winning me any points in his eyes, by the way, but I can't seem to stop."

"I think you're much more than that. I think you love him."

Evan placed his hand over hers and pressed it into his chest.

Juliet smiled. "He's got two people who love him, whether he realizes it or not, so we'll have to trust that love will conquer all somehow. Someday. Did that sound very old and wise?"

"Yes."

"Can we leave the old and wise Juliet out here while

you take the young and sexy me to bed? It's been a horrible day, and I'd like to do something that feels good."

"Insanely good." Evan stood with her cradled in his arms. "I have one more question. What made you decide I was father material?"

"Don't you remember how you found out I was allergic to cats? I found those abandoned kittens junior year, but they made me so sneezy and itchy, you made me give them to you. You took care of them for me until we could get them to the pet rescue."

"Kittens." Evan laughed softly. "Better than a puppy, after all."

He carried his bride over the patio's threshold, all the way up the stairs and into his bed.

Chapter Eighteen

Evan sat at his desk, busy with paperwork, but nothing could chase the thoughts out of his mind.

He was a family man, and his family was in pain.

Sunday had been just as hard for Matthew as Saturday. Juliet's patience had won out by the end of the day, and Matthew had finally told her a little bit of what he was thinking as she'd tucked him into the security of his bed. Evan had stayed in the hallway to listen, because Matthew seemed to be barely able to look at him.

"Dad said he didn't recognize me. I'm nothing like him. I'm just a little off-ff-offshoot of you and Evan."

"Not true. You are Rob Jones's son, and nothing will change that. He said that because he was mad at me. When people are angry, they don't always say things that are true."

"It was true. Dad meant it. I don't do anything like him."

"Let's think about this. He played baseball at school, and you play baseball, too, don't you?"

"That's 'cause of Evan, not Dad."

"You played baseball before you ever met Evan."

"Yeah, but I wasn't any good at it until Evan."

Juliet had gone silent for a moment. Evan had imagined she was as nonplussed by that argument as he was.

"Are you mad at Evan because you're getting better at baseball? That makes no sense."

"I'm mad because he pushed Dad out the door! I s-saw it from my window."

"Oh, honey. Dad wasn't supposed to be in our house. He was shouting at me. I think he wanted to pick a fight, but Evan made him leave instead. Evan was protecting us."

Yes, Evan had been doing just that. He couldn't regret pulling Rob away from Juliet, not when the man had been casing their house, waiting until Evan had left before convincing a child to let him in. None of that was going to make sense in an eleven-year-old's world, though.

Evan flipped to the last page of the police blotter and signed it. He tossed it into the outbox on his desk.

Sergeant Hadithi appeared in his door. "Sir, the watch commander is on the back line."

That was a surprise, the kind that made Evan avoid surprises.

The watch commander ran the actual police station on post. He was in Evan's battalion, but there was no reason for the station to call the battalion commander about routine law enforcement. None. If a soldier was in a holding cell, the watch commander would call someone in that soldier's chain of command to come get him. That person had to be at least two ranks higher than the detainee. For Evan to be the one getting the call, the detainee would have to be a captain.

It was inconceivable that one of his company commanders was in a holding cell. That left only one other possibility: a soldier in his battalion had been killed on duty.

The moment of surprise passed. This was going to be news of the worst kind.

Evan took the call. "Colonel Stephens here. Go ahead."

"Sir, this is Sergeant First Class Montoya at the station. I'm sorry to bother you, sir."

Sorry to bother me?

"We dispatched a unit in response to a call of vandalism in progress."

What in the actual hell…? Why would he be getting a call about vandalism?

"We took juveniles into custody at the middle school."

Evan had already figured it out and come to his feet before the word *juveniles. Middle school* was unnecessary.

"One of them, a Matthew Jones, age eleven, according to self-report, has been asking where you are, referring to you as Evan. I can't tell if he wants you to be here or if he's afraid you're here at the station. Do you know him, sir?"

"Yes. It's Grayson-Jones, hyphenated last name, for the record. Have you contacted his mother yet?"

"No, sir. He's only given us his father's name and number, a Robert Jones. The area code is out of state. We left messages, but so far, no call back."

Of course not.

"Is he hurt?"

"Just scared to death. Trying not to cry."

That description of Matthew squeezed Evan's heart like a fist. The watch commander didn't know Matthew was Evan's family. He was only speaking as Sergeant First Class Montoya to Colonel Stephens, an MP to an MP. He probably wouldn't say such a thing to any kid's real parent.

"I'll be there in five."

Hell, he could run there in five. The station was less than a mile away, but he'd take his car, because he wouldn't be leaving without Juliet's child, the child he'd always wanted. His child.

Evan parked in the middle of the patrol cars behind the station and shoved open the back door to the briefing room. The MPs who were on their way out were startled to see him. They said their "good afternoon, sir"s and pressed their backs against the wall to let him pass.

It still took an eternity to reach the watch commander's desk.

Sergeant First Class Montoya stood as soon as he spotted him. "Good afternoon, sir. There's been no call back from the father yet."

"Don't hold your breath waiting for it. I already called Matthew's mother. She'll be here any minute. Let me see the report."

Evan looked at the preliminary accounting of damages. Spray paint, of course. Juliet had described how Rob had bragged over doughnuts about raising hell at Matthew's age.

Curse words had been spray painted on the outside of the school, words that were almost innocent in their mildness. *Ass. School sucks. Damn.*

Meaningless, except to express the desperation of a child who'd been told he bore no resemblance to his father, a father who'd once spray painted his own school.

Evan handed the list of damages back to the watch commander. "How many kids involved?"

"Three, sir. The other two have already been released into their parents' custody. MPs responded to a call from someone living near the school. The juveniles were caught outside the building as they painted. One tried to run."

Evan braced himself. Running from law enforcement never went well for the runner. They tripped, they fell, they ran into traffic. They got tackled. K-9s sent after them—no, the MPs wouldn't send K-9s after juveniles, but *damn.* "Who ran?"

"The oldest one. It was his father's spray paint. Guess he had more reason to be scared than the rest."

"He was still on school property when he was apprehended?"

"Yes, sir. He didn't get far. Sergeant Koch ran him down. She cornered him by a fence that he couldn't get over, and he gave up. She didn't want to tackle anyone in front of the student body if she could help it."

"Outstanding." Evan made a mental note to commend Sergeant Koch for showing good judgment—and for being a fast runner. "We could turn jurisdiction for all three of them back to the school instead of dragging them in front of a judge. This sounds like a kid's prank. The juvenile courts have enough of a backlog for bigger crimes."

"Yes, sir. I thought so, too. I spoke to the principal. He's going to call the parents now and ask them to report first thing in the morning. I could call him and let him know we're going to defer to his judgment instead of pursuing any charges."

"That sounds reasonable."

That keeps my wife's son out of court for a stupid prank.

The principal would be deciding Matthew's fate tomorrow. Detention, internal suspension, expulsion? Evan had no idea. He was about to find out, because he'd be going to the principal's office with Matthew.

The words *principal's office* touched some long-buried bit of his psyche. It sounded as bad now as it had when he was a kid.

Kids don't scare me.

He almost smiled. Kids? No. Being called to the principal's office? Maybe.

The police station, however, was his turf. He could wait until Juliet got here, then explain everything to her and ask what she wanted to do next, but he knew the legal and procedural options better than she did. There was no need to put that on her shoulders. Matthew had probably had enough of a scare to last him for the rest of his adolescence. Evan didn't want to leave him alone any longer.

"I'm sure they'll be spending tomorrow finding out

how much elbow grease it takes to get paint off a wall. If that's everything, I'll be taking custody of Matthew Grayson-Jones."

"Sir?" The watch commander couldn't release a juvenile to just anybody, not even the commander of the MP battalion.

"He's my stepson. He didn't tell you?"

"No, sir. I thought you were maybe a neighbor or a friend of his parents."

"I married his mother a week ago, because I'm luckier than I deserve to be. He'll get used to it sooner or later. Got any paperwork for me to sign?"

The watch commander handed him the release papers. "He's the last one left. I'm sorry, sir. He only asked where you were as if he wanted to make sure you weren't here, like he was afraid you'd tell his parents about this, so I had a hunch maybe you'd know who his parents were."

"Good hunch. I'm glad you called me." Evan handed him the signed paperwork.

"You'll find him in the first office on the right. He's all yours now."

Yes, he is.

"My wife is Lieutenant Colonel Grayson. You can send her back when she arrives. Thanks again for following your hunch."

"Yes, sir."

Evan paused outside the office door that the watch commander had indicated. They didn't lock juveniles in the station's holding cells unless they were truly violent or suspected of felonies. Matthew and his new spray-painting posse had been seated in a lineup of chairs against the wall of an empty office. Through the rectangle of the door's reinforced glass window, Evan saw the row of chairs, all empty but one. Matthew had never looked younger or smaller. Lost.

You're not alone, Matthew.

Evan opened the door and walked in.

Matthew looked up—and gasped. "I told them to call my dad."

"They did. You mentioned my name, too. It's a good thing you did. I would have gone crazy with worry when you didn't come home from school when I expected you to. So would your mom, right?"

"But I thought Dad would come because…because I did something just like him."

"You hoped he would come. No one can blame you for that, but call me, too, from now on. I will always come for you."

"Because you're an MP?"

"Because I would never leave my kid all alone at a police station."

"I'm not really your kid."

Evan rested his hands on his hips. "Yeah, Matthew, actually, you are. You're my stepson. You, me and your mom all live together. We're a family, like it or not. In case you wondered, I like it."

Matthew thought about it, looking for loopholes, no doubt. "So, am I not in trouble? Because you're king of the MPs and all?"

The kid was too damned clever—and wrong. "You are in serious trouble. You spray painted a school wall. You have to go see the principal tomorrow."

Matthew hung his head.

Evan didn't know if it would comfort Matthew or not, but it wouldn't hurt to try. "I'm going to the principal with you. We'll find out what he thinks is a fair punishment."

"You'll be there," Matthew muttered. "Instead of Dad."

Evan sat down. Rather than stare at the top of Matthew's head, he turned his patrol cap in his hands and shaped the brim a little, as he'd done to ball caps since he was Matthew's age. "You know, at the courthouse, when I married your mom, I can understand that you might have felt like I was taking your dad's place. I didn't. Your parents got divorced years ago."

"I know."

"Your mom and I promised that from now on, we'd be each other's one and only, because that's how marriage works. You can only be married to one person, right?"

Matthew's head bobbed a little, even with his chin in his chest.

"But that's not how family works."

Matthew looked up.

"Here's the thing. You can make your family as big as you want. I'll always have my parents and my sister, but I've added you and your mom now, too. You didn't replace anyone in my family. You just made my family bigger. It means there are more people in the world who care about me."

He resisted the urge to ruffle Matthew's hair. "More people for me to care about, too. Maybe you'll decide to make your family bigger. You've already got a dad and a fantastic mom, and you can add me as a stepfather. I'll be married to your mother forever. I'll be your stepfather forever."

Matthew looked more than sad or scared. He looked pale. His breathing was shallow.

"Matthew..." Evan wished he could hug the poor kid, but after the last two days, he knew it would only make Matthew even more unhappy. Instead, he stood. "Are you ready to go home now?"

Hope touched his terribly young face. "Really? You can take me home because you're an MP?"

"I can take you home because you're my stepson. Because I'm an MP, I have the Vette parked right outside the station door."

Matthew stood, trembling like a leaf. Evan held an arm out, thinking only to steady him if his knees should give way, but Matthew threw himself across the few feet of linoleum between them and plastered himself to Evan, arms around his waist, face buried somewhere in Evan's lower ribs. The fabric of Evan's ACU jacket muffled the boy's sobs.

Evan had never been more surprised in his life.

Matthew clung to him with a grip that was shockingly fierce for someone who was barely tall enough to ride the Fireball roller coaster. Evan hugged him back just as tightly. If Matthew needed to hang on to something solid, then Evan was glad to be it.

Eventually, Evan turned at the feeling that someone was watching him. Juliet, one of his oldest friends, now his beautiful wife, was standing outside the office. Her hands were clasped over her heart. Without saying a word, she walked up to them and joined them, one arm around Evan, one arm around her son, and they stood there in a hug for a long, long time.

Party of three.

When they left the station, Colonel Grayson hooked her pinkie finger with Colonel Stephens's, and they began living the best years of their lives.

Epilogue

Evan watched patiently as Matthew struggled to learn a new skill.

"Got it," Matthew said. "That took forever."

"The more you do it, the faster you'll get. It's a good skill for a man to have."

Matthew looked skeptical. "Getting a stroller out of a car is a man skill?"

"If you don't know how, then you have to hold the baby. The first time I held you, actually, was to help your mom while she got your stroller out of her car."

"But I wasn't a baby."

Matthew loved the story of Evan's first impression of him at a long-ago tailgate. Evan retold it as often as Matthew hinted that he wanted to hear it.

"Right. You were four times as big as Maggie is." Evan patted his daughter's diapered and ruffle-covered bottom as she slept on his shoulder. "You were a toddler who knew what he wanted. I'd already seen you steal your mom's hamburger." *And I was reeling from the impact.*

Later that day, Juliet had needed a hand with her stroller, and since Evan had known nothing about the things back then, Juliet had plopped Matthew in his arms and dealt with the stroller herself.

"All right, let's go. Your mom's plane is landing. Maggie's asleep, so I'll keep carrying her, because what is Rule Number One?"

"Never wake the baby."

They grinned at each other.

"You are a very wise eighth grader. I've got the baby. You get the stroller."

Juliet was returning from her latest assignment. She'd been sent out of the state, but not across the world and not to an area of conflict, thankfully. Her staff officer course had taken three long weeks, but not a year. She was returning home on a regular civilian flight, so they'd come to meet her at the airport, not at a military hangar.

But when Juliet caught sight of her husband and her son and her baby girl, the explosion of joy was the same as they ran to each other for a group hug.

Party of four.

It was one of life's perfect moments.

* * * * *